PRAISE FOR *NO FURY LIKE THAT*

Imagine if characters from ~~...~~ ped in Sartre's play *No Exit*, whe~~...~~ ...o *Fury Like That* uses the lens of female ~~...~~ ...gatory to examine loss, love, rage, angst, and wha~~...~~ ...y is to live for. Alternately funny, melancholy, philosophica~~...~~, and raunchy, it's a wild ride and another gutsy novel from Lisa de Nikolits.
—JOHN OUGHTON, author of *Death by Triangulation*

Suspenseful, surprising, thrilling and at times laugh-out-loud funny, *No Fury Like That* takes you on a page-turning ride into another world—with Lisa de Nikolits' skillful writing keeping you belted in.
—JACQUELINE KOVACS, *Metroland Media*

Afraid to die? Worse is yet to come! Julia, a ruthless business woman, suddenly finds herself in Purgatory not remembering if she has died, or how. Left with no choice but to make friends with other lost souls, she never dreams she will not only become their saviour, but also an avenger. In this brilliantly written book, you will hold your breath when Julia realizes she should have made things right at the primary crime scene where it all started—Earth.
—SUZANA TRATNIK, author of *Games with Greta*

No Fury Like That is de Nikolits at her best. She has taken the question, "What if you had a second chance?" and given her imagination free rein to answer it. The result is a novel full of colourful characters who grapple with their lives, their deaths, and what it is to be human. By the final page the reader has not only witnessed Julia Redner's metamorphic journey, but has also taken a personal step forward.
—LIZ BUGG, author of the Calli Barnow Mystery Series

Lisa de Nikolits is one of my most fascinating discoveries of Canadian literature. Her writing is fresh and attractive, but deep in ideas and thought-provoking. *No Fury Like That* is an example of this duality: under the appearance of a paranormal story set in Purgatory we face a brilliant psychological exploration of a human soul questioning our certitudes about the world: Who are we really? How do we find responsibility for our past? What are the implications of our acts? Big questions presented through captivating prose displayed in a perfect plot that catches the reader from the very beginning. De Nikolits knows how to combine the oppressive atmosphere of Beckett or Kafka with the contemporaneous form of a thriller-narrative, always with a touch of humour and sensibility. And of course, with an extraordinary capacity to capture the essence of human emotions.
—MIGUEL ÁNGEL HERNÁNDEZ, author of *Escape Attempt*

Lisa de Nikolits' serio-comedic interpretation of Purgatory, with a subplot of suspense and revenge make *No Fury Like That* an intriguing novel and a fascinating read. To date, I have read three of Ms. de Nikolits' novels and it has been interesting to see her develop her serio-comedic style that really hits its stride in *The Nearly Girl* and has continued with *No Fury Like That*. In this novel, as with the earlier novel, we have a similar disparate cast of characters united in the afterlife, who for the most part are attempting to make sense of their earthly lives in a "coffee klatch" type of atmosphere, gently guided along by the more experienced Helpers. It is this "stand-back-and-take-a-look-at-your-life" message that is the biggest takeaway from *No Fury Like That*. It is about realizations: how an altruistic life is better than a self-centered mean-spirited one; the struggle for recognition is often futile; your family does need you, even if they don't know it; one act of indiscretion can have fatal consequences, and the list goes on. Bottom line: don't dismiss *No Fury Like That* as a light, entertaining read. There are nuances to Ms. de Nikolits' writing that could be missed with such a viewpoint. This book is really about second chances that we may never get the first time around on our trek along Eternity's Road.
—JAMES FISHER, *The Miramichi Reader*

Julia Redner seemed to have it all: stunning good looks, a fantastic job, and enough money and perks to live in the style she'd grown accustomed to. But after it all went down and she finds herself in the afterlife, Julia realizes that she didn't have a single friend and now has a whack of unfinished business to settle. *No Fury Like That* is a cautionary tale about the perils of rising to the top at any cost. It's also a smart, satisfying read that's laced with humour, peopled with quirky characters and moves along at a fast clip. Readers will root for its plucky heroine, hoping she'll get a shot at a second chance. Another spellbinder from Lisa de Nikolits!
—ROSEMARY MCCRACKEN, author of the Pat Tierney Mysteries

An intriguing and edgy idea where Purgatory is re-imagined as a pleasant spot where souls progress toward redemption through lattes, friendship and therapy. The book engages us from the first page when we meet Julia struggling to explore the strange airport where she has landed through her fight to solve the mystery of her own life and death. A beautifully written exploration of the metaphysical and of the many serious social issues faced by today's women.
—M.H. CALLWAY, author of *Windigo Fire,* Arthur Ellis Best First Novel finalist

Lisa de Nikolits is the perfect travel companion we all search for; she is funny without being mean, wise without being boring, and so good at getting both into and out of trouble. I have let her lead me onto a coach bus heading *West of Wawa,* I have stolen away with her to an abandoned school when *Between the Cracks She Fell,* and now I know I will follow her even to Purgatory where there is *No Fury Like That* of her betrayed but unsurmounted protagonist, Julia Redner. If you can, I recommend seizing this chance to take a trip with Lisa de Nikolits.
—JADE WALLACE, contributing author to *PAC 'N HEAT,* a *Ms PacMan Noir Anthology*

No Fury Like That is a a bold tale of comeuppance....
—SHIRLEY MCDANIEL, artist at art-explorations.com

No Fury Like That

We gratefully acknowledge the support of the Canada Council for the Arts and the Ontario Arts Council for our publishing program. We also acknowledge the financial support of the Government of Canada.

Cover design: Lisa de Nikolits

No Fury Like That is a work of fiction. All the characters and situations portrayed in this book are fictitious and any resemblance to persons living or dead is purely coincidental.

Library and Archives Canada Cataloguing in Publication

De Nikolits, Lisa, 1966-, author
          No fury like that / Lisa de Nikolits.

(Inanna poetry and fiction series)
Issued in print and electronic formats.
ISBN 978-1-77133-413-6 (paperback).-- ISBN 978-1-77133-414-3 (epub). --
ISBN 978-1-77133-415-0 (kindle).-- ISBN 978-1-77133-416-7 (pdf)

          I. Title. II. Series: Inanna poetry and fiction series

PS8607.E63N6 2017   C813'.6   C2017-905367-1
                                                                        C2017-905368-X

Printed and bound in Canada

MIX
Paper from
responsible sources
FSC® C004071

Inanna Publications and Education Inc.
210 Founders College, York University
4700 Keele Street, Toronto, Ontario, Canada M3J 1P3
Telephone: (416) 736-5356 Fax: (416) 736-5765
Email: inanna.publications@inanna.ca   Website: www.inanna.ca

No Fury Like That

a novel by

Lisa de Nikolits

inanna poetry & fiction series

INANNA PUBLICATIONS AND EDUCATION INC.
TORONTO, CANADA

To Bradford Dunlop.
And all my friends and family, in this world and the next.

TABLE OF CONTENTS

PART I: THERE

PART II: HERE

PART III: HERE AND THERE

Heav'n has no Rage, like Love to Hatred turn'd,
Nor Hell a Fury, like a Woman scorn'd.
                                    —William Congreve (1697)

PART I: **THERE**

1. WAKING

I WAKE. EVERYTHING HURTS. I'm locked in darkness, submerged. I'm breathing, yes, but the burn bites deep into my bones. I want to lift my head but it's too heavy; it's a giant tree stump buried in the roots of my arms. My arms are stinging. My elbow feels like shattered wreckage. Am I broken? Why can't I move?

I focus on my mouth. Teeth are clenched, jaw is locked. Prison. The prison of my face is buried in the stump log of my head that is handcuffed to my arms.

But, yes, I can breathe and I do. It feels good to breathe and, like a balloon, my head fills with air and becomes lighter, light enough that I can nearly imagine moving it. But only nearly.

I am wedged. I breathe into the darkness of my hot, exhaled air and I wonder if I am dreaming or floating slowly towards the light of wakefulness, at the surface of consciousness.

I wait, expecting to burst through like a drowning man freed after an interminable time of clawing upwards but there's no reprieve, and I'm not going anywhere. Although my head is a balloon, lighter, still, there's nothing but the burning, the sting, the darkness, and the air I breathe in and out.

Unclench jaw. Teeth snap apart with a click and the sandpaper of broken tooth enamel is gritty in my mouth. My tongue is a giant snake lodged in an earthworm's burrow and I want to move my giant python tongue but I can't. All I can do is sandpaper my palette with the tiny enamel tooth shavings that I ground down during the night. The night? Is that why it's so dark? It's night, I must be asleep but I panic, where is my surface?

I want out, away from the pain that burns from my elbow, which is crushed underneath me, crushed awkwardly, bent, twisted and broken. *Please,* I implore my limbs, my tongue, my head, my hand, *please, something move.*

My head budges a fraction, enough to make me believe that some movement now will equal all movement soon.

And it is so. Slowly, slowly, like a car being dredged up from the depths of a lake, my head is lifted by an invisible crane, lifted out of the dark, wet prehistoric roots of my burning, stinging, broken arms.

My eyelids are glued tight, but my head is upright and I can straighten my arms although it hurts like hell and I want to scream but I've yet to open my mouth.

My python tongue finally forces its way between my teeth, and I hiss inwards. The sound gives me strength and I snap my mouth open, a letterbox unhinged.

Pins and needles like boiling water, fingers pierced by cactus thorns of poisonous pain.

I am going to open my eyes. I tell myself this in no uncertain terms. I force my eyelids apart and stare blindly into the fierce flame of the unforgiving sun. I slam the shutters closed and hiss again.

Burning pain, broken teeth, searing light, why can't I find the surface of this terrible dream? Why can't I find the escape hatch of air, that geyser that will shoot me back into the land of daytime sanity and boring, reassuring normalcy?

My torso is twisted like a pretzel. Chair. I'm in a chair. Did I fall asleep at work? Am I at my desk, drooling, gritty-eyed and dishevelled for all the world to see?

I straighten my spine. Yes, that's definitely the arm of a chair.

I command my eyes to open again but I take it slowly this time, and I peek gingerly through slitted blinds, see fuzzy movement. People. There are people. I open the blinds just that much more. Yes, people.

Oh my god, I'm in an airport.

Floor-to-ceiling windows tower to the left, and I see planes lined up outside, white shark capsules ready to swallow sardines, ship them through the sky and spit them out on the other side.

But I notice something strange. None of the planes have any markings. They are void of Air Canada logos, there are no American flags, or British Airways or WestJet decals. There's nothing, only white sharks lined up on flawless licorice, the tarmac so fresh it looks chewy. Green lawns divide the runways under skies of the purest blue, accessorized by perfect cotton wool clouds, so pretty. I stare through Vaseline-smeared eyes and I blink a few times, hoping my vision will clear and that something will make sense, but there's nothing familiar about the world outside.

Was I in a plane crash? Is that what had happened? Maybe I'd been on my way somewhere—but where? And the plane crashed or maybe it had to make an emergency landing? The outdoors is reminiscent of the Caribbean and yet it also looks like nothing I have ever seen before.

I turn back to the world inside the airport, and I recoil. It's as if I have been punched in the gut, my already tender gut. The noise, the noise, the noise. It's like being slammed by a Mac truck, such is the impact of this harsh wall of noise. How could I have mistaken this chaotic inferno for the cool, quiet world of underwater blackness?

A crowd is gathered in front of me and they're screaming and jostling while airport staff make loud, unintelligible announcements over the intercom. Everybody's shouting at the same time.

I blink again, still trying to clear my eyes, and I unwind my body until I'm sitting straight up in my chair, well, nearly straight. My elbow is still stinging and I reach for it, fearing I will encounter sheer bone jutting through the flesh but the skin is as smooth and intact as ever. My arm aches as if I crushed it beneath me when I slept and it needs to ease the kinks out in its own time. But it is still hard to breathe. I feel winded, as if I've taken a bad fall from a horse and broken a few ribs.

I let my fingers explore the rest of my body. I reach for my face first, again, frightened by what I might find. But my hair is soft and silky and there are no cuts or bruises on my scalp. I brush my bangs aside and check my forehead. Undamaged. I slide my fingers down my nose. My nose is reassuringly my nose, long, with that tiny pinch at the tip. My cheekbones are high and rounded and familiar under my fingertips and my mouth is free of cuts although my lips feel chapped and dry, and this confuses me. I wet my lips with my tongue and again I taste the sandpapery grit of broken enamel. I explore my teeth and the inside of my mouth, but nothing is broken, nothing explains the sandy grit. My front teeth have always stuck out slightly, much to my annoyance, because I think it makes me look friendly and approachable, which I am not. My overbite and full lips give me a slightly open-mouthed, Marilyn-pout and my theory is that men find me irresistible because I look like I'm halfway ready to give them head, and I've got no feminist problems with that. Men and their predictable desires for my assets have made my life so much easier. I've always pitied the plain Janes. I gnaw on my bottom lip, a gesture that Martin finds so alluring and, reminded of him, I shoot up in my seat.

Martin! My husband! Where is he? Panic fills my chest and I stand up quickly. The room spins to black and I fall back into my chair. I lean forward, with my head over my knees and take shallow, little breaths.

I tell myself that I am fine. I got up too quickly, that's all. I must find Martin but I need a moment.

While I rest my head on my knees, my right hand searches my left for my wedding band and engagement ring, and, to my horror, I find nothing. Where are my rings? I would never have lost them. They, like Martin, mean the world to me.

I raise my head slowly and sit up. My vision has cleared and everything is in sharp focus.

I look around wildly, hoping to see Martin in the crowd. He must be there. I bet he's trying to find out what happened and he'll be back soon, back with directives and solutions. I can always rely on Martin.

I look at the seats next to me. They are the usual, steel-framed airport chairs, sectioned off by armrests. The black, padded, plastic-covered seats are empty.

I wonder where our luggage is. And, for that matter, where is my purse? I lean down again, taking my time, but there is nothing under the chairs.

I turn to look at the lounge area behind me. I am the only person in a sea of seats and the clamouring crowd is still in front me, but they are white noise now. Voices scream in my head: Where is Martin? What happened? What's going on? And where is my fabulous white leather Prada purse with the snake-print accordioned sides that I had bought only days before? Where are my Cartier rings, the startlingly huge emerald set high in a bank of diamonds, embedded in rose gold, with a wedding ring to match, a ring inscribed with the date of our wedding and, *Us, Always* in scripted font?

I focus on the crowd in front of me. A Noah's ark of the world's people are assembled, but there is no camaraderie or friendly intimacy. Kids in their twenties, old folks with walking sticks, businessmen, housewives, a rock star, a construction worker, an executive power-woman, a middle-aged lady in a cleaner's uniform, and a supermodel.

The surreal nature of the situation puzzles me and then I am further punched in the gut by three realizations. None of these people is dressed for a holiday, none of them has a companion, and none of them has any luggage.

I look down at myself and shrink back into my chair. What was I thinking, leaving the house like this? My navy blue sweatpants have seen better days and the pink T-shirt should have been thrown in the trash a long time ago. And I don't even have any shoes on, for god's sake.

I pull my feet up onto the chair and hug my knees to my chest and I am shocked anew by my pedicure, which is chipped and worn, as are my fingernails.

It's a tight fit, tall me scrunched up in the chair, but I fold into myself like a scrawny bird, wings hugging in tight and I chew on a fingernail, something I haven't done in years, but I need to gather my thoughts and try to make sense of what's going on.

Where's Martin? Why doesn't he come and find me? Why am I here alone?

And where on earth is here? Perhaps I had decided to go on a yoga retreat, it must have been something like that. Yes, I bet I was on my way to a spa and Martin was going to meet up with me once I had done ten days of downward dogging and nibbling on exotic fruit. But there's no way I would have gone with nails like this. My explanation doesn't make sense and I don't even like yoga—it's a sorry excuse for people who can't handle real exercise. Once again, I bury my head in my arms and try to focus on my breathing.

At least the pain has left my body. The pins and needles have gone, and there is no burning and no stinging. So that's good, but my distressed heart is thumping like an angry fist, and I cup my hand under my left breast, trying to calm myself down.

I am not sure how long I stay like that, but I finally decide, from the sanctity of my dark and cozy place, that I am going to find out just what the fuck happened.

2. AGNES

I UNFURL FROM MY PROTECTIVE BALL and lower my feet to the floor. The sharp, scratchy carpet pokes at my toes with synthetic fibers. I stand slowly and my head remains clear.

I raise myself to my full height, six-foot-one, and scan the room. I've always loved being tall. I've never been one to stoop on the arm of a shorter man, trying to diminish my height and Martin, bless him, short as he is, never wants me to either. He loves me in stilettos, towering, getting a bird's eye view of the world, and telling him what I can see.

Which, in this instance, isn't a lot.

Tall windows to the left show the same white, unmarked planes I noticed earlier, green astro turf, and black runways. Nothing moves. Planes are neither landing nor taking off, and there are no baggage carts scuttling about.

I walk over to the window, and cool linoleum replaces scratchy carpeting under my feet. I press my face up against the glass. The cotton wool clouds haven't moved since I first noticed them, but surely that isn't possible?

I will the clouds to move, even slightly, then study them for evidence of the tiniest shape change, but nothing happens, nothing at all.

I turn towards the crowd at the information desk. Where, I wonder, are the arrival and departure boards? The ground crew behind the desk are in uniform but there are no logos or badges, and their suits are dull navy and old-fashioned. Even their jaunty sailor hats are reminiscent of a 1970's poster, retro and boxy.

I need to speak to one of the crew.

I push my way to the front of the crowd, elbowing people aside, but a strange thing happens: as soon as I reach the counter, an invisible rubber band snaps me back to the end of the line. It happens so fast that I can't put the brakes on. The fourth time I reach the counter, I grab it with all my might, fingers digging in, but still, I find myself being flung backwards. It doesn't hurt, it's more like I am rewound, like a film clip that keeps jumping back.

After a dozen times, I lose my cool. "What the fuck? Seriously? What the fuck is going on here?" I am shouting but I don't care. "Is there some goddamned vortex or what? What the fuck?"

"She's a new arrival," someone says, and I spin around.

"Who said that?" I snarl. "Can someone please explain what's going on?"

"Your Introducer will show up eventually," someone else offers. "You have to wait."

"My what?"

"Better hope you don't get Agnes," an elderly woman with a Jamaican accent and a tight yellow perm says. "She's a crazy girl, that one."

"Martin!" I scream, "Martin, I'm here! Where are you? Please, I'm here, I'm here!"

"I'll get someone for you," a tall bony woman in her sixties says and she pats my shoulder. "Agnes? Agneessss!" She bellows, and I am astounded at the strength of her lungs, given that she looks skeletal. I also notice that she is sporting a snow-white billy goat beard that matches her brows and bouffant hair. I shrink back. I want to tell her that there are many ways to deal with unwanted facial hair, but she is yelling again and wouldn't have heard me anyway.

"Agneessss!"

"Yeah?" A tiny gothic girl pops up from under the Jamaican woman's arm.

"Help this woman," my bearded friend tells her. "How come we've got to tell you how to do your job? How you think you ever gonna get out of here?"

The girl shrugs and snaps gum. She eyes me. "That her?"

"How many other new ones you see?"

I am ping-ponging between them, my head bopping this way and that, like I am watching a tennis match.

The gothic girl looks at me and sighs. "Come with me," she says.

"Why?" I am suspicious.

"Because I've got the answers you're looking for. Don't get me wrong, I don't give a shit but it's my job to be your Introducer. We'll find a Lounge Room and you can take a load off and I'll tell you what's what but I'll be upfront, you're making me nervous, man, you're so freaked out."

"For god's sake," I snap at her, "forget the stupid fucking lounge. I need to know where I am, how I got here and what's going on."

"Julia," Agnes says kindly, "the sooner you shut the fuck up and follow me, the sooner you will be enlightened, whatever joy that may bring you."

That the girl knows my name both horrifies and silences me. I decide that the best course of action is to follow her away from the crowd and hear what she has to say.

We walk down a long, spotlessly clean corridor and I hear an odd beeping sound, like a truck reversing. The sound gets louder and I turn around in time to avoid being mowed down by a small airport buggy with flashing orange lights. A blonde woman is perched forward, hanging onto the steering wheel, pedal to the metal. She is in her late fifties, with a Maggie Thatcher helmet of hair. Her pug-dog eyes are popping and unblinking, and her grin would scare off monsters at Halloween.

"Who the fuck was that?" I ask, still pressed against the wall.

"Shirley the Driver. Who knows what she really does. I never see her actually giving anyone a ride. Come on, we're here."

Agnes leads us into a lounge with red walls. Lamps in various shapes and sizes create soft shapes of light in the room. It is like being inside a red lava lamp only nothing is moving. The room is filled with red bean bags and there are hanging basket chairs with fuzzy red cushions, and the floor is covered with soft, rectangular pieces of red foam.

"Is this a playroom for kids?" I ask, but Agnes shakes her head.

"There are hardly any kids here and they've got slides and nets and balls and shit. Stuff to climb on and break their necks, if they could, which they can't. But they're on the other side, they're not in this nook."

"Nook?"

"Where folks like us hang out. The kids move along quickly anyways, it's different for them."

This girl is making no sense at all. She waves me to sit and I sink down into a bean bag and cross my arms, thinking that the sooner I let her do her spiel, the sooner I'll be out of here.

"Ready whenever you are," I comment, with no small amount of sarcasm, and I watch in horror as she pulls out a pack of cigarettes.

"You can't smoke in an airport!" I protest, but she lights up and exhales a cloud in my direction.

"Sure you can," she says. "You want one?"

I shake my head. "What's the scoop here, Agnes?"

"What's your hurry, Lady Jane? I'll tell you this for starters, you've got all the time in the world, we both have."

She shakes with laughter and I want to hit her. I glare at her, hating her muffin-top belly that spills over the waistband of her tight black jeans. I hate her sleeve tattoos, her red and purple hair and most of all, I hate her piercings, all of which look infected. Nose, chin, ears, brows, they are disgusting.

"I tell you what, you motherfucking annoying child," I say evenly, "talk now, or I'm leaving."

"You can't leave," she says and she blows a smoke ring.

I lunge for her, knock her off her bean bag, and pin her to the ground. Her eyes are wide, like a panicked raccoon and the cigarette burns a hole in the carpet but I don't care.

Agnes stops moving. She lies underneath me and she looks up at me and grins without warmth or humour. "You're dead, Julia, dead, dead, dead."

"How do you know my name?" I dig my knees into her spongy upper arms, wanting to hurt her for saying such stupid things.

"I know, because I'm your Introducer. I'm here to show you the ins and outs of this life. Although, it's not a real life in the way you are used to. It's a no-man's land of wait and count your sins, and try to find the right way to atone, so you can get the heck out of here."

I bounce on her a few times, as heavily as I can, and I watch her face for a reaction. I'm trying to get her to tell the truth but she doesn't speak or move, and I cross my arms and wait.

"You can't hurt me," she says and she reaches for the cigarette and lies on her back, smoking, with me pinning her to the ground.

I notice that the cigarette burn on the carpet has vanished and I stare at the spot where it was. I'm about to ask Agnes about that, but she starts talking.

"I'm dead too," she says. "I think I've been here for a while but I don't know how long. Time is weird. It's like that thing that happened to you when you got to the front of the counter and you got bounced back. That happens a lot. Groundhog day, only not in any world you know."

"You. Are. Full. Of. Shit." I say, slowly, and I roll off her and sit cross-legged on the floor.

But something in what she says rings horribly true. "Where's my husband? How come he's not here?"

She gives me an inscrutable look. "You'll figure that one

out for yourself. I'm just here to give you the guided tour: *Purgatory for Dummies*."

"This is Purgatory?"

"It's no island cruise, I'll tell you that much."

"Why didn't I go to heaven?" I sound childish and forlorn and Agnes laughs like I have said something hilarious.

"Because you were a bad girl! We, all of us here, we were crap people." She stands up. "Come on, time for the tour, I'll show you around."

I stand up, numb, and I nod. I tell myself that by the time she gets to the end of her tour, I will have woken up and I'll recognize this for the bad dream that it is. And my husband will be by my side and my life will return to normal. Oh Martin. I can see you so clearly. All I want is for you to come and find me.

3. VERSACE

WE WALK DOWN A LONG HALLWAY. White institutional walls look like they have been painted with high gloss enamel. The floor is snowy linoleum and everything gleams. Steel beams hold a warehouse ceiling some twelve feet above me, and large silver pipes intersect like fat serpents, connected by shiny concertina folds.

"This is the Clothes Room," Agnes says and she opens a door.

We go inside and I gasp. I have stepped into a department store of the highest order, and it's filled, floor to ceiling, with endless couture. The shelves are piled high and a dozen full-length mirrors echo the opulence.

"This is utterly fantastic," I say. "Oh my god, look, it's vintage Dior! That's unbelievable. Do you know how much that dress is worth? What's it doing here?"

"It's doing the same thing as all the other shit," Agnes says lighting another cigarette. "Nothing."

"And this, oh my god, beaded Versace. It's impossible, this dress was one of a kind, no one knows what happened to it and now, here it is."

"You can wear it, if you like," Agnes says. She looks bored and leans against the wall, picking at her nail polish and letting her ash drop onto the floor.

"I can? But doesn't it belong to somebody?"

"Not anybody who gives a shit. The rules are, you can wear anything you like, but you can't take extras out of here."

"Who takes care of the clothes?" I ask, and Agnes shrugs.

"No idea. But they get cleaned and rehung."

"How will I choose?" I wail, holding up the beaded Versace cocktail dress and the Dior ball gown. "Look, two treasures! I can't possibly choose. I'll hold onto both of them while you finish giving me the guided tour, and we'll figure the rest out later."

"Julia," Agnes says patiently, "read my lips. You can't take anything with you. You get changed into the clothes here and wear them out. That's it."

I look around. "Isn't there someone I can leave one of them with? Like a holds counter or something?"

Agnes shakes her head. "There's no one. So put one of them on, or both of them if you're that in love with them, and we'll move on. You'll find this fascination with dead people's fancy leftovers wears off pretty quickly."

I look at the two creations. "I have to try them on," I say. "Where's the change room?"

Agnes points at a curtained corner and I shoot inside taking the garments with me.

I zip up the Versace and fit the Dior gown on top of the tight-fitting cocktail dress. It looks a bit odd but it works. No way am I letting go of either of them. I head back to Agnes who eyes my ensemble but doesn't say anything. "What must I do with my things?" I ask her.

I feel oddly detached from my old sweatpants and my pink T-shirt. Once again, I try to remember where we could have been going, my husband and I, that I would have been so poorly dressed. It annoys me that I can't remember what happened. I stare at the sad bundle of clothes I am about to get rid of and I wonder if I can come back and find them again if I want to, but I tell myself that I don't care. I have triumphantly scored not one, but two couture outfits, each worth thousands of dollars, so who cares about a pair of stupid old sweatpants and a faded pink T-shirt?

"Dump your stuff in the bin," Agnes points.

"I know the value of these garments," I tell Agnes, running my hands appreciatively over my Dior. "And I'm not going to let items like these go to waste. Do you have any idea what they'd sell for online? Let me tell you, I do know and I could even tell you in various foreign currencies."

Agnes shrugs and turns to leave and I follow her out into the hallway when I stop abruptly.

There is something I know for sure. These are not my feet. I am never without shoes, and I would never have gone anywhere with a pedicure in such a sorry state. These are not my feet.

I stand there, holding the hem of my ball gown, staring at some stranger's feet when I hear Agnes clear her throat.

"Gotta move on," she says. "C'mon."

"Wait," I say and I point, "those feet. They are not my feet."

"They are so your feet and I'm getting seriously bored, okay? We've got a lot of ground to cover, so please, accept the fact that those feet are your feet and let's move on."

"But something's very wrong," I say, and she laughs.

"Yeah, like you've only noticed now. Look, Queen Julia, if you don't come with me, I'm going to leave you here and they can get some other asshole to intro you."

All of a sudden, I feel strangely drugged, woolly, and confused, and I can't think straight. Where did those feet come from? Am I trapped in a stranger's body?

I lean against the wall and close my eyes. I shake my head, trying to dislodge the stoner brain swamp, but my nerve endings feel as if they have been soaked in soap suds and everything is blurry and slippery. I've lost my grip on reality. This is it: I've lost my mind.

"I wondered when this was going to happen," I hear Agnes sigh. "Stay where you are. I'm going to get a Soother. You need help. Don't move."

As if I could. I lean against the wall, and the finery of my ill-chosen garments feels stiff and prickly against my skin. At least the wall is cool and solid and I tell myself that as long as there are cool, solid walls, everything will be fine. I slide down to the floor and rest my head on my knees.

"Julia?" Agnes returns. "This is Intruiga. She's a Soother."

I open my eyes slightly and see an angel wearing a white hijab. She's also wearing an old-fashioned all-white nun's habit.

She takes my hand and strokes my arm lightly and the bones in my body melt. I hate arbitrary body contact but Intruiga's touch renders me helpless. She smells of oranges and tangerines, lavender and vanilla.

"You smell wonderful," I say, and my voice sounds oddly throaty.

"Cocoa bean base," she murmurs.

Her eyes are so dark they're nearly black, and I wonder if she's a witch of some kind.

She blows lightly on my arm and small currents of cool air caress my skin and I am incredibly aroused, entirely embraced, and utterly loved. I couldn't move even if I wanted to, but I don't want to. All I want is to sit still forever, and have this woman blow softly on my skin.

After too short a time, Intruiga stands up and she pulls me to my feet.

"You'll be fine," she says with a small smile and she raises my wrist to my nose. She has transferred her fragrance to me.

"Beautiful," I whisper.

"It will help you," she tells me and she slowly lowers my hand, running her thumb down my skin as she does so.

"Well," I say, at a loss to express everything I am feeling, "thank you."

Intruiga turns and walks a few feet down the corridor, and then she vanishes. She doesn't turn into a doorway, she simply evaporates.

"Wow," I say to Agnes. "That felt amazing. But where did she go?"

"Too hard to explain but yeah, she's good. Let's move on."

I nod and gather up the skirts of my gown, distracted once more by those traitor feet. There's a nail bar I go to every two weeks, mani/pedi, regular as clockwork. The mere thought of chipped nail polish is intolerable. God knows I have fired interns for arriving at work with less than perfect nails. A prospective copywriter showed up for an interview with an outdated French manicure and talon-length nails and I told her right there and then that if she did that sort of thing, how on earth could she expect to make it in the big leagues? She left weeping, the stupid girl, when she should have thanked me for giving her valuable advice. And, if she had admitted that her manicure was ridiculous, there might have been a chance for her but instead she melted into tears and that was when I really lost my patience. Who comes to an interview and cries? No one with any kind of backbone.

I continue to follow Agnes down the endless hallway, past countless closed doors but there is something I have to know.

"Wait," I call out and she stops right where she is, with her back to me, and I can see her heave a great sigh.

"Tell me where we are," I say. "I won't freak out. Just tell me what's going on here."

Agnes turns to face me. "This is Purgatory and you are dead," she says matter-of-factly. "We all are. Everyone here is in different stages of the process. I don't know where you are on the scale of things or how fast you'll move through. And don't ask me what comes next, because I've got no idea. None of us knows. And none of us knows what we have to do to get out of here. I don't have those answers."

"How did I die?"

"I don't know that, either. You'll figure it out, or you won't. There are people here who can help you with that, and I'll introduce you to them."

"I'm really dead," I say, and the Intruiga-infused calm leaves me. I am dizzy and I lean against the wall. I sink down onto my haunches.

"I'm not dead," I tell Agnes, and I close my eyes. "I can feel things physically, therefore, I am extremely undead."

She doesn't reply. From the sounds of it, she sits down next to me. I hear her light a cigarette and the smoke wafts towards me.

"Give me one," I say, and I sit up and hold out my hand.

She hands over the pack and I light up, inhaling deeply. The intoxicating head rush floods my brain and lungs, and I exhale slowly. Clarity returns, panic subsides.

"Thank god for smoking," I say, "I love it. I have since I was twelve."

"Me too," Agnes says and it seems we have found common ground.

"Fact," I say, inhaling deeply, "if we were dead, we wouldn't be smoking or enjoying it."

"I'm not going to argue with you," Agnes says. "That's not my job description. I'm here to intro you, that's it, and then you have to deal with it."

"Do you get to leave here once you've done your job with me?"

"Hell no. It's not that easy. You'll see. I got promoted because I made progress and I accepted the job for the perks. More privileges. But none of it means shit to me. I don't care about anything."

"I see." I take another drag. Agnes is beginning to bore me. "Why don't we continue? I'll try to stop interrupting you and let you do your job."

She stands up. "The next stop on our guided tour of Purgatorial Delights is the Rest Room."

"We still use the washrooms even though we're dead?'

"We do. But the washrooms are not the Rest Rooms. The Rest Rooms are where you go to rest, like really, rest."

We finish our cigarettes and grind the butts into white enamel sand buckets that hang from the walls. I wonder what Purgatory has to offer next.

4. CANTEEN, REST ROOMS, ABLUTION BLOCKS

AGNES OPENS A RANDOM DOOR and I follow her, but I can't see a thing. It's as dark as a black sky reserve that a boyfriend took me to so we could make out under a meteor shower. Only there are no meteors here, only dense blackness.

"A black hole?" I joke in a whisper.

"Shh." She pulls me to one side. "You can't talk in here. Follow me, okay?"

I nod and she leads me to a second door, which is black and as thick as a bank vault. She touches a tiny glowing amber button and the door swings outwards without making a sound. We step inside the room and the door closes behind us, equally silently.

I can see even less inside the dark room than I had in the preceding foyer. I hug my arms to my chest, overwhelmed by the cloth of darkness enfolding me. I'm about to turn and start pounding on the door to be let out, when my eyes start distinguishing tiny lights. I see orange fireflies, like cigarette cherries dotting the night.

Agnes takes my hand, which I do not expect, and I jump with surprise, and nearly scream. She quickly guides my fingers to a switch near one of the lights. I flick the button and a warm nightlight, shaped like a Halloween pumpkin, emits a reassuring warmth. The colour isn't exactly orange—it's richer and softer, more like the saffron of a Buddhist monk's robes, and I am soothed by its presence. I am about to ask Agnes about the lights and she must sense it, because she shakes her head, holds a finger to her lips and points to a curtain which she pulls around us, much like a hospital enclosure. The curtain slots into place with a magnetic grip and I can't say how it happens, but an even more solid silence settles in the small space. My eyes adjust further and I see an oval-shaped king-sized bed. The sheets, comforter, and pillows are all black and I am reminded of a discussion I had with my annoying art director who was trying to explain the difference between rich black and a single colour black.

"If you mix black with cyan and magenta and some yellow," he said, showing me the swatches on his computer screen, "you get a rich black. Look at how much deeper it is—it's got layers to it, like liquid velvet."

I saw exactly what he meant but I didn't want to give him the satisfaction of having been able to teach me anything, so I nodded and walked off as if he had been wasting my time.

But this bed linen is a deep, rich black and I want to touch it, stroke it.

I take a step closer to the bed and Agnes tugs me down with her. I lie back on what feels like velvet and immediately I am weightless, floating on a beautiful sea of buoyant warmth. My worries, my fears, and my anger are a distant memory. Agnes seems content too.

I drift peacefully until the curtain soundlessly opens. Drat. Agnes flicks a switch and the pumpkin glows again, and we can see well enough to find our way out of the room. We walk through the dark foyer and out into the startlingly white hallway and I blink, trying to adjust to the snowy glare.

"You can see why it's called the Rest Room," Agnes says. "You go there when you need a time-out. Don't worry about making the beds; it's done after you leave. You're allowed to stay for four hours max, and then the curtains open like they did now, and you have to leave or you get bounced. I wish I could stay in there all the time."

"It was amazing," I admit. "Why only four hours?"

"Because they know we'd never leave if they didn't give us rules. I don't know why it's four instead of two or eight or six. I guess they figured four is the perfect amount of time to keep us constantly in limbo. Haha, in limbo in Purgatory!" Her own joke cracks her up, but I am not amused. My fears, worries, and anger are back and it's clear that the soothing effects of the Rest Room have no staying power.

"Who are 'they'?"

"The Regulators."

I decide to let that slide for the moment.

"Smoke break?" I ask, and she hands me the pack.

We light up. "We get endless cigarettes?" I ask, and she shakes her head.

"Privileges. You've got to earn them."

Rules. Regulators. Four-hour rest sessions. Privileges. It's all so complicated. "What's next?" I ask.

"The Canteen," she says. "But we all call it the caf."

We finish our cigarettes in silence and I take the time to look around. I notice skylights high up in the warehouse ceilings, skylights that show patches of that eerie, bold blue. The swell of a green hillside and more of the unchanging blue is visible through a window at the end of the hallway.

"Does it ever rain?" I ask, and Agnes shakes her head.

"It's always like this. There is a Rain Room though."

"Of course there is," I say, and I laugh although I don't think anything is even remotely amusing. "Let me ask you this. None of the doors have any signs on them. How will I know which one is which one?"

"It's a bit tricky at first," she admits. "They should have come up with a system. Eventually, you just know what's where, but it does take a while."

Attention, please! May I have your attention, please? An airport announcer speaks loudly through the intercom and I jump.

"What the fuck?" I look around.

"No one knows," Agnes says helpfully. "It just says that now and then. None of us knows who says it or why. Come on, the Canteen, which, if you ask me, should be called the Food Room, in keeping with all the other Rooms. But no, and that's Purgatory for you."

Attention, please! May I have your attention, please? The disembodied voice echoes its command.

Agnes ignores it and opens another unmarked door and we enter a sprawling, Ikea-style cafeteria. A seaside mural flanks one wall, with a palm tree on an airbrushed, eggshell-coloured beach, and two red Adirondack chairs face a burning sunset.

On the other side of the room, windows showcase the rolling St. Paddy's Day green hills with deep, sloping valleys carpeted in that relentless, verdant, springy clover.

Something occurs to me and I walk over to the windows.

"Where's the sun?" I ask Agnes. "And where are the shadows? Look, there are clouds but they cast no shadows. That's unnatural."

Agnes finds this hilarious. "That's unnatural? Of all the bat shit crazy crap in here, that's what you find unnatural?" She can't stop laughing and I think of a thousand terrible things to say to her but I manage not to say any of them. I walk around, inspecting the cafeteria.

Unsurprisingly, the tables are white, with white-framed foldout chairs with three white wooden slats for seats and a single slat to support one's back.

I test one and while it is not exactly a Herman Miller, it isn't terrible either.

My fury simmers down and I rejoin Agnes.

"Where's the menu?" I ask, and Agnes points to a Kleenex-sized box on the table, which I had mistaken for a stainless steel napkin dispenser. But it is a computer of sorts, with a continuously scrolling menu. I pull it towards me and study it.

There are pasta dishes, with meatballs and vegetarian options. There are stews, chicken dishes, pizza, sandwiches, fruit, desserts, casseroles, muffins, cookies, sweet buns, yoghurt, cheese platters, fish dishes, ribs, burgers, hot dogs, French fries, and baked potatoes. Soups and salads. There are waffles and pancakes and crêpes, with all kinds of toppings. There are scrambled eggs, fried eggs, bacon, hash browns, the works. Ice cream, cakes, scones, and pastries. There are stir-fries and burritos and then there are dishes classified by nationality; Indian, Thai, Mexican, Japanese and Jamaican. The list is endless and I get tired of scrolling through the options.

"There's so much to choose from," I say, but Agnes shakes her head.

"Not really, not once you've done the loop a dozen times. Then it all starts to taste the same."

"How do you order? The menu isn't organized numerically or alphabetically or by food groupings. I don't get it."

"Another one of the joys of Purgatory is the inconsistency with things like that. Things can be so random, but you'll get used to it." She scoots around so she's sitting next to me. "Here's how you search for something." She shows me on the screen. "Then you make a note of the number. For example, the code for macaroni and cheese is #3641. You punch it in here," she points to the screen, "and when you hear a wind chime, you grab a tray from over there, go to the microwave number on the screen, and there it is. Very simple really. You put your dirty plates in that bin, and your trays on that console and that's it. Most of us who have been here for a while don't seem to get hungry. Eating is more of a habit than anything, or just something to do when you're bored, but there are people who eat for comfort. If you come here often, you'll see a lot of regulars."

"And it's never dark in here and the view never changes?"

"It's never dark and the view never changes." Agnes affirms and she sounds tired.

"How long have you been here?" I ask. "I know you said something about it before, but I don't remember."

"I don't know. We don't have clocks or watches or calendars or anything. It's endless really."

I don't know what to make of that, or what to say. By all rights, I should be panicking, after all, this is really fucked up, but I have moved from hysteria to numbness.

"How many people are here?" I ask. The cafeteria is deserted and there is no sign of the crowd I saw when I first arrived.

Agnes shrugs. "Hard to say. You'll see more people as time goes on. It's weird that way. It's like people know to leave you alone until you get settled and then it gets busy and you wonder where everybody came from."

"And who are the Regulators?" I ask.

"I don't know. We never see them. They enforce things, but they never do anything in person. It's like you suddenly just know the new rule is here."

"Is the food any good?" I ask.

"Pretty good. We'll get a test dish for you. What's your favourite thing?"

"I'm the furtherest thing from hungry," I comment. "But fine, let's test. I'll have a platter of nigiri and a bottle of Moët & Chandon Don Pérignon White Gold champagne."

"Nice try," Agnes says. "No drugs or alcohol in Purgatory. We'd all be off our faces all the time. But sushi, yes."

She punches in a number and, in short order, I have a large platter of saki nigiri in front of me. I want to find fault with it but it's the best sushi I have ever eaten. For some reason, this infuriates me. I refuse to finish it and I push the plate aside. Agnes gets up and deposits it in the console she pointed out.

My double-layer outfit is beginning to chafe under my arms and I yank at the ball gown to try to loosen it. I am about to tell Agnes that we need to return the Dior when the doors to the caf open and a group of women enters, identically dressed in white. "The bowling ladies," Agnes explains. The group looks like they've stepped off the pages of a bowling catalogue with their pristine outfits, from the hats down to the shoes.

"They're regulars," Agnes says. "There's a Bowling Room for them and they pretty much live there unless they're in here. I've never seen a bowling lady anywhere by herself. They always travel together. They died together, maybe that's why. Their bus went off the side of a mountain when they were on a tour in Italy and none of them wants to move on. They've been here for longer than me, I know that much."

I watch the bowling ladies line up. They order crustless cucumber sandwiches, Petit Fours, Bavarian chocolate cake, scones and crumpets with whipped cream and jam, and several pots of tea.

"They look happy," I say, and Agnes shakes her head.

"They've made their peace with it. That's not happy. I don't want to be here forever but I can't seem to move on. I try to, but I'm stuck and I don't know why. I hope I don't end up like them, here forever, not happy but just doing it. It's true, though, you can get comfortable."

"Can we see the washrooms?" I ask, not knowing how to respond to her comments.

"Sure. They are called Ablution Blocks. This way."

We leave the cafeteria and walk down the endless hallway again.

As we pass one of the doors, I hear a piercing scream and I stop, horrified. It sounds like someone is being tortured alive.

"What the fuck was that?"

"The Scream Room," Agnes says calmly. "It's supposed to be soundproof but as you can hear, it's not. I tried to free my inner scream but all that comes out is a little squeak. Says loads about me, I suppose. Maybe one day when I can scream at the top of my lungs, I'll be able to move on."

"How old are you?"

"Twenty-four."

"So young," I say. "How did you die?"

"I'll tell you one day," Agnes says. "Maybe. Here we are, at an Ablution Block. There are a few of them around and they aren't signposted as being male or female but the correct one will appear for you. Purgatory isn't in favour of gender-neutral facilities, although I've never bumped into anyone inside, male or female. "

"What if you're trans?"

"Then a trans one would pop up. Purgatory knows everybody's shit inside and out. It's freaky that way. You'll see."

The Ablution Block reminds me of a corporate gym changing room. Industrial grey carpeting lines the floor and there are steel lockers and wooden benches. Showers are to one side, with lilac curtains and pale grey tiles.

"No bathtubs?" I am dismayed.

"No bathtubs," Agnes confirms. "I guess they think showers are less luxurious or something. This isn't supposed to be a spa vacay in the Bahamas."

"But the bowling ladies have their version of heaven," I object. "Bowl all day, enjoy high tea, and do whatever they want."

"Even they can only have a room for four hours, and then they have to leave."

"I have a question: How can you calculate four hours if there's no such thing as time here?" I feel smug, as if I have found the flaw in Purgatory and, in so doing, have solved the mystery of the whole place. I'm confident I will soon find myself back in my own bed, with all this nothing more than a very odd, very intricate dream.

Agnes isn't impressed by my insightful discovery. "Everybody just knows it's four hours," she says.

"How long before you can go back?"

"There's no definitive number. You just know."

I inspect the showers. "Very utilitarian," I say. The showerheads are small and nothing like the sunflower-sized, five-star hotel designs that I am used to. Hanging wire baskets are filled with mini bottles of no-name shampoos and conditioners. I inspect the individually wrapped bars of soap and I rip the plastic off one and sniff it. Nothing. How can soap smell of nothing? I sniff it again and catch the vaguest scent of a memory of clean and I look at Agnes in horror. I take my soaps very seriously.

"Not exactly *Pré de Provence*," I say sarcastically and although Agnes looks blank at the reference, she understands what I mean. She shrugs, takes the soap from me and throws it in a steel trashcan. I catch sight of myself in the bank of mirrors and I recoil in horror. My skin is dull and pasty, my hair looks like it got caught in a wind tunnel, and my eyes are bloodshot.

"What the fuck happened?" I ask. "Look at me." My eyes fill with tears and I look away, unable to deal with my bedraggled and sorry self. There are hair dryers on the counter, next to two steel trays, one filled with hairbrushes and a sign that says USE, while the empty tray bears the sign USED.

"You put your used hair brushes into that one," Agnes states the obvious.

I know I should pick up a brush and fix my hair but I am flooded with exhaustion.

"I need a break," I say, and I sound grumpy.

"We can go back to the Rest Room," Agnes suggests, but I shake my head.

"Let's go for a walk," I say. "I think best when I'm walking. Actually, running. I suppose there's a Running Room too?"

Agnes nods. "Yeah, but you need special privileges for it. There are endless Rooms, but you can't get into them unless your Helper gives you a voucher."

"I shouldn't have worn this stupid ball gown." I am angry with myself. "It's uncomfortable and hot and scratchy. I don't give a fuck if it's vintage Dior. I don't care if I never see it again."

I wrench it off, ripping it in the process and I feel childishly satisfied. I tear the bodice from the skirt for good measure and fling the torn pieces on the floor.

"Let the cleaners deal with that," I announce scornfully and Agnes smiles.

"They will. They don't care if you break things. No one cares about stuff here."

I look at the ruined ball gown on the floor and give it a kick for good measure.

"I want a pedicure," I say petulantly and Agnes sighs.

"There's a Room for that," she begins, but just as quickly I lose interest.

"Actually, forget the mani/pedi crap. How do I get out of here? I want to get the fuck out of Purgatory, so tell me how to do that."

"You have to come to an epic realization," Agnes says. "I can introduce you to your Helper. He'll guide you through the process. Let's go. Now is a good a time as any."

"Are Helpers therapists?"

"Sort of, only they are ordinary people who have been promoted."

"So they haven't reached their own realization but they tell us how to?" I am sarcastic.

"They may or may not have. Once you've reached your realization, they say you can choose whether or not to stay. You might be surprised, but many want to stay."

We leave the Ablution Block and Agnes leads me down the corridor, another airport runway of polished linoleum. We finally turn a corner and I see a row of glass brick offices.

It looks like the human resources department at work. The décor is impersonal and bland and there's a ubiquitous leafy Boston fern that I can tell is a fake. An enormous signboard dominates the area. It is a slogan-bearer, much like the signs you see outside churches, trying to entice you to attend Sunday mass with a clever quip. This sign says: *Mere religion does not take away the penalty of sin.*

"Who's in charge of the sign?" I ask.

"What sign?"

How can she not see the sign? I point to it and she shrugs. "I never noticed it before," she says.

She is tapping a code onto an electronic whiteboard that I had failed to see, and she studies the screen.

"Ha!" she laughs.

"What?" I walk up to her and stare at the board.

"You've got Cedar Mountain Eagle."

"Male or female?"

"Male. Hippie dude as you can probably tell by his name. You ready to meet him?"

"Why did you laugh?"

"He takes some getting used to, but he's good. You ready?"

"He's my ticket out of here?"

"I guess."

"Then, yeah, I'd like to meet him, pronto-haste."

Agnes points down the narrow hallway of glass bricks.

"Third office on the left. His name's on the door."

"You aren't coming with me?" I am alarmed at the thought of Agnes leaving.

"Nope."

"Where will I find you afterwards? No, ditch that. Will you wait out here for me?"

"You don't need me to wait for you. You'll be fine. I'll be at the Canteen. Or the Card Room. I like to play poker. We use jellybeans for money."

"Oh, for god's sake," I say. "I'll never find you. This place is an endless maze of halls and unmarked rooms. I'll never see you again, will I?" I am panic-stricken and I grab at Agnes's arm.

"Sure you will," Agnes says and she pats my hand. "I'll come and find you. Don't worry, I won't abandon you. This is my designated job, remember."

That a midget-sized, overweight gothic girl with a face full of piercings, a head of red and purple hair, and a variety of senseless tattoos has fast become my best friend, says a lot about my current situation.

I watch her walk away and I feel more alone than I ever have in my entire life, and let me tell you, I have done alone.

I figure the sooner I get my meeting with the hippie dude done and dusted, the sooner I will be able to make my way back down to Earth and I turn towards the door.

5. CEDAR MOUNTAIN EAGLE

I KNOCK ON THE DOOR. "Come in, come in, we don't stand on ceremony here," a high-pitched male voice calls out and I instantly hate him. I like deep, chocolate, radio-rich baritones. There's something about a shrill man that invites disrespect.

I open the door and my dislike is confirmed by what I see. A tall, old hippie stands before me. His greying hair is pulled back into a ponytail, and he has a weirdly elongated torso that accounts for most of his body, long simian arms, short corduroy-clad legs, Jesus sandals, and an ornate feather necklace.

"Julia! I've been waiting for you! I'm Cedar Mountain Eagle and I will be your Helper during your time in Purgatory. Of course, Agnes isn't one of the more speedy Introducers but be that as it may. No disrespect intended of course. Agnes and I go way back. I'm very open and honest about my feelings with, and to her, and I encourage you to be the same with regards to all your relationships in Purgatory. I encourage you to be absolutely honest with me."

In which case, I should probably tell him that I already hate him but I'm fairly certain that will be counter-productive. There is always time for insults later.

I sit down on a brown corduroy sofa that sags in the centre but is surprisingly comfortable. I immediately feel sleepy.

"To start, I'd like to clarify that this isn't therapy," Cedar says. "This is open, honest communication that will hopefully help you move towards the healing light of realization, thereby setting you free from the prison chains that hold your soul captive."

"And in specific, practical terms, that means what?"

He chuckles and I grit my teeth. "Ah, now, Julia, I encourage you to leave those rigid thought-patterns behind you. Specific, practical, etcetera etcetera. Who needs the constraints of such boundaries? I encourage you to open your heart and mind to new ideas, new thought patterns, and new motivations. And do you know what the only real motivator is, Julia? Can you guess?"

"Money? Power?" I know he won't go for those but I have to throw them out there anyway, and he gives that shrill chuckle again.

"Oh my dear, you are in so much pain. No, sweetie, it's love. Love is all you need. You may think it's a cliché but it's true!"

"I don't believe anybody has ever called me sweetie in my life," I say.

"Well, there we go," he says cheerfully. "Breaking new ground already. That's what we're here to do, break new ground. What would you like to talk about today?"

"Why the fuck I'm here."

He frowns and shakes his head emphatically. "I don't have many rules, Julia, in fact I am well-known for being Mr. Easy Going, but I draw the line at profanity. Please, no swearing."

"And what if I do swear?"

"Then our session will be terminated until the following day."

"I thought you guys don't have time here. How will I know it's been a day?"

"The door will not open," he says. "The door will remain shut. Now, if you'd like to talk about how and why you are here, over to you. I encourage you to say anything you wish."

"Without swearing, of course."

"Yes, no profanity."

"I thought you hippies swore like troopers, man." I am mocking him but he just looks at me.

"I encourage you to respect the rights of the individual, Julia, and I personally don't approve of swearing."

"Do you put the signs up on the board outside the therapy office?"

"These aren't therapy offices," he corrects me. "They're Help-Facilitation Centres. What sign are you talking about?"

"The one—" I give up. "So, Cedar Bear,"

"Cedar Mountain Eagle," he corrects me. "And you know it. I encourage you to respect my name, just as I respect yours."

"Don't you have a more normal name? Like Dave or Judas or something?"

His eyes narrow. "You see me as your betrayer?"

"It was a joke, man. You guys aren't big on humour, are you?"

"Depends on the humour," he fires back, deadpan. "I'll tell you honestly, Julia, that I don't believe you and I will be sharing much by way of humour. However, that will not impede the healing process, unless you let it."

"How do I get out of here?" I ask. "I want to go back home."

He looks at me steadily. "You weren't exactly happy back home," he says.

"What's that supposed to mean? What do you know about me? What happened to me?"

"Life happened, Julia. And it's not what happens, it's how we deal with it."

"And I dealt with it how?"

"You don't remember?"

"No, Dave, I don't. Give me a clue."

He sighs. "This isn't a game, Julia." He looks out the window.

"Don't you ever get tired of the same fucking view?" I ask without thinking, and Cedar Mountain Eagle stands up.

"See you tomorrow," he says courteously and I find myself outside his door, with no idea how I got there.

"Fuck me gently with a barge pole," I say to the door. I am tempted to knock but I don't want to give Cedar the pleasure of knowing that I am trying to get back in.

I stop in front of the sign, which now says: *There is more hope for a fool than for someone who speaks without thinking.*

"Ha ha, very fucking funny," I say. "Well, that was a blast, wasn't it?" I turn to leave, hoping I am heading in the right direction.

6. MAKEOVER

I SAUNTER DOWN THE HALLWAY, away from Dave the Mountain Man and his fucking therapy office, and I enjoy the feeling of my bare feet slapping against the coolness of the linoleum. But I feel horribly lost. All the corridors look the same.

"Card Room," I say, out loud. "Card Room, appear, toot sweet." But nothing happens. It seems Purgatory hasn't granted me any magical powers.

On impulse, I open the next door and a group of men look up at me from the floor. They are playing with model trains and I can tell by their expressions that "playing" is the wrong terminology. They glare at me with an expression close to hatred.

"Can we help you?" one of the men asks, clearly wanting me to leave.

"I'm looking for Agnes," I say, and he shrugs.

"In that case, I'll close this door and open another," I joke, but they don't respond. They just glare at me and I leave, baffled. I lean against the wall and try to process what just happened.

Here's the thing. I am, by my own or any definition really, extremely beautiful. Women hate me and men love me and that's what I'm used to. Therefore, the reaction of those guys was beyond unusual. Never, and I do mean never, not since my blossoming adulthood anyway, have I entered a room full of men and encountered such nothingness. Well, it wasn't entirely nothingness, there was an ounce of disinterest, coloured by a smidgeon of disdain.

Disdain? For me?

I look down at myself. I am still wearing the fantastically bright, tiny Versace dress and it clings in all the right places and reveals all the right things. How could they have resisted me? Granted, I am barefoot with the chipped remains of a pedicure, but surely my beautiful legs make up for that fashion misdemeanor?

My faith is shaken. I had forgotten to ask Agnes about sex and I hope this isn't the kind of place where beauty, sex appeal, and physical charms hold no sway, because if that's the case, I'll be in deep shit.

I try another door and find a group of women knitting and crocheting.

"Come in, come in!" They are too welcoming and I back out as if I've stumbled into a room full of bees.

These doors. Why can't they have signs on them?

I try another one. Ah! Mecca! This must be the Makeup Room. It's an enormous cavern filled with makeup, nail polish, fragrances, hair styling products, creams, lotions and potions. I feel right at home and I figure I may as well take care of my awful pedicure before trying to find Agnes again.

I pluck a bottle of nail polish remover and some cotton balls off a shelf and sit down on the sofa. I'll give Purgatory this: it's one helluva comfortable place. Well, parts of it are, anyway.

I bend down to clean the chipped aqua polish off my toes and maybe I lean down too quickly, but I suddenly feel dizzy and everything goes black. I have a fleeting vision or thought or something, of me getting my nails done with the lovely aqua polish and I was happy at that moment but then something went horribly wrong. What had happened? Something very bad but I can't remember what.

My husband! Martin! I shoot upright. My vision is still black and my ears are ringing. How could I have forgotten about him? He must be here somewhere but where? How can I find him? I can see him clearly: he's a little man, not very tall at all, blonde and handsome as a movie star. He's particularly well-dressed. He wears bespoke suits and he's never without his monogrammed cufflinks. He drives a Lamborghini convertible and he loves to laugh. And I've lost him.

Did we have an accident? Is he dead? If he's dead, why isn't he here with me? I sit motionless on the sofa, wishing I had the answers to my questions. The door opens and Agnes strolls in.

"Hi," she says. "How did it go with Cedar?"

I shrug. "He kicked me out for dropping the f-bomb."

"Yeah, he does that. He's alright though, you'll see."

"He says you're a very slow Introducer." I feel the need to be spiteful but Agnes just laughs.

"I would encourage Cedar to accept me as I am," she says. She takes out the pack of cigarettes and offers me one and I accept gratefully.

"I'm so confused," I say. "I want to know what happened to my husband."

"Can't help you," Agnes says blowing smoke rings. "What do you want to do now? There's the Reading Room, if you like, or we could hit the Disco Room and boogie for a bit. I've got privileges, I could take you."

"Boogie? I wouldn't have thought you'd be the type to boogie."

"Desperate times call for desperate measures," she tells me. "Anyway, disco was a very cheerful era. I'm going to paint my nails while I'm here."

She picks up a bottle of black nail varnish and starts to haphazardly paint her nails while I watch in horror.

"Good thing you never applied for a job with me," I comment. "A sloppy manicure is the sign of a sloppy mind."

"Were you a bitch to work for?"

I laugh. "Yes, I was. Everybody in power is mean. You don't get respect unless you act like a bitch. People expect it. My staff were instructed not to say good morning to me, unless I greeted them first. Oh my god, Agnes, come here, I've never seen such a botched job." I pull her closer to me and scrub her nails with varnish remover until they are perfectly clean. I neatly apply a single coat, with precise little strokes.

"Don't move until they're dry," I say.

"Thanks, Mom," she says and the word "mom" triggers a nasty feeling in my gut and I shrug.

"You ever had kids?" Agnes eyes me while she blows on her nails.

"I don't think so. I'd remember if I did, wouldn't I?" I frown.

"Sometimes it takes a while," she says. "I didn't remember stuff for ages and it was no party when I did, I'll tell you that much. Stay ignorant for as long as you can, my friend." She licks her freshly-painted fingernails.

"What are you doing?" I grab her hand.

"It helps it dry faster," she says.

"Yeah, by poisoning yourself," I tell her and she laughs, a carefree, pretty sound at odds with her tough-girl appearance.

"You should have seen all the drugs I took," she says. "No one could party like me. I could drink a whole bottle of nail polish and my body wouldn't notice."

"Is that how you died? Drugs?"

"Drug related," she acknowledges. "Are you going to do your toes?"

I look down and shake my head. "No. Come here, time for a second coat. What do you do around here for fun?"

"This is Purgatory," Agnes says reprovingly. "We're not here to have fun."

I finish her nails and apply some make-up to my face while we wait for her polish to dry. I style my hair and I start to look more familiar to myself.

"Funny how much I know about this shit," I tell Agnes. "The latest face creams, fragrances, eyeliners, you name it. I was wined and dined by the cosmetics industry, you've got no idea. I took bags of products home daily. I could have shared them with the staff, sure I could have but no, I took everything home. Chanel, La Prairie, Dior, Givenchy. I had more shit at home than I knew what to do with. I'd open a moisturizer that cost nearly $500, try it for a night and never use it again. And it wasn't only product. I got cashmere blankets, towels, briefcases, purses, designer earrings, jewelry, couture, and shoes. And that's not the end of the list either."

"How did they know what size your feet were?" Agnes asks, licking her black nails again.

"Stop that," I say. "They emailed and asked me. I got tickets to all the concerts. I got to see everybody. I saw Lady Gaga five times and Beyoncé more times than I can remember. Everybody. Even people I never cared about, or had never heard of."

I pick out a bottle of topcoat, sit next to Agnes, and apply the final coat to her nails.

"My apartment is like something out of hoarders," I laugh. "Only it is worth thousands, all the shit I have."

"You didn't have a sister or mother to share it with?"

I think hard. "I may have. Something about that feels familiar but I don't know what. How come I can remember all the free shit I got, but I can't remember who my family were?

Agnes shrugs. "You will. It will come back to you. You'll see. Like I say, be glad you don't remember."

I look at her. "Why? Surely it's better to know?"

"Don't call me Shirley," she jokes. "Just trust me, it hurts when it starts to come back. Like getting feeling back when you've had bad pins and needles. It burns."

I nod, remembering the stinging burn of arriving in Purgatory.

"Listen," Agnes says getting up, "It's time you met some of the other inmates, apart from me and Cedar Mountain Sage Brush. You ready?"

"I don't know," I say. "Hey, where's Intrigua? She was cool."

Agnes laughs. "Everyone loves her. But she's only for emergencies and newbies who are freaking out. You were freaking out big time, that's why you got her. You were lucky."

"I'll never see her again?" I am disappointed.

"Only if you have a major meltdown."

I pick up a bottle of Guerlain's Habit Rouge and show it to Agnes. "This fragrance has the same notes as the one she was wearing," I say, and I spray myself liberally while Agnes ducks.

"None of that stinking crap for me," she says. "Reminds me of my mother. Too rich for her own blood, stingy as a nun. Now, anything with roses, that's what I like."

"Roses are for old ladies," I say unthinkingly, and Agnes's eyes fill with tears.

"Exactly," she says. She walks over to the fragrances, picks up Moroccan Rose, and sprays herself liberally, and this time *I* dive out of the way.

"Now that you smell like a horde from an old-age home," I say, "let's go and meet some other fun people. Lead the way."

7. MY NEW CREW

W E WALK THROUGH THE MAZE of wide hallways, past dozens of closed doors, and into the vast, nether regions of the building. Purgatory is like an endless airport hanger, broken up into dozens of tiny rooms, each housing a strange piece of the world we have left behind.

I hear that crazy beeping and I jump out of the way just in time to let Shirley the Driver go by on her buggy, lights flashing. She is still grinning that horrible grin, teeth bared like a wolf under a full moon, her hands white-knuckling it on the steering wheel.

I have, strangely, accepted my current life, such as it is. It would be fruitless to try and smash my way out by denying its existence. Like a bad dream, I have to let it play itself out until I wake up and get my real life back.

Agnes stops and reaches for a door handle. "They're dying to meet you," she says with a lopsided grin. "Or, should I say, they died to meet you?" She chortles and opens the door.

"Wow, this is nice," I say as I step into a small, boutique coffee shop. There are overstuffed leather chairs and a low, rustic wooden table. A bookcase lines one wall and there is a sideboard with milk and canisters of sugar, vanilla powder, nutmeg, and cinnamon. It's a miniaturized Starbucks.

"Special privileges," Agnes says. "You are here as our guest. Samia was a barista back on Earth. She can whip up anything."

Samia is a short, strikingly lovely girl with a geometric sweep of dark hair pulled to one side and perfect eye makeup that meets my approval.

"Not many people can do a cat's eye as well as that," I tell her and she thanks me.

"Practice," she says. "The one thing we have here is time. What can I get for you?"

"Venti, non-fat, no foam, 180 degree latte," I immediately reply. "That would be fantastic. I might even mistake this for Heaven."

The gathered lot don't smile at my joke and I sigh. More humourless people. I am annoyed that they don't appreciate my attempts at levity and I sink down into a chair and study my surroundings. I smooth my dress over my knees and realize I should take a shower soon in that awful washroom. Agnes hasn't said anything about my needing to wash up so perhaps body odour doesn't exist in Purgatory? I give my armpits a surreptitious sniff and things seem fine.

"We don't have the same needs as we did on Earth," Samia comments as she comes out from behind the counter to give me my drink.

I flush, embarrassed that she noticed my armpit sniff.

"Don't worry," she smiles. "It's what I do. I notice things."

She's kind and gentle and I'm glad when she sits down next to me.

"Where were you from, on Earth?" I ask.

"Pakistan. Although I lived in Canada my whole life. But my family were originally from Pakistan."

"How old are you?"

"Twenty-five. And next, you're going to ask me how I died. I went to a concert and took some bad drugs. It was the only time I'd ever taken drugs and I died. The newspaper said I had 'ingested substances' which would be one way to put it. I felt bad for my parents, though. I was an only child and now they are all alone."

"I'm sorry," I tell her.

"Julia doesn't remember anything yet," Agnes announces, having yet to introduce me to the others.

"Lucky bitch," one of the girls says. "Try not to remember," she adds. "It's much easier if you don't."

"We have to remember," Samia says. "It's why we're here."

The door opens and a tall elegant woman floats into the room. I sit up straighter. This woman moves like one of my peers and I can't be found slouching with the teenage outcasts.

I cross my legs and wish I had picked up a pair of shoes in the Clothes Room. This woman is impeccable. Narrow trousers, a businesslike blouse tied in an elaborate bow at the neck, high-heeled shoes, tinkly bracelets, and dark hair smartly fashioned in a chignon.

"Hello," she says holding out her hand. "I'm Grace."

"Julia," I reply, but I am distracted. This woman is the most sensationally reconstructed Barbie doll I have ever seen. Huge, clearly fake breasts; pert, high, rounded buttocks; a nose that looks eerily similar to mine; the wide-eyed stare of a victim of a too-tight face-lift; squirrely cheeks plumped with implants; and strange, trout-pout, full lips.

I immediately conclude that she must have died under a plastic surgeon's knife, after one too many procedures. I am repulsed by her vanity and her greed for youth and beauty and yet, there is something very sad about her.

"Samia dear," she says, and it is painful to watch those swollen lips struggle to talk, "may I have a chamomile tea, no milk?"

"Of course," Samia darts back behind the counter.

"Have you met everyone?" Grace asks, and I shake my head.

"I was going to introduce her, but she was too busy grilling Samia about her life and death," Agnes says.

"I'm interested," I say.

"Curious," Agnes corrects me.

"Never mind," Grace puts a stop to our bickering. "I'm Grace, You know Agnes and Samia, and this is Fat Tracey and Isabelle."

I look at Fat Tracey. Doesn't she mind being called that?

"Well, face it," she says "I am fat."

It is freaky, the way some of them can read your mind. But Tracey is right. She is fat. Her eyes are deep-set raisins in a pretty pudding bowl face.

"Yeah," she says reading my mind again. "I'd be lovely if I lost about a gazillion pounds. But this is me."

Body shaming in Purgatory? This doesn't sit right with me. I've always judged a book by its cover, yes, but never by its heft, or the lack thereof. Keep your manicures polished, but back off when it comes to body shapes and sizes. I have always been clear on this point and I'm about to say something else, but Fat Tracey holds up her hand.

"Don't," she says. "Just drop it."

I try to focus on something else. "Nice setup you've got here," I say, looking around. We are seated around the coffee table.

"Had to get special permission from Beatrice, that bitch," Fat Tracey comments, blowing on her hot chocolate. "And we had to ask her if you could join us."

"Beatrice is the Administrator," Samia explains.

"One of them," Grace says. "She's ours."

"Is an Administrator a Regulator?"

"No," Grace says. "No one knows who the Regulators are."

I give up. "What did you have to do, to get this?" I ask.

"Time," Grace says. "We did time."

Well, this is a fun lot. A laugh a minute. I cross my legs and look at my toes, figuring that right after this little coffee klatch, I'll go to find some shoes in the Clothes Room.

"I'm Isabelle," a skinny little creature says, and I stop thinking about what I will do next and focus on her. She is birdlike and angelic, as delicate and ethereal as wild grass.

"I liked having sex with strange men," she tells me. "Men I met online. You know that website for people who are married but want to have sex with other people? I joined that one. Actually, my partner at the time made me join, but it turned out I loved it. It was a dangerous thing to do. I knew that, but I loved it and I couldn't stop. I had sex all over the city: in parking lots, under bridges, and in cars, a lot of cars. The trouble with me was that I fell in love with the men I had sex with and I wanted them to leave their wives." She sighs. "And of course they didn't, which really hurt."

"Why didn't you go online and look for single guys to have a relationship with?" This is a no-brainer to me.

"Because I didn't want a relationship. At least, I didn't think I did. I thought I was just in it for the sex, but then I fell in love with whoever I was sleeping with. Well, I didn't love all of them, really. I fell in love with about four. And they texted me and promised to leave their wives but they never did. I tell you, I spent a fortune on underwear. Good underwear is SO expensive and they like it, you know, the corsets, the bras, and little panties. I got into big debt from that. And I got a tattoo because men love tattoos. Look!"

She jumps up and pulls her dress over her head. She isn't wearing a bra and she flashes tiny little bud breasts. She is wearing a thong, a strip of lace between her perfect buttocks, and I am taken aback by her brazen exhibitionism.

"You see?" she says.

It is hard to miss. An intricately detailed dragon caresses the side of her torso.

"The girl with the dragon tattoo!" I am amused, while she is less so.

"I didn't know about that shitty book when I got it," she says and she pulls her dress back on and sits down, ignoring me. I must have offended her, but I can't think of anything to say to put it right, not that I care overly much.

The others are unsurprised by her behaviour or her revelations.

"We must talk to Beatrice about Viewing privileges," Grace says changing the subject.

"What are Viewing privileges?" I ask.

"It's kind of like Google Earth for the dead," Samia explains.

"You can watch someone you loved, check in with their lives, and see how they are doing."

"Creepy," I say.

"I heard they can do it in Heaven whenever they want," Samia tells me.

"You've spoken to someone in Heaven?" I am skeptical.

"You hear things," Samia says. "I can't remember from where exactly but that's what I heard."

"I wouldn't have anyone to watch," I say.

"Beatrice is such a bitch," Fat Tracey pipes up. "She said flat-out 'no' the last time we asked her."

"That was a while ago," Grace says. "You never know, now."

"What's changed?" Fat Tracey counters.

"Time." Grace is unperturbed. "It's all about time."

"No, it's not." Fat Tracey is angry. "It's about fucking realizations."

I burst out laughing and they look at me.

"I'm just happy to hear someone swear," I say. "Cedar kicked me out of a session because I swore."

"Fucking Cedar," Fat Tracey says cleaning out the inside of her mug out with her finger. "Thinks he knows fucking everything."

"Are there other Helpers?" I ask, and they nod.

"Can you change Helpers, ask for a new one?"

They shake their heads. So much for that idea.

"What about sex?" I ask, thinking about the Train Room men and their absolute non-reaction to me.

"Doesn't exist," Isabelle says and she sounds sad. "Not on the menu. It's like it never existed at all. None of the men here even notice me."

"I know what you mean," I tell her. "Me too. I've never experienced that."

"Bummer," Fat Tracey says with a hint of a smile.

After that the conversations picks up and Agnes fills the others in on what we did after I woke. "And she gave me an awesome mani," she says, showing the others.

They give me a rundown on their favourite fare from the canteen and for a moment, I forget where I am, and what has happened. But I need to ask another question. "How do we go outside?" I ask, and they all look at me.

"There is no outside," Agnes says.

"The runways, the grass. The planes. How do we get out there?"

"It doesn't exist," Grace says gently. "It's like the backdrop of a movie."

"None of the doors lead outside?"

"She's like this a lot," Agnes tells the others. "She asks you a thing in different ways, like that will score her the answer she wants. Julia, hear me loud and clear: There is no outside, there is no sky, there are no planes or clouds. There's just this weird building we're in, wherever it is, we don't know."

My latte rises in my throat and I think I am going to throw up.

"Try not to think about it," Samia advises me and she comes over and rubs my back. "Focus on your breathing."

But that only makes it worse. "What kind of air is it anyway?" I say and even I can hear the hysteria in my voice.

"Oh, for fuck's sake Julia, grow a pair," Fat Tracey tells me and the shock of her words helps jolt me out of my fear and I swallow hard.

I am about to reply when I notice a strange thing happening to Grace. She is slowly dimming and fading, going ghostly right before my eyes. I lean towards her. "What's happening?" I ask and I reach out to touch her, but I pull my hand back as if she might infect me with her transparency.

"It's something only Grace does," Agnes explains to me. "Please don't freak out, Julia. It's perfectly normal for Grace. As you can tell, Julia freaks very easily," she informs the others.

"I do not." I am defensive. "This is all very weird. Cut me some slack, will you?" By this time, Grace has vaporized and I stare at the empty spot where she had sat.

"Hang onto your hat, Julia," Agnes advises me. "We about to bounce, which means our time is up and we'll scatter who knows where in the building."

"But..." I start to say when I am interrupted by Samia.

"See you tomorrow," she sings out, and next thing, we all bounce away from one another; bouncing is, I think, an accurate term.

I end up back in the Makeup Room and I wonder if we are responsible for projecting where we want to be, once we are expelled from whatever room deems we are out of time.

With nothing better to do, I give myself a mani/pedi. I lie back on the sofa, with my feet up on the armrest, watching the polish dry, and I think about the group.

I wonder how Isabelle, Fat Tracey, and Grace died. I suppose I'll find out eventually. I don't even know how Agnes died, except that it was drug-related. Short, square-bodied Agnes with her gothic glam and her love of old-fashioned rose perfumes.

I am curious as to how the others fill their time. I had meant to ask them. One can only play girly in the Makeup Room for so long.

I wish I could remember more about my life than my job. Clearly, my job had meant a lot to me, along with all the stuff I was given. So much stuff. I think about my swag. And yet, I remember always wanting more. More, more, and more. When I wasn't gathering freebies and having them couriered home, I was ordering stuff online. You name it, I bought it. Dresses, shoes, watches, sunglasses, belts, purses, coats, and hats. I maxed out my credit cards. I was an unstoppable spender.

I held a beauty sale at work once and I sold the remnants of a season's haul to my colleagues. It was only the shit I didn't want of course, leftover crap like Avon, Mary Kay, Pantene, and Dove, but my staff descended on it like famished vultures and picked it clean.

I made nearly two thousand dollars. I told everyone the money would go to charity but I kept it. I figured that if it wasn't for me, none of those people would have got any of that shit at such good prices. So it was win-win. But instead of paying some of my debts with it, I ordered a pair of Givenchy sweatpants with a matching hoodie, and then I had to throw in an extra thousand bucks to cover the bill. I wonder what happened to my belongings after I died? I hadn't made a will, because who thinks about that when they're going to die? Do I have any family? Are they sharing my estate? I can't remember a thing. And my husband? Martin? Where does he figure in all of this? My little blond god. Where is he? I am getting a pretty good picture of an über-cluttered apartment with no one in it but me. I can't see it so much as feel it. But I know Martin exists. He's a big part of my life.

It's frustrating, not being able to figure it out. I wonder how much time I have left in the Makeup Room and where I should go after that.

"You're boring as fuck," I say out loud to Purgatory, but nothing happens. I'm not struck by lightning, nor does entertainment arrive on the arm of a butler bearing a silver tray. Sigh.

8. THERAPY, TAKE TWO

THE NEXT DAY, or what I assume to be the next day, I find myself outside Cedar's door. The sign says: *If only you would be altogether silent! For you, that would be wisdom.*

Of course, I pay it no heed.

I knock on Cedar's door.

"Come on in, Julia!" he cries, and that voice, oh, how that voice annoys me.

I open the door.

"Fuck," I say, "fuck, fuckity fuck. And a fucking good—"I don't even get to finish before I am booted out.

"Oh shit," I say. I hadn't meant to do that. Now I will have to wait a whole extra day until I can broach my realization and get the heck out of Dodge.

I walk past the sign. "Yeah, yeah, yeah," I say, and I stomp off to try to find Agnes and the others.

9. FAT TRACEY BAKES

AFTER CEDAR BOUNCES ME, I wander the halls, hoping to bump into one of the gang. I open endless doors and annoy the train men again and I am once more eagerly welcomed by the knitting women.

I find the Puzzle Room, the Weight Lifting Room, the Needlepoint Room (these women aren't nearly as friendly as the knitters), the Beading and Jewellery-making Room, the Sewing Room, and the Painting Room. There is even a Play-Doh Room for adults. Apparently you don't need special credits for these activities. Purgatory could easily be mistaken for an endless amateur arts and crafts festival.

I open another door and the heavenly smell of baked goods wafts my way. Caramel mixed with butter, vanilla, and butterscotch. I close my eyes and inhale deeply.

"Julia," an unenthusiastic voice greets me and I open my eyes.

"Hi," I reply and I wander in, in spite of Fat Tracey's lackluster greeting. I'm delighted to see someone I know. "How are you? Baking?"

She grunts in reply and sifts flour into a large china bowl. "You probably think a fat chick like me shouldn't be baking," she says, and she spoons large chunks of butter into the flour.

"I didn't think that," I say. "But I do wonder why you let people call you Fat Tracey, and not just Tracey."

"I don't *let* them. I *make* them say it. Because they fucking think it, don't they?" She looks at me calmly, and there is knowledge and spite in those eyes that frighten me a little. "I'd rather people were honest. I make them say what they are thinking, even if they don't want to admit it."

I want to argue with her, but I know that if I do it will be the end of whatever fragile friendship we are forging. So, I sit down on a high stool and watch her work.

"It's like Williams Sonoma in here," I say. There are dozens of pots, pans, and utensils hanging from the walls and in the cabinets, with state-of-the-art, stainless steel eye-level ovens and granite counters, but Fat Tracey is alone in this cavernous place.

"I don't eat it," she says abruptly. "I make it for the cafeteria."

I look up. "What?"

"I don't eat what I bake, if that's what you're thinking."

"I wasn't," I say. "I was thinking that's it's very peaceful in here."

Fat Tracey gives a snort and loads a tray of cookies into an oven. She sets a timer and starts to clean up and I jump when another timer unexpectedly sounds. Fat Tracey removes a load of fresh bread rolls and puts them on the counter and my mouth waters. She tips one onto a napkin and hands it to me.

"Don't burn yourself," she says. "They're piping hot when they come out."

I tear the bun into bits and watch the steam rise. I blow on a tiny piece and pop it into my mouth.

"Fucking amazing," I say, and she smiles.

"The miracle of butter, flour, and salt," she replies, and she leans her elbows on the counter and rests her chin in her hands.

"I died in my car," she tells me. "My uncle killed himself in a car. He gassed himself while the family was at the movies. He was only nineteen. I always wondered why he chose the car and not some other way, but then one day I knew. One day I pulled into my garage and I sat there and I knew. I mean, he could have done it in so many other ways. He knew about drugs and things; he took quite a lot of them and he could easily have done it with heroin or something.

I never knew if he sat in the back or the front seat and I always wondered. I chose the front seat, the driver's seat. I like to be in control."

I am not sure what to say. I break off more of my bread and let her continue.

"I drove home one day from work and it came to me—the comfort that a car can bring. I pulled into my garage and sat there, facing the wall, the wall of my life, and I looked around at my car. My car was always tidy and clean. I spent a fortune getting it detailed. My kids knew I'd beat the living shit out of them if they so much as wiped a dirty hand on the seats. They knew better."

She stops and traces a pattern in the spilled flour on the countertop. She draws a heart with kisses under it. "My car knew all my hopes and dreams. It took me everywhere, to places where I had high hopes that came to nothing. My husband bought me the car, brand new, out of the box, and I loved it. I could talk to myself in that car, or cry or laugh or anything I felt like. I could be away from the world in my car; no kids, no husband, no job to let me down."

She stops and again, I don't want to say anything that might cut the thread of her story, so I remain silent and she continues.

"I loved my job," she says. "It meant everything to me. I was the accounting girl at a law firm and I thought I mattered to them. I had been there for ten years and then I heard they had planned a brainstorming weekend away, to figure out the company's future, a weekend at a really swanky hotel in the city and they didn't invite me. It wasn't like they forgot. They just didn't see a reason for me to be there. Meanwhile I had helped build the business for ten fucking years.

"They broke my heart. And the main guy there, he was like a father to me, but I didn't mean anything to him.

"I phoned my husband and I cried and he said 'their loss' or some stupid shit like that. He never understood what it meant to me, being part of something important. My sister said I should resign immediately but then what? I'd have less than I did before. But there was no way for them to make it right, not even after I told them I was upset. Yes, I told them, and they looked at me like they had no idea why I was making such a big fuss over such a small thing.

"I told them that I would never have done that to them, excluded them like that. I got home, and parked in my garage and that's when I knew that I would kill myself in my car."

She stops talking.

"Did you gas yourself?" I ask. Tactless, yes, but I always need to know the details. She shakes her head.

"I pretended to go to work the next day. I drove back when I knew no one was home. I had a bunch of oxys. There was never a problem getting pills in our family. I crushed them up and mixed them into some ice cream. I took them and I sat in in my car and waited. It didn't hurt."

"Did you leave a note?"

She nods. "I said I couldn't live in a world that didn't want me. I wrote a letter to each of my boys, telling them I was sorry, and saying I hoped they'd grow up to be good men, men who stuck to their word and didn't hurt people with disloyalty."

"How old were they?"

"Eight and twelve."

"They weren't reason enough to live?"

She frowns and shakes her head. "No one else is ever reason enough to live. I don't think so, anyway. I was worried about the damage I would do to the kids by killing myself, but I wrote them that they had a choice. They could carry my shit for the rest of their lives or they could accept that my decision was my decision, and make their own lives have meaning. I said I couldn't have given their lives meaning anyway, that was up to them."

"What about your husband?"

She shrugs. "I knew he'd get over it. He loved me more than he should have, but that wasn't my fault. And I cared more about being appreciated at work than anything else, and maybe that was my fault."

The cookie oven beeps and Fat Tracey opens the door and pulls out the tray.

I eat more of my bread roll and think about what she has said. "Do you think suicide is genetic?" I ask, thinking about her brother.

She dumps the cookies into a large container and I don't think she heard me but then she replies. "No idea. Lots of death in our family. Death is one of us for sure." She laughs. "Come with me to the cafeteria to drop these off?"

I jump off my stool and pick up the bread rolls she has tucked into a basket. We leave the kitchen, and walk down a hallway. We turn right and then left, and she opens the door to the cafeteria. "I wish I could do that," I say. "Know what's behind each door."

She smiles. "You will, you're still a newbie, it takes time."

"Do you miss your boys?" I ask.

"Yeah. That's why I want Viewing privileges from that bitch, Beatrice. She's got no right to keep me from my boys. She's got no right, but she's got the power and man, does she ever use and abuse it."

She takes me behind the main counter and I get to see how the cafeteria works behind the scenes. There are large vending machines behind the dispensing windows and she shows me how to stack the bread rolls and cookies. Then she dusts off her hands. "Let's go and find the others," she says.

10. BEATRICE, THE ADMINISTRATOR

"I GOT KICKED OUT OF CEDAR'S again," I tell the others. I expect them to find this funny but they don't. Of course they don't. "I didn't mean to," I acknowledge. "It's like I had Tourette's or something."

"Cedar's alright," Grace comments. "You should try to work with him."

"Why? So I can have a so-called realization? That clearly worked well for you. Look, you're all still here." They have no answer for that.

"What are everybody's plans for the day?" Samia asks, brightly.

"Rest Room, Reading Room, Rest Room, cafeteria," Fat Tracey says and she sounds grumpy. "I don't know why you bother to ask us, Samia. It's not like I can say oh, I'm going to Bermuda to lie on a beach or fuck it, let's go to the mall and spend money we don't have."

"You are in a mood," Grace says.

Fat Tracey nods her head in my direction. "I was telling her my life story and I guess it got to me a bit."

"Oh, I am sorry, dear," Grace says and Fat Tracey's eyes fill with tears.

"I shouldn't have left my boys," she says and she starts keening quietly. "Julia said so, and she was right."

They all turn to look at me.

"I never said that!" I am indignant. "I asked her if they

couldn't have been reason enough to make her stay."

"Well, obviously not," Isabelle is scornful. "That's a stupid thing to say, don't you think?" I feel like she just slapped me across the face.

How dare she speak to me like that? But what am I supposed to do, these are the only people I have in my life right now, and so instead of asking her just who the fuck she thinks she is talking to me like that, I simply nod. "I see that now," I say meekly and the others accept this apology of sorts.

"I want my fucking Viewing time," Fat Tracey says.

"Let's go and see Beatrice again," Grace suggests, and I am glad she does because any kind of activity will help pass the day, or whatever our strange allotments of time are.

"Enjoy your lattes first," Fat Tracey says. "No point in wasting them."

We sit and drink in silence. I notice that Agnes has gnawed away the perfect manicure I gave her and I sigh.

"You okay?" Samia asks.

"Still trying to get my bearings on things," I say, and she nods sympathetically.

"It takes a while."

"I don't suppose there's a Massage Room here?" I am wistful. "I wouldn't mind a four hour massage, that's for sure."

"No, dear, no Massage Room," Grace tells me.

"No movie theatre either," Isabelle says.

Then they all chime in: "No animals, sauna, hot tub, swimming pool, beach, no real grass or thunderstorms—"

"There is the Rain Room," Grace interrupts the long list, and I gather this isn't the first conversation they've had that went like this.

"Yeah, it's super depressing," Samia comments, and it is unlike her to say anything negative.

"Why?" I ask. "Rain can be soothing."

She shakes her head. "I'll take you one day and you'll see. The whole place is grey and gloomy."

"There are chapels," Grace says "and there's even a cathedral. It's enormous, like St. Peter's in Rome."

"I don't see the point in praying," Isabelle says and the others fall silent.

"We're not supposed to talk about religion," Agnes explains to me.

"Why not? That doesn't make any sense. Of all the places, you'd think religion would be first on the list here." I am baffled. "Are there priests and nuns?" I think about Intrigua with her hajib and nun's outfit.

Agnes shakes her head. "Only Helpers like Cedar."

"I find that weird," I say, and I finally get the group to laugh.

"Ah, yeah, Purgatory is weird," Samia agrees. "That might be the point."

"If you're all finished, let's go and see the bitch," Fat Tracey says. "But I'm not going to do the talking, someone else will have to."

"I will," Grace is firm. "I want to see my family too."

"We're not going to get anywhere," Agnes says with a warning tone in her voice, "I can feel it."

"Well, we're going to try," Grace insists and she stands up and brushes biscotti crumbs from her skirt. "We're most certainly going to try."

This time we don't enter the maze. We walk the perimeter of the building, and we pass those eerie planes, those white sharks lined up on the licorice black, lined up and waiting for god knows what. We pass the counter where a group of people are still gathered and they are arguing and jostling, while harried flight attendants shout from behind the counter.

I want to check if it's the same group of people or a new lot but we walk by too quickly. Besides, I hadn't noticed much the first time.

I spot the womb that birthed my arrival, that steel and black leatherette chair, and I can still feel the burning pain as I surfaced. I look out the window. The immaculate green astro turf between the runways is unchanged, as are the cotton wool clouds that are two-dimensional and cartoon-like in their perfection. A movie backdrop, Grace had said. Sometimes, it's as if I've stepped into a graphic novel that's been assembled using clipart.

We walk for what feels like hours but of course, there's no way of telling. Shirley the Driver passes us, beeping and squawking, her lights flashing like a Christmas tree and we all press up against the wall.

"We're nearly there," Agnes tells me and I nod.

We turn down an unusually dark hallway. "Everything's on one level here," I remark. "No escalators, elevators, stairs or ramps." No one finds my observation worthy of comment and I fall silent.

"We're here," Grace says after we turn a corner and walk past a series of yellow doors with yellow half-moon handles. I want to ask what's with the yellow all of a sudden, but I sense it's not a good time for questions. I don't want the others to bounce me. They haven't said they can do that, but I'm certain they have the power.

We stop in front of a door, and no one wants to be the first to venture inside. But then something creepy happens—the door handle twists down and the door swings quietly open.

"I know you lot are out there," a hoarse voice bellows, "so come on in, you ninnies. I know what you're going to ask me and I can tell you now that the answer is still the same, it's no, nada, zip, zero, and I've got no idea why you wasted your time coming out all this way. I guess you had nothing better to do or you wanted to introduce me to your new friend. Hear this, Julia, you're a longer ways off from a Viewing than you can imagine. You, with your ego the size of Jupiter, well, you'll have to wait in line like the rest of them. Your charms hold no currency here."

I feel as if someone has thrown a bucket of ice water on me. I can't move or speak. I just stand there, dripping with the venom of this woman's sarcasm. "Come on in," the voice bellows again. "Bloody rude to stand out there and make me shout."

"Hardly a point in coming in, is there?" Fragile little Isabelle shouts back and I am surprised. The mouse has roared. But then again, this is a girl who had sex with a lot of strangers—she isn't afraid of anything.

"You should at least give us a timeline," Isabelle says loudly, and she marches inside and I can see that her fists are clenched and her face is white.

The others creep in behind her and I bring up the rear.

"Should? Fuck should," Beatrice says and I guess she's never had Cedar as her Helper.

Beatrice is sitting behind a desk, with her feet up. She's wearing Birkenstocks and her toenails are as thick and gnarly as old tortoise shells. They are also inexplicably filthy. There is no dirt in Purgatory, so how did her feet get to be that dirty? Did she arrive like that, and never wash?

Beatrice is chomping on a large apple and bits of it are spraying everywhere. She chews loudly with her mouth open and I look away, studying her office instead. Her bookcase filled is with works by Dorothy Parker, Charles Bukowski, Ernest Hemingway, F. Scott Fitzgerald, Hunter S. Thompson, and Raymond Chandler, and I wonder if she had been a drunk back on Earth. That, and heavy smoking, would explain her less-than-dulcet tones.

A large poster of a Hawaiian sunset covers one wall along with a framed picture of an old Cadillac convertible. A stack of needlepoint cushions is piled in the corner and I wonder if Beatrice was in the Needlepoint Room when I barged in looking for Agnes. A large framed embroidered canvas has a green alligator baring its teeth, with the slogan, *Come In, The Water's Fine!*

Everything is pristine and polished but the items are old and show wear: the Scrabble set, the stacked, empty margarine tubs, the cans of Sanka. A tiny black toy cat is perched inside a glass bell jar on the edge of Beatrice's desk and behind Beatrice's head is a framed picture of a vase and a bowl of fruit and the artwork, if you can call it that, is so dreadful that I am mesmerized. It looks like it was drawn with thick crayon and then melted over an open fire.

Beatrice stops chewing for a moment and the silence is so thick that I stop my inventory of the place and glance at the others to see what is going on, but they are fearfully looking at Beatrice who is calmly watching me.

"Enjoying yourself?" she asks. "Very nosy, aren't you? Nosy parker." Beatrice, resplendent in shiny black shorts and a red and black man's checked shirt, cocks her head to one side and I can't think of anything to say. She shrugs and returns enthusiastically to her apple and juice spurts out in an arc onto Grace's blouse and Grace flinches.

"Well, when?" Fat Tracey can hold back no longer. "When can I see them?"

"Should have thought of that when you left them," Beatrice counters. "It's not up to me, anyway."

"It is so," Isabelle insists. "We all know that."

"You don't know fuck all," Beatrice aims the apple core at a bin in the corner and slam dunks it. "You think you do, but you don't. Who would you View, Isabelle? Huh? Tell me?"

"No one. It's not for me. It's for Fat Tracey and Grace and Agnes," Isabelle says. "I never had anyone, I don't care. I'm fine with things the way they are, but it's not fair to the others."

"Fair? Fair? Like life was ever fair?" Beatrice is mocking. She whips her feet off the desk and pulls her chair close to her desk. She gives her mouse a thwack, to wake up the computer. She peers at the screen and then she fumbles for a pair of reading glasses, searching on her desk until she realizes they are strung around her neck on a beaded cord.

She puts them on and examines the screen, using the rough, thick nail of her forefinger to scroll down. She mutters all the while, and we stand there, silent and unmoving. She taps furiously at the keyboard, so hard I am surprised it isn't damaged, and then she slams a fist on the Enter key. The printer next to the desk springs into life and jerkily delivers a single page.

We hold our breath.

"Here," she says handing the sheet to Agnes. "Access for you for the Viewing Room. You've got half an hour tomorrow."

Agnes looks stunned. "But I'm not ready," she says.

"I am!" Fat Tracey and Grace both chorus at the same time.

"You're ready when I say you are," Beatrice retorts. She looks at Agnes and holds out her hand. "You want to give it back?"

"No." Agnes clutches the paper to her chest.

"Thought so. Well then, goodbye all of you. Don't come again, why don't you?" She laughs and coughs up a wedge of phlegm that she spits into a Kleenex and lobs at the bin, narrowly missing my head.

"Go on, shoo! Out you go!"

We turn and file out slowly, and the yellow-handled door swings firmly shut behind us. We stand in the corridor for a while, in silence.

"I can't do it today," Agnes says. "I'm not ready."

"Yeah, well, you heard her, it's for tomorrow in any case," Samia points out.

"When you do it, do you want us to come with you?" Grace asks and Agnes nods.

"Yes, I can't do it alone. We'll go after coffee."

"Will you wait to have coffee with me?" I ask, sounding unfamiliarly unsure of myself. "I have to go and see Cedar, first thing."

"Of course we'll wait," Samia says when no one else replies, and my confidence level drops even further. "I'll come and find you," Samia reassures me. "We'll wait. Don't worry."

I thank her, and before I can say anything else or ask the others what they're going to do next, I am back in the Makeup Room, alone.

11. DUCHESS

THE NEXT DAY, THERE I AM, back at Cedar's door. *Go on up, you baldhead!* the sign says. Yeah, well, whatever.

"Come on in, Julia!" Cedar is his usual, cheery self.

I ease the door open and slip inside, carefully closing it behind me. I keep my mouth zipped. I am not going to screw up this time. I need to hear what Cedar has to say, I need to have my realization, and get the fuck out of here. I mean, get the heck out of here. Surely heck is okay? I sit down silently and look at him.

He is beaming at me. "And how are we today?"

I mumble something.

"Settling in? Great! So, Julia, what do you think brings you here?"

I look at him. "What do you mean?" I slur, fearful that an obscenity will fly out if I open my mouth any wider.

"To Purgatory. Why not Hell? Why not Heaven? Why to this place of in-between? You don't strike me as an in-betweener."

"I'm not," I mumble. "I don't know what I'm doing here."

"Hmmm." He is seated in a grey wingback chair, wearing his beige corduroy trousers and his expression is earnest. His close-set eyes peer at me, his hands are clasped and his feathers are aflutter. "You don't remember anything before you achieved consciousness in Purgatory?"

I shake my head. "Where's my husband?" I ask.

Cedar shakes his head. "I can't tell you."

"But you do know."

He nods. "But it's vital that you remember on your own. I can't impede your progress." He falls silent and leans back in his chair, his hands steepled in prayer.

"How about we do a little exercise?" he asks. "I'm going to encourage you to open your mind, close your eyes, and listen to my breathing guidance. Can you do that?"

I nod, still not trusting myself to say anything.

"Close your eyes, breathe in for the count of five. Hold for five and out for five. I'll guide you."

We do this for a while and I start to feel sleepy.

"What do you remember, Julia?" he asks softly. "Before you came here, what do you remember? Were you making a cup of tea? Were you on the telephone to your mother? Were you stroking your kitty cat?"

My eyes fly open. Cat? "I had a cat?"

"Concentrate, Julia. Let's start again."

I sigh. In for five, hold, out for five.

The image of a cat comes to my mind. I see a large, incredibly grumpy, beautifully ugly cat with a squashed face and a pug nose. An immensely hairy, immensely fat, immensely angry cat. I can't keep my eyes shut. "Cat. Oh."

I get up and pace around the room.

Cedar doesn't say anything, he just watches me.

I fold my arms across my chest. "Yes," I say. "A cat."

Before I can stop myself, tears are pouring down my face.

"Lady Marmalade. But I called him Duchess. He was my baby. My joy. I got him from a pet store. I swore I'd never buy from them, such a rip-off, you know, and pet store animals are all demented or deformed in some way. Too much inbreeding or something or they keep them in cages too long. But I was in a mall and I walked past him and he meowed at me and I stopped and I couldn't help myself. I got them to take him out of his cage and he climbed up my shirt, and I paid two thousand dollars for a kitten, right then and there."

By now, my nose is running and Cedar gets up and hands me a box of Kleenex.

I grab a fistful, blow my nose and continue.

"But he was demented, of course he was. He peed everywhere. He'd go right in front of me, on the carpets. He'd saunter into the room, give me a filthy look, and pee. But what could I do? I loved him. So I cleaned up after him or, I tried to. He peed in places I couldn't find until I discovered wiring and cables had been eaten away by his puddles. He could have started a fire or something.

"I took him to the vet, and we put him on drugs and they helped, we drugged the shit, oh sorry Cedar—" I look at him, my face wet with tears and I stand there, waiting to be bounced out the room but Cedar just nods and I carry on.

"And it helped, it lessened the problem. And he was my baby, my buddy, my friend, for nine and a half years, and then he got sick; his liver started to give out. I tried everything. I took him to homeopathy. I must have spent thousands of dollars on him, maybe even tens of thousands, I'm not exaggerating, but in the end, oh, in the end, nothing helped."

I sink down next to Cedar, sobbing. I am shaking and howling in a way I've never cried before. "He died. I held him and he died. His heavy, grumpy, angry body just gave out. One minute he was purring, and the next, he left me. He got light as a feather and I didn't know where his weight went, but I knew it was his anger and it was gone. And his anger was like my anger, and my anger is what grounds me. Without it, I too would be nothing and I'd float away, and I still miss him so much."

I am wailing and Cedar is rubbing my back like I'm a baby and I don't care. Snot runs down my face and I cry like my heart is broken. And just when I think I can't cry any more, I start all over again, wailing that ungodly sound and Cedar sits there patiently, rubbing me.

Finally, I get to hiccupping. "I loved him so much," I say.

"There wasn't a day I didn't miss him. I had him cremated and I have an urn and I talk to him every day. I ask him why he left me. I know that sounds stupid but I do. I talk to him every day, so if you're asking me if I was talking to my kitty cat before I came here, yes, I most likely was. He was the only friend I could rely on in this world."

"But he left you," Cedar points out.

"He did," I wail. "Why? He wasn't even ten years old. Didn't he love me? Didn't I make him happy? I tried so hard."

I start to cry again.

"This is excellent progress," Cedar says and he hands me the box of Kleenex. I blow my nose again. I am exhausted.

"We've done enough for the day. What you should do now," Cedar says kindly, "is have a lie-down in the Rest Room. Would you like me to walk you there?"

I nod. "Yes, please."

I get up and touch my swollen face. "I don't want anybody to see me like this," I say, and Cedar laughs.

"You are so concerned with all the wrong things. But don't worry, we won't bump into anyone. I can arrange that."

I don't ask him what he means. I let him lead me down the corridor, past several doors until he finally opens the door to the Rest Room. He guides me through the foyer and into an enclosed circled curtain and I lie down and he rubs my back.

I start crying again. And this time, I am not even sure what for.

12. VIEWING AUNTIE MIRIAM

A FEW HOURS LATER, I suppose it is the scheduled four, I find myself outside the Rest Room, my face still swollen and my eyes gritty and burning.

Cedar is nowhere to be seen and I suppose I must have slept or whatever the equivalent thereof is.

I suddenly remember that I was supposed to meet Samia, or she was going to find me, after my session with Cedar but Duchess had derailed everything.

I am utterly miserable and I have no idea what to do. I have missed out on coffee, on Agnes's Viewing, on everything.

I walk aimlessly down the hallway, thinking I might try to find the Ablution Block and have a shower, and then find something new to wear in the Clothes Room.

I still feel the loss of Duchess keenly, as if his death had happened that very morning, and I can't find the Makeup Room, or the Ablution Block or the Canteen or the Coffee Room. I feel as bereft and as sad as I have ever been. I lean against the wall and close my eyes, thinking I'll apologize to Agnes when I see her again, and I'll explain.

"Hello!" It's Samia. She pops up beside me, and stands there, grinning. Much to both our surprise, I grab her and hug her, and then I start crying again.

"I'm sorry," I am wailing and splashing her with tears. "I got caught up with Cedar, and I couldn't find you and—"

"Don't worry," she says and she reaches up and pats my arm.

I am nearly twice her height and bending down to hug her is killing my back, so I straighten up and wish I had a Kleenex and I sniff loudly instead.

"We wouldn't have gone without you," Samia says. "I came to fetch you, the others are waiting. Come on, coffee first and then the Viewing. There's time, we've got all the time in the world! Well, in four-hour segments anyway."

Samia leads me to a door that I swear I opened, but all I found for my troubles was a couple playing Scrabble.

I greet the others in the coffee shop but I am distracted and while Samia makes me a latte, I try to figure out what's on my mind. Scrabble. It has something to do with Scrabble.

I think back to the box I saw on Beatrice's bookshelf. I was good at Scrabble back in the day and I wouldn't mind finding a partner. A truly bizarre thought crosses my mind. I wonder if Beatrice would like to have a game or two. Ferocious though the old duck is, there is something about her meanness I can relate to.

Back on Earth, my rules were the only rules, and you played by them or you left. And usually, if you left, you left in tears. I was single-minded in my focus. Work was my life. My apartment was right next door to the office and my working hours were ten a.m. to nine p.m. with at least two weekends a month thrown in, and if that didn't work for you, well then, so long and thanks for all the fish. I was upfront about the hours but most people thought I was kidding or exaggerating, but they soon found out it was no joke.

And I may have been a diva but I was one of the best and I cleaned up at award shows. I expected my team to know all the trends, who was fucking whom, who was wearing what, and where were the bodies buried? I didn't expect anything from them that I didn't demand of myself.

When I got home, I'd work out for an hour to a killer Jillian Michaels video, followed by a ten-kilometre run on the treadmill, finishing up with a half an hour of stretching while I watched TV. Then I'd have a lengthy soak in the tub, followed by take-out, sushi mainly, and I'd watch TV again while I ate and chatted to Duchess who generally ignored me.

I'd finish up my day with some pricey online shopping, hunting for couture treasures while I drank Scotch. I went to bed around one a.m. and such was my life, and it was a good one.

I had no need for people and I knew that my demeanor was such that staff members preferred to take detours to the washroom simply so they wouldn't have to pass my office. They thought I didn't know that, but I knew everything.

I couldn't be bothered with niceties and I sent out a directive instructing people to cut the crap from their emails: no "dear" this or that, no fluff, no embellishments, just get to the point and tell me whatever the fuck it is you need to tell me.

Of course, there were complaints to human resources but I was protected by—Actually who had I been protected by? I stopped short in my reminiscing, confused. Who protected me?

"Purgatory to Julia," Fat Tracey says and I blink. "Your 180 degree coffee is getting cold."

I shake my head as if I am trying to dislodge water from my ears. "I just had a weird experience," I say. "A piece of my Earth life flashed before my eyes but it isn't what I thought it was. I am missing my husband."

"Maybe I was having sex with him in a basement parking lot somewhere," Isabelle jokes.

Grace looks horrified. "I am sure she wasn't, dear," she says to me, but I brush off her comment.

"Of course he wasn't. But I can't find him. I remember what he looks like, right down to his monogrammed cufflinks, but I can't see him at home with me. My home was just me and Duchess before he died. Duchess was my cat," I explain. "My best friend, really."

"Confusion is the norm," Fat Tracey says. "Don't overthink it. It'll come to you. Anyway, today is Agnes's big day, so let's leave you and your past for the moment, and support Agnes."

I feel abashed. "I am sorry Agnes, I really am. How are you doing? How is everyone doing? I am sorry I was in such a fog when I arrived."

"S'okay," Agnes waves a hand at me. "I'm freaked out to be honest. Now's when I need a toke or a couple of beers, not this caffeinated excuse for a beverage."

Samia looks hurt and Agnes rushes to make amends. "You know what I mean. I'm not sure I am ready for this. Actually, maybe I just won't do it."

"Can't we use it to log on to Grace or Fat Tracey's lives?" I ask, but the others shake their heads.

"It's non-transferable and non-refundable," Fat Tracey says. "Trust me, I already tried to bribe my way on, and Beatrice found out and she tore a strip off me."

"Besides, if Beatrice gave it to you, it means you're ready," Grace argues. "She wouldn't do it unless it was going to help move you on."

"Or set me back," Agnes says. "I wouldn't put anything past Beatrice."

We mull in silence for a bit.

"Who are you going to look at?" I ask.

"It will choose," Fat Tracey says. "You can't pick who or what you want to view. Apparently, it will show you what you need to see to move forward in your healing." She snorts.

"What I need to see is my Great-Auntie Miriam." Agnes looks glum. "There isn't anybody else. I wonder how much time has passed. I hope she's okay."

She puts her cup down and stands up. "Come on," she says. "Let's do this thing before I lose my nerve."

She walks out and we scramble to our feet and follow her.

We find the Viewing Room quickly enough and it is decorated much like the red Lounge Room that Agnes first took me to, although the setup is different. The room is divided into four sections and computers in each corner face a movie-sized screen attached to the wall. There are four curved retro-style, red banquette benches, with their backs butting neatly up against one another, and there are thick, red Perspex floor-to-ceiling panels separating the four segments of the room. I am reminded of a Larry Bell installation exhibit I saw in New York.

"Soundproofing," Isabelle says when she sees me looking.

"Pick a booth," Grace tells Agnes and she sounds nervous.

Agnes points to the furthermost corner and we slide into the banquette, with her in the centre.

"Have any of you ever done this before?" I ask, and, to my surprise, they shake their heads.

Agnes sighs. "I hope I see Auntie Miriam," she says, unfolding her piece of paper and touching a small computer screen on the bar countertop that runs the length of the banquette.

The computer comes to life and Agnes taps in a code off the printout and we lean forward and stare at the movie screen on the wall facing us.

At first, the screen remains black and then a greeting appears: WELCOME, AGNES! WE HOPE YOU WILL ENJOY YOUR VIEWING TODAY!

The screen fades to back to black and we are in travelling in outer space, narrowing in on the Earth. We all comment that we feel a bit dizzy as the camera, or whatever it is, zooms in closer to the ground, and before we know it, we are gliding up the walkway of Benevolent Lives old-age home.

The viewing experience is, of course, like nothing we've seen before. It's 3D, yes, and it's as if we are actually there, on the ground, eye level with the action. It should feel crowded, all of us on the walkway but it doesn't. I guess ghosts don't take up much space.

"There's Granny Jean," Agnes whispers as we pass an old lady leaning on a walker, sucking hard on a cigarette.

"God, how I miss Earth," Grace says. "Look at those rose bushes." We are so close to them that she reaches out to touch them but she's grasping at air.

"I don't miss it one bit," Isabelle gives a shudder. "Look at it. Life is just about growing old and dying alone. I'm glad I'm not there any more. It's a relief to be done with it."

I don't know what I feel. In a way, I feel unpleasantly locked out of my own life but on the other hand, it's like watching a home movie of a time and place you are glad to have left behind.

Fat Tracey and Samia are silent and I sneak a quick glance at them and wish I hadn't when I see they are both crying quietly.

The View moves us inside the old age home and we float down a corridor. We pass the dining room that is empty except for a janitor cleaning the floor. Something about this sets Agnes off and she begins to cry and she's not quiet about it either. I sense that Agnes would like to stop in the dining room but the View relentlessly pushes us forward. Grace has come prepared and passes Agnes a handful of Kleenex.

Agnes blows her nose and the View propels us down a dark, narrow hallway. We stop outside Room 216 and then we float through the door.

We are completely unprepared for what we see and we jerk back in our seats, hands to our hearts, eyes wide open. The View has put us in a position of terrible danger, but then, as one, we remember that we're not really there.

We are inside that tiny room with three burly men who are systematically ripping the place apart. They crack open books and throw them on the floor. Shoeboxes of photographs are emptied, and vases are overturned and flung down to join other discarded knick knacks. The men leave nothing intact.

A very tiny old lady is cowering on the bed, hugging her knees to her chest and clutching a large tapestry cushion.

"The fuckers," Agnes wails. "Leave Auntie Miriam alone!" She wants to rush over to Auntie Miriam but she can't move. None of us can move. All we can do is stand there, shoulder to shoulder with those thugs and watch as they open drawers, scatter letters, break mugs, and rip the cushions apart.

"What are they looking for?" Grace asks, but Agnes can't speak.

It doesn't take long before the room is destroyed. The men stand ankle-deep in the aftermath of their destruction and, as one, they turn and look at Auntie Miriam.

She sees the look in their eyes and she shoots off the bed with surprising speed for a ninety-year-old woman and she rushes into the bathroom, still clutching her cushion, and we hear the door lock.

"Call mother," Agnes shouts at the closed door. "Call her! Call her now from the phone in the bathroom."

Meanwhile, the three men start attacking Auntie Miriam's bed with knives, and stuffing, torn fabric, and ripped cotton swirls around the room like a snowstorm.

Without warning, the door to the room flies opens and a woman stands there, open-mouthed, aghast. It is hard to say who is more shocked, the three thugs or the woman.

"What on earth are you doing?" she asks, and one of the men reaches over, through us, and he grabs her and flings her to the far side of the tiny room. She hits her head on the sideboard and crumples into a heap.

"Mom?" Agnes whispers, hardly able to speak. "Mom, are you dead?"

We watch in horror and in silence as the woman lies unmoving, as boneless as a rag doll.

"What the fuck?" One of the men says. "Let's get out of here, *now*." They scramble over the mess and make a dash for it, rushing through us and leaving us alone with Agnes' unconscious mother.

A man appears at the open doorway and he looks in, as if assessing the damage.

"Mr. Healey," Agnes hisses. "This is you! You did this." At the sight of him, Agnes starts to shake and although she can't take her eyes off him, she is as white as bleached linen and she's making a strange sound, like a trapped and wounded animal.

The man steps casually into the room, as if he's there for an afternoon tea and his actions are unhurried until the washroom door opens and Auntie Miriam peers out hesitantly. She casts a glance at Mr. Healey, making it very clear what she thinks of him, and she looks around for her niece. "I heard her," she says wildly. "I'm certain I heard her."

"She's over there!" Mr. Healey bellows, and he makes it sound as if he's the cavalry that arrived in the nick of time to rescue them. He pulls his phone out of his pocket and calls 911.

"Ambulance and paramedics," he says and he gives the address. "A woman has been attacked by burglars, how they got past security, I've got no idea. Come quickly, she's unconscious and I hope she's not dead."

"Dead," Agnes says, but just then, her mother moves. She gives a groan and rolls over onto her back.

"Cheryl, love, don't move. Help is coming," Auntie Miriam rushes over to her niece and kneels down. "Stay still, lovie, you'll be fine, don't move."

We watch in silence as the paramedics arrive and load Agnes's mother onto a stretcher.

"I'm going with her," Auntie Miriam tells Mr. Healey as they strap Cheryl in. "And you will send the minibus to follow us so Andrew can drive me home."

Mr. Healey nods in agreement. "I'll get someone to clean up in here," he says.

"Don't you touch one single thread," Auntie Miriam tells him. "You think I don't know it was you who sent those men? Of course it was you. How else would they have got past security?"

"Don't be ridiculous," Mr. Healey says dismissively, but Agnes's mother raises her head off the stretcher.

"She's right. And let me add this, you scumbag," she says. "You're done working here. I'm on the board of directors and I'm phoning my husband now to get you removed from the property." Cheryl has a large welt on her forehead and a trickle of blood snakes down her face.

Just then the police show up.

"Who called them?" Isabelle asks but none of us knows.

"Maybe someone heard the noise to or saw those men leaving," Grace says.

"It was all that man's doing," Agnes' mother says to the cops and she points at Healey. "Auntie Miriam, please find my phone in my purse and give it to me."

"You should wait and get checked out before making any calls," one of the paramedics says, but Cheryl ignores him.

She takes the phone from Auntie Miriam and presses the speed dial. While she waits for it to ring, she turns to Auntie Miriam. "Auntie Miriam, I need you to stay here and explain everything to Daniel. Will you do that?"

Auntie Miriam nods as Agnes's stepfather answers the phone.

"Daniel, you must come to Benevolent's, it's urgent, okay? Auntie Miriam will explain. The cops are here. Make sure Healey is booted off the premises and never allowed near the place again. Auntie Miriam will explain it all. I'll talk to you later." She listens for a moment and nods. "Yes," is all she says, then she ends the call and lies back on the stretcher.

"Don't worry, Auntie Miriam," she says closing her eyes, "Daniel's on his way. I'll be fine. I'll come and see you tomorrow." The paramedics cart her off and we remain in the destroyed room with Auntie Miriam but then the View starts to pull back.

"No! Don't go!" Agnes shouts at the screen. "I need to see that she's okay."

But the View keeps pulling back until finally the screen is black. GOODBYE AGNES! WE HOPE YOU ENJOYED YOUR VIEWING TODAY!

"We had better leave soon," Grace's voice jolts us into action. "If we don't leave together, we'll be bounced all over the building away from each other and we need to stick together. Come on."

She herds us out and Fat Tracey takes Agnes by the arm and holds on tightly. Agnes leans into her, looking glazed and shell-shocked.

"Follow me," Grace says and like obedient ducklings, we fall in behind her.

13. AGNES'S STORY

GRACE LEADS US TO THE CANTEEN. We sit Agnes down and Samia and Isabelle go and get tea. Agnes doesn't say anything, her eyes fill with tears that gather and spill and roll down her cheeks and drip off her chin. She could also do with blowing her nose.

We wait until the other two come back and we encourage Agnes to drink some tea but she just stares off into space and doesn't say a word.

"She's in shock," Fat Tracey says, dabbing at Agnes's chin and mopping up tears and mucus.

"I don't know what to do," Grace is worried. "Maybe we should go and get one of the Helpers or something."

I pat Agnes on the back and rub between her shoulders.

"Look," Fat Tracey says. "There's that bitch, Beatrice. I bet she knew exactly what was going to happen."

We turn and stare at Beatrice who is lining up for the dessert special of the day. Peach cobbler with rum custard and whipped cream. We watch her punch in her order and she waits patiently for the machine to sound the wind chime. When it does, she loads the bowl onto a tray, pours herself a large coffee, adds a good few inches of milk and a couple of packets of sugar. Then she turns and heads straight for us.

"Oh my god," Samia says, and she sounds terrified. We are all terrified.

Beatrice plunks her tray down in the centre of our table and pulls up a chair. "She's fine," she says without ceremony to Agnes. "Your Auntie Miriam is fine. So is your mother. Your mother had a nasty bruise, that's all. And Mr. Healey was escorted off the premises with directives by the police to never return. But," she says spooning cobbler and custard into her mouth, "that's not the end of it, is it?"

I wish Beatrice wouldn't eat and talk at the same time. I look over at Agnes instead, wondering if she knows what Beatrice means and she clearly does because she nods, still silent.

"What's going on?" Samia asks, her voice small and her eyes enormous.

"Spit it out, Agnes," Beatrice says and she eats more dessert and a blob of custard drips onto her chin, but she doesn't notice. "It will help you to get it out."

"I..." Agnes begins and we stare at her.

"Carry on," Beatrice says unmindful of the dessert on her face.

"It's all my fault," Agnes manages. She pulls out a pack of cigarettes and I help myself to one. I wonder if we are allowed to smoke in the canteen, but if we aren't, Beatrice isn't stopping us.

Agnes inhales so deeply that I think she is going to finish the cigarette off in two drags. She blows out a truckload of smoke and picks at a fingernail.

"Okay. So, Auntie Miriam, who is my great aunt really, she lives in that old-age home and I visit her a lot. She's amazing and she loves me and I love her. My mom's an uptight bitch and my stepfather thinks I'm a loser because I put food colouring in my hair and I've got piercings and tattoos. I was never very good at school, unlike his kids, because I was always hanging out with the potheads, and I'm not saying I was right and he was wrong, but let's just say we never got along.

"Auntie Miriam doesn't have any family left except us. Mom visits her maybe once a month, meanwhile I went twice a week at least. I'm not trying to sound like a goody-two-shoes, I did it for me, because she loved me and she thought I was interesting and funny and clever.

"One day I met a guy there. He was working as a janitor and before you think 'loser', let me tell you, he was a musician and he was incredible. He was all set for the big time, there was no doubt in anyone's mind. But he was only working at the home to make money until he could get off the ground with his band."

She pauses and Samia hands her a cup of now-tepid tea and she downs it in one go. "I fell in love with him. Josh. He was so cool." She looks away and blows a piece of hair off her face. "He was so beautiful. I don't know what he saw in me. But he liked *me* even though he had these amazing girls falling all over him."

She lights another cigarette from the remnants of her first. "One day, he says he's got a present for me. And he gives me a jewellery box and it's got this enormous diamond ring in it. Real diamonds. I asked him where he got it and he said he found it. He said he was out walking and there it was.

"Now, stuff had been going missing from the old-age home, everybody knew about it, and I thought he had taken it from one of the old ladies. I admit it, I did. But I didn't have any proof so I figured if I could get into Mr. Healey's office, then maybe I could find a list or something of what was reported missing.

"I waited for Mr. Healey to go home and I watched the nurses' station outside his office. I knew where they kept the spare key. As soon as I could, I let myself in and I locked the door from the inside.

"I started searching and I didn't find a list but I found a huge load of heroin in the filing cabinet. Later, I found out it was about a thousand bricks."

Fat Tracey lets out a low whistle. "Man. That's a lot."

"How much is it?" Samia asks.

"A bundle is ten bags, there are five bundles in a brick and a bag is like the size of your little finger," Fat Tracey explains.

"What would a thousand bricks be worth?" I ask.

"I guess around half a million to a million dollars," Fat Tracey says. "Depends on what it's cut with."

"Tracey, how do you know so much?" I ask.

"That's Fat Tracey to you," she retorts, but I shake my head.

"Fuck the fat," I say. "You're too damn gorgeous." It's true, and I am sick of her demeaning herself. It's time to fight this battle and win.

Tracey looks annoyed. "Why do you even care?"

I get why she's surprised. I come across as the most superficial person on the planet and for the most part, I am. But this kind of self-denigration is never okay.

"Your fat does not define you," I say. "We are more than the bodies we were born with. I had everything come my way because I turned out to be beautiful, but no one liked me and I was a bitch. I still am. All I am saying is that you're Tracey to me."

I know there is a reason I feel this strongly about it. I try to pinpoint a memory, to probe it for clues but it drifts away. I stare at Tracey, resolute.

"Well, okay. Whatever," Tracey says. "Focus on Agnes, will you? Shit, Julia, you're like a fucking magpie, distracted by the weirdest shit, try to stay on track here."

"I wish I still had the body I was born with," Grace says. "Instead, I'm Frankenstein's monster and that's not easy to live with, I'll tell you. But never mind that, what did you do?" she asks Agnes. "What did you do about the heroin?"

"I took it. I grabbed a smelly old gym bag that he had there and I took it all."

"Motherfucker," Tracey says. "You've got balls, girl."

"I went back to Auntie Miriam's room," Agnes continues, "and I stuffed as much as I could into that cushion that Auntie Miriam was holding when they were tearing up the place. I stashed about half of it."

"Did she know what is in it?" Grace asks and Agnes shakes her head.

"No, she was asleep when I did it. I went home and I phoned Josh."

"Was home with your mom and stepdad?" Samia asks and Agnes shakes her head again.

"I had this roommate who was oblivious to me, to life, to everything. She hardly spoke any English. Anyways, I called Josh and he came over and I showed him the stuff. He nearly had a hernia. He said he knew a guy who'd get us hooked up and we'd make a killing. Yeah, right."

She starts crying again and Beatrice, who finished her dessert and has thankfully wiped her chin, hands her a couple of napkins.

Agnes blows her nose and wipes her face.

"About a week later, it's arranged for us to meet up with a guy in Niagara. There's an abandoned hotel on the lakeshore with a parking lot and that's where the deal was going to be made, at midnight. We were supposed to get half a million in cash and that's just for the half of the stuff. I didn't tell Josh about the rest that I left in Auntie Miriam's cushion. I guess I wanted to make sure we got the money and then, if everything went okay, we could do another deal. Big mistake.

"We get there and the place is pretty scary and we wait. We're the first to arrive. Then this big SUV pulls up and guess who gets out? Mr. Fucking Healey. I nearly died. My heart was going so hard I thought it was going to blow a valve. I say to Josh, what the fuck, and I can see he's as terrified as I am.

"Mr. Healey says 'oh, it's you, Joshua, I should have guessed. Who's your girlfriend?' Because no one at the home knew we were seeing each other and I had on a toque and it was dark and I had removed my piercings. And then Mr. Healey pulls out this gun and he says 'give me back my fucking drugs or you're dead.'

"And I've got no fucking clue how we're going to get out of this shit and it's all my fault we're there in the first place.

"Mr. Healey tells Josh to take the drugs to him and I say no, he shouldn't, but what else can he do? He takes the bag over and of course, Mr. Healey notices there's a bunch missing.

"And that's when he shoots Josh in the foot." Agnes is sobbing and it's hard for her to talk. "He shot him in the fucking foot."

"Do you want to stop for a bit?" Grace asks and we look at her, incredulous at her suggestion. Stop? We need to know what happened next.

Agnes shakes her head. "I need to finish. Josh is lying on the ground and he's screaming and Mr. Healey's shouting at him, 'where's my drugs, where's my drugs?' and Josh is saying he doesn't know and I can't tell them because they'll kill Auntie Miriam."

She lets out a shuddering sigh. "I guess he figured Josh was the mastermind behind the whole thing because he didn't pay me much mind up to then, not about asking me where the drugs were anyway. But he turns to me and he says 'do you know?' He says 'don't you lie to me, little girl,' and I throw up and he waits and then he says 'tell me, and don't lie now.' I shake my head, I say I don't know, God help me, I don't know. He asks Josh again and of course, Josh can't tell him because he doesn't know, but Mr. Healey just figures he is being a tough guy. So he shoots him in the knee. I'm terrified that Josh will tell him I was the one who found the drugs in the first place, because then of course, Mr. Healey will know that I have the missing stash.

"But Josh is in so much pain he can't talk, and he's screaming so loud and Mr. Healey shouts at him to shut the fuck up, but Josh can't even hear him.

"Then Mr. Healey shoots Josh in the chest and in the head and the bullet goes right through his eyeball and out the other side.

"And the only person left screaming is me and I hear Mr. Healey say 'what a bunch of fucking baby amateurs' and he turns the gun on me and he shoots me three times in the chest.

"And then I woke up here."

None of us know what to say.

"I loved him so much," Agnes says crying. "Josh. I loved him so much and he was so beautiful and everything, and he was going to be a great musician and he's dead, because of me. And Mr. Healey must have somehow figured out the connection between me and him because why else would they have done that to Auntie Miriam's room?"

"But your mother got them kicked out," Beatrice says calmly. "I'm telling you, Auntie Miriam is fine."

"But I killed Josh," Agnes says twisting her hands in her lap. "He's dead because of me."

"He's dead because he chose to sell the drugs," Beatrice says. "It was dangerous for both of you. Neither of you had any idea what you were doing, but Josh knew it was dangerous, of course he did. The truth is that you died because you were young and stupid and that's not your fault."

"That's not a very nice thing to say," Isabelle objects, glaring at Beatrice who shrugs.

"It's the truth," she says. "Nice or not." She gets up and walks away.

"So gentle, so loving," Tracey says watching her go. She pulls her chair around to where Agnes is sitting and puts her arms around her.

"Listen, baby, it really wasn't your fault, okay? My mum was a drug mule and trust me, it's a risky game even for those who've been at it a long time." She strokes Agnes's hair, but Agnes cannot be consoled.

A drug mule? I want to ask her more but it's clearly not the right time.

"She's back," Isabelle says watching Beatrice striding across the canteen floor.

"Intrigua's with her," I said. "She'll take care of Agnes."

"We're taking you to the Rest Room," Beatrice says, in what are for her, kind tones. "Come on, Agnes."

Intrigua takes Agnes by the hand and she immediately relaxes, as if hypnotized. After they leave, we look around at one another. "I don't think I ever want a Viewing," I comment, and Samia agrees.

"I don't think they're all as bad as that," Tracey says. "Coffee tomorrow?"

"I never know where to find you," I say, panicked.

"One of us will come and get you," Tracey assures me. "Grace is fading. Grace, you've lasted longer than usual."

"The power of adrenalin is effective, even to us dead folk," Grace says faintly and she smiles as she disappears.

"We're all going to get bounced soon. Who needs a watch when you've got Grace?" I hear Tracey joke and it's the last thing I hear before I find myself lying in the darkness of the Rest Room, with the thick black curtains pulled around my bed. I guess Purgatory decided that I needed a break and for once, I'm in agreement.

14. I RUN AWAY FOR A WHILE

THE SIGN SAYS: *God, being Love, is also Happiness.* I thought we weren't supposed to talk about God here? Although Purgatory does seem to change the rules without rhyme or reason. Agnes warned me about the inconsistency and she was right.

I stand outside Cedar's door for a bit, thinking. Then I knock.

"Julia! Come on in."

I sidle in, still fearful that an obscenity will jump out of my mouth like a toad. I sit down and look at him.

"Quite the day you had yesterday," he says and I nod.

"Anything you'd like to talk about?"

I shake my head. "I ... I think maybe I need a day off. I can't do this today."

"Fair enough," he says and he stands up. "I've got something you might like. Come with me."

I follow him down a different hallway to another door that looks exactly the same as all the others. He opens it and holds the door aside, so I can enter first. The room is plain and white and it's empty except for a running machine exactly like the one I had at home. "Yeah," I say, exhaling. "Good thinking."

Cedar points to a basket. "Clothes and running shoes are in there. You can change in here once I'm gone, no one will disturb you. And here," he says "put these on."

He hands me a pair of sunglasses.

"My future's so bright?" I joke but when I put them on, I

am immediately transported to another world. I am back on Earth, on a winding road that follows the pale caramel curves of a sandy beach, with breakers crashing and rolling off an ocean of aqua and teal. The sky above me is blue but it isn't the weird flat cyan of Purgatory, no, this sky is cobalt and rich and deep and the clouds are real, they're alive and bursting with energy. Seagulls cry and swoop for fish and behind me, mountains soar with majestic beauty.

I can hardly speak. "Thank you, Cedar," I finally manage and he grins.

"My pleasure. And there's music too, if you like. Just say whatever song you want, and it will play. See you later, alligator." He leaves me alone with my heaven on Earth.

I yank off my Versace dress and pull on the running clothes with a feeling akin to a craving. The shoes are exactly the same as mine, of course, and the running gear is also a mirror image of my Earth apparel.

I do some stretches, then I hop on the treadmill and start jogging slowly to warm up. I am stiff from lying around and not doing much of anything in Purgatory but I quickly loosen up.

I jog down the road, and I can smell the salt coming off the ocean. I smell the asphalt heating up beneath my feet, and the happy fragrance of suntan lotion hangs in the air along with French fries, evening bonfires, sea sand, and the burnt caramel of toasted marshmallows.

Apart from the fragrances in the Makeup Room, Purgatory is without scent. The only aroma can be found in Tracey's kitchen. The canteen is completely odourless despite the variety of dishes served. The hallways and rooms never carry the scent of cleaning products or furniture polish or anything at all, and I've yet to see a live flower.

As if reading my mind, Earth obligingly coughs up the goods, and I run past bushes of sweet honey jasmine and daydreamy lilac, past trees with cherry and plum blossoms and the sweetness and purity nearly make me cry.

"I've missed you so fucking much," I tell the Earth. "I'm so fucking sorry I didn't appreciate you properly when I was here. I miss the trees. I miss real grass. I miss mud. I miss dogs even although I hated the fuckers, and I miss the sound of kids playing although it annoyed the shit out of me back then. I miss seeing people playing baseball at night in the summer and walking on the boardwalk. I know that the only thing I was thinking about was myself and what I wanted to acquire next, and I hardly seemed to notice the beauty around me but I did notice it, I did."

The road veers into a forest and I run into the tangled undergrowth, with the sun struggling to shine through the twisted and knotted vines of the treetops. I brush at tiny cobwebs as I run, and the sound of breaking twigs and crunching loam crackles under my feet as I pick up even more speed and pound forward. I run for miles in that forest, through sunlit glades and back into the cool shade of the forest.

The path curves and I find myself at the ocean once again, on a boardwalk this time, with the weathered old wood bouncing slightly beneath my feet and I run harder and faster than I have ever run, and I can hardly breathe. I stop pacing myself and I push until I think my lungs will burst. I finally have to stop and I throw myself down on the sandy beach. I lie there, looking at the sky, listening to the crashing waves, and the cries of the seagulls echo the loneliness I feel.

I close my eyes and suddenly there is no longer sand under me but cushiony foam, and from the jumble of scents, I know that I am back in the Makeup Room.

I lie on the sofa, not wanting to open my eyes. I never want to leave that ocean road and I want to be able to run in that forest forever.

But all good things come to an end. The door opens and in walks Beatrice, with a Scrabble board under her arm.

15. SCRABBLE AND MURDER

"COME ON, CUPCAKE," she announces brusquely. "This was your idea, so let's have at her."

"Here?" I swear my voice squeaked.

"Of course not. I've got no time for girly doodads. Follow me."

I am still in my running gear and, unbelievably, there is a dusting of beach sand under my T-shirt and on my joggers. I touch this miraculous substance and I want to show Beatrice but she walks away too quickly.

She leads me to a room with white Formica coffee tables and large red leather armchairs.

"Purgatory has a very rudimentary colour palette," I comment. "Grass is green, clouds are white, sky is blue, and décor is red."

She shrugs, empties the letters into a bag and shakes it vigorously.

"I would have thought red would be saved for Hell," I say meditatively but she simply holds out the bag and won't engage. I lean down and sniff the leather chair I am sitting on.

"Why doesn't Purgatory replicate what Earth smells like?" I ask. "But no, there's nothing." I sit back, triumphant at pointing out this shortcoming, but Beatrice just shakes the bag again.

"Closest to letter 'a' starts and you can keep the letter if you want to."

I get an "i," my least favourite Scrabble letter, while Beatrice gets a "j."

I sigh, throw my letter back and let her choose hers. God-damn it. I get three "i's," two "e's," a "g," and an "f." And it goes downhill from there.

"I used to be good at this," I wail, and Beatrice gives me a vicious smile.

"Best of seven?" she asks and proceeds to whip my arse six to one.

"At least I won one," I say, trying to make myself feel mar-ginally better. "Beatrice, I swear we've been were here longer than four hours. You don't get bounced?"

She shakes her head. "Not when you've been here as long as I have."

She lights up a cigarette and offers me the pack and I take one gratefully.

"How long have you been here?" I ask.

"Hard to say. Put it this way, I've seen hundreds of you new-bies come and go. Course, it took me a while to get to admin, that didn't happen overnight."

"How did you die?"

"Miss Nosy Parker, at it again. Fine, if you must know, I got Alzheimer's and the doctors wanted to put me in a home. Except for my sister, who died before me, I always lived alone, quite happily thank you very much. When the chips were down and I was going to lose my marbles, I decided to take my own life while I could still remember what a sunset in Hawaii looked like."

"How did you kill yourself?"

"Jesus, you're a morbid one. I gassed myself in the garage, sitting in my big Cadillac convertible, top up, needless to say. And I took my cat with me, if you must know. All for one and one for all. My house is still there, rotting away on Chuckery Hill Road. I didn't leave a will. I thought it'd be fun to leave a mess since I lived such a neat and tidy life and where the hell did that get me? I visit the old shack when I get a Viewing now and then. Great little place it was, on the edge of a lake.

You probably won't believe me when I tell you the name of the lake."

"Try me."

"Ecum Secum."

"Pardon me?"

"Told you. Ecum Secum."

"Memorable."

"Yes. A little house on the edge of Lake Ecum Secum. I was very happy there for many years."

Beatrice starts gathering the pieces.

"I will improve," I say, trying to let her know that I am open to playing again.

"Fine. I'll come and get you," she says not specifying when, and she gathers her things and stands up.

"There is a Reading Room," she says helpfully. "You might want to look through a few dictionaries for some ideas." And she leaves.

A weird tingling sensation floods my body and the room acquires the haze of a late summer afternoon when the humidity is high. *I'm going to bounce,* I think, and that's exactly what happens.

I come to in the Coffee Room with the others and I am inordinately proud of myself.

"I knew I was going to bounce," I announce proudly. "And I even got myself here!"

Only Samia acknowledges what I've said, and she smiles and gives me a thumbs-up. "I'll get your latte," she says, and she starts steaming the milk.

I look around. Agnes is pale and swollen-eyed, staring off into space, chewing on a finger. Grace is digging in the huge purse she always carries with her. She's the only person I've seen with a purse, and I wonder what's inside. I save that question for another time.

Isabelle is studying her hands and Tracey is watching Agnes with a worried look.

"Agnes? How are you?" I ask. "I know it's a stupid question. I guess I mean, are you going to be okay?"

She looks at me and her eyes well up with tears. "I killed him," she says. "And I put my Auntie Miriam in terrible danger. Look at all the terrible shit I did. I deserve the worst things to happen to me. I should never be allowed to be happy again."

"Yeah, well, that's bullshit, and if you keep telling yourself that, then you're going to carve out a very miserable life for yourself. Josh set up the drug buy, he knew what he was doing," I tell her.

"But he didn't know. He thought he was so cool, but he was just a nice guy, a really nice, even geeky guy, and he probably thought I expected him to be in the know, and he tried his best and he paid with his life. I was much more druggy than he was. I'd take anything people gave me, but Josh never even smoked weed. And look at Auntie Miriam. Look at what I did there."

I have no reply to that.

"My mother was murdered," Tracey says and we turn and stare at her.

I recall Tracey saying that her mother was a drug mule and I had meant to ask her about it but I had forgotten until now.

"She used to go to Hong Kong a lot," Tracey says, dipping her finger into her hot chocolate that couldn't have been that hot. "She said she worked for an import export store, a home décor thing, but it was just a front. She'd come back with all kinds of crap for the store and there were never any drugs in the vases or ornaments, but she'd buy fluffy toys and shit like that and fill them up with heroin, and put them in her luggage and because customs were so busy checking her papers and what she was declaring, her bags were never searched. She wasn't bringing in millions of dollars but she got paid enough money so us kids could live in a nice house growing up. We weren't rich but we weren't poor either. We got by.

"Then one night, out of nowhere, on her birthday, her throat was slit, and if that wasn't enough, she was stabbed half a dozen times as well. I had moved out a long time before, got married, had my two kids, but I still saw her pretty much every day. But I wasn't at her place when it happened.

"The police thought her boyfriend did it. They'd been together for a couple of years and my mom went to Hong Kong with him a bunch of time, but a few months before she's killed, she suddenly breaks it off with him and marries some other guy that none of us even knew. My husband said he had heard that this guy was violent, and I told the police it could have been her fucking husband or her fucking boyfriend, and they told me, 'Listen Missy, don't you talk to us like that. As far as we're concerned, you're a suspect too.' But the boyfriend took a lot of pills all the time; he took about five Prozacs a day as well as truckloads of other stuff. He always talked really slowly and he even moved slowly. But you never know, he could have got angry and had an energy spurt or something."

Tracey is talking quietly and she's relating her story in a monotone and we lean forward, concentrating hard to hear her.

"The boyfriend was very wealthy, at least his ex-wife was. She owned a few carpet cleaning places. I told him, just days before my mom died, that he should come and clean my carpets but he never replied. I told him not to be so lazy. It was the last thing I said to him before my mother was killed. The cops decided it must have been him, not the new husband, but they didn't have any evidence except that he'd had a nervous breakdown two weeks before he killed my mother, and when she got married, he told her, 'If I can't have you, then no one can.' So they locked him in a psych ward while they tried to find more evidence.

"But my mom always hung out with violent men. It turned her on. Made her life exciting."

She falls silent and I wonder if that is the end of it. The whole thing sounds extremely bizarre to me. I glance over at Agnes. She is caught up in Tracey's story, and she has some colour in her cheeks and looks more relaxed.

"Apparently the husband said that the boyfriend had written a letter saying that my mom was his or no one's, and the whole case hinged on that, but the letter was missing. I tried to find it but I couldn't. My sister had told me there was blood everywhere in the flat, on the couch, the walls, the ceiling, on the phone where my mother tried to call for help, and on the door where she tried to get out. I had to see for myself and I went there, but what my sister said wasn't true; there was only blood on the couch and there wasn't much of it either.

"My mother wasn't even properly dressed when she was killed. She was in her bra and panties, her stockings and her jewellery.

"I wanted to see the body. I wanted to see where she was stabbed and how bad it was but they wouldn't let me see her. We had a eulogy for her and I was disappointed because hardly anybody said anything. My mother was no angel, but still. Her husband ran out as soon as it was over, and my sister was crying too much to talk, and only I said something. My dad told me that my mother was in limbo, and that we had to have another mass for her because she needed a minister to tell her soul where to go, but I told them, who the fuck were they to tell my mother where to go?

"I've looked for her here but I've never found her. My mother was a drunk and all I can say is that I hope she was three sheets to the wind when it happened so she didn't feel a thing."

"If they never found the letter, did they convict the guy?" Isabelle asks.

"A couple of days after he was locked up. The cops phoned us in the middle of the night and they said they had found my mother's house keys in his house and nearly a thousand dollars in cash that he had stolen from her, and some of her jewellery with her blood on it. So that was a slam dunk. But he only ever ended up in a mental home, which was too good for him if you ask me.

"My birthday is the day after my mother's and she was murdered on her birthday. They think she was killed between five-thirty and seven p.m., while I was out shopping. I was shopping for her birthday while she was getting killed." She falls silent again and this time she doesn't have anything to add.

"That's too terrible, dear," Grace says. "I am more sorry than I can say."

We echo the same and Tracey nods. The cynic in me is voicing objections, the story sounds disjointed and uneven, and I have a hundred questions but I know I can't ask any of them.

"I miss my kids," Tracey says and she wipes the tears from her eyes.

But I think about what she had told me before, about how she killed herself because no one at work appreciated her and the thing about Tracey, and I feel disloyal even thinking this, is that you can't be sure what's true. That's the way I feel, anyway. But, on a good note, Agnes seems much more cheerful, and at least Tracey took her mind off Josh and Auntie Miriam.

"Did you ever ask your Helper about trying to find your mother here?" Grace asks and Tracey nods.

"It's not like we all end up in the same nook," she says. "And Mom was killed, meanwhile I killed myself, so there's that difference for a start. And also, part of me doesn't want to see her again because I don't want to have to explain to her why I killed myself. She thought the guys I worked for were a poncey lot of wankers, and she would have said I was a stupid twat for letting my feelings get hurt by them. It wouldn't have been a good enough reason to kill myself, not to her, anyway. I don't think Mom would have thought any reason was good enough, not with me leaving the boys behind, and I don't want to have to face her, so that's probably why I haven't found her."

The others nod and I realize they know the story of Tracey's suicide, but I wonder why the details about her mother's murder are only coming out now? Surely they would have talked about this before? But then again, none of them had had any idea about what had happened to Agnes either.

I want to ask them how long they have been hanging out together and what they talked about before I came, when such important details to their stories are only coming out now? Beatrice would probably call me a nosy parker again, but if you don't talk about the nitty gritty real stuff, then what else is there?

Which is a bit rich coming from me, me who used to only talk about celebrities and their trending tattoos, and what nail varnish colour ruled the season.

"You know what I miss," Isabelle says wistfully, apropos of nothing, "I miss thunderstorms. Purple clouds. Lightning."

"There's the Rain Room," Agnes points out.

"I've never been," Isabelle says.

"It's depressing," Samia pipes up.

"I'd still like to go," I say. "Isabelle, you want to go? Can someone show us?"

"Let's all go," Grace says. "We need the healing power of water to soothe us."

I want to tell her that she sounds like Cedar and we're are about to get up when Tracey starts to speak again.

"I don't believe that guy killed my mother. The ex-boyfriend, I mean." Her voice is the same strange monotone, and we sit down again. "He was too fucked up on pills and shit. She could easily have overpowered him if he attacked her. And I don't think it was her husband. Even though he had an alibi that he could easily have faked. He said he was in bed with his ex-wife and she would have lied for him. But still, I don't think it was either of them."

"Who do you think it was?" Agnes asks.

"The guy she carried drugs for. I met him a few times. What a piece of work. Tattoos everywhere on his neck and up the back of his skull. Snakes and ladders. Thinks he's a British gangster out of a Guy Ritchie movie, he's got this stupid fake Cockney accent and he wears shiny suits and lots of gold rings. I think he fancied my mom and she thought she could take advantage of it. After her last trip to Hong Kong, she was throwing around way too much cash. Of course, a guy like that, he's untouchable by the cops. He'd have alibis up the arse. He never even came to her funeral. He sent a huge big bouquet of lilies, which I can still smell today. What a fucker. Wore his hair in a little stripe down his head, like a Mohawk, only a crew cut. I bet it was him, the fucker. I bet it was him. And I bet he planted the evidence in the ex-boyfriend's house. "

"Dear, I'm beginning to fade," Grace says gently. "Let's go the Rain Room and we can carry on talking there."

We get up and Tracey is lost in her own world. Agnes puts her arm around her and that brings her back to us and she gives us a small smile.

"Sorry for being such a downer," she says as we walk along the corridor and Agnes jostles her.

"You aren't a downer. You helped me. Thank you."

Isabelle starts singing "That's What Friends Are For" and we join in and silly as it is, it feels good.

A run on an ocean boulevard, Scrabble with Beatrice, coffee and a sing-along with friends. I am actually having the nicest day I've had since I can remember.

But then I chastise myself. Murder. Drugs. Tales of tragedy and broken families. What kind of sick puppy has a happy day in the midst of all that?

16. RAIN

SAMIA IS RIGHT. The Rain Room is weird and depressing. We're in a glass gazebo and rain drizzles down from all sides, rain that is more like mist, and I miss the tapping sound of drops as they land. I feel like I'm in a glass tent, being hugged by a humid fog. There's no foliage outside. It's just grey. It reminds me of the time I did a photo shoot in a small seaside town, out of season. I had the bright idea that it would be romantic, and lend a note of mystery to the fashion, to have models coming out of the rain and the mist, all very moody. But it was just damp and dull and the only highlight I had was sex with the boy model who was a vision of androgynous beauty. But that was before Martin, I am sure of that. I never stepped out on Martin, I would bet my life on that.

I kept the model in my room for the weekend, then we went back to the city, reshot in a studio and the results were fantastic. Win-win. At least that's what I thought of as a win, in those days.

I don't enjoy remembering that side of myself. I told myself the boy was flattered that I had chosen him to share my bed, but had I given him a choice? Maybe he'd thought he had to screw me royally or I'd fire him and, if so, he'd have been correct. I would have fired him for sure. I thought of William Congreve's line from *The Mourning Bride*, "Heaven has no rage like love to hatred turned, Nor hell a fury like a woman scorned."

"No fury like that…" I mutter and I let the thought peter out. I settle down on one of the giant red beanbag pillows on the floor. Samia looks enquiringly at me.

"You're right," I say. "I prefer not to remember. Some things are forcing their way to the top of my mind and I'd rather they didn't."

"Yeah. Ignorance is bliss," Tracey agrees.

"I played Scrabble with Beatrice today," I say and the others look at me open-mouthed.

"Why would you do that?" Agnes asks. "Socialize with her?"

"I didn't plan on it. I admit that the idea occurred to me when we were in her office. Well, it didn't so much as occur as flit across my mind like a cloud on a sunny day, and I never thought about it again until she arrived in the Makeup Room with her Scrabble board under her arm."

"Maybe you can ask her for a Viewing for me," Grace says and she sounds desperate.

"You want a Viewing? After what happened yesterday?" Tracey is astounded.

"Now, more than ever, because of yesterday," Grace says and her poor, ruined face is sad.

"If I can, then I will." I am cautious about promising anything. "Beatrice is so powerful, I don't want to upset her."

"She must like you if she plays board games with you," Agnes says. "I've never heard of her hanging out with anybody before. Hey, why are you wearing running gear?"

I can't tell a lie. Not in Purgatory. "Cedar hooked me up with a Running Room," I say. "Gear and everything. It was fantastic. I don't know why he did it, but it was great."

"Motherfucker," Tracey says and she shakes her head. "Looks aren't supposed to count here but all of a sardine, Miss Supermodel is playing board games with the Wicked Witch of the West and Cedar's giving her special privileges that most of us have never had."

"You want the Running Room?" Agnes asks her.

"That's not the point. The point is, how come she gets things like that, when she's only been here three farts from a sparrow's arse and we've been here for like a fucking century and we get nada, zip, banana fudgesicle, el zilcho? I'm splitting. I've had enough of the goodwill of mankind for one day. See you guys tomorrow." She marches out of the Rain Room, muttering under her breath.

"I'm fading," Grace says. "Please, Julia, if you can—" and then she is gone, leaving Isabelle, Agnes, Samia, and myself.

"I don't want a Viewing," Samia says sadly. "The only people I have to look at are my parents and I know I ruined their lives."

"Let's take this to the caf," Agnes suggests, "before we lose each other."

17. SAMIA

WE LEAVE THE RAIN ROOM and go to the cafeteria where we load up on cookies that have most probably been baked by Tracey. Samia seems down in the dumps and I push the plate of cookies towards her. "You okay?"

She puts her face in her hands and starts to cry. I scoot around the table and put my arms around her. She is tiny, and I hold her while she sobs. "I ruined everything. And seriously, I'd never even done drugs before. I went to a concert with a friend of mine, a guy I've known forever and he does a lot of drugs. Well, not a lot, but he does coke and ecstasy and he loves it. And he said here, try it, you'll feel fantastic, and he gave me a capsule full of white stuff and a little brown pill. Funny, a little brown pill for a little brown girl." She blows her nose. "I had a job that I loved. I had just turned twenty-five. And then I died. And shamed my poor parents too. I was an only child and I broke their hearts. I never got to live out any of my dreams. I wanted to travel the world, learn how to cook exotic dishes, volunteer and make a difference to people's lives. Now, I am just dead, and stuck in Purgatory."

"I am very sorry," I say and I am. "That's so unfair. Did your friend not take the drugs too?"

"No. He said he had taken stuff before we met up and that he didn't need to but he said he'd score some for me. Five people died that night. But lots of people took it, not just the five of us who died."

"Have you met any of the others here, who died that night?"

Samia shakes her head. "I don't know. I don't know who they were. There were thousands of people there that night. I was so stupid. Why didn't I say no, like I had so many times before? It's not like my friend cared if I did or didn't do the drugs; he always asked me. It was like he was being polite, in case I wanted some. And I probably ruined his life too."

"Are we here because we're supposed to make amends?" I ask.

Agnes pours sugar onto the table and dips her finger into the pile and licks it clean. "Who the fuck knows?"

"But you're an Introducer, you should know."

"Introducers just show newbies around. We don't have any inside info or anything."

I sigh. "How do we move on?"

"Ask Cedar. I bet he'll say something like, 'I encourage you to open yourself to the realm of simply being here now, and try not to be distracted by what's to come.'" She mimics him so perfectly that we burst out laughing.

"Here's another question," I ask. "How do I get myself to bounce to where I want to go? My default is the Makeup Room. How do I change that?"

They shake their heads. "My default is the Rest Room," Isabelle says. "And I am sure it lets me stay longer than four hours."

"Mine is the Reading Room," Samia says.

"I get the Introducer's Lounge," Agnes chips in. "It's a pretty cool place, so I guess I do get to have some extra privileges. When you feel you're going to bounce, try to picture the room you'd like to be in," she advises me.

"Which is about to happen," I say. "Rest Room, Rest Room, Rest Room!"

And astoundingly, it works.

18. TIME ALONE TO THINK

I LIE IN THE SOOTHING DARKNESS of the Rest Room, and I think about recent events. I am not tired and I wish Intruiga would wander by and relax me, soothe me. I am wound up by the story of Tracey's mother's murder and I am still freaked out by seeing Agnes's Viewing, and I feel terrible for Samia and Agnes, both of whom have brought such sadness to their families' lives. I am ambivalent about Tracey though—how much of what she had said was true?

And I think about Grace and the weird way she has of fading that no one even comments on. Does it have to do with her freakish looks, because she is so full of plastic and fillers? And I wonder about Isabelle—how did she die? And how had Grace died?

I wonder about the six of us, and I ask myself why we have formed the bond that we have. Is there some common denominator that links us together or is it just random? We are a strange, odd mix of people. And why do I even care about them? Since when do I care about anybody except myself? I should be looking out for number one, figuring out how to get out of here, meanwhile, I am obsessed with everyone else's issues.

I lie in the darkness, feeling increasingly restless. Eventually I get up and tiptoe out.

I stand in the hallway, and I don't know what to do with myself. I resolve to ask Cedar for a pack of cigarettes. I need something to calm my nerves.

A long hot bath, that's what I need. A long hot bath. But baths are nowhere to be found unless they too are hidden within the elusive club of privileges.

Ablution Block, with its showers and utilitarian fixtures, will have to do, if only I can find it.

I open a door and find a room filled with intense chess players, none of whom look up.

I find a Yoga Room, with people in all manner of twisted poses: handstands, pretzels, odd squatting frog poses, or whatever they are called. The yogis glance up and freeze me with their collective icy glares and I back out, thinking they're not very zen.

Once again, I find the knitting ladies and I recoil from the wave of their boisterous welcome. "Come in, come in! Beginners welcome!"

"No!" I shout and they look at me somewhat puzzled, taken aback by my rudeness.

"I'm looking for the Ablution Block," I say, certain that I look wild-eyed and crazy. "I can't find any of these bloody rooms like the rest of you can."

"There's a trick to it, dear," one of them says, and she gets up and puts her knitting on her chair. "Come on. Ablution Block, you say? Okay, now concentrate hard. Focus on the bottom of the doors, and try to hold the whole corridor in your vision, as if you are looking at one of those trick pictures where you see a vase but there's also two faces. You with me so far?"

"Yes," I say, and I squint slightly, trying not to focus on a particular door.

"Now, say the words 'Ablution Block' quietly in your mind, over and over, and see if a faint light starts to shine from under a door."

"Ablution Block, Ablution Block," I chant quietly, while gazing blankly down the corridor. "Nothing is happening."

"Keep trying."

"Ablution Block, Ablution Block," I say. I feel stupid and

despairing and I am about to give up when I see a glimmer of light glow for a nano-second under one of the doors. "I saw it! But now it's gone and I can't remember which one it was."

"Try again." For an affable old knitting biddy, she is awfully stern.

I give her a quick glare and I try again. Nothing. I try yet again and this time when the light glows faintly, I don't lose sight of it, I keep it in my peripheral vision and walk slowly towards it.

"What's the bet it's the wrong door?" I joke and I open it, fully expecting to find the train men or something else but, remarkably, there I am, inside the Ablution Block.

"Whoa! Cool!" I turn to thank the knitting lady but she has vanished, gone back to her needles, I suppose.

I however, have erred in my thinking. I should have gone to the Clothes Room and picked up a fresh outfit first. What is the point of getting buffed and clean and getting back into smelly running sweats?

I stand outside the washroom, not keen to leave, in case I lose it, and I try the Clothes Room trick on the bottom of the doors. But I remember that there are a bunch of hallways, some of which intersect so how can I be sure that I am in the right corridor for the Clothes Room? And, if I leave this hall, how will I find my way back?

"Attention, please! May I have your attention, please?" The airport announcer speaks loudly through the intercom and I jump.

"I need to find an Ablution Block," I tell the disembodied voice. "Do something useful and help me."

But the voice just repeats its message, and then there is silence.

I figure nothing ventured, nothing gained, and I try once more to summon the Clothes Room in the corridor I am in, but there is nary a glimmer.

I walk down a passage of shiny linoleum and I stop. "Clothes Room, Clothes Room."

Nothing.

I have no idea how long I try to make this work. Eventually I resort to begging.

"Help me," I implore, not exactly sure who I am talking to. The god of the Clothes Room? "Help me, please."

A light glimmers and I rush towards the door and find myself in the cafeteria. Great. I may as well have a cup of herbal tea and a cookie and then, once fortified, I'll get back out into the maze again.

"Looking for some company?"

My eyes are closed and I am inhaling the sweetness of chamomile with honey and I look up, not happy to be disturbed. The voice is an unfamiliar one, male but it isn't Cedar's reassuringly high-pitched nasal whine, this voice is deep and sensual.

No, this certainly isn't Cedar. This guy is about twenty-six and he looks like an Armani model. My weakness has come calling.

"Jaimie," he says grinning, his forelock doing all the casual, cool, floppy things it is supposed to. He holds out his hand.

I pick up my cookie and take a bite, and he withdraws his hand and sits down.

"How did you die?" I ask, thinking my rudeness will drive him away but he isn't deterred.

"Went water skiing and I drowned. I couldn't actually swim but I figured it would be okay. Which it wasn't."

He has dimples and a cleft in his chin and the greatest cheekbones I have ever seen.

"Do you know how to find the Clothes Room?" I ask him and he nods.

"Yeah, sure. You want me to take you?"

"Please." I get up, abandoning my drink and my cookie, silently apologizing to Tracey for wasting her baked goods.

I follow Jaimie down the hallway, trying to memorize the route he is taking. First left, second right, first right, third left. Ye gods.

"*Voila*!" he says and there we are, in the couture clothing section of Goodwill in Purgatory. "Here," he says holding up a Dior cocktail dress that my former Earth self would have killed to lay her hands on.

"I'm looking for comfort," I say, and I can see he isn't impressed.

I find an acid yellow Lululemon ensemble with stylishly tapered track pants and a zippered hoodie.

"Perfect," I say and I bound off to the change room.

When I come out, Jaimie is nowhere to be seen. Which is fine, but now I will have to find the washroom all by my lonesome.

I try to retrace our route but we came from the cafeteria not the washroom. I am ready to weep. Any why is there never a single soul in these hallways? I never see anybody walking by, never. What is with that? I sink down on my haunches and wait for the bouncing sensation that isn't quick to arrive, let me tell you. As soon as I get the tingle, I chant Ablution Block, Ablution Block and I manage to emerge in the washroom. I guess I should be proud of myself but instead, I just feel exhausted.

I turn on the shower and I stand under the hot water and let it run down my scalp and my neck and my back. It feels wonderful. The small bar of soap is remarkably ordinary but it lathers well and the shampoo has a faint smell of roses which must make Agnes happy, remind her of Auntie Miriam. At least I hope that's a good thing.

I dry myself and my hair and wait to bounce, thinking I'm finally ready for the Rest Room and when I arrive there, I am well and truly delighted to be back in that safe cave of soft blackness and comforting warmth.

19. JUNIOR

WHERE HAVE YOU COME FROM and where are you going? The sign asks. I came from Earth and I'm on my way to Cedar's office, smartass. Shows how much you know.

I am not in the mood for Cedar today. I am not in the mood for anything today. I wish I hadn't given pretty boy Jaimie the brush off because who knows, maybe I could have found a way to have wild sex with him in the privacy of some nameless faceless white room in this limbo land of eternally boring days. Maybe I am horny, but whatever the cause, I feel unsettled and dislocated. Fine, so yesterday was a good day, but days like that were scarce while days like this one go on forever.

I stand outside the door and glare at the handle. I guess Cedar realizes I am there and I guess he also realizes I am not going to come in because the door swings open and he stands up behind his desk, and smiles. "Julia! Welcome! Nice outfit!"

I scowl and slouch in like a rebellious teenager, but I think of his generosity the day before and I want to thank him. First, I have to remember to keep my unruly tongue in check.

"Thank you very much for yesterday," I say formally, and his smile morphs into a grin.

"A pleasure," he says. "How are you today?"

"Cigarettes. How do I get cigarettes?"

"Privileges," is his reply, not that I don't expect it.

"Darn. So what do I have to do to graduate and get myself some privileges?"

"We carry on doing the hard work," Cedar says. "Shall we continue?"

I nod and slump deep into the sofa and close my eyes.

"We're not going to do breathing today," Cedar says. "We're going to try something different. Word association. Are you ready?"

"Ready as I'll ever be," I reply, and I open my eyes and try to look alert.

"Just say the first thing that pops into your head when I say a word."

"Yeah, well Cedar, the first word that usually pops into my head is profane and you know it, so I guess this session is going to be a short one."

"You're a grown woman," Cedar tells me. "You've got the power to control what comes out of your mouth, trust me. Actually, trust yourself."

"*Work,*" he says.

"Play."

"*Men.*"

"Power."

"*Woman.*"

"Beauty."

"*Love.*"

"Stupid."

"*Family.*"

"Dead."

"*Cat.*"

"Friend."

"*Power.*"

"Necessary."

"*Greed.*"

"Everywhere."

"*Legs.*"

"Parted."

"*Desk.*"

"Sex."

"Stairwell."

"Affair."

"Cufflinks."

"Betrayal."

I stop and sit up. "Oh my god. Cedar. I never had a husband, did I? There is no Martin. Martin was a boy at university I should have married but he was nice, much too nice for me. Meanwhile, Junior ... Junior ... well."

Cedar doesn't say anything; he just looks at me.

"That short little piece of ... *excrement*. What a ... totally ridiculous excuse for a man! Wow, he really hurt me."

"Let it come," Cedar says. "Just let it come."

I get up and pace around the room and it does come to me, whether I want it to or not. Yeah, there was me, Ms. ÜberPower, Queen of the castle, happily ruling my roost, when in walks the new chairman of the board—the newest saviour, bright-eyed, bushy-tailed, and ready to springboard us into the future. Not that we weren't doing just fine in the present, but everybody's only really focused on the future. So in he walks, like some manic Duracell bunny, a tiny Adonis who tells us that our present state is doomed but no worries, he's here to save us.

He isn't clear on the details, and he speaks in riddles and vagaries but he does allude to cuts, yep, sorry about that but a couple of people are going to have to go, not immediately of course, but...

I am not overly worried. In the first place, my group is making money hand over fist, and in the second place, I am fucking him.

Despite my craving for power, I hadn't actually planned the latter, but he literally fell into my lap when we met by sheer chance in the stairwell.

One of the many ways I keep in shape is to skip the elevators and take the stairs, stilettos and all, and there I was, navigating down while he was jogging up.

Our paths met outside the fire door of Stairwell Exit #8. We both stopped. He looked at me. "Julia Redner."

"You gonna fire my ass or what?"

He laughed. "It's too fine an ass, but perhaps I should take a more detailed look."

I turned around and placed my hands three stairs up and I leaned down, with my legs spread, my buttocks in the air, my skirt stretching tight and my calves pumped in silk stockings.

"What's the verdict?" I asked, looking back at him, over my shoulder.

"Fucking beautiful." He could hardly talk and I was about to straighten up when he moved in and put his hands on either side of my hips.

It sounds crazy but the electricity between us was immediate.

Without thinking, I thrust my buttocks back into his groin and he groaned. He lifted my skirt with one hand and he pulled down my panties, and unzipped his trousers with the other.

Sadly, the man was hung like a chipmunk but I used my hand and came, and despite his lack of size, there was something about him that I got off on. Something? There was actually only one thing. Power. He was *the* guy, the guy who held our jobs in the palm of his hand.

We straightened up and looked at each other. "My secretary will call you," he said, and he bounded up the stairs without looking back.

His secretary would call me? About what? That hadn't ended like I had wanted it to, and I, disconcerted, walked back up to my office instead of going down to have that smoke I had been craving.

I didn't hear from him or his secretary for two hellishly long nail-biting days. Days in which I was the worst bitch to work for ever, even by own standards.

I sent the creative director out to get my dry cleaning. I got the art director to vacuum my office. I got the copywriters to go shopping for fresh flowers and then I sent them back because they had bought the wrong ones. I spent double online at night and I came up with an ad campaign that the client called unreservedly genius.

Just when my staff were ready to kill me and I was about to implode, having checked my emails every two minutes since we parted in the stairwell, my phone rang. I recognized the caller ID—it was the Chipmunk's secretary. I let it ring for a while and then I picked it up.

"Junior wants to schedule lunch with you on Monday," she said.

Patrick Ralph Davidson-Loach IV. Who liked to be called Junior, as if we all already knew his blue-blooded lineage, it was so imprinted in curves of our brain matter that nothing more was needed, only the utterance "Junior."

"I'm sorry but I'm busy that day," I said.

"Surely you can reschedule whatever appointment you have?"

"Absolutely not. It's a standing appointment with my manicurist. There must be an alternative time that he is free?" I was casual, as if I was taking about a mere mortal instead of a god.

His secretary sounded stunned. "I'll have to get back to you," she said. I thanked her and hung up.

The whole thing was childish and stupid and clichéd and I knew it, but I didn't care. I loved it. I loved the power play, the adrenalin. I didn't hear anything more that day and by evening I was worried that I had overplayed my hand.

I gave the staff an early night off, sending them home at seven p.m, and some of them wondered if I was sick. And I was! Like a schoolgirl, I was sick with the longing of a schoolgirl crush and I was nearly at the point of doodling his name on my desk, with hearts and flowers. The way he smelled, so fresh, so cool, so spicy. And the excitement that had shuddered through me when he held my hips as if he had every right. I wanted him and I wanted him to want me, me above all else.

I decided to leave for the day, go home and run double my usual distance, try to get him out of my head for a bit. I stood up, grabbed my purse and swung around and there he was, in the doorway, watching me.

"You leaving? Half-day worker." He smiled and I looked at him, narrowed my eyes to suggest he get to the point, and he did. "Be my date tonight," he said.

"To what?"

"Charity ball hosted by the mayor. Come on, we're already late."

"Wait." I opened my office closet and took out an Yves Saint Laurent cocktail dress that left nothing to the imagination.

His eyes widened.

"Back in a flash," I said, and I escaped to the washroom to change and I tried to steady my heart. I shimmied into the dress, touched up my make up, and slipped on killer heels. I'd be about three feet taller than him.

"Fuck me," he said when I came out, "don't you look sensational."

"I plan to, later," I replied and was gratified to see a red flush spread across his middle-aged pretty boy features.

We rode the elevator in silence, standing far apart and looking at the lit up floor numbers as if they held the secret to the universe.

We sat sedately in the back of his limo and the only movement was his hand riding higher and higher up towards my snatch, easing my skirt up, and pushing his fingers inside. I closed my eyes and flooded my panties with orgasms.

We arrived and he cleaned his hands off with a Wet Wipe as if he had been eating fried chicken and we went inside.

Oh, the clamour and the acclaim that rode the wave that was Junior! Cameras flashing, lights exploding, hugging, back-slapping, high-fiving. The only thing they didn't do was carry him aloft and chant their love for him, but I guessed that the evening was still young.

The women associated with the power boys came over to interrogate me while their men paid homage to their tiny chief.

At first, I downplayed my role. But that didn't last long and I soon assumed the full reins of power while modestly insisting I was simply a worker bee, a lowly cog in Junior's powerful wheel.

"I'm sure the missus isn't going to be too fond of you," one of them commented. "She was a model too, back in the day."

"I was never a model," I said. "I fire models."

The evening ended with Junior ostentatiously calling me a cab and waving goodnight while he went off to gamble at some after-hours men's club with his buddies.

But the next day, I got a text message from him: *Stairwell#8 in 5?* The question mark was a good thing; it meant he wasn't that sure of himself.

Yes, I typed back and I got up. I was waiting in the stairwell when he arrived and we fell on each other, tonguing like school kids, grabbing furiously at each other.

"You got a passport?" he asked when we finally drew apart, our chests heaving like we'd run a marathon.

"Of course."

"I need to go to Geneva for the weekend. Mary Ellen will call you and set it up. Officially, you'll be there to consult. I'm promoting you. Vice President of Global Marketing Strategies. You like it?"

"I love it."

I returned to my desk. There was no stopping me now.

And, for two, glorious, power-frenzied, high-flying years in which we fucked and fingered and hired and fired and threw our weight this way and that, there was no stopping me. Junior and I were feared and envied and I moved into a corner office close to his, taking my team with me to the seventeenth floor.

We had the greatest view and we practically lived at work, unless we were out gathering intel in five-star hotels in international cities. We were the self–crowned Emperor and Empress of Media, Publishing, Marketing, and Advertising, and the rush was better than any drug on the planet.

"What happened?" Cedar asks when I fall silent and I turn to face him. I pick up a sharp piece of amber from the basket of colourful stones on Cedar's desk and I dig it deep into the palm of my hand.

"Well, he fired me, didn't he?" I sit down. "Actually, he didn't do the dirty work. He was probably busy cleaning his fingers with Wet Wipes somewhere else.

"I got to work one morning and he wasn't there, which immediately struck me as odd. He was always there. And, I had had no early morning text message either. Junior never came to my place, even though I had given him a key. He never even saw my apartment the whole time we were together, which was a good thing because it was always in such a mess. I never had time to tidy it and the place was filled, floor to ceiling with all my swag. Plus, Duchess was going downhill fast and he was throwing up everywhere and peeing again and the place stank. And my clothes were all over the floor and the tables and I never had time to get anything dry-cleaned or sorted, I just kept buying new stuff.

"But anyway, that morning, I hadn't got a message and the office was quiet. Dead quiet. None of my staff were there either, which really made me mad, and I couldn't understand what was going on.

"Then my phone rang and Mary Ellen said that a new guy from accounts was coming up to see me and that I should wait in my office. She rang off before I could say or ask anything.

"And that's when I knew. I felt sick, I was perspiring like crazy and my silk blouse was stuck to me. I thought of leaving before the guy got there but I knew I couldn't. I waited and then he arrived and he sat down across from me, he sat without invitation.

"He was tall and fat, like a food-addicted ex-football player and his suit was too small for him, and his tie was badly knotted. Not to mention that his cheaply-cut hair hadn't been washed in a few weeks. Not someone I would have taken seriously under any other circumstances. This unstylish doofus was going to fire *me*?

"It's a pleasure to meet you—" he said and he quickly paged through a folder with his horrible fat fingers and he was sweating more than I was. "Julia. Right, Julia. I am Derek DeWitt and I am sorry we have to meet under these conditions. A number of jobs have been cut today and yours, I'm afraid, is one of them."

I didn't say anything. I just looked at him thinking that if I stared him down, he would apologize and tell me this was a huge mistake.

"Here's a package for you to review," he said, and he pushed an envelope towards me.

"You've been given a year's severance," he said, "which is extremely generous and you've got benefits for another three months and vacation pay for any days you did not take. Do you have any questions?"

I shook my head.

"Do you have anybody you can call for support?"

I shook my head again.

"Are you okay to get home or do you need a cab?"

"I live next door. I'll walk. Where are my staff?"

"You no longer need to worry about that."

"What about the contents of my office?"

"Everything will be packed up and sent to your home within the next two to three business days."

I turned to shut off my computer and found the screen was black.

"You have been de-activated and deleted from the system," he said.

"But I have files on there that I need."

He shrugged. "You can email HR and request specific files but if they are work related, you will have no right to them and your personal files have already been deleted."

I picked up my purse, straightened my skirt, and walked out.

He stuck close to my side and he stank like the Stink-Stopper I used to clean up Duchess's pee.

"Can I have your phone please?" he asked. "It's company property."

"But it's got all my phone numbers on it."

"Fine. You've got two weeks to return it, along with a signed copy of your severance package. Thank you for your service to this company and we wish you the best with your future endeavours. May I have your security pass card?"

I handed it to him and he walked me out and I stood there for a moment, hoping no one had seen me.

It wasn't even noon and I was already on my way home. I had no job. Clearly, I had no lover either. I had nothing. I walked towards my condo and that's when I saw Junior and I ducked behind a marble pillar, grateful for a place to hide.

Junior was heading towards a breakfast bar, with a bunch of smiling acolytes in tow, some of whom were my former team. They were hanging onto his every word, and everyone was laughing.

I dig the piece of amber into the palm of my hand and stop talking for a while, and then I turn to Cedar. I feel utterly sick. "Would you consider that progress has been made, today?" I ask and I sound bitter.

He nods. "I know that wasn't easy for you, Julia. Well done."

"Yeah, sure."

He goes behind his desk and pulls open a drawer. He grabs something and then he throws a pack of cigarettes at me, followed by a lighter and I catch them in quick succession.

"No smoking in here," he says. "See you tomorrow."

In other words, bye bye, birdie, off you go, deal with your own issues, but here's some nicotine to ease the pain, a little reward for being a good girl.

I stand up and leave without saying another word.

20. GRACE, THE LIVING BARBIE DOLL

I TRY TO FIND THE GANG but of course I get lost and I am aimlessly wandering the halls when Samia finds me. I am chain-smoking my third cigarette. "Hello," she says and just seeing her makes me feel better. "Come on, I'll take you to the others. And how are you today?"

I growl something indiscernible and feel even worse for being awful to her when she is so sweet to me.

"I'm sorry to hear that," she says.

"Just a bad day," I mumble and I follow her.

For some reason, the others appear to be similarly glum.

"Nice pajamas," Tracey says to me.

"Lululemon," I counter, but neither of us can be bothered to carry it further.

Samia brings us our lattes and we drink in silence.

"No sign of Beatrice?" Grace asks me and I shake my head.

"What's your story, Grace?" Tracey asks. She is antagonistic, looking for a fight and I don't understand why she's picking on Grace.

"I thought you guys knew each other's stories?" I ask. "I thought you go way back?"

They look around at each other. "It's never a straight line in Purgatory," Samia says and they all nod.

Grace looks down and holds her large purse tightly on her lap. "I don't have a story," she says softly.

"Sure you do. You're here, aren't you?"

"Leave her alone," Samia says from behind the counter where she is cleaning up, but Agnes disagrees.

"You know our dirty secrets," she says. "And you know it's because we care."

"Do you?" Grace asks, trying to raise an eyebrow. "Maybe you're just bored."

"I remembered some vicious shit today," I say. "It was brutal."

I am trying to get their attention away from Grace.

"That's why you've got cigs," Agnes says. "They reward you when it was heavyweight. What was yours?"

"I don't feel ready to go there right now," I reply. "And I'm not sure where 'there' is, actually. I got to a point where bad things went down but I don't know what happened after that."

"If you haven't got to the part where you die, then you can be sure there's a lot more crapola to come," Tracey is confident. "Whatever happened today, it's only going to get worse."

"Yeah, thanks for that," I tell her and she grins and sticks her tongue out at me.

"Forewarned is forearmed," she offers, and I light up a cigarette and offer the pack around.

"Nah, I've got lots," Agnes says and the others decline.

"I was married," Grace says softly, and we turn to her and wait. "I was married to a surgeon. A plastic surgeon, actually. He made a lot of money. We lived in the suburbs and we had a huge house and I had a Mercedes SUV and we had three children: two boys and a girl. I'm a fan of the Royal family and my children were all named after royals: Harry and William and Beatrice. Harry was nearly thirteen when I left. William was nearly twelve and Beatrice was ten. Everybody thought I had the perfect life. But Richard, that's my husband, he changed me. And I do mean literally. Everybody thought I was so lucky, that I'd never have to grow old because Richard would give me facelifts and things, but he made me have surgeries I never wanted and every time I woke up from an operation, I looked different and less like myself."

She stops.

Samia comes out from behind the counter and sits down next to her.

"He said I needed a breast job after Beatrice was born and he also made me have a hysterectomy so I wouldn't get pregnant again. He said three kids were enough and he didn't want to worry about it. He gave me liposuction on my legs and tummy. I had breast and buttock implants and he took a rib out, to give me a longer waist. But the body ones weren't the worst, it was how he took away my face."

"How does anyone 'make' a person have surgery?" Tracey asks. Clearly she doesn't believe a word of it. "You could have said no, this is my body, my face, leave it the fuck alone."

Grace shakes her head. "You've clearly never been at the mercy of a manipulative, cruel, psychopathic bully. It starts very slowly and once you take that first little step, you are rewarded. I don't mean with gifts, although there were lots of those too. The first surgery he suggested was liposuction, to get rid of the baby fat. I argued. I said I would lose the weight over time, with diet and exercise, that it would come off. But he was so persuasive. This was much, much quicker, and didn't I know how many women would kill for this opportunity? That it was incredibly expensive and such a wonderful solution and it would save me a lot of hard work and trouble.

"I said no, I was fine. I was healthy and strong and I would lose the weight, he'd see. He didn't say anything, but he got really cold. We'd had a very loving, intimate, affectionate relationship up until that point, but he froze me out. He'd chat with the nanny, and the children, and anyone who came to visit, but he was icy to me. And he wouldn't touch me. When I tried to talk to him about it, he would just look at me and say 'you know,' and he'd leave the room.

"Eventually, I gave in. I thought well, fine, it's only liposuction and he was right, lots of women would have given anything to have it done. I told my best friend and my sister and they couldn't understand why I was arguing about it. To them, it was a no-brainer, have the surgery. They both volunteered to go in my place and made me feel very stupid, and I felt ostracized by them too."

She takes a sip of her tea.

"I had the surgery. It hurt like crazy. You have no idea how painful it was. And Richard was so kind, so loving, supportive, generous, and gentle. Being loved and pampered by him like that was unbelievable, especially after his cruelty. I was more relieved and happy than I can tell you."

"How long before he wanted you to do another one?" Isabelle asks.

"About four months. Buttock implants. What could I say? It wasn't like I could change the shape and size of my bottom myself. And there was that ice about him when he suggested it, as if he was waiting for me to say no, so he could freeze me out. And when I agreed, it was like sunshine pouring down on me with all its might. And that's how it went. And then came the breast jobs. Lifts, implants. Then the ribs were taken out. My friends and family thought I looked fantastic. Everyone was envious. No one understood. I had to follow a strict diet, no sugar, no sodas, no white flour, very few carbs, and no fat. Richard had a chef prepare meals for me. Sugar ages you, he told me. All that stuff ages you, and he couldn't have me eating garbage, not after he had done all the work he had done.

"But he was happy to keep me drugged. Painkillers, tranquillizers, you name it. Never anti-depressants though, he was violently opposed to those. He said they messed with your brain and he'd never go there.

"One night, we had just finished having sex and he was examining his handiwork, very pleased with himself and he started caressing my face, pulling my hair back, running his thumb around my ears, and stroking my nose. It was extremely pleasurable and I lay there, enjoying every minute until he said, Graceful, we have to fix that bump on your nose.

"I sat up and grabbed the sheet up around me and I said no, Richard. Not my face. My face is mine. And he looked at me coldly and said have it your way, and he left and all that cruelty started like it had never ended. And again, no one supported me. And I had three babies, they were so little at the time and Richard even turned the nanny against me. I had no one, no friends, no support, nothing. It was terrible.

"I asked him one night if it would stop at my nose. If I do this, I asked, will you leave me alone? And he lied, he said yes, he promised. Just this one tiny thing, this one tiny, tiny thing. What could I say?

"Of course it wasn't only the one tiny thing. He was like an addict, always wanting more, just one more tiny thing, one more tiny thing. And the worst thing was seeing myself vanish. I had no idea who was looking back at me in the mirror. Lips, cheeks, face lift, I didn't look like myself. He made me change my hairstyle and my hair colour. My babies hated it. Harry asked me once, 'where's mommy? I want mommy,' he said. 'I do too, baby, I told him, I do too.'"

"How could your sister let this happen?" Tracey asks. "My sister would never have put up with that. She would have belted my husband."

"Eventually even my sister hated it. She told me he was turning me into a freak. Even she used that word—freak. She said she'd talk to him and make him stop but by then, you must understand, I was too tired to fight. The pain of all those surgeries was grueling. And I had lost myself. I could never get the old me back. And if I lost Richard, how would I support myself and the babies?"

"He would have had to pay child support," Tracey argues. "You could have sued him for mental and physical cruelty."

"And paid for a lawyer how? I didn't have any money. My sister didn't have any money. Both our parents were dead. I was trapped. And there were days when I was happy, or I told myself I was. We went on a cruise with the babies and it was lovely, and I even forgot my troubles for a short time. Richard was loving, and I thought I would never be unhappy again. I told God I was sorry I had been ungrateful and miserable when I had so much in life. But then I overheard people whispering about me, and pointing, and saying I looked like that cat woman who had changed her face and that I was a freak and I should be ashamed. And it went on and on and I went to the cabin and cried and I wouldn't come out.

"Richard thought I was being ridiculous. He said they were jealous of my beauty. Who cares what people think? he said. He said I was perfect, I was his beautiful lady doll and he loved me with all his heart. That's what he called me, his 'lady doll.' He made me come out of the cabin and it was terrible. All I could see were people laughing at me.

"But he paraded me. And when we got back home, I had to carry on going to dinners and balls and galas to be shown off, his finest piece of artistry.

"I told myself that it wasn't me. I pretended I was wearing a mask, that the real me was behind the mask, but when you can never take a mask off and you can never look at the real you, well, then you don't really exist anymore, do you?"

"Grace," Isabelle says urgently, "you're beginning to fade. We must bounce together, where do you want to go?"

"Let's go to the Rain Room," Grace says and she gets up and we follow her out into the corridor. "I need that gloominess if I must finish this story."

"Come on," I say and I put my arm around her, but she flinches.

"I hate being touched," she apologizes. "Don't take it personally. It reminds me that I am trapped inside this body that isn't mine."

"I understand," I say "I'm sorry."

We get to Rain Room and settle down on the giant red pillows in the glass gazebo. Grace is right, it's a perfect place for her sad story and she continues.

"I found a walk-in clinic and I told the doctor the whole story. I told her that I couldn't let my husband know I was seeing her and I explained that I needed anti-depressants and she happily obliged. Richard was right about that, how casually she prescribed them.

"I never took them but I kept filling the prescription. I also stockpiled the sleeping pills, painkillers, and tranquillizers that Richard gave me. He never used to give me much money but I saved small amounts here and there, until I had enough for a hotel room.

"It had been more than ten years since the first surgery. I didn't want to leave my babies, I loved them. Harry was fiercely loyal to me. His friends would tease him about his freak mommy and he got into fights in the playground, and he'd come home bloodied and battered, which devastated me. I'd comfort him and then I'd go to my room and cry.

"Richard was a good father. He helped them with their home-work, he took them cycling, he played baseball with them, he took Beatrice to horse riding lessons, and ballet.

"And he was faithful to me until one day I saw the way he was looking at one of Harry's teachers and I knew that I would lose him. I would lose everything. It was only a matter of time. How could the children grow up to love and respect me, after what I had let their father do to me? I was weak and pathetic and a bad role model. What kind of person was I for Beatrice to look up to? How could she learn to love her own body and her own face? And, much worse, what if Richard wanted to 'fix' her? I wouldn't be able to stop it from happening. I was a joke, a clown."

I look at her. She is struggling not to cry. I feel terrible. I had thought those things about her, that she was a freak and a vain narcissist who couldn't bear the thought of growing old.

"Oh, Grace," I say, and she knows I am apologizing, and the others nod.

"What did you do?" Isabelle asks.

"I went to a hotel, a good hotel, and I got a room with a lovely view of the city. I had started taking the anti-depressants a few days earlier, so they would be in my system along with the tranquillizers and sleeping pills. You see, I never took the anti-depressants, but I wanted to lay the blame on them for me having killed myself. Richard was the first to say they caused suicides and I wanted him and the children to think that I had become depressed and unbalanced by them. I wanted the children to have a good reason as to why I killed myself, something other than my weakness. The last thing I wanted was to give them another reason to hate me.

"I wrote each of the kids a note telling them how sorry I was, and I wrote to Richard, saying that I had been feeling depressed for some time but I was too afraid to tell him. I told him I had been prescribed anti-depressants by another doctor, and I knew how he felt about them, so I kept it a secret. But, I said, instead of making me feel better, they made me feel even worse, until I couldn't face being alive any longer. I said I knew he'd find another wife who'd be a good mother to the children and that I was sorry to let the children down, but I just couldn't bear to live any more.

"I left my phone at home, so he couldn't track me and I had the nanny drop me at a mall to do some shopping and I told her I would take a cab home. I took a bus to the hotel and there was no way anyone would be able to find me. I had only checked in for the one night, so I knew housekeeping would find me the following day.

"I left the notes on the dresser and a note on my purse with 'call the police' on it and Richard's cellphone number.

"And that was that."

She falls silent and stares ahead, and I look at her perfect nose that is the twin of mine with its little upturned tip and those tiny pinched nostrils.

My Candice Bergen nose, my surgeon had called it. "One of my most popular," he said, "and one of my personal favourites."

I force my attention away from Grace's nose and I try to think of something comforting to say to her.

"I'm sorry Grace," Tracey says. "I said a lot of shit I shouldn't have."

"Oh, don't worry about it," Grace says lightly. She bites her lip. "I just want to see what happened to my babies," she says. "I need to know. That's why I can't move on. I don't know if I'll end up in Heaven or Hell. I don't think God can look too kindly on me for being so weak as to let someone destroy His work, dismantle and reshape the face and body that He gave me. I don't think I'll be forgiven for that. But it wasn't as if He protected me, did He? I prayed so hard. God, I said, please, make him stop. I am weak but You are strong. Help me, please help me. But there was no help, not from anyone. And God will no doubt stand in judgment of me, like everybody else and I will be condemned to live my afterlife with everybody laughing at me for my weakness and my stupidity."

"That's a load of bullshit," Agnes says. "I don't know God too personally but I do know that what you just said is rubbish. You were the victim, Grace, it wasn't your fault."

But Grace cannot hear her.

We sit in silence and when Grace begins to fade, we let her go and we all silently bounce in different directions.

21. ISABELLE, ENO, AND BOWLING

I END UP WITH BEATRICE. She finds me in the Makeup Room. "C'mon, sad sack," she says. "Get up and let me whip your sorry ass."

I follow her and we find the room with large red leather armchairs. I watch her shaking the bag of letters, a cigarette hanging from her mouth. "Beatrice," I ask. "What's your take on God?"

She exhales a plume of smoke. "Never met him," she replies. "Not my pay grade."

She holds out the bag. I get the "z" and she gets an "i."

"I do believe the tables have turned," I grin and she scowls at me.

I win the first three games with speed and witty precision. I am so proud of myself, I nearly inflate to twice my size, while Beatrice seethes with annoyed fury.

"Did you know," I say, thinking I had better ask about Grace's Viewing before things deteriorate further, "that you and Grace's daughter share the same name? You're both Beatrice."

"Only I was named for my granny, not for some ponced-up rich royal brat. And the answer is no." There is no pulling the wool over her eyes. She knows what I am after.

"Yeah, well," I deflate slightly, recalling who is in power here. "She's desperate, Beatrice. She really is."

Beatrice doesn't reply, she just holds out the bag and I take a letter.

I win the next game but barely, and then Beatrice rebounds to win the following two. "Y'all come and see me tomorrow," she says, "after your Starbucks convention and I'll see what I can do, okay? But no promises. If she's not ready, she's not ready and I can't change that."

"Great!" I say. "Thank you."

"Yeah, yeah. And now you're due at Cedar's."

"I'm thinking of skipping a day," I say. "A lot came up yesterday and I'm not in the mood."

"Suit yourself," Beatrice says and she leaves.

The only trouble is, I don't know what to do with myself.

I decide to find the Clothes Room to pick out something else to wear. Tracey is right. I look like I am wearing pajamas. I manage to get to the room and to my surprise, I find Isabelle poking around, trying on stiletto heels and admiring herself in the mirror.

"Manolo Blahniks," she says happily.

I flick through the cocktail dresses and find a black and white sequined Chanel number that I recognize from Vogue and I look at myself gloomily in the mirror.

"You look fantastic!" Isabelle compliments me. "You're so beautiful."

She brushes her fingers through my hair. "Let's go to the Makeup Room and I'll do your face for you. Come on, you look like you need cheering up."

"I do feel down," I admit. "Grace's story made me terribly sad."

"None of us is here because we lived happy lives," Isabelle says. "Most people's lives aren't happy."

"Everyone thinks they're entitled to happiness."

"And then we screw up, trying to find it. I thought I was happy, having sex with a bunch of men I'd never met before. And look where that got me. It got me killed. When all I really wanted was a nice guy, a house, and babies."

"How did you die?"

We reach the Makeup Room and I lie down in a chair while Isabelle smooths moisturizer on my face. I hadn't realized how much I had missed being touched by another person, and my whole body relaxes.

"Some guy had this Bettie Page fantasy. We went to a sleazy motel and he had me put on a wig and the rest of the bondage crap that she was wearing in that one photo— you know the one, she's on her hands and knees and she's trussed up like a turkey and she's got that ball in her mouth? Well, like that. So he ties me up, he jerks off on my back and then he leaves."

"He left you tied up?"

"Yep." She was dabbing foundation and tapping it on with her fingertips.

"The bad news was that I had eaten KFC and fries before, because I had no idea what he had planned, he only showed me when I got there and I didn't want to say no. I didn't think what I had eaten would be a problem anyway. But he leaves and I throw up, it's got nowhere to go and I choke. Pretty embarrassing really. I had friends at work but they never checked up on me, everybody thought I went off with a guy or something, I don't know. That's why I'm not interested in a Viewing, who would I look at?"

"Does it make you sad? That you had no one?" Immediately, I know it is a tactless thing to say and I wish I could take it back. She was brushing powder onto my face and she falters. "Sorry," I say quickly. "That was a very stupid thing for me to say. I'm sorry."

"It's okay," she tells me but her voice is unsteady.

"Beatrice said we could go and see her after coffee tomorrow," I say, trying to change the subject. "She said maybe she can get Grace a Viewing."

"Good," Isabelle says, but I have lost her with my thoughtless remark.

"I didn't go and see Cedar today," I babble, trying to find any topic to bring her back to me. "I couldn't face it. I had the realization that I was having an affair with my boss and I got fired. I got to the bit where I was in a cab, going home and I couldn't face more yet."

"You were fired?" I feel her cheer up a little. "What happened?"

I tell her the whole story.

"I was such an arrogant bitch," I say. "I thought I was invincible and there I was, going home all by myself. Kicked out before lunchtime. That job was my life. I'd been there for nearly seventeen years. Seventeen years. And they kicked me out in half an hour. Some smelly fat stranger showed me to the door. And I saw him, Junior, on his way into a breakfast bar and he was laughing, that fucker, and he looked so happy."

"Wow. What did you do? Keep your eyes open and look up." She is brushing mascara onto my lashes.

"I don't know what came next. I don't want to know. I can't face it. Clearly, it wasn't good. I don't want to go there. I may avoid Cedar for a while."

Now I am the one who is subdued and Isabelle is once again cheerful.

"There, you're done," she dusts me off. "Sit up, I'll brush your hair."

I do as she says but my mood doesn't improve.

"Let's go and find Tracey's kitchen," she says. "You need a fresh cookie."

I follow her in silence. I don't want to be alone with my thoughts although I can't seem to escape them no matter how hard I try. The only thing I can see is me hiding behind that marble pillar, and Junior laughing and walking away and leaving me so alone.

"Hey, looking good!" I hear someone drawl and who should we bump into but Armani Jaimie. He's got some skanky looking fellow in tow.

"A Chanel frock is way more you," he says. "Sweatpants are for depressed housewives. I never got your name."

"Julia," I reply, and I try to send sexual vibes his way, just to test if it is at all possible, and I am rewarded by a big, solid nothing. Yep, sex is clearly banned from the province of Purgatory.

"I'm Isabelle," Isabelle sticks out her hand, nearly elbowing me out the way.

"Jaimie." He kisses her hand and she giggles. "What are you two delectable ladies up to?"

"Just hanging," Isabelle says. She has brightened up even further with the appearance of the two boys, whereas my mood sinks.

"This is Eno," Jaimie introduces the skanky fellow.

"You in the mood to do something?" Eno asks.

"Yeah, like what?" Isabelle asks. "Come on, wow me."

She is batting her eyelashes at him and swinging her hips and it's strange to see her in flirtatious action. I hadn't seen the side of her that liked to have sex with strangers but I recalled her stripping down to her panties to show me her tattoo when we met, and I shouldn't be surprised by her manner now. But I wonder what the point is, unless she's just looking to extend our circle.

"I scored myself PRIVILEGES, dude and dudettes, to ... wait for this ... a bowling alley in the sky!" Eno is overjoyed.

"Bowling?" I cannot understand his enthusiasm.

"Yeah, yeah, bowling! I made some realization or shit and I got REWARDED!" Eno is dressed like a skater punk, his jeans are torn and hanging low on his ass, an oversized black hoodie frames his face and his sneakers are Yeezy's that cost a small fortune on Earth. He pushes back the hoodie and looks at us earnestly. He has a goatee, a long narrow nose, and big soulful eyes that are slightly too close together. With flashy sideburns and his hair brushed flat across his forehead, he's street-cred personified. When he talks, he accents a word now and then with doubled enthusiasm and adds an extra drawl and weight to it.

"Wait. You two hang out?" I am surprised. "Cover boy, skater boy, what do you have in common?" Purgatory is making me tactless. Actually, I was pretty tactless back on Earth too. I wonder if this observation counts as a realization but there are no bells or whistles or free cigarettes falling from the sky, so I guess not.

"DEATH, lady," Eno says. "Death is what we've got."

"How'd you die?" I ask Eno. "I know Jaimie the brain surgeon went water skiing when he couldn't swim but how about you?"

"Man, she's a righteous bitch," Eno comments to Jaimie.

"Yeah, but she's gorgeous," Jaimie points out.

"You want to come bowling or WHAT?" Eno asks, and Isabelle and I look at one another and shrug.

"Yeah, sure, why not," I reply and we follow them down the hallway and Eno opens a door.

"Party time! Don't say I don't know how to treat the ladies! Yeah man! Look, sodas, French fries, hot dogs. Only thing missing is the BEER!"

Of course Purgatory knows we are coming and our shoes are already laid out.

"I wish I'd worn something more glamorous than this," Isabelle says looking down at her white micro shorts, with her purple Flashdance top sliding off one shoulder.

"You look fine," I say. "So, who do you fancy, Jaimie or the junkie?"

"Jaimie! For god's sake, Julia! I do have taste you know!"

"Well, he's all yours, for whatever good it will do, since sex is an activity *non grata*, here."

"I know but it will be nice to have some conversation that isn't about murder or husbands making their wives into Barbie dolls or stuff like that. Me, I could do with some FUN!" she imitates Eno's drawl and I laugh.

"Point taken," I say. "Point taken."

"How does this work again?" I ask when we rejoin the guys.

"I don't think I've been bowling since I was about ten."

"You aim for those things there at the end of the runway," Eno says pointing. "It's not like it's complicated. Okay, here goes." He gets in position, fires a ball, and scores a perfect strike.

"I guess we can figure out what you did when you weren't smoking meth," Jaimie comments and he gets up. Jaimie fares less well, his ball dribbles into the gutter, as does mine.

Isabelle, however, scores a beautiful strike and she dances around Eno, pointing fingers and giggling.

"Yeah, little girl, bring it ON!" Eno stands and he hitches up his pants. "You wanna have a friendly BET or something?"

"What you got?" Isabelle says and it seems like she has lost interest in Jaimie, and maybe there is something more to Eno.

"I got THIS, little girl, I got THIS," Eno grabs his crotch and makes thrusting actions.

"Yeah, like that works here," I comment and Eno turns to me. "Hey, NAMASTE bitch, lighten up, okay?"

He takes the measure of his ball and fires another strike and he turns to Isabelle. "Your turn, little girl, you show Daddy what you GOT!"

Pretty soon, it is just Eno and Isabelle playing, while Jaimie and I watch.

"What's your story, Princess Julia?" Jaimie asks. "Let's you and me get up close and personal."

"Why? Nothing to see here, move along, cover boy."

"Aw, now, be nice."

"Nice? Well, for starters nice is the furthermost thing from me. Eno is right, I'm a bitch and there ain't no NAMASTE happening here." I mimic Eno's way of speaking and I expect Jaimie to smile but he does not.

"For example?"

"I beg your pardon?"

"Give me one example of this so-called bitchiness."

I am quiet for a moment. "Why, don't you believe me?"

"I don't. You don't strike me as a nasty person. Hurt yes, damaged by life maybe, but not nasty."

"When my sister and her husband died in a car accident, I put my four-year-old niece into a foster home, rather than have her come and live with me. She had no one except for me and that's what I did. How's that for a good example, Jaimie? That'll do?"

"Fuck, yeah," he says and he looks away. "Why? You didn't have the money to take care of her?"

"I had lots of money. Well, correction, I would have had lots of money if I didn't spend it on couture dresses I found online. No, I just couldn't be bothered. I was happy working all hours of the day and half the night and I liked spending my money on myself. I couldn't be bothered to talk to a child, or bring up a child or listen to her chatter or take care of her homework or meet with her teachers or buy her a dog or any of that. The only person I was interested in was me, me, me."

"And how did that work out for you?"

"I'm here, aren't I? Am I sorry about what I did? Yeah, I am. Now. Only now. I was never sorry before. What's weird is that I never even thought about it until you asked me. Give me one example you said, and that came to mind. I had pushed it so far away that I never even thought about it, until now."

"You never visited her?"

"I never thought about her. Seriously, I never did. My sister and I were largely estranged. Jan wasn't like me. She didn't have the blessing or the curse of being beautiful. Funny thing was, she was the pretty one growing up, not me. All the boys came to see her. She had shiny blonde hair and big green eyes and this perfect, turned-up nose, but somewhere around twenty, it all dulled out and she became ordinary. Very ordinary. She was a hardworking accountant and she married a hardworking bald accountant and they had Emma. And he had no family either so they left the kid to me, never figuring they would actually die. But they did, and I walked away, and yeah, I'm sorry. Listen, Jaimie, I'm going for a walk okay? I'll leave you guys to party. Tell Isabelle I'll see her tomorrow."

I walk out, still wearing my bowling shoes with my Chanel cocktail dress and I head straight for Cedar's. His office is the one place that Purgatory doesn't keep me guessing to find. I silently thank it for being helpful that way.

22. EMMA, JAN, AND AUNT GWEN

FREEDOM IS NEVER FREE, said the sign. "No shit, Sherlock," I tell the sign and I knock on Cedar's door.

"Julia! What a lovely surprise! Come on in! I just lit a fresh stick of mulberry incense, come on in and breathe!"

"Why aren't I in Hell?" I ask, still standing at the door, with my fists clenched at my sides. "Why am I here and not in Hell? I should be in Hell. I'm getting a good look at myself, Cedar and it's not exactly pretty."

He nods and waves me to a chair and I sit down. "It's easy to get caught up in the greed of life," he says gently. "What's on your mind today, Julia?"

"Emma. My niece. I gave her away like a purse I didn't want. I dropped a four-year-old child off like she was a sack of used-clothing and I haven't even thought about her in six years. How could I have done that? What kind of rabid animal am I?"

I can't sit. I jump up and pace, getting more and more worked up and Cedar watches me. "This realization came to you today?"

"Yes. I was in a bowling alley with Jaimie and Isabelle and that meth-head guy, and Jaimie asked me to give him one example of a bad thing I had done and before I could even think about what I was saying, it popped out of my mouth. I am a sick fucker, Cedar, that's all there is to it."

Wham. I am outside his door.

I knock. "Cedar, listen, I am very sorry. Please, let me back in, I'll be more careful, I promise. Please, let me back in. I need to see you. Please, I'm sorry."

The door swings open slowly and Cedar looks at me. "Generally, there are no second chances," he tells me, "but you are in a lot of pain today."

"I really am sorry. How can I make up for what I did to Emma? I want a Viewing. I want to see how she is. I need to see if she's okay. I arranged to meet Beatrice with the others tomorrow to get Grace a Viewing but I need it. I need it more than she does."

Cedar studies his hands. "Why do you think it's necessary for you to View her before Grace Views her children? You seemed to think it was vitally important for her but now, your needs trump that?"

"Don't give me a hard time, Cedar. I hadn't realized until now, what I've done. What if Emma's in danger? What if she's dead?"

"What if she is? There's nothing you can do to help her anymore. The only thing you can do is watch from a distance."

I raise my hand before I can stop to consider what I am doing and I swing with all my might, wanting to strike this kindly hippie across the face as hard as I can. But he catches my hand in mid air. "You don't want to do that," he says. "And we'll both forget that the idea ever occurred to you. Now, sit down."

Shocked by my actions, I sit down and clasp my hands between my knees, as if imprisoning them will help keep them in check.

"You're not in Hell for reasons that will be revealed to you later, during your stay here. Your niece is fine. You will get a Viewing but not tomorrow. Tomorrow belongs to Grace and you will be supportive and kind to her."

I am humiliated. I look down at my hands.

"I want to ask you something," Cedar says "and I encourage you to open your mind, okay? Put today's incident out of your thoughts and see our meeting with a clear slate. Can you do that?"

I nod.

"What do you remember about your life after your parents died?"

I am startled and I look up at him. "Um, I don't really know."

"You were how old? Eight?"

"Yes, I guess."

"And what happened to you and Jan?"

This is like unlocking Pandora's box and I don't like it one bit. "We went to live with Aunt Gwen."

"And how old was Jan?"

"She was six."

"Did you like living with Aunt Gwen?"

"Not really. Well, that's unfair; she did her best. She was a career woman, so she didn't have much time for us. We had a lot of nannies. Aunt Gwen seemed to find fault with the nannies just when we were getting used to them." I give a small laugh.

"What did she do, for a living?"

"It's more like what she did for a passion. She was a banker, high finance and she loved it. She worked even when she was at home and we weren't allowed to disturb her. And she was very particular about her house. It was a huge mansion of a place, all polished and sparse. She didn't care for knick-knacks; she was a minimalist. She said that space encouraged clarity of mind and gave you freedom to think. The house was dark—there was a lot of brown with the wood-paneled walls, the shiny parquet floors, teak tables, and dark leather chairs. It looked like a private men's club. Aunt Gwen's only concession to femininity was flowers. She loved enormous vases filled with lilies and pink roses. The flowers were delivered weekly and she had the old ones thrown out even if they were still good."

"Did Jan like living there?"

I shrug. "Jan was adorable as a baby and pretty as a picture when she was a little girl. Everybody loved her, even Aunt

Gwen. Aunt Gwen was always buying Jan presents, girly things, fluffy toys, clothes."

"But not you."

"Not me. I was this little dark stork, you see, bony and unattractive and beaky. I had a nose out to here," I wave my hand to show him a big nose. "And I was all limbs that didn't know how to fold gracefully and I was not, in any way, adorable. I tried to make up for it by being clever. I worked really hard, trying to win Aunt Gwen's approval that way. I wanted to show her that I was the one who mattered, I was the clever one and that was more important."

"And did she see?"

"She told me I was like the son she never had. Sometimes she'd buy me books on economics and marketing."

"When you were a child?"

"When I was a child. But don't get me wrong, she was generous. She paid for me to go to university and she paid for Jan too. When Jan went from pretty to plain, Aunt Gwen lost interest in her and started ignoring her, but it didn't bother Jan. She never really cared for Aunt Gwen. Jan lived in her own head, she was so sure of who she was that she never even seemed to mind when her looks faded early. She had a kind of inner contentment. And then she met her husband and she was happy."

"Did you have any friends at school?"

I laugh again. "Nope. Why would I? I didn't have much going for me. I wasn't funny or personable. I wasn't pretty. Later, when I grew into my body, and my face became quite lovely, except for my nose, which I got fixed, people treated me differently and it made me angry. I wanted to shout at them that I was the same person I'd been when I was ugly, that I hadn't become any more interesting or loveable, but they assumed I had. Or maybe they didn't care. I tell you, Cedar, looks are currency in this world and you have to maximize your returns before you're left with nothing."

"And love?"

"Love is a myth. I thought for a moment that I had love with Junior. I did, how stupid was that? There was this one morning, he and I had stayed up all night at a ball and then we went down to the lake to watch the sunrise. We sat there, holding hands, looking out at the water and the world was filled with golden light. I thought I had finally found the meaning of life. I thought that he was my meaning and then he threw me out like a piece of garbage."

"What happened to Aunt Gwen?" Cedar asks, not too interested in my love for Junior.

"She got cancer. She died shortly after Jan and I finished university. Turned out she didn't have any money after all. She invested badly and lost everything. If she hadn't died, she would have been kicked out of her house."

"I would like to ask you this," Cedar says. "Perhaps you didn't offer your niece a home because you were afraid you would become like Aunt Gwen? That you would hurt her, like Aunt Gwen hurt you."

I thought about it. "Maybe, but that doesn't make it right. It was still better that Aunt Gwen took us in, rather than handing us off to strangers, so, no matter what, it was disgusting, what I did."

"You didn't feel in a position to offer love," Cedar argues. "You've felt unlovable your whole life."

I shake my head. "But still. I should have tried harder. It's like when people say 'I tried my best.' You know what I say to that? I say, well, clearly your best isn't good enough. Try harder, be better."

"Very harsh," Cedar observes.

"Being a bitch is all I know." I smile at him.

"It's all you think you know," Cedar says. "I would encourage you to practice not being a bitch, in small increments. For example, you will now go back to the bowling alley and you will show your friend Isabelle that you can be a good sport and that you can play a game that you hate, and you can lose at it and you can let her have some fun. That's what you can do, and I will see you tomorrow."

Before I have the chance to nod, I find myself back in the bowling alley, with Jaimie and Eno and Isabelle.

23. CONVINCING GRACE

"WHAT DID I MISS?" I ask brightly.

"Me, man, being MAGNIFICENT!" Eno crows happily and I force a smile.

"Are you losing?" I ask Isabelle and she shakes her head and grins.

"I am WINNING!" she says mimicking Eno and he swats at her. Jaimie is looking at me curiously.

"Come on, Jaimie, I challenge you. Rack 'em up," I say.

"I think that's what you say when you're playing pool," he says, but he gets up. "I propose we start again. Fresh. Isabelle is queen of that round and Eno, you get to try again? What do you say?"

"Sure thing BOSS man," Eno grins. "But first, I'm gonna get me some French fries and a BURGER! Man, privileges ROCK!"

Once I get going, the whole thing isn't so bad and I am even grateful to Cedar for suggesting it because it stops me from thinking about my unloved, ugly duckling childhood.

And the next day, I smile, watching Isabelle tell our coffee klatch about the party we had. "And then, I won again, and it was such fun," Isabelle tells Agnes and Tracey while Samia whips up lattes and we wait for Grace.

"Eno is so cool and—"

"He's COOL?" I ask it Eno-style and Isabelle blushes. "I thought Jaimie boy would be more up your alley," I say.

"Jaimie's boring," Isabelle says. "I was wrong about Eno.

He's funny. And he's kind. He was a cop, you know, a narc, and he got hooked on meth because of his job. He's got a huge Italian family and lots of nieces and nephews and he loves them all. He feels terrible about having disappointed them."

"Isabelle's got a boyfriend," Tracey grins. "Isabelle's got herself a ghost for a boyfriend, a ghost relationship in a ghost town called Purgatory."

"I'll take it," Isabelle says fervently. "I like him. He makes me happy. More than you lot, anyway."

"Nice," Agnes says lighting a cigarette. "Knows a guy for two seconds and dumps her homegirls. Nice one, IzzyBella."

"I haven't dumped any of you. I'm just saying that I had fun."

"And you, Julia, did you enjoy your bowling adventure? I wouldn't have thought you'd be a keen bowler?"

"It was great," I lie and before I have to continue with my fabrications, the door opens and Grace glides in.

"Hello, all," she says. "I am sorry I was such a downer yesterday. I'm not sure why I was so dismal. None of that today!"

"Beatrice said we should go and see her after coffee," I say. "We *might*, and I do emphasize the might bit, be able to get you a Viewing today."

She looks flabbergasted. "Oh. Now I'm not sure. I might not be ready. I don't think I can. Thank you, Julia, thank you very much but I can't."

She gets up to leave but Tracey pulls her down and Grace flinches and shakes Tracey's hand off her arm. But she does sit.

"Stay for some java," Tracey is conversational. "Okay, no Viewing, but stay anyway."

Grace sits down and nods at Samia who brews her chamomile tea.

"Isabelle and Julia went bowling yesterday, and now Izzy's got a new boyfriend," Tracey tells Grace.

"What? What do you mean?" Grace turns to Isabelle who eagerly blurts out the whole story, elaborating what a nice guy Eno is, how funny and cool.

"A boyfriend, you are so lucky," Samia sighs. "He sounds very nice."

"He does sound lovely, dear," Grace says. "When will you see him again?"

I stop listening to them and Tracey looks at me and we both nod. We are determined to get Grace to her Viewing.

"Look, if you don't want it, fine, we'll ask Beatrice if I can take it," Tracey interrupts Isabelle's litany of Eno's many favourable qualities. "But we can't miss out on the opportunity of a Viewing."

"Not since we had such fun last time," Agnes points out.

"All I'm saying is that we have to go and see Beatrice or we'll piss her off and we don't want that," Tracey says.

"True," I agree fervently. "I asked her for a favour, and if I don't turn up today, I'm toast and it's not like there's anywhere to hide in this godforsaken town."

"Come on, Grace," Tracey says. "Julia did this for you. The least you can do is come with us and tell Beatrice yourself that you're not ready and we can see about transferring it."

"You think you can trick me," Grace says and her chin quivers, as much as the surgical implants will allow. "You think I am stupid. Fine, let's go. I will do my stupid Viewing. How much worse can my life get? And maybe Beatrice will say I'm not ready, which I'm not."

She gets up and grabs her purse. "Let's go and get this over with."

"Try not to worry," Samia tells her, "we are right here with you."

But Grace does not look particularly comforted by this comment.

24. GRACE'S VIEWING

BEATRICE HAS HER FEET UP on the desk and she stares at us. "Plead your case," she says to Grace. Poor Grace's botoxed, plastic face is expressionless but her eyes are filled with pain. "Screw you, Beatrice," she says crudely for her. "You know why this is important to me. But I won't beg. I don't even know if I really want to do this. In fact, I know I don't, but I feel as if I must."

"Fair enough," Beatrice replies and she takes her feet off the table, puts on a pair of reading glasses, and peers at her computer screen. She scowls, punches in a few numbers, backspaces a few times, and pounds a couple more keys. Then she stares at the screen and waits. "Processing," she says. The printer squawks to life and spits out a page which Beatrice hands to Grace who takes it wordlessly.

"Thank you," I say and we leave and make our way to the Viewing Room. We are anxious, not sure what we are going to get.

We sit down in the same booth as the previous time, and Grace takes the centre seat on the curved red bench. I punch the numbers in for her and the screen flashes black and then the writing appears: WELCOME GRACE! WE HOPE YOU WILL ENJOY YOUR VIEWING TODAY!

"We bloody hope so too," Tracey mutters and we all nod.

The camera zooms closer to Earth and soon we are in a garden in front of a large house, standing on real grass only we can't feel it. Three kids are playing with a hose, spraying each other in the heat of the summer's evening and Grace tries to rush over to them, but she cannot move.

The garden is immaculate, with neatly pruned rose bushes and brightly coloured flower beds surrounded by manicured green lawns.

"At least he kept my garden maintained," Grace whispers. "Oh, look at Harry," she says and her eyes fill with tears and she brushes them away, not wanting to miss anything. "He's gotten so big. Oh my god, how long have I been gone?" She blows her nose on a Kleenex that Tracey shoves into her hand.

"And there's William, he looks so healthy. And my baby girl, my princess, Beatrice! Oh, they look so good! Everything's fine. And there's their nanny, the same one. Richard managed to keep her. That's good too. And look, there's my sister. Doesn't she look lovely? I wonder if Richard has offered to 'fix' her. I bet she would have told him where to get off. I wonder where Richard is?"

As if in answer to her question, the View propels us up the garden path and inside the front door. We move down the hallway, past the living room on the left that looks as if it has never been visited by a single soul. We pass the TV room on the right, with a far more lived-in look. We pass a study filled with leather furniture, bookcases, and brass library lamps.

"You didn't hold back on spending," Tracey comments. "It's like being inside a Restoration Hardware catalogue."

I nudge her sharply.

"What? I'm just saying. It's very nice."

The View stops.

"We're outside the downstairs washroom," Grace tells us. "If Richard's having a bowel movement, we don't need to see that."

"Maybe the View's stuck," Tracey says as we remain outside the door.

"I don't think it can get stuck," Agnes replies. "I think it's wondering if it should show you something."

"Show me already," Grace instructs the View and we move through the door and into the washroom on the other side.

"Oh my god!" Isabelle, Grace, Samia and I chorus at the same time while Agnes and Tracey don't say a thing.

We are all crowded into the small washroom with Richard who has a hypodermic needle in his arm and a belt tied tightly around his bicep. His eyes roll back in head and his mouth is open with pleasure.

"What the fuck?" Grace says and I have never heard her swear.

"I know him," I say weakly.

"Me too," Isabelle says.

"What? How?" Grace's eyes can't leave the screen but the man does not move.

"He gave me your nose," I admit. "The Candice Bergen special. I thought it was odd, that we have exactly the same nose."

We turn and look at one another.

"Holy moly," Isabelle says staring at us. "It's true!"

"Fuck a duck," Tracey said. "Your noses are identical. I never noticed it till now. Isabelle, how do you know him?"

"I saw him kill a man."

"Impossible," Grace says. "As evil as he is, I know him. He's not capable of murder."

"I saw him," Isabelle insists. "He killed a drug dealer named Foxtrot Four. I was in a motel with this guy and we came out and that guy, your husband, was beating up Foxtrot Four. I knew Foxtrot because he was always very charming to me and I used that motel a lot and he always said he was looking out for me. And your husband was smashing his head in with a rock. I yelled at him and he looked straight at me and then he ran away, and the guy he was with ran away too. I called 911 and the cops came, and the ambulance came, but Foxtrot Four was dead. The cops said it was most likely a guy looking to score, who got angry because there was nothing to be had. The streets were apparently dry. You know," she says accusingly to Grace, "if your husband hadn't killed Foxtrot, I'd probably still be alive today. Foxtrot would have come and untied me. Like I said, he always looked out for me."

"I can't believe it was Richard," Grace says her eyes still glued to the unmoving Richard. She reaches out and tries to prod him but just like when she tried to touch the roses outside Auntie Miriam's old-age home, her fingers encounter nothing but air.

"Is he dead?" I ask.

"Just high," Tracey replies. "Enjoying himself. But he nearly went too far, leaving the needle in like that, and the belt so tight."

"The cops wanted me to sit with a sketch artist, and I did, but they never found the guy," Isabelle says.

Richard finally stirs and we all press back in fright. The View is so convincing, it's as if we are truly in the room with him. He's a handsome man with an aquiline nose, blond hair, and big blue eyes. He is losing his hair but his high cheekbones and sensual lips dominate his features. He looks directly at us and we recoil and grab each other.

"For the love of god," Tracey says, "This View is fucking nerve-racking. I nearly peed in my pants there."

"It's too intense," Isabelle agrees. "Why can't it be like a normal TV screen? Why do we have to be right *in* it?"

Richard looks down and flicks the needle out of his arm, and he snaps the belt open. He shakes his head, as if agreeing with Tracey that he'd nearly gone too far. He puts his syringe and needle back into a cookie tin, along with a spoon, cotton ball, and a lighter. He snaps the tin shut and kneels down, hiding the box under a bunch of toilet rolls in the closet underneath the basin. "The kids could find it there," Grace says hardly able to breathe.

Richard rolls down his sleeve and buttons the cuff. He stands up and looks at himself in the mirror and smooths his hair. He takes a big breath and opens the door.

He saunters down the hallway, with us right behind him. He stops to straighten a picture and he steps out into the sunshine where the kids have stopped horsing around with the hose and are chasing each other.

"Baseball in the backyard," he yells. "Who wants to play?"

"Me, me, me!" they reply and gallop through the house.

"Thanks Michelle," Richard speaks to the nanny. "See you tomorrow, have a great night."

"I'll get my purse from the kitchen," Michelle says and we follow the three adults into the house. "I made a salmon casserole with red beans. Good night, Hope. See you tomorrow."

"Grace and Hope?" Tracey asks.

"My mother was Catholic," Grace says squinting. "Hope has certainly made herself at home. I wonder how long I've been gone?"

As if answering her question, Richard moves over to Hope and he puts his arms around her, holds her tight, and kisses the top of her head.

"Have I told you what a wonderful woman you are and how much you mean to me?" he asks.

"Where have I heard that before?" Grace mutters.

"Thank you again for taking care of us," Richard says standing back and brushing Hope's hair from her face. "Grace left a big hole and you've filled it and I thank you."

"I think you mean you've filled Hope's hole," Grace comments.

"Hard to believe it's been a year, isn't it?" Hope says hooking her arms around Richard's neck and hugging him close. "I really miss her."

"Yeah, it looks like it," Grace says.

"Dad! We're waiting."

"Come on, honey," Richard says. "Let's go and play some ball." He grins.

"*Honey?* I never got *honey.*" Grace is seething.

We follow them out to the back yard and watch the baseball game get started, with Hope cheering from the sidelines and the kids running and jumping.

"Psycho junkie," Grace says quietly. "My poor, poor babies."

The View starts to pull out, and the garden shrinks, and we are treated an aerial view of the million-dollar homes with their perfect lawns and their flowerbeds and their big SUVs in the driveways. The paved roads are intersected with small emerald parks, and we see the lakeshore and the city in the distance. We pull back even further and look at a blue-green Earth covered by gauzy swirling clouds and then, back still further, until there is nothing but blackness and the message: *GOODBYE GRACE! WE HOPE YOU ENJOYED YOUR VIEWING TODAY!*

We stare at the screen, none of us able to move.

"I could really use a drink," Grace finally says and we get up.

"They lay this shit on you but they don't exactly help you process it," Tracey comments. "It's like look, this is what is happening, and oh, there's nothing you can do about it."

We walk out of the Viewing room and head for the cafeteria.

"A heroin addict," Grace says still in disbelief. "I guess it explains a lot. I wonder how far back it goes. Because we don't know how long Isabelle has been here or when Foxtrot Four was killed. You're sure he died?" she asks Isabelle who nods.

"Definitely, very dead."

"I think it's just dead," Agnes says.

"I mean I'm very sure."

"The kids look happy and well," Tracey says. "And I know you're not too happy about your sister stepping into your panties while they were still warm, but at least the kids have got a mom and they've got the same nanny and they live in a great house and play ball with their dad. He might be an addict and a scumbag, but you must feel better, knowing the kids are okay?"

Grace nods. "It doesn't help my pain though. The hurt I suffered at his hands. It doesn't help how he ruined my life and took everything away from me and turned me into a freak. It doesn't help that I lost the kids I love. It helps and it doesn't."

We get to the caf. Isabelle spots Eno and Jaimie at the far end and abandons us. "That one's her boy," I point out Eno although by the time I do, Isabelle has reached them and it is clear to all of us who is who.

"Cute," Tracey says. "For a tweeker."

"He's gorgeous," Samia sighs.

"Shh, they're coming over," Agnes says.

"I want you to meet Eno," Isabelle introduces him, smiling broadly.

"Yo, ladies, how they're hanging?" Eno says and he gives us each an elaborate handshake. "Hey Julia, styling as always. I hear you ladies been to a Viewing. Always good for a party, that shit. You all okay?"

He, Isabelle, and Jaimie pull up chairs and I see Tracey stiffen when Jaimie sits down.

"You were a narcotics cop?" Grace asks Eno and he nods.

"Yeah, that was my gig. I was pretty good too, till I got hooked on the shit. I wanted to be in homicide but I screwed that up and here I am. But hey, I got to meet the gorgeous Isabelle, so life ain't so bad!"

I notice that he has lessened his strange and strong inflections, but he still speaks with a rapper-style sing-song.

"We just learned my husband is a heroin addict," Grace says and Eno shakes his head.

"That's heavy shit, man. I'm sorry."

"But how can he be an addict and still function?"

"Two ways. First off, you got your functioning addict—he takes as much as he needs to keep himself even. Or there's scenario numero duo, which is that he's only just started partying with heroin, in which case, he's on a downhill road, it just hasn't hit him bad yet. What does he do for his day job?"

"He's a plastic surgeon."

"Whoa, man, I wouldn't like to be under his knife, man. What if he gets the itch and loses it that tiny bit?"

Grace sighs and gets up. "I need to be alone for a while. I'll see everyone tomorrow." We watch her walk out the cafeteria.

"I need to meet Cedar," I say, and I also get up and push my chair away.

"Come by later for cookies," Tracey calls out to me.

"If I can find the room," I tell her. "I still can't do it like you."

"I'll find you," she says.

"Yo, Namaste," Eno calls out after me, "I've still got a bowling privilege for later if you're interested."

"Why don't you take Tracey, Agnes, and Samia with you?" I reply. "They deserve to have some fun." The girls clearly love my idea and Eno nods.

"Sure, why not. Big old party, mamas!"

When I leave, they are chattering like sparrows on a picket fence, as if it's a normal, happy day on Earth.

25. GOODBYE DUCHESS

*G*OD EXPECTS SPIRITUAL FRUIT, *not religious nuts.* Good for God, I tell the sign.

"Julia! How are you?" Gone is the stern man from the previous day, telling me that it was Grace's day, and that I needed to toughen up and stop being such a selfish bitch. In a manner of speaking.

"I'm okay," I say and I lie down on the sofa. "Actually, I am tired, Cedar. This place is rough. You never get to rest properly and it's like cannonballs of reality keep blasting you."

"It's not Heaven, this is true," Cedar agrees. "How did Grace's Viewing go?"

"Oh, I'm sure you know," I reply. "There's nothing you guys don't know."

"True," Cedar acknowledges. "I guess what I mean to say was this, how do you feel about what happened at Grace's Viewing?"

"I don't feel anything except tired," I tell him, and it is true. "I wish we had music here. Or TV, or the internet. I get bored. There's nothing to do here."

"That's not true," Cedar says. "But the point is, we aren't here to entertain you. Have you given more thought to your niece?"

"What's there to think about? I was a bitch. I am a bitch. There's nothing I can do to change what I did. Like you keep pointing out, I'm *here*, and Earth is just a part of my previous, long-distance life."

"Just out of curiosity, if you went back, would you look her up?"

"In a heartbeat. I'd make it up to her, for sure, in every way I could. But what happened to me? How come I'm here? I still don't get that part."

"Would you like to know? You weren't ready before, you didn't want to go there."

I sigh. "I'm as ready as I'll ever be, I guess," I tell him. "So there I was, hiding behind a marble pillar, watching Junior and the others laughing, and I was on my way home. Then I can't see anything."

"I can help you," Cedar says. "This process isn't a Viewing as such, it's what we call a Rewind. Close your eyes and try to relax. "

I do as he says and I see myself behind the pillar. I see my own stunned, shocked incredulity as I watch Junior's bubbly joy walk away. I watch myself walk home, let myself into my apartment, and sink down onto the sofa. Cedar's right. This isn't like the in-your-face, 3D experience of a Viewing, it's like watching a movie on a high-def TV. And there, on that screen is award-winning, powerful me, fuck buddy to the CEO, unstoppable, incredible me, home alone, with no one in the world to call. *Better get used to it*, a little voice whispers.

I look around my apartment as if seeing it for the first time. It's like something out of *Hoarders*, only everything is Chanel or Dior or Yves Saint Laurent. The place stinks of cat pee and there is cat throw-up everywhere. It is unnervingly quiet. I call Duchess but he doesn't appear, which is unusual, and I go to find him. My poor boy is lying under the bed and I have to pull the bed away from the wall to get to him. He is lying on his side and his little tongue is hanging out and I pick him up, grab my purse, and run downstairs.

I had known that the treatments were failing him but I can't bear to lose him, not now. I hail a cab and rush to the vet and fortunately they take us straight to the back. Duchess is heavy and limp in my arms but he is purring and his eyes are closed, and I hug him to me.

The vet calls up his file and I put Duchess on the steel table and the vet examines him and when he turns to me, I can't bear to read the message that his eyes are so clearly giving me.

"There's no choice," he says. "I am very sorry, Julia. It's time for you to say goodbye. Do you want us to take him and do it, or do you want to be with him?"

I am crying, rivers of hot tears. "I must be with him," I say and I follow the vet into another room.

"I am sorry, baby," I tell Duchess, "I love you so much, you've always been my best friend, you crazy boy. Mommy's going to miss you so much."

The vet gives him the injection and Duchess purrs and he slowly goes to sleep and all the weight leaves his body and he is so light, while I feel as heavy as lead, and I can't stop crying.

"Would you like him cremated? You can keep the ashes."

I nod that I would.

"It will take a week," the vet says. "We'll call you. I'll take him from you now."

I can hardly bear to let Duchess go. I finally hand him over and when he is gone and my arms are empty, my whole life feels bereft and without hope or meaning.

I walk out and find a cab and somehow, I get myself home.

Now, everything is gone. Everything. But surely Junior will have called? Surely he will have texted me or contacted me or something? I can't believe that after everything, he would just dump me like that, cut me off, and leave me bleeding.

I sit down on the sofa and pick up my phone but the screen is insultingly blank and I wish I could smash the phone into a thousand pieces. I think of calling him but I stop myself. No. Never. Fuck him. I will not pander to his ego. I want to kill him.

I scroll through the pictures I have of him, flicking through selfies of us smiling, holding champagne glasses, decked out in fine evening wear, at formal dinners with celebrities, him sleeping next to me, him holding his dick, his tiny Chapstick dick, with his monogrammed cufflinks clearly visible and his sparse ginger-blond pubes a fine fuzz on those tiny, acorn-like balls.

Filled with vicious glee, I have an idea. I want to email that picture to everybody in the company but I can't do it from my phone.

I jump up and hurry out. I go to an internet café and I sit in the darkness among the gamers and the backpackers and I create an anonymous email account, *janesmith1234@eezymail. com,* and I email the pic to myself from my phone.

I painstakingly type in the addresses of my team along with Junior's Board of Directors and every other contact that I can find on my phone. It takes a while.

I type the subject line, *It takes big balls (or not) to be a great leader.* I pause for a moment. Is this a terrible thing to do? But then I have a vision of myself hiding behind a pillar while he danced off to breakfast and there is no doubt in my mind. I press send.

I delete the anonymous account and I don't have to wait long before my phone buzzes and "Junior" flashes onto the screen.

I leave the café and I stand outside in the glaring sun, holding my phone and watching it vibrate like a crazy thing while he calls and calls and I don't pick up.

26. THE FIRST TIME JUNIOR TRIES TO KILL ME

I SIT DOWN ON A PARK BENCH and shake my head as if I'm trying to get water out of my ears. I feel really weird, stoned and in a fog. I guess the shock is finally kicking in. I need sugar.

I spot The Artful Dodger across the street and I am grateful for the cool quiet of the empty pub. I order a triple Woodford Reserve, figuring that alcohol has sugar in it. My phone continues to buzz and by now, the text messages are pouring in.

I down my triple and order another. I start reading my text messages and to my surprise, some of my team express dismay at what had happened to me. But they are the obsequious ass-creepers who probably think they'd better say something or I'll hold it against them forever, not knowing, as I do, that my days of power and glory are gone.

I sip the second drink more slowly and read the messages from Junior. To say he was livid was an understatement. He called me names I didn't even know he knew. I didn't even know I knew. I grin. I finish my second drink and think about having another but I am feeling really out of it and when I get off my chair, I stagger slightly.

"You okay?" the bartender asks.

"Yeah. Just had my ass fired today," I tell him. "A bit of a shock to the system."

"No kidding." He looks sympathetic. "But I can tell, if anybody will land on their feet, it's you. I know these things," he taps his nose and I smile weakly.

"Great, thanks."

I walk unsteadily home and make my way up to my apartment. I live above a pizza parlour and the narrow old wooden stairs are a challenge in my weakened state and I pause for a moment, gathering strength.

The pizza joint is a family-owned affair, proudly in business since 1971. Carlos, the granddad, comes out and asks me if I am okay and I sit down on one of the stairs and face him.

"I got fired, Carlos," I say. "I feel kind of weird. And I lost Duchess, the vet had to put him down." I start crying again.

"Ah, I am very sorry, bella," he said. "Come back down, have a soda. You need some sugar. You're in shock."

"Thanks Carlos, but I just need to lie down. I'll be alright."

He looks at me. "You want Marcello to walk you up? I keep meaning to get those stairs fixed." Carlos owns the building.

"No, really, I'm fine. Thank you, Carlos."

"Okay, but come down later, we make you a pie. You gotta eat, you too thin. You work too hard. Maybe this a good thing, you learn to live a little bit. Life is good, Julia, life is more than work."

I am going to throw up. I haul myself up. "Yes, Carlos. See you later, thank you."

I hold tightly onto the railing and crawl up the rest of the stairs. I have just reached the top when I hear a commotion below and I peer down the dimly-lit stairs. It is hard to see what is going on but I don't have to wait long to find out what is causing the racket. Junior, much like a small, rabid, red-eyed bull, is charging up the stairs, his face purple and swollen with rage, his eyes bulging.

"You fucking BITCH," he yells and he lunges for me, and grabs me by the throat. I am taken aback by how strong he is and I claw at his hands, trying to scratch him but my fists flail uselessly.

I can't breathe and my legs are kicking out wildly and I finally manage to scratch his arms and his hands. My chest feels like it is going to explode and every cell in my body is screaming for oxygen. I grunt and thrash about as much as I can, but I am dying. Junior has me pinned up against the wall and he is throttling me and the world starts to turn black and I vaguely hear a voice shouting. I think it's Junior but then I hear a pounding noise and Junior drops me, and I fall in a crumpled heap on the floor.

Marcello has saved me. He saw Junior pull up in his Lamborghini and he saw him run up the stairs. He had called out to Junior, asking him what he wanted, but all he got in reply was a furious growl.

"Something's not right," Marcello said to Carlos.

"So, go look," Carlos had grunted and, in that tiny window of time, Junior nearly killed me.

When I come to, I am in a hospital bed with a security guard outside my door. My throat is on fire and I can't swallow and even my eyes hurt. Everything hurts. How can everything hurt so much?

"You're awake," a cheerful nurse appears at my side. "Good. I'll call the doctor."

"You're lucky to be alive," the doctor tells me, and I want to say something but I can't talk.

"No permanent damage done," he says. "You'll be fine but it will take some time before you will get your voice back. Don't even try to speak now. You need to rest and relax and recover. We'll keep you here for another day, as a precaution. Do you have anybody we can call? We couldn't find any next of kin."

I shake my head.

"Try to sip on some iced water," the doctor says. "We've got you on hydration fluids and this button activates your painkiller, you can press it every hour. If you press it more, it won't work." He smiles briefly and leaves.

I want to ask him about Junior. I wave my hand in the air and the nurse stops and looks at me.

"Sweetie, I'll get a notepad, hang on, two shakes of a lamb's tail." She reappears, raises the bed and hands me a notepad and a pen.

Junior? Man who tried to kill me—what happened to him? It is such a terrible scrawl that I'm surprised she can even read it.

"He was arrested," she says "but he made bail. He wanted to have you arrested for slander, bullying, social media abuse, defamation of character, and a bunch of other things but he tried to kill you and that trumps what you did. I tell you, it's been the only thing people have been talking about."

How long have I been here?

"You came in on Thursday evening, it's now Saturday morning. Here," she says and she hands me a remote, "you can watch it on TV. They've still got it on a loop, you can't miss it."

I flick the TV on and there we are, Junior and I, in all our sordid glory.

"Her revenge nearly killed her! Fired media mogul's mistress seeks revenge and nearly pays the price with her life." There are pictures of Junior and me at various events, laughing, not a care in the world. Then there's a clip of Junior being led into the police department, hands cuffed behind his back, his face impassive.

The reporter said that Mrs. Davidson-Loach could not be reached for comment but she asked that the media respect the family's privacy during this challenging time.

Junior's lawyer explains in great detail, using tangled legalese, that his client had become momentarily unhinged, and had acted extremely uncharacteristically as a consequence of the abuse he had suffered. "Clearly, he wasn't thinking straight," the lawyer adds. "The attack was in no way planned or premeditated, Mr. Davidson-Loach merely wanted to talk to Ms. Redner and explain the level of pain and trauma that she had caused, but when he saw her, he momentarily lost control of his mental faculties. If anybody is to blame, it's Ms. Redner."

"But she had just been fired," the reporter points out. "She too was under a lot of stress that day. She had worked for the company for over seventeen years and he gave her the boot. I heard he didn't fire her in person, that she was walked out by some hired axe. You have to acknowledge that would be tough."

"Tough yes, but there's no excuse for what she did."

"She emailed a picture," the reporter challenges. "He tried to kill her. There's a difference."

"She murdered his reputation," the lawyer counters. "She murdered his career."

"Will you be pressing charges against her?"

The lawyer is silent for a moment. "I am urging my client to drop the charges and we are hoping Ms. Redner will do the same. They both acted in haste, from a place of pain and momentary insanity, and it would be best if they got on with their lives and put this whole sorry incident behind them."

"That was legal representation for Patrick Ralph Davidson-Loach IV, the full name of the man known as Junior. We've interviewed former employees of Ms. Redner and Mr. Davidson-Loach, and while there is full support for him, who people have characterized as a fun-loving go-getter and risk-taker, the views of Ms. Redner are not as kind."

The camera turns to my art director who already looks as if he's been spitting venom for hours. He is not one of the ones who emailed me with regrets about what had happened. "Bitch," he said. "I'm not sure if I am allowed to say that on TV, but she was the meanest bitch I have ever worked for. We weren't allowed to say good morning to her. We had to tiptoe around her, and we had to fetch her dry cleaning, get her lattes. I'm an art director not an editorial assistant. And the way she could talk to you! She got off on it. And stuff … man, she took everything: pens, pencils, post-it notes, and all the stuff the agencies would send her. She got tons of free stuff, high-end makeup and cosmetics and fragrances and only once did we see any of it, the rest of the time, she took it all. The one time, she had a beauty sale and I swear she made over a thousand bucks, maybe two, and she said she was giving the money to Sick Kids but I swear she took it."

I am not coming across in a good light.

Next they have one of the copywriters, a girl I nearly even liked. I wait to hear what she has to say. "Well, she's very damaged. I don't know anything about her childhood or her past but she's clearly damaged. All she did was work although she did enjoy having sex. Before she took up with Junior, she had sex with the boy models on shoots and she was quite blatant about it. In the middle of shooting, she'd say she needed to give the model some direction and she'd lead him away, but everyone knew what they were doing. And some of these guys were like twenty and she must be what, nearly fifty?"

Nearly fifty? I would have choked but my poor broken throat can't manage it. I thought they thought I was thirty. I'm not fifty, I am forty-two, and I thought I looked much younger than that.

"But I liked her," the girl adds. "I did. In a way."

"Sounds like not many people liked her," the reporter comments and she swings her focus back to the camera.

"We haven't been able to find out much about Ms. Redner's past, or her private life. We do know that her very public affair with Mr. Davidson-Loach went on for two years. Davidson-Loach the IV comes from old money, bankers who lost everything because his father gambled it away. Davidson-Loach married Sharon Besting, heiress to the Besting discount furniture chain. Davidson-Loach is unavailable for comment and we assume he is at the family cottage, trying to put the pieces of his life back together. He has officially taken a leave of absence from work, and we are unclear as to how long that will be in effect for, or whether, in fact, he will be returning at all. The acting-CEO of the company where both Ms. Redner and Junior worked has declined to comment."

I turn off the television and lie there, surrounded by hospital sounds. Unsurprisingly, popular opinion is not in my favour, not that it ever has ever been but it hasn't mattered before. I had the power to make up for it and I hadn't given a damn.

My throat is killing me. I hit the painkiller button but I am sure nothing is happening so I summon the nurse by hanging onto her bell.

"I heard you the first time, Julia," she says and I want to tell her that she is being overly familiar by calling me by my first name but I can't talk.

I hold up the pain button and she shakes her head. "You're maxed out," she says. "You'll have to wait." And she walks out. She walks out!

I buzz her again and again and she comes back. "Listen," she says "I'm legally not allowed to turn the call button off in case you have a real emergency, but if you call me again to ask me for drugs that I can't give you, I'm going to yank that thing out of the wall and pretend that the cleaners forgot to put it back when they were polishing the floor. Are we clear?"

I nod and she walks out again. I lie in my bed thinking. There are no flowers, no calls, and no visitors. Back in the day, the day of my sweet reign, if I had so much as stubbed my toe, the room would have been filled with designer bouquets from boutique flower stores. I would have been besieged by fawning underlings who I would have sent rushing to Victoria's Secret for bed jackets. I would have imperiously dictated notes and instructions and they would have fallen all over themselves to scurry and obey.

Now, I have nothing. And there is no one.

"Code Orange, Code Orange, looking for a missing patient, patient is in his early thirties, has short dark hair, is five-foot six, wearing a fedora hat, green sweatpants, and a black leather jacket. If you see this man, call security immediately. Code Orange, Code Orange."

The message is repeated and I wonder about the missing man wearing a fedora hat and green sweatpants Is he dangerous? Mentally deranged? I don't care. I want more drugs. I push the button again but nothing happens.

I sit up slowly and take stock of my situation. My IV machine is on wheels and there are two thick cables plugged into the wall. I work at yanking them out, which isn't easy—they are wedged in tight and my whole body hurts with the effort. I loop the cables onto my IV trolley and ease myself off the bed, hanging onto it for a moment for support, but I don't feel dizzy and I slowly make my way to the washroom. I am in a room for two but the other bed is empty.

When I look in the mirror, an ungodly sound fills the room and I realize that the moan of horror is coming from me. My hand fly to my throat, my poor, damaged, bruised throat. The bruising extends down to my chest but the worst of it are my eyes. The whites of my eyes are a vivid, blood-filled red and there are motley scarlet patches on my cheeks.

I touch my face slowly. Junior really did try to kill me. I wonder if the police are obliged to press charges or if, as the lawyer had said, it is up to me. I don't want to drop the charges. I want the son-of-a-bitch to go to prison for the rest of his life and while I know that will never happen, the least I can do is try.

27. BLESSED ARE THOSE WHO

I STAND IN THE HOSPITAL WASHROOM and hold my hands under the hot, running water and try not to look at the broken woman in the mirror. My body has been attacked, but my spirit is more determined than ever to make Junior pay. I ease the door open and walk slowly back to my bed. As I round a corner, I see a news reporter standing at the doorway of my room, with a cameraman at her side. Their eyes widen when they see me and the reporter starts talking but I hold up an imperious hand and she falls silent.

I climb back into bed and gesture for the reporter to plug the cables back into the wall, which she does. *Do you want a picture?* I write on my notepad and she nods.

I get to choose which one. She nods again.

I pull the top of my hospital gown down to show my bruising, and I tilt my head back slightly to show the full extent of the damage to my neck. My hair is tangled and wild but this will be good for the shot. I stare into the camera with all my hatred and bloodshot ugliness and I hold that pose while the photographer fires a series of shots.

When he is done, I reach for the camera and flip through the shots. I find a perfect one. I look frail, ravaged and full of anger.

I pick up the notepad and write: *Use pic 334. Hed: "I will press charges" former ad exec vows after strangling attempt. "He will not get away with this. He tried to kill me."*

I write this on two separate pieces of paper and I have the

reporter and the photographer sign and add their telephone numbers and I wave them away.

I want to go home. I unplug the cables and pull the IV out of my hand. I dig around in the bedside table and find the clothes I was wearing when I got fired, along with my shoes and my purse. I take my phone and grab my clothes and I go to the washroom where I take selfies of all the damage, making sure I get every angle.

I get dressed and I ease on my crystal-embellished platform Miu-Miu sandals, wishing I had flats instead. I pick up my purse and I walk to the elevator and no one notices me at all.

I take the notepad and pen with me and I hail a cab and write my address down and show the driver.

He drops me off and I take my shoes off and slowly climb the stairs. I stop midway. I don't think I can face the landing where Junior tried to kill me but I have no choice and I force myself up the remaining stairs. The shattered pottery fragments of an empty pot plant holder lie scattered on the floor. I must have kicked it when I was fighting to breathe.

I open the door and head straight for the sofa. At that moment, I wish I had asked for liquid painkillers at the hospital and not left surreptitiously. I wonder if there is anyone I can call who will help me. I scroll through my phone and decide to take a chance on the copywriter who had been marginally more positive about me than the others. The only thing is, I can't let her see my filthy apartment, filled with all the stuff I have accumulated.

I send her a text. *Margie, I'm home. Can I ask a favour? I'll reimburse you, I need meds and baby food....*

Sure, the reply comes immediately and I send her a list, along with my address. I tell her she has to get liquid meds because I can't swallow pills. If there's no other choice, she's to bring a couple of quarts of NyQuill, but liquid codeine would be preferable.

I change into my favourite Alexander McQueen sweatpants

and matching tribal print sweatshirt and I put fifty dollars into an envelope with Margie's name on it and then, I wait.

When she buzzes from downstairs, I stand outside my front door at the top of the landing, and I take the bag from her. I can tell she wants to come in and chat, but I have a note prepared. *Can't speak. Thank you. Must rest.* She nods, takes the envelope, and leaves.

I chug a generous swig of meds and feel relief as it burns its way down. I lie on the sofa and stare at the ceiling until I fall asleep.

I don't move and I am worried that I have died but then I realize where I really am. I am in Purgatory, watching myself. I am not there in my apartment.

"I've made it stop for now. That's enough for one day," Cedar says softly. "In fact, that was too much, but I couldn't see a way to break it off sooner. How are you?"

I am speechless. "He tried to kill me," I say and I am relieved I can talk, because in my mind, I can feel the raw, sandpapered pain of the woman I had been watching.

"But you did email a picture of his inadequate private parts to nearly a hundred employees, some of whom saw fit to post it on social media where it went viral."

"Are you defending him?" I can't believe my ears. "The fucker tried to kill me and—"

Whoops. There I am, outside the door.

"And he fired me," I shout. "He fired me. He fucked me sideways, up and down and left, right and centre, and then he fired me. The fuck! And you defend him? Fuck you too, Cedar!" But I feel bad as soon as I say that.

"I didn't mean that," I shout. "I'm sorry, Cedar. Let me in, so I can apologize."

The door opens and Cedar looks out. "It's okay," he says. "But that's it for the day. See you tomorrow." And he closes the door again.

God expects spiritual fruit, not religious nuts.

I glare at the sign, filled with the desire to vandalize something, anything. I take the letters off and rearrange them but *life is nuts* is the best I can come up with, and I throw the rest of the letters on the floor.

I march off and when I reach the end of the hallway, I turn back to look at the sign. There is a new message. The letters silently rearranged themselves and there is nothing on the floor.

Blessed are those who...

And that is all. I give the sign the finger and as I do, Tracey appears. She laughs.

"Having a good day I see. We're in my kitchen. Eno nearly ate a whole batch of cookies. I had to make more. A good session with the Grateful Dead?"

"Just spiffy," I tell her. "As you can tell." But I don't elaborate and she doesn't ask.

We reach her kitchen and the warm, comforting smell of baking is like a hug.

"Yo, Namaste, how're they hanging, Mamacita? We got a fresh batch of dead people's cookies coming up soon, I've been helping Trace bake."

"Hindering," Tracey says with a smile. "Eating raw cookie dough isn't helping."

"I am the royal tester," Eno says. "Hey, Julia, seriously, you okay?"

I sigh and sit down. "It seems that back on Earth, after I was fired, I emailed a picture of my boss's miniature crown jewels to a hundred employees and they shared it and it went viral. And then he tried to strangle me to death."

There is silence. And then Eno bursts out laughing. "Whoa, let me not piss you off! But hey, how did you have the picture?"

"We had an affair for two years. And he didn't have the balls, small or otherwise, to fire me himself or even talk to me and I wanted to humiliate the gutless bastard."

"But how did they know it was his dick?" Agnes asks.

"Because he wears these ostentatious monogrammed cufflinks

and they were in the picture. He was holding himself and also, he's a gingery blond and his pubes are that colour too."

Samia giggles, her hand to her mouth.

"You got some henna done," I say to her, noticing the lovely designs on her hands. "How come?"

She raises her eyebrows. "Privileges for brown people. Some people get bowling, we brown ladies get henna, like for a wedding that will never happen. I'd rather have bowling privileges. I told Cedar but he said it's not up to him."

The oven alarm sounds and Tracey removes the tray and she glares at Eno. "At least let these ones cool down."

He raises his hands in surrender. "I couldn't eat one more thing."

"Well," Jaimie says and he blushes. "I'm not saying I'm not well hung or anything but I can understand a man's chagrin at being outed like that."

"He tried to KILL me," I am outraged. "I was in hospital. If the pizza guy from downstairs hadn't come up, I would have died. I had bruises around my neck down to my chest. The blood vessels in my eyes and my cheeks burst and I couldn't eat or swallow for two weeks. And yet, you think what he did was justifiable?"

"I said it's understandable," Jaimie says and Eno agrees.

"Yeah. Julia, there are some boundaries that should not be crossed."

"Oh, bullshit," Agnes says. "He got what he deserved."

"I agree," Tracey nods, rolling dough into buns. "He'd had an affair with you for two years, and if he didn't know what you were capable of by that time, then he got what was coming. What did he think you would do? He was arrogant and he deserved it."

Isabelle doesn't say anything. She is leaning against Eno, off in her own world.

"You said he nearly killed you," Eno points out. "If it was only nearly, how come you're here?"

"I don't know. I haven't got to that part yet, and I can't wait," I say. "It's sure to be a barrel of laughs." I take a caramel white-chocolate-chip cookie and bite into it but just as quickly I spit it out into a napkin.

"What the fuck?" Tracey is furious.

"My throat feels sore," I say, and it does. "I'm sorry. I can't swallow anything. I can still feel that pain."

She hardly looks mollified but the door opens and Beatrice peers in. "Smells good," she says sniffing the air like an old bulldog. "You want a game?" she asks me and she comes in and takes a cookie.

"Sure," I say.

Beatrice piles four more cookies onto a napkin and leaves.

"Bye gang, see you tomorrow," I say and I follow in Beatrice's generous wake, preparing to do word battle and relieved to have a distraction from my woes for the moment.

28. THE SECOND TIME JUNIOR TRIES TO KILL ME

WHO IS THIS KING OF GLORY? "Fucked if I know," I say and I immediately slam my hand to my mouth and resolve to watch my language. The door opens, and there stands Cedar, kindly, stern, and welcoming.

"Julia! How are you?"

"Ready to continue, thank you very much," I say and I lie down on the sofa. I cross my hands over my chest and close my eyes.

"I see. Fine. You had returned home and Margie brought you medicine and food and you were lying on the couch, and you fell asleep."

The Rewind starts and the scene unfolds before me and, yes, there I am, lying in a similar position to the one I'm in now.

"Is there a fast-forward button?" I ask Cedar after we watch me do nothing for what seems like half an hour.

"Tell me when to stop," Cedar says obligingly, and he speeds up the passing of time. "Actually, you do it."

I give it a try and find it surprisingly easy. I speed through that night and the following week and I lie on the sofa for the duration and drink liquid painkiller and eventually I eat some Gerber puréed apple.

The only time I leave the apartment is to collect Duchess's urn and I pick up a few supplies at the pharmacy and grocery store and return home.

"I'm hoping this gets more interesting," I remark and I

fast-forward to me starting to watch TV, with Duchess's urn next to the sofa. Apparently I tap into Netflix and get into binge watching. I appear to be disinclined to change my clothes or bathe, or even look at my phone. I avoid news channels and I choose series with three or four seasons to them and I watch episode after mind-numbing episode. I'm not eating properly or keeping hydrated. "Do I die of malnutrition?" I ask Cedar. "Or, do I die from overdosing on TV?"

I watch the bruising around my neck fade and still, I do not bathe and still, I do not change my clothing. I finish the painkillers and I finish the baby food and all the supplies that I have bought.

"Surely I'll pull myself together soon?" I ask. "This is deadly. I've been like this for nearly a month. And now I don't have any food. I'll have to go out soon."

But I don't. I go online and order a bunch of stuff and get it delivered. Then I carry on watching TV, sleeping on the sofa and living off snacks and sodas. I can drink scotch again and I drink that too but thankfully only at night. I was worried I'd see myself downing neat whiskey for breakfast.

"Wait," I say, "back up a bit."

The View obligingly rewinds and I press play, real time. I am lying on the sofa and my phone rings. It actually rings. I pick it up. It is Junior.

Junior.

"What does he want?" I ask Cedar suspiciously. As far as I can tell, I'd received no other calls about his attempt to kill me, not even from the police. Maybe everybody just wanted it to go away. I had seen the picture of myself on the news, the one I got the photographer to take but that was as far as it had gone, and I hadn't had the energy to pursue anything myself.

"Hello?" my poor voice is still damaged and I sound like a hundred-year-old smoker.

"Julia?"

"Yeah."

"You don't sound like yourself."

"You broke my voice when you tried to strangle me."

There is silence.

"I'm sorry about that," he says. "Look, I want to see you."

"I don't want to see you. You fired me and then you tried to kill me."

"And yet," he says conversationally, "I still love you."

I am gobsmacked. "You've got a weird way of showing it," I say. "I never asked you for anything. Never. I thought we had an understanding. And then you fucked me over and hung me out to dry. And then you tried to kill me."

"I am sorry," he says again. "What are you up to, these days?"

"Nothing. I am resting. I need to rest after my ordeal."

"It's been six weeks," he says.

"It was a big ordeal."

"Yeah. Well, can I come and see you?"

"No, you can't. Are you back at work?"

"I can't go back. You took care of that."

"Good."

"I did underestimate your … passion."

"My viciousness, you mean. Your mistake, buster."

"I know. Listen, I really want to see you."

"Dream on. I'm hanging up now. Have a good life."

I hang up and return to my TV watching.

"Time to fast-forward again," I say and the view speeds up.

I watch more TV. I order more food. I finally, thank god, have a bath and wash my hair and launder my clothes.

And then, I stop and stare at my front door.

"Slow to present time," I say and the Rewind obliges and I hear knocking at the door.

"Julia? I know you're in there." It's Junior. "I know you're in there and I'm not going away. I need to see you."

"No," I say. "I'm sorry I ever met you. I thought we understood and respected each other. You don't know what the words mean."

"I've got flowers for you," he says. "And a gift from Cartier. Come on, you love Cartier and this will match the emerald promise rings I bought you. Let me in."

"If you don't leave, I'm calling the cops," I say. "I mean it. Go away."

"No, baby, please, please let me in. I love you. I'm begging you."

"Go away. I'm not your baby anymore. Go away, I mean it. I'm dialing 911 now and I want my key back."

"What key?"

"The key I gave you to my apartment."

"You gave me a key? I must have lost it. Listen, Julia, please let me in. I need to see you. Sharon's kicked me out. I've lost everything."

"Yeah? Well, I lost everything too and you are to blame. Don't expect sympathy from me. Sharon will take you back. For some reason, she'll forgive you anything."

"Not this time. Come on, baby, let me in."

He's lying. I know him too well. There are two dead give-aways when Junior is lying. The one is that his lower lip does a strange tiny sideways twitch and the other is that his voice changes. It's almost as if he acquires a faint European accent of some kind, his intonations are different.

"You're lying, you fuck," I tell him. "I know you. Your voice is doing that funny thing, you sound like a bad mafioso in a B-grade movie."

"What the fuck are you talking about?"

"When we were pitching big and someone asked you a question and you replied with a lie, your voice changed. I never told you I noticed but I did. You never lied to me before but I can hear it in your voice now. There's no way I'm letting you in."

There is silence.

"Think you're so fucking clever, you stupid bitch? Well, you're right. I am lying. I never loved you and Sharon never kicked me out. She's much more of a woman than you'll ever be. And I want to come in so I can finish what I started."

"Get the fuck away from me, Junior," I say. "Go now or I am calling the cops." I am shaking and my body is drenched with cold, vinegar sweat. I press my ear against the front door. "You aren't leaving," I say. "I will hear the stairs creak when you go, so go."

I hear creaking noises. "Oh, for fuck's sake, Junior, you're walking up and down the top two stairs. Do you think I'm an idiot? Get the fuck out of here and make sure to close the door of the vestibule so I can hear that too."

"Julia," he says softly. "This isn't over." And he pounds loudly down the stairs and I hear the door slam.

I get the locks changed in case he finds the key I gave him all that time ago. I think about calling the cops but I figure no one will believe me.

The next time I open the door, it's to accept a load of groceries I have ordered, and I wait until I hear the guy's familiar voice.

"See you in a couple of weeks, Mike," I say to the grocery guy and I give him a big tip.

"Take care," he says.

More fast-forwarding. No more Junior. More TV. More sleeping on the sofa. More doing nothing with my life. More ordering groceries.

Mike, back at the front door. "Julia? I've got your stuff. You want me to bring it in?"

I sit up. He's early. And more than that, his voice sounds odd. My paranoia is in full swing.

"Leave it out there," I say. "I'll push the cash out under the door."

"Julia! It's me, Mike! And there's stuff here that'll go bad. C'mon, let me in."

"It will survive until you get into your truck and I watch you drive away," I say and I push the money under the door. "I'm going to the window now to watch you leave."

"Nutcase," I hear him mutter, and I think I'd be well advised to order my groceries from somewhere else in the future.

"Tell Junior he can't get to me," I shriek. "I won't let him. He had his shot at killing me and it won't come around again. Fuck you, Mike and tell Junior fuck him too!"

I hear the front door slam and I run to the window but despite what I have said, I can't see the truck at all.

I go back to the front door and I listen but I can't hear anything but just to be safe, I don't open the door until halfway through the next day. My fresh produce has wilted and my frozen pizzas have spoiled but I don't care. I throw it out and place a new order with another company.

More fast-forwarding. More TV. More groceries from the new place and finally, another bath, hair wash, and fresh clothes. I have run out of couture, and I'm wearing generic navy blue yoga sweatpants that have seen better days and a pink t-shirt that I should have thrown in the trash.

I am asleep on the sofa and nothing out of the ordinary is happening but I suddenly slow the Rewind down.

"I have a bad feeling," I say to Cedar.

I watch closely. I am fast asleep, with a fleece throw pulled up to my chin, and my feet are sticking out from under the blanket. I watch the front door open. "But how?" I ask Cedar. "I got the locks changed."

"It's not that hard to get in to a place," Cedar says quietly "and anyone could climb up those stairs while you had the TV on, and you wouldn't have heard."

My front door swings open. The room is brightly lit, with the streetlights shining in. I am amazed I could sleep at all with so much light.

Two men slide inside my apartment. They approach the sofa, one on each side of the coffee table. One man stands at my head and the other is at my feet. They look at each other, exchange a nod and swoop. The one man covers my mouth while the other sits on my legs, grabs my arms and holds me down. I watch myself wake and register the terrible danger. I am unable to move, pinned down and wide-eyed like a terrified cat and I am making mewling sounds.

Of course it is Junior who has his hand over my mouth. "Nice to see you, Julia," he says softly.

The man pinning my arms down with his knees, reaches for a bag, digs out a roll of duct tape and tears off a large strip. Junior grabs me by my hair, lifts up my head and removes his hand and the man slaps the duct tape onto my mouth, pressing down for good measure. He gets up and flips me over as easily as if he is flipping sofa cushions, looking for spare change. He ties my hands tightly behind my back and he binds my ankles.

He props me up into a sitting position and Junior sits down in front of me on the coffee table, and he stares at me for a while without saying anything.

"Such a bitch," he says and he almost sounds affectionate and he runs a finger up my cheek. "Such a god-almighty bitch. How powerful are you now, bitch?"

The other man doesn't say anything. I don't recognize him. He is tall and burly, with a massive barrel chest.

I can't move and my heart is going to explode. *Thud, thud, thud*, it's like the pounding hooves at the Kentucky Derby and I struggle to hear what Junior is saying.

"I'm going to kill you, bitch," he says. "And I'm going to take my time doing it. I'm not here. I'm with my buddies in Vegas. We're playing poker in a private room as we speak, so in case you're thinking there'll be any kind of justice for you, dream on. But the whole world will know that you got what was coming to you. Or maybe they won't know. I don't care. I'll know."

And then he punches me, and he breaks my nose and I hear it crack and my eyes fill with tears and blood pours down my face. It's hard to breathe, with the duct tape covering my mouth, and I am suffocating. My face feels as if it has been stung by a hundred bees.

"Not so pretty now," he says. "I'm going to break every bone in your body, Julia, every fucking bone, and I'm going to smash your face in so hard that no one will be sure it's even you."

He gets up and pulls the coffee table to one side. He nods at the man who grabs me and throws me on the floor. I'm on my back and Junior sits on top of me. He is wearing black gloves and he pulls them tighter on his hands and he smiles at me. He takes aim and punches my right cheekbone and I hear a terrible crunch and the pain is worse than I could have imagined. I wish I could pass out but I am a long way from that.

And then he proceeds to do exactly what he said he would do. He breaks every bone in my body. I am powerless to do anything except watch, while he slowly works me over. He takes his time. He even stops to drink a bottle of water that he pulls out of the bag.

The other man just stands there, watching. He doesn't say or do anything.

"I'm getting tired," Junior jokes at one point, and he stands up, his chest heaving. "I'm getting a good workout! Won't need to go to the gym today!" He kicks my ribs and brings his foot down hard on my stomach.

"I can't watch any more," I say to Cedar. "I can't."

The Rewind jumps forward and I am a tangled, bloody heap, curled up on my side. My face is a mashed pulp of blood and bone, and my body is broken.

"Time to go," Junior says. "We don't want anyone to see us."

He and the man are wearing toques and although it is still dark outside, they put on wraparound sunglasses that make them unrecognizable.

"Those fucking stairs are noisy," the man says. It is the first thing I have heard him say and his voice is whiny and high-pitched.

"Yeah. Well, nothing we can do about that except be quick. Come on."

Junior grabs the bag and they walk out, closing the door behind them.

"But who will find me?" I ask Cedar in a small voice. "No one will find me."

The Rewind speeds up and the morning light pours into the room. And no one comes. Why would they? Who would come? I have no one. I am going to die in that room, die by my own hand because I have no friends and no one cares about me. There will be no rescue in sight and the only person I can blame is myself.

But then the Rewind slows down. There is someone at the door. Mike, the grocery man. I had thought Junior had sent him to kill me but now, there he is, at my door.

"She hasn't ordered groceries in too long," he sounds worried. "And last time I was here, she sounded scared, like she thought someone was trying to kill her. Like she thought that guy who tried to strangle her was back. I just want to check, make sure she's alright, okay?"

He bangs his fist on the door and I see that he is there with Carlos and Marcello. I pray that Carlos will open the door.

"Come on," Mike begs him. "Open it. And if she's inside and yells at us, so what? Come on."

Marcello grabs the keys from his grandfather and opens the door and even from where they are standing, they can see me on the floor, a bloodied mess with my hands and feet still bound.

"Holy Christ," Mike says and he rushes in and puts a finger to my neck. "She's alive but I don't know ... call 911."

Marcello is already talking into a phone. Carlos just stands there, unable to speak or move.

"Julia?" Mike speaks softly to me. "We're here, okay? Stay very still, help is coming."

"What are the odds," I say to Cedar, "that Mike would come? Maybe two percent?"

"Believe it or not," Cedar replies, "there is such a thing as Divine Intervention."

We watch the paramedics arrive and load me up and take me down the stairs on a stretcher, which in itself, is no easy feat. We watch them put me in an ambulance and we watch Carlos and Mike and Marcello stand on the sidewalk after I am taken away.

Then the Rewind fades to black and that's it. Gingerly, I sit up.

"Did I die? Is that why I'm here? I died?" I touch my face with my fingers and run my hands along my arms, down my legs, over my torso. "He hurt me so badly. He broke me with such deliberation." I am relieved to feel myself in one piece, smooth, uncut, unbruised, unbroken.

"I can't tell you any more," Cedar says. "Not at this point anyway. How does all of this make you feel?"

Ordinarily, a question like that would have resulted in me shouting profanities at him but I am numb, shocked. "He hated me so much," I say. "He hated me so much."

"He did," Cedar agrees.

There doesn't seem like there is anything left to say and I get up.

"See you tomorrow," I say and he nods.

Forgiveness is the Key to Happiness.

"Go and suck an egg," I tell the sign and I go and try to find the others, and if I can't, I hope that one of them will come and get me.

29. EARTH IS AN OPTION

"WE WANT TO GO BACK to Earth," Isabelle says and we look at her.

Tracey sighs. "Oh, what love does to your brain. Izzy, we is here, baby, because we is dead. Get with the program, girl, okay? I know you and Eno-licious here are in the raptures of true romance but we don't get to go back."

"And you, baby, is wrong," Eno drawls. His long legs are stretched out in front of him and he is chewing on a toothpick.

I had found them all in the cafeteria, even Grace was there. "What do you mean?" Grace asks, leaning forward.

I have an image of Grace dropping back down to Earth, walking up the garden path, knocking on the front door and saying, "Hey honey, I'm home." I can't see Hope and Richard being too delighted to see her.

"You don't go back as you," Eno says. "You can go back as someone like you."

"Reincarnation?"

"Nope. It's still you but you're in a new body, with a new name. It's you, but you're a different person."

"And you know this how?" Agnes asks.

Eno shrugs. "I was a detective in the real world. So I did some detecting here."

"We want to go back and get married," Isabelle says. "And have babies and be happy."

"Oh, sweetie," Grace says and she reaches over and pats

Isabelle on the hand. "You poor thing. We all struggle with being here, we do. But we know we can't have what we want, that's just the reality."

"I've called a meeting of the Board of Regulators," Eno says. "They'll tell us what's real and what's not."

"And who are the Board of Regulators when they're home?" Tracey asks, her eyes narrowed.

Eno shrugs. "I know Cedar's one of them. I asked him to set up the meeting."

"I don't want to go back," Tracey says. "I don't want to stay here, making cookies forever, but I don't want to go back."

"Me neither," Jaimie says and we look at him in surprise.

"I would have thought you'd leap at the chance," I say. "A pretty boy like you, you'd have the world at your feet."

"I was supposed to die when I did," Jaimie says. "And now I'm supposed to be here and when it's time, I'll go to the next place. It is what it is."

"It is what it is for you, bro," Eno says high-fiving him. "But me and Izzy, we want our shot at it. We want babies and diapers and cash flow problems and all that shit. Don't get me wrong, I was happy with it is what it is until I met Izzy. Then I saw what my life could and should have been and I need to do it. We both need to do it."

"I don't want to go back either," Agnes says. "I am worried about Auntie Miriam and I want her to be safe but I want to go on and find Josh. I know he's somewhere. My Earth life was only good because of him. I wouldn't want it without Josh."

"Love is all you need," Tracey is bitter. "What's wrong with me? I don't love my husband and my kids, is that what you're all saying?"

"No one is saying that, Tracey," I tell her. "I want to go back too," I add, "and I don't have anybody."

"Then why?"

"Because it was *my* life and I want it back. Junior had no right to take it. I'd like to find my niece. I'd like to listen to music and dance and walk on real grass with bare feet, and get a dog and feel the hot sunshine on my face and swim in lakes and learn to rollerblade and take walks in the snow in winter and smell the leaves in fall. I want it back. I'd do it better, I would."

I don't mention that I'd also track down Junior, that fucker, and kill the shit out of him. Never mind dogs and sunshine, I want to go back to kill Junior, pure and simple. Wait, I correct myself. First, I'd make him suffer and then I'd kill him.

"All that live in the moment crap," Tracey is scornful.

"Hey, you have your opinions, I have mine," I say. "Eno, when does this Board meet?"

"Don't know. We're waiting for the call so we can plead our case. I've got my whole speech ready," he says and he looks earnest and is about to launch into his speech when Jaimie holds up a hand.

"Spare us," Jaimie says. "I can imagine. Grace, would you go back?"

She shakes her head. "No. For a moment, I thought it might be a good idea but no, going back is not for me. I'd like to get my husband to stop being a drug addict so my kids are safe but other than that, there's nothing I'd want to do on Earth. I suffered too much there. Everything hurt me. No, I wouldn't go back. Samia, would you?"

"I don't know," Samia replies softly. "I thought I would want to, but now that there's some kind of option, I don't know. I feel like I should want to go back but it wouldn't feel right for me. I agree with Jaimie. It was my time to go, as much as it hurt my parents. But I am very happy for both of you," she says to Isabelle and Eno. "It will be wonderful for you."

"If they say yes. I'm so afraid they will say no," Isabelle says, and Eno strokes her back.

"Don't worry, baby," he said. "Here or there, they'll never tear us apart."

"Isn't that a song?" Tracey asks. "Don't you have any original lyrics, Eno?"

"Be your bitter self, Mamacita," Eno says without rancour. "Isabelle and me choose happiness."

"Yeah? Well good for you. I'm going to bake more cookies for you to stuff into your fat face." Tracey gets up and leaves and Samia follows her.

"If you go back, do you get to say goodbye to us or do you just vanish?" I ask. "How will we know?"

"I don't know that either," Eno admits. "I guess we will see what we will see."

We sit there in silence, each lost in our own thoughts until a voice interrupts us.

"Greetings campers!" It is Beatrice, sounding uncharacteristically chirpy. "Eno and Isabelle, follow me, please."

Isabelle looks terrified and even Eno looked nervous. They stand up and Isabelle looks like she's about to faint.

"Julia," she looks at me pleadingly. "Please come with us. You know how to do this stuff, make presentations to directors. We need you. You know why we want to do this and you'll know how to say it best."

"Yeah, Julia," Eno says. "Making sense to a bunch of higher ups isn't what I do best. And you know what this means to us. Izzy's right, you'll say it better than we can."

I look at Beatrice. I admit I am curious about the process and I'd love to find out what happens. But more than that, I want this for Isabelle and Eno.

"Can I come?" I ask Beatrice and she nods. "If it makes these little chickies feel better, then sure."

"See you later, amigos," Eno says and he, Isabelle and I follow Beatrice. She leads us to a side door we hadn't noticed was there.

"Exciting," I hear Agnes says idly. "I'm getting more tea."

30. FLYING COWS AND BOARD OF REGULATORS

THE BOARD OF REGULATORS conduct their meetings in an underground bunker. Eno, Isabelle, and I follow Beatrice to an elevator with stainless steel doors and Beatrice pushes the only button with a downward-facing arrow. "You sure we're not going to Hell just because we asked to go back?" Eno jokes, but he is holding Isabelle tightly and they are both trembling.

"Relax," Beatrice says and she lights a cigarette.

The elevator arrives and we step in. There are two rows of blue-lit arrows, one row pointing up, the other pointing down. Beatrice presses the third downward-facing arrow and it flashes a neon green. The walls in the elevator are mirrored and our apprehension is evident in all of our reflections.

"What's on the top floors?" Eno asks.

"None of your beeswax," Beatrice says, exhaling a cloud of smoke.

"Yo, is that like real live elevator music?" Eno chatters.

"It's supposed to calm you down," Beatrice says pointedly.

"There are no floors being shown," Eno says studying the elevator panel. "How will the arrow know when we will get there?"

"Because it will stop," Beatrice says. "You claustrophobic, Eno?"

"I don't care for being stuck in a box, I will admit to that. And why, in a place of such whiteness, is this elevator so dark? What's with this mood lighting?"

He's got a point. The elevator is as dark as an after-hours booze can. I focus on the bright green button and fold my arms across my chest.

"Eno," Beatrice says, "have mercy and shut the fuck up. You are hurting my ears. And here's a tip, Cedar's on the Board, no cussing."

"Got it," Eno says and he falls silent and the elevator's seventies' jazz hums quietly and we stand there, descending forever but seemingly going nowhere. Isabelle's eyes are wide and she's clinging to Eno like a barnacle.

"Destination arrival has been achieved!" A woman's automated voice exclaims triumphantly and the doors open. We tumble out, gulping like dying fish except for Beatrice who looks at us with annoyance. "Such drama queens," she says, flicking ash on the floor.

"Why we couldn't just bounce here, I've got no idea," Eno says to Beatrice. "Just sayin', that's all."

We follow Beatrice down a wide hallway carpeted with thick white shag. The walls are covered with enormous prints of flying cows—black and white comic book cows with pink angel wings, and the cows are sailing through blue skies with happy smiles on their tremulous bovine faces.

Eno, Isabelle, and I exchange a glance but we don't say anything.

We arrive at a double-wide set of frosted glass doors with a split black and white cow handle, with pink wings. Beatrice grabs the cow's butt and leads us inside.

The room is enormous. Acres of polished marble flooring sparkles, and the glass boardroom table in the centre of the room is the size of a football field. Wicker chairs around the table look like they've been imported from a tropical island, with high, round peacock-fan backs and brightly-coloured floral cushions.

Beatrice leads us to face the Regulators and she takes her seat at the table, next to Cedar.

Shirley the Driver is there and there are three people that Eno and Isabelle have never seen, but I recognize two of them, an elderly woman with a tufted snow-white billy-goat beard and a large Jamaican woman with yellow dreadlocks. There's an enormously obese young man wearing paint-splattered overalls and thick glasses. His spray-on tan makes him look like a large tangerine. No one is smiling and even Shirley the Driver looks stern under her helmet of Margaret Thatcher hair.

Beatrice selects a red apple from the bowl of fruit and apart from a loud crunch as she takes a bite, there is silence.

Shirley the Driver hits a round silver desk bell.

Attention, please! May I have your attention, please? The announcement sounds loudly and repeats its message and Eno, Isabelle, and I jump, startled.

Eno and Isabelle are both shaking. I can feel them because I am leaning into Isabelle, more for my own comfort than hers. They are holding hands tightly and are practically glued to one another.

"Eno, you requested this meeting," Cedar says sitting back in his chair, his hands clasped in front of him. "Let's hear what you've got to say."

I look at Eno, wondering if he wants me to jump in but he shakes his head.

"We want to go back," Eno says earnestly. "We've heard we can, we're not sure how but however it works, we'd like to apply. But we want to go back together."

"Impossible," Beatrice says chewing her apple in her inimitable spewy way.

"What Beatrice means," Cedar says removing a piece of mashed apple from his arm, "is that, in case neither of you had noticed, you're both dead."

"Yeah but we heard you can go back," Eno insists.

"That's the only thing you've got to go on?" Cedar asks. "And you called a honking big meeting, on the basis of an urban legend?"

"I did some digging," Eno says and he looks down. "Well, it wasn't digging exactly but I asked someone in the know and they said it can be done. They said we can go back, not as ourselves exactly but as replica souls. We will have the same mannerisms, be the same age as we are now, come from the same kinds of families, have the same histories. Basically, we would be us but in new bodies with no memory of any of this shit. And things will be different, like I'll be a cop but I won't be an addict and Isabelle will work in admin and we'll meet each other and fall in love and have kids and live the life like we were supposed to."

"Let's say this was even remotely possible," Cedar says, "you'd both still have the same appetites, the same hungers, and the same problems. What do you say to that?"

"Yeah but lots of people have addict tendencies but they don't end up being addicts. I'm not excusing us by blaming bad luck but we were unlucky. Lots of people play sex games, and not all of them choke on their own vomit because they've been tied up and left by some loser. And me, well, I take responsibility. No one put that pipe in my mouth except me but I wouldn't do it again. And I would take this knowledge back with me, I know I would. I'm asking for a second chance for us. We don't want to stay here. We don't want to go to Heaven and we don't deserve Hell. Please, give us a second chance."

"Isabelle?" Cedar asks.

"Look," Isabelle sounds desperate. "I'm not even thirty. I got mixed up in something because I was lonely. I was so lonely and now, I love Eno. All I want is to be with him and have some babies and be a family together. That's not a lot to ask in the bigger scheme of things. Life isn't easy, I know that. I know we'll have our own difficulties but I never got to experience life the way that I really wanted to, and all we're asking is to be given that chance."

"And what if, and it's still a huge if, you were to go back and you were asked to put your lives in danger to help a friend who needed you and, in so doing, you may not live a long life but end up back here?" The Jamaican woman asks the question and I bristle with anger. How can anyone answer that?

I look at Isabelle and Eno who are silent. "What about the children?" Isabelle asks. "Would they die too?"

"No. And you wouldn't both die," Cedar says. "Actually, neither of you might. But there is a chance that one of you may."

"I'll take that chance," Isabelle says looking at Eno and he puts his arm around her.

"Me too," he says. "Me too. Come on, people, please, let us go back."

"We need to confer," Cedar says. "If you do get to go back, we won't alert you, you'll just be back. You'll bounce and the rest is up to you. If you're still here, you'll know you're here, and that the answer is no. If the answer is no, we won't respond to your calls for a meeting again. This was your one shot at the title, get it?"

"This is no time for jokes, man," Eno looks angry. "This is life or death. Don't joke. You don't know what it means to us."

"I think we do," Cedar says. "Now, out you go."

Shirley the Driver pumps the nipple on the desk bell and the silvery ping sounds and Eno, Isabelle, and I find ourselves back in the cafeteria.

31. ISABELLE, ENO, AND OPTIONS

"IT DIDN'T GO WELL?" Jaimie asks, sounding sympathetic. Eno and Isabelle look pale and I collect a round of hot chocolates for us. I feel weirdly hungover. When I get back, Jaimie is still asking Eno questions and Eno is shrugging. "If we bounce to Earth, the answer is yes, but if we stay here, it's no."

"When will you know?"

"Don't know that either."

"What was it like?"

Eno, Isabelle, and I look at each other. "Do you remember?" Eno asks and we shake our heads.

"There was a bell?" Isabelle says. "I don't remember anything else."

"Me neither," Eno says. "Freaky deaky, man."

"I think there were flying cows and apples," I say. "But I can't even remember who was there. Cedar and Beatrice were but I can't remember the others. If there even were others."

"You want to go bowling?" Jaimie offers. "It will help pass the time."

Eno and Isabelle shake their heads. "Thanks, bro, but no," Eno says and he tips back in his chair, his hands behind his head, and exchanges a worried look with Isabelle.

"I'd go skiing in Vail," I say dreamily. "I'd learn to ride a bike again, and I'd scuba dive and eat in five-star restaurants and try all different kinds of foods and I'd travel and see the world and read the classics—"

"And you'd grow old and wrinkly and get all kinds of weird splotches and blotches and your breasts would sag down by your knees, and you'd grow three chins and your arms would be flabby with loose skin that's got nowhere to go," Jaimie says.

"That's why you don't want to go back," I am triumphant. "Narcissus doesn't want to get old."

"So, shoot me," Jaimie is complacent. "I like how I am. Only the beautiful die young."

"Not true," Agnes comments. "Look at me."

"You'd be very presentable if you didn't have a hardware store attached to your face. And the demon punk eyeliner has to go. And ditch the colours in your hair. Laser off the tats, hook you up with a personal trainer, dress you up in something nice, and you'd be a hottie, I'm telling you."

"Screw you, Mom," Agnes says, and she gives him the finger. "This is me."

"That's my point," Jaimie retorts. "It doesn't have to be. This is just one version of you. There are countless versions of who we can be and what we can look like."

"Tell me about it," Grace agrees, sounding none too happy.

"I'm fine with—" Agnes starts to say, but she is interrupted.

"It's working!" Isabelle screams at the top of her lungs and Eno grabs her hand.

"Stay with me, baby, stay with me," he yells and next thing, they are both gone.

"Fuck me," Jaimie says staring at the two empty seats. "They did it. They really did it."

"May they live long and prosper," Agnes says giving the Vulcan salute.

Grace has tears in her eyes. "I hope they are happy," she says. "Well, I'm fading, see you tomorrow."

"How does she do that?" Jaimie asks as the last of Grace shimmers and disappears.

"She's never said," Agnes tells him. "I gotta go—got an

appointment with my personal trainer, Tracey. She's training me in cookie eating."

"An admirable pursuit," Jaimie says. "I'll come with you. Julia?"

I shake my head. "No. I'll stay here a while. I'm hoping Beatrice will come and find me with her Scrabble set. I'm sending out mental invitations."

Jaimie shudders. "Why you want to hang out with that battle-axe is beyond me," he says. "She scares the living daylights out of me. Reminds me of my algebra teacher. *Stop being such an airy fairy, Jaimie,'* eughh!

"Airy fairy!" Agnes is delighted. "Come on, my little fairy, let's go."

"You do know I'm straight," I hear Jaimie say as they walk off.

"That's what all the girls say," Agnes replies.

I am left alone and I look at the empty seats where Eno and Isabelle had been only moments before.

And I too, like Grace, wish them every happiness in the world. In fact, I wish them the world, the whole complicated, topsy-turvy, difficult as hell, loveable as cherry-pie world.

"Wishing you could go back too?" Beatrice answers my thoughts as she arrives, Scrabble in hand. "Come on, let's go somewhere more comfortable. But I want to take a pudding with me, give me a moment."

Oh lord, she's going to eat. Well, it's a small price to pay for her company that I do enjoy.

"Hot fudge pudding with ice cream," she says gleefully, returning with a soup bowl serving. "Sure you don't want some?"

"I'm sure. You know that Isabelle and Eno have gone back to Earth?"

"Of course I know. Good luck to them. They gave a good argument and seemed earnest."

"Will they be okay?" I follow her out of the caf to our usual room and we get settled.

"I can't say."

"You can say but you won't?"

"No, I could, but I can't."

I have no idea what she means and I let it go.

"Do you want to go back to Earth?" she asks me again, holding out the bag of letters.

I nod.

"Why?"

"I'd find my niece and make things right, whatever that takes. I'd walk on a beach and feel the sand between my toes. Go to a music festival and eat hot dogs. Do all the stuff I thought was stupid. Have a family, friends, get a dog. Learn to play a musical instrument, see the pyramids of Egypt."

"Well, you could do it, you know," Beatrice drops this bombshell while putting *quaint* on a triple word score and she beams. "Look! I'm going to beat the pants off you today, girlie."

"Beatrice," I ask, stupefied, "what do you mean, I could?"

"You're not dead," she says selecting more letters and frowning. "Bloody 'i's and 'g's. I hate them both."

"I'm not dead? But then why am I here?"

"Because you need to choose. You need to know that you won't be as pretty as you are now. And they had to remove a lung, so there's that. And the vision in one of your eyes is reduced and you'll have to wear glasses."

"I see," I reply slowly. "Will I reunite with my niece?" I admit that reunite is a fairly strong word because in reality, I only saw Emma once, shortly after her birth.

"Yes, you will."

"What about money?"

"You'll be okay but you won't be rolling in moola," Beatrice says and her words fall like sledgehammers.

"What will I do for a living?"

"Once your life settles, you'll find a job in a small marketing firm. You'll handle the publicity for trade shows and conventions."

"That sounds terrible," I say. "I don't know, Beatrice. You're not exactly selling it here."

"Play your turn," she points at the board. "Life's not easy for most people. You had it good, but you never realized it. Not that you're alone in that regard."

"It wasn't my fault," I say, and I sound whiny. "I did what I could, to survive."

Beatrice snorts. "Yeah, right. Poor little princess. You had a well-to-do childhood, a nice home."

"My parents died when I was eight," I object. "They left me and Jan all alone, at the mercy of the ice queen, Aunt Gwen. I worked hard for my degree, then I interned in an ad agency, and I worked like a dog to get to where I was. And my looks helped—I remember what it was like to be unattractive. It made things much harder and now you're telling me that if I go back, I'll be an ugly, scarred, old gimp."

"You will still have your skills," Beatrice says studying her letters with a frown, "that's true. And you're right, none of the cool kids will hire you because you're too old and you don't look the part anymore."

"Can't I get plastic surgery?" I ask.

"You'll get some out of necessity but you won't look anything like you do now, like you did before. Junior really worked you over."

"Where is he now?" I can hardly get the words out.

"He's playing the links on St. Andrews golf course," she says. "Ten points for me."

"The fucker," I say.

"Good thing you're not playing with Cedar," Beatrice comments. "Take your time, you don't need to decide now."

"No, I'm ready, 'frolic' on a double word score."

"I meant about going back to Earth," Beatrice says.

"Oh. Yes. Can I see what I look like?"

"You'll have to ask Cedar."

"And my niece is happy?"

"She is. But she'd happier with you in her life," she adds.

"Happy," I mutter. "Happier, happiest. What's the difference?" I am unsettled. None of my options are wonderful.

"Such is life," Beatrice says. "And the after-life. None of the options are wonderful," she chortles.

"I hate it when you read my mind," I say.

"I answer your invitations to come and play," she reminds me. "You don't mind then."

"You're right." I sit back in my chair and sigh. "Things were much easier when I was young and beautiful and intoxicated by my own greatness and working eighteen hours a day. Life was so simple."

Beatrice doesn't reply. I think she is getting bored by my whining and self-absorption. As if to confirm my thoughts, she finishes me off brusquely, leaving me with a thirty-point deduction and another game that I've lost.

"I've got to run," she says getting up. "Places to go, Viewings to organize. See you around. Try not to sweat it too much."

"Sure thing," I say, and I hope I don't sound too sarcastic.

32. THINKING

I WANDER DOWN THE HALLWAY after Beatrice has left, not sure what to do with myself. I decide that Purgatory isn't so much an airport as a combined warehouse, hospital, and airport, with shiny white linoleum and glossy walls. Everything is white, white, white, and I want to scream. I need to escape but I am not in the mood for the suffocating blackness of the Rest Room and it feels like there's nowhere for me to go.

I suddenly remember the Rain Room and I try to get in touch with Samia and it works.

"You called?" she smiles as she pops up next to me.

"How come I can get in touch with people but I can't find the rooms?" I grouch and she smiles again.

"Patience," she says. "You want to go to the Rain Room?"

"I do. But I know it depresses you, so do you mind? If you're not in the mood, maybe you can help me find it and I'll go alone."

"I actually don't mind at all," Samia says. "I could do with some rain. I admit it. I envy Isabelle. I wish I could have a boyfriend like Eno but he'd never look at someone like me. Isabelle's cool, I'm not. My parents tried to find me a boyfriend and they set me up with their friends' son, but he was like the kiss of death. I'm too quiet and boring for someone fun like Eno."

"You are not," I protest. "I agree that Isabelle and Eno are a good match but there's a match for everybody."

"Maybe," Samia says, but I think she is just agreeing with me to be polite. "Here we are, the fantastic Rain Room!"

We sink down on the big red pillows that are piled onto the soft grey carpet of the gazebo's floor. Today, the misty clouds that swirl around the glass are comforting. Unlike the previous time we were there, I can hear the sound of the rain, and the sharp, tiny taps are soothing. Samia and I pull soft blankets over our knees and get comfortable.

We sit in silence for a while and I wonder if Samia has nodded off and I glance at her but she is wide awake, staring out into space.

"Beatrice says I can go back too," I tell her and she turns to me. She doesn't look too surprised and I continue.

"But I will be deformed, ugly, and poor," I add. "I'll have a beaten-up face and a bad job."

"Lovely," Samia says. "Lots to look forward to."

I laugh. "Exactly." I fall silent for a moment. "If you were me, what would you do?"

"Well, I wouldn't go back as me, but I can't say for you."

"You know why I'd like to go back, Samia?"

She shakes her head.

"I'd like to kill the fucker who killed me," I say. "I'd like to kill him very slowly and very painfully."

"Don't tell them that," she advises me. "Not if you want to go back."

"I bet they know," I reply. "They know everything."

"True."

We sit in silence again, watching the rain blowing in gusts, as if it is coming off an ocean. The room grows darker and I welcome this cocoon, this shelter in the storm of my life. Well, my afterlife.

"It depends on how badly my face is damaged," I say after a while. "Beatrice said I've lost a lot of vision in my left eye and I'll have to wear glasses. Me, wearing glasses! Of course Junior ruined my beautiful Candice Bergen nose. What will my niece think of me? And will she come and live with me or what? I have a spare room, but it's full of clothes and shoes and purses and makeup. Everything would be need to be cleaned out." My thoughts change track. "And there I'd be, injured and ugly. And how will I feel being back in that apartment where I was brutally attacked and nearly died?"

"You wouldn't have to do everything at once," Samia says. "You could take your time."

"I still have money coming in from my severance," I say, calculating. "I had only been off for three months and they gave me a year, with benefits too, so there is that, which will help. But no more online shopping, not that I'd want to. I have credit card debts up the yin yang."

"You could have a yard sale," Samia suggests. "Or sell stuff online. I bet you could make a lot of money."

"I wouldn't have a clue how to go about it. I was a shopper, not a seller."

"Things change," Samia says.

"They do, they do." I slide down among the cushions. "I'm very tired, I'm going to close my eyes for a bit."

"Yes, have a nap, that will help. If you wake up and I'm not here, don't worry, okay?"

"I won't worry. See you tomorrow at coffee?"

"For sure. I'm not leaving now though. Lie down and try to sleep."

I am glad she is going to stay. I settle down and before I know it, I am drifting as peacefully as if I were in the Rest Room.

33. MY VIEWING

IT IS THE POWER OF THE MIND to be Unconquerable. Whatever that means. I knock on Cedar's door and he welcomes me with his usual good cheer. "I need to see what I look like," I say, without a preamble.

"Then you'll need to ask Beatrice for a Viewing," he replies with equanimity.

"She said to ask you. What is this, the government? You two are like civil servants, bouncing me back and forth."

"Seeing the damage will help you determine whether you want to go back or not?"

"Yes. Wouldn't it make a difference to you?"

He cocks his head. "Not really. I'd either want to go back or I wouldn't."

"I think I do want to go back. I'm simply doing due diligence on what the situation would be, for real."

"One can never prepare," Cedar advises, "even though we mistakenly think we can."

"Indulge me," I say, and I am angry and pleading at the same time.

"Just ask Beatrice," he repeats.

"Here's what I don't understand," I say. "You were the one who showed me everything. I lay on this very sofa and we watched me being fired and we watched me being attacked on the Rewind. Why do I need a Viewing now? Why can't we do a Rewind like we did before?"

"One-on-one sessions using the Rewind are intended to guide you towards Realizations," he replies. "The View can only be accessed once certain Realizations have been reached. There are different stages to the healing process and there are aspects of group therapy that are optimal at certain points. Viewings are also present tense, they happen in real Earth time, while Rewinds are exactly that, rewinds of past events. Also, it's more helpful to do Viewings in groups, with supportive friends rather than being alone or one-on-one, like we do here. It may not seem like it, but there are systems in place to truly help and support you through all of this. We, the Helpers and the Board of Regulators, have been doing this for a while."

He pauses. "You're looking for revenge, aren't you?"

Rather than tell a lie, I remain silent.

"And what good would that do?" he asks.

"It would make me feel better," I say, through gritted teeth. "And don't tell me it wouldn't. I know myself better than you know me, and I'm telling you, it would. I would love nothing more than to have the f... the asswipe on his knees, begging for mercy."

"Asswipe is close to swearing," Cedar says. "And, know this. We can't stop you from going back, even if your goal is revenge. It doesn't sway us one way or another. Your going back is entirely your choice."

"It wasn't Isabelle's and Eno's choice, you decided."

"Agree, but they were fully dead. You're in a coma. It's different."

"If I go back, can I see Eno and Isabelle?"

"It's possible. You could."

"I would or I could or there's what, a two percent chance or a ninety-two percent chance?"

"You're very into specifics," Cedar comments.

"Human nature," I reply. "We're big on that."

"Some of you," Cedar grins. "Do you think you'd be a good aunt to your niece?"

"I'd like to try. Look, Cedar, I'm going to find Beatrice and ask her for a Viewing and if she sends me back to you, I'll..." I can't think of anything threatening that I'd be able to action, and I fall silent, feeling foolish.

"You'll what?" he smiles. "If you go back to Earth, you won't be in any position to demand anything from anybody and I suggest you get used to that idea, starting now. Use me to practice on, I don't mind."

"Gee, thanks." I get up. "See you tomorrow."

"Perhaps," he says enigmatically and he waves me out the door.

I glare at the nonsensical sign as I go by and I wander around the white maze trying to find the gang for coffee. But the room eludes me, no matter how hard I focus and I am about to give up when Samia appears.

"Come on," she says. "Everyone's there."

"Bless you for rescuing me again," I say. "And how are you today?"

"Fine, the usual." She shrugs and opens a door.

Jaimie, Agnes, Tracey, and Grace are sitting in a circle, mugs in hand. "Got lost, did you?" Jaimie grins and I glare at him.

"Maybe I haven't been here as long as you have." I change the subject. "Will you guys come with me to see Beatrice after we're done here? I need to ask for a Viewing and I don't want to watch by myself."

They agree and I sit restlessly, bouncing my left leg up and down until the others are ready to leave. I even leave half of Samia's perfect latte unfinished.

I follow Tracey's lead, and wish that she would pick up the pace. She seems to be ambling and I wonder if she is doing it on purpose to annoy me, but I remind myself that she always moves slowly. After what feels like a decade, we arrive at Beatrice's door.

"Sent you to me, did he?" Beatrice sounds unsurprised. "Okay, let's take a look." She puts on her glasses, peers at the screen, and mutters something I can't make out. Then she punches in some numbers and peers at the screen again.

"How does this work anyway?" I ask. "What are you doing?"

"Configuring latitudes and time," she says. "It's more complicated than you might think. Then you add duration and you subtract the speed of light and multiply by probability."

"Okey-dokey," I say. "So is it ready?"

"It's ready," she replies and the printer coughs out a page. "You can go right now, if you like."

I grab it and pause. "Beatrice," I ask, "will you come with us?"

She looks surprised, as do the others. "Sure, why not." She gets up and we file down to the Viewing Room.

I am surprised by how terrified I feel. I ease my way into the centre of the red banquette, with Samia on one side and Beatrice on the other.

WELCOME, JULIA! WE HOPE YOU WILL ENJOY YOUR VIEW-ING TODAY!

I take a deep breath and the View starts moving in from the black. It flies towards the Earth and floats through the gauzy outer curtain. It hovers over blue oceans and continues down to the ground of my home city. We get closer and closer, until it comes to a hospital, where it slides us in through the front door and we land on our feet, in a manner of speaking.

The View glides us down a hallway and we come to a stop in the intensive care unit.

We move towards a woman who I cannot recognize as myself. She is lying on her back, with one leg up in a sling and we close in so we are standing right next to her bed. Seeing myself from the View's angle is much harder to take than the Rewind that had kept its distance. My arms and hands are bandaged and my head is secured by a sturdy neck brace. I can hardly make out my body for the tubes and wiring coming off me. Both my eyes are swollen shut, and the rest of my face is bandaged. My mouth is cut and bruised, and a line of stitches traces from my top lip to under my nose.

Bile fills my mouth and I choke it down. "I need a moment," I say and Beatrice presses pause.

"I didn't know you could do that," Tracey sounds annoyed. "Teacher's pet gets special treatment as usual."

Beatrice shrugs. "Agnes and Grace weren't Viewing themselves. And this is past present tense, not present live. That's about a week after you were first brought in," she says to me. "We are moving towards real Earth time."

"I'm ready to move on," I say, weakly.

"Now we'll go further forward in time, to three weeks later."

We stand next to the bed and watch as things change slightly but not by much, except that my face is no longer bandaged and the mess of broken bones, lacerated skin, and bruised flesh is out in the open.

"You had a lot of internal bleeding at this point," Beatrice says. "They still weren't sure you were even going to make it."

"Was I in Purgatory yet?"

"You were."

"I was playing with dresses and makeup while I was lying there like that?" A wave of self-disgust washes over me.

"You didn't know," Samia says and she squeezes my hand and I hold on tight.

Time moves forward and the swelling lessens on my eyes and my face loses its balloon-inflated appearance but it's misshapen in a horrible way. My nose is flattened and squashed to one side, my left eyelid droops down and the scars crisscrossing my skin make me look like a monster.

"Please tell me it improves," I whisper.

"It does," Beatrice says, but her tone isn't exactly reassuring. "Viewing, show present day."

The View moves forward and I look down at the broken face of the woman that Junior has created. The bruising has largely disappeared and so have I. I, me, my face—it's all gone.

My nose is still flattened. I am lined with red and purple scars, my mouth is twisted and ruined, my cheekbones are out of alignment and even my chin is a strange shape, as if a thumb has pushed into cookie dough. There is no symmetry to this face, no even lines, no lovely curves or pleasing angles. I am horrific. And I am all alone.

I study the woman for a long time and the others patiently sit with me. I turn to Beatrice. "I want to go back to Earth now," I say. "I choose Earth."

I look around at the others. "Goodbye gang, I'll miss you. You mean a lot to me but there's someone down there who needs me. Beatrice, send me back, NOW." Then, just to be polite, I add, "Please."

PART II: **HERE**

34. BACK AGAIN

I AM NOT SURPRISED to wake up in my hospital bed. I guess Beatrice realized I really meant what I said. I wish I had thanked Cedar for his help but, thinking back to his cryptic message at our last meeting, he knew what was going to happen.

It is strange how fiercely protective I feel about my poor battered body and I want to be fully present to help it heal. Help it heal, so I can get back to the real world and kill the fucker responsible.

It is still a shock, how badly I am hurt. Seeing the extent of the damage at my Viewing helped prepare me, but what I'm not prepared for is how much it hurts and how strange it feels to be behind that damaged and scarred face.

Even without looking or probing, my face and body feel different. I am misshapen, tight, swollen, and tender. I run my tongue along my lips. The stitches have been removed but the skin is rough and bumpy. My arms are no longer in casts and I flex my muscles and fingers and am relieved to find everything moving as it should. I explore my rib cage and gently prod my stomach and I'm amazed and relieved to find no pain. The internal damage has healed better than the visible wounds.

"Ah, you're awake!" A nurse comes in and smiles widely as she nears the bed. "I am so glad to see you. How are you?" She pulls out a thermometer and takes my temperature, then scribbles something on a clipboard that is sitting at the foot of the bed.

I look at her and Beatrice was right. The vision in my left eye is blurry, as if an optometrist has inserted a weak lens while testing. Right now, I'd welcome glasses—so much for my famous vanity. "Okay, I guess," I reply, and my voice is raspy and old.

She nods and smiles again. "Excellent. I'm going to get the doctor. He'll be thrilled that you're awake!"

I pat my fingertips along my squashed nose, my flattened cheekbones and my poor, droopy, damaged eye.

The doctor arrives and also greets me with a broad smile. "You will get reconstructive surgery to help you," the doctor says after he has thoroughly examined me. "Of course, we have to be realistic about our expectations but things will improve. We're going to take the cast off your leg today, you woke up just in time. And next week, we'll start with physio and help you get back on your feet."

"How much longer will I be here?"

"Four to six weeks. That will include the work our man will do on your nose and cheekbones. You'll need the rhinoplasty to breathe better, it's not simply a cosmetic procedure."

He is right. I am snuffling like a French bulldog on a hot day. I am humiliated by the disgusting noise I am making, and I try to breathe through my mouth instead.

"The cops will be happy you're awake too," the doctor says. "Are you up to talking to them?"

I nod, a micro-movement that sends waves of pain pulsating through my skull.

"Good for you. Try to eat something. I'll get a soft meal brought to you and, as I say, we'll be removing the leg cast later today."

He and the nurse leave and I notice that neither of them suggested getting me a mirror. They must have felt it was better for me not to see the extent of the damage.

I close my eyes and wonder how the others are doing. It was strange and unsettling when Eno and Isabelle vanished like that, and at least with them, there was some forewarning of their possible departure, whereas I just rushed out. Which was more my style, but I wish I had hugged Samia and thanked her for being my friend. I wish I had thanked Agnes for being my Introducer and for sticking by me, and Tracey for her salt-of-the-earth directness, and Grace and Jaimie and Cedar and Beatrice for the many ways in which they had helped me.

I am glad they haven't been wiped from my memory because thinking about them brings me comfort. It's as if they are with me, helping me. I am not alone. Maybe Purgatory knows I need them.

I doze off and when I wake, two policemen are standing next to my bed. "Sorry to disturb you," the one says awkwardly, and he sounds genuinely apologetic. "We have a few questions if you don't mind."

Eno! Tall and skinny, with those big, slightly close-set dark eyes, that scruffy goatee and long sideburns, and the slightly greasy forelock pulled in a sideways across his forehead. Only this guy is much better dressed than his counterpart in Purgatory, with dark grey trousers, a white shirt with a grey tie, and a black stylish overcoat with a turned-up collar.

I want to smile and tell him that it is great to see him and that he's really styling it, but then I remember that I can't say anything, and I think about the ruin of a woman he is facing and my eyes fill with tears.

"It's okay, Ma'am," he says, but I interrupt him.

"You can call me Julia."

"Julia. Thank you." He hands me a box of tissues and I dab my eyes.

"I'm Detective Joe Moretto and this is my partner, Detective Dan Harms. Do you remember anything about the night you were attacked?"

"No. I was asleep on the sofa," I say, hating my horrible dry raspy voice. "I was asleep and then I was being attacked and I was tied up. There were two men. They were dressed in black. It happened so fast."

"Did any of them say anything?"

"No. Didn't anybody see anything?"

"We're investigating some possibilities," Joe says vaguely. "No witnesses as yet, but we haven't stopped digging. Neither of the men said anything to you?"

"No. They were very prepared. They had a bag with duct tape. They wore gloves. They were dressed in black, I remember that."

"No distinguishing features on either of them?"

"No."

"Height?"

"They were both quite tall, I think. And big, they were both big."

"Hmm. And you didn't see their faces?"

"It happened so fast," I say. "Only the one man beat me up. The other one stood to the side and watched."

"That's helpful," Joe says, but I notice that he isn't writing anything down.

"Do you remember what time this happened?"

I sigh. "No. I was asleep. I don't remember anything else. I'm sorry. I can't help you as much as I want to. They didn't leave anything behind to help you identify them?"

"Not a thing. Like you said, they were prepared. Here's my card in case you think of anything else, okay? You've just woken up. You never know, you might remember more in a few days."

"Thank you." I want to ask him if he has a girlfriend and if they are happy and then I notice that he is wearing a shiny new wedding ring. "Recently married?" I ask, and he looks surprised.

"Yeah, still trying to get used to wearing a ring." He looks at it with surprise and clear delight.

"Congratulations," I say and he smiles.

His partner, Dan Harms, has not said anything; he just stands there, unmoving, watching me. They turn to leave and clearly Dan thinks I am deaf as well as battered because I hear him clearly. "She's lying," he says and Joe grunts.

"She just woke up," Joe replies.

"She's lying and you know it."

I watch them through the glass window of my room. They stop and talk to the nurse holding a tray. She nods and they leave and she comes in.

"Mashed potato, mashed chicken, mashed carrots, and vanilla pudding," she says and she puts the tray down. The food looks terrible and I think back to Purgatory's menu with longing. I should have taken advantage of it.

I try a tiny piece of the chicken which succeeds in being tasteless and creamy at the same time, and I wonder if the cops think it is odd that I haven't mentioned the most obvious suspect, Junior.

I wonder if Junior knows I am still alive. He must. I try a forkful of mashed potato and it is so dry, I have to wash it down with water.

"This food is dreadful," I tell the nurse when she returns and she smiles.

"Maybe I could get takeout?" my former self suggests, but then I remember that she is gone and her vanished beauty and diva demands hold no sway in this world.

"Aw, it's not that bad," the nurse says. "You'll get used to it."

I am moving the carrots around on the plate when Joe comes back.

"One thing I forgot to ask," he says. "You're sure it wasn't Patrick Ralph Davidson-Loach IV who did this? I understand you have some history."

I shake my head, but I immediately stop because it hurts. "Which doesn't mean to say he wasn't behind it."

"Davidson-Loach says he was at a private poker game in Vegas and his buddies confirm that, but they'd lie for him. There are hotel reservations in their names but that doesn't mean Junior was actually there. We can't find records of him having spent any money while he was supposedly there, there are no credit card receipts or ATM withdrawals. He says his buddies comped him and they support that claim. And we couldn't find any credit card activity on this end either, so it's not like we could prove he was in town when you were attacked. We couldn't find a single thing to tie him to this. But who else could it have been?" He looks at me.

"You're the detective," I tell him. "Look at me. I've got enough problems dealing with my injuries and trying to heal my body. Don't you think I want you catch the guys? Of course I do. Do I think you will? No. Therefore, I don't want to waste any more time on it. I need to get better. I need to get on with my life, such as it is."

My voice sounds less like a rusty old truck than it did before, and if the tasteless, creamed chicken helps, I will eat it by the pound.

"You're not afraid that whoever did it will come back?"

"They've ruined me," I say simply. "They've ruined me. They did what they wanted to do. I wasn't exactly Miss Popularity and someone made me pay."

"Well, call me if you need anything," he says. "I feel like we've met before. Have we?"

I shake my head gently. "We haven't. But thank you."

"And let me know if you want me to bring you a shawarma or a burger from McDonald's. That glop on your plate looks pretty crappy."

I laugh, my first laugh back on Earth. He sounds so much like Eno that it is funny. He tips a mock hat at me and leaves.

"You've got a fan," the nurse teases me. "Your reconstructive surgeon will be down shortly after you've had your lunch."

I do what I can to finish the food and I doze off, waking when I hear voices next to my bed. I struggle to focus and sit up. I blink and I see Richard, Grace's husband.

"I'm Doctor Silino," he tells me, "and I'm here to give you a new nose and hopefully a few other reconstructions to help the healing process."

"We've met before," I say. "You gave me a Candice Bergen nose."

He looks surprised. "I did? I don't remember."

"You've probably got a lot of patients and it was a long time ago."

He seems to be functioning fine for a heroin addict and I think about what Eno had said, how that was possible. I also think about what Eno had said, about him getting the itch while I was under the knife, but I push that thought from my mind. Besides, whatever he does, it can only be an improvement.

I first met Richard Silino when I was twenty five. I had decided to give myself a nose job for my birthday, a self-gift I had wanted for a very long time. The rest of my face and body had grown up beautifully but my nose was a big, awful hook, a witch's nose.

In what was my first episode of online shopping, I researched top plastic surgeons and he came out far ahead of the others. I sat in his office and told him what I wanted, and I recalled seeing the framed portrait of his perfect family on the bookshelf behind his desk. And I remember thinking that his wife was lucky, that she could get all the surgeries she wanted for free. Little did I know.

"The good news is that there's still cartilage for me to work with. However, I'll still need to take material from your ear or your rib to for the rebuild, or I could use silicon rubber. The advantage of using your tissues is that your body is less likely to reject them. However, the cartilage may later be absorbed by your body, and further surgery might be needed. Silicon is less likely to shift but there may be the chance of infection at the site, but this is a minimal risk."

"Which one do you think is better?"

"In your case, silicon. I'll create a new bridge for your nose and I can't promise it will be a Candice Bergen special but it will be much better than the one you have now."He smiles.

"Thank you," I say, and I mean it. "And my cheekbones? Can you fix them?"No one has noticed that I have an intimate knowledge of my injuries, despite not having access to a mirror.

"I will do the best I can," he says. "Each of us has asymmetry but not to the degree inflicted on you here. In years to come, the work I do may need to be touched up. As I say, the body shifts and moves and things can change. However, sometimes they don't change at all, it's hard to know in advance."

"Buyer beware," I say. "I am very grateful for this and I'm lucky to have you as my surgeon." I feel disloyal to Grace but if flattery will help, then I am willing to pay that small price for now. I'll collect the debts later.

"My pleasure," he says. "I hope they find the men who did this to you. See you in surgery."

He leaves and I spend the remainder of the day having the cast taken off my leg and making the long journey of eight steps to the washroom, unassisted. I am determined to get out of the hospital as soon as I can. Thoughts of revenge will have to wait. What I need to do now is to heal.

34. HEALING

I MAKE GREAT PROGRESS. And, with Eno Joe's help, I change my name. "I get why you need to do this," he says as he helps me fill out the paperwork. "I do."

Julia Redner for only a few days longer, I stand in the parking lot of the hospital, my arms crossed against my chest, smoking a cigarette. I know that smoking retards the healing process but right now, it's my only source of pleasure. Joe and I agreed it would be best if Julia left the hospital and vanished, and only once she was gone, would Lula Jane Harris emerge.

"Sounds like a country and western singer," Joe had grumbled. "You should be June or at least Jane. That way when you start saying the 'j', people won't think it's odd when you get your own name slightly wrong. But if you start with 'j' and then swerve into Lula like a bad lady driver, you'll be calling attention to yourself."

I laughed. "I won't get it wrong. I like Jane, but Lula means famous warrior, and I need something with meaning. I fought hard to stay alive and I'm going to fight to build a new life."

"Yeah, see now, that's the spirit!"

Joe has been a real help to me, visiting and counseling, and so has his new wife, Ella. Ella, unlike Isabelle, doesn't remove her clothing when we meet.

Ella is, by Isabelle's standards, conservatively, even primly dressed and she's initially shy and reserved but she quickly warms to me. "Lovely to meet you," she said. "Joe's told me a lot about you. When you get out of hospital, you must come over for supper."

"I'd really love that," I said and she grinned.

It's clear that she and Joe dote on one another and I want to tell them how delighted I am that it all worked out, but of course I can't say anything.

When Ella turned to leave, she paused with a perplexed look on her face, as if she thought we'd met me somewhere before, but couldn't quite remember where. "I'll be back tomorrow with a bedside picnic," she said, and that was all it took for us to become firm friends.

I am thinking about her and Joe and the glad news of their baby on the way, when I spot Richard, my plastic surgeon, across the parking lot. I am about to wave and thank him again for my new face but he's with another man and they are arguing furiously.

The vision in my right eye is still fuzzy and I have been fitted with a new pair of glasses but I can't wear them until my reconstructed nose is fully healed. I close my bad eye and strain with the good one, hoping to catch sight of who it is that Richard is arguing with. I can hear his raised voice from where I am standing.

I duck around the side of a parked ambulance, and it is then that I recognize the man. It's Mr. Healey, the man who killed Agnes and Josh, the man who tossed Auntie Miriam's room and was thrown out by Agnes's mother. Mr. Healey, the drug dealer. Clearly, Richard is still in the grip of his heroin addiction.

I can hear their voices raised in anger, but I can't make out what they are saying.

Mr. Healey shrugs and turns to leave but Richard catches him by the sleeve and yanks him back. Mr. Healey doesn't like that and he grabs Richard by the lapels of his doctor's coat and shoves him against a parked car.

"Dr. Silino!" A security guard dashes across the parking lot. "Hey, let him go!" he shouts.

Mr. Healey releases Richard and raises his hands. "Just leaving," he says. "See you around, doctor."

Richard looks more upset than angry, and he adjusts his clothing and waves off the security guard. Then he looks up and sees me watching him.

We stare at each other until he turns and strides off into the hospital.

"I'm not surprised," one of my nurses says. She has come up next to me without my having noticed. She takes a deep drag of her cigarette. "He's a moody bastard. Never know what you're going to get with him. Sometimes he's like your best friend, the next minute, he's biting your head off."

"The pressure of being a brilliant surgeon," I murmur but she shakes her head.

"Psycho is more like it. Anyway, I've said too much." She grinds her cigarette out and walks away, and I shade my eyes, and look over to where the argument had taken place.

I have been so busy attending to my healing that I have forgotten certain things—well, not forgotten, but I pushed them to the back of my mind. But it is nearly time to remember. And once Lula is in place, she is going to set a few things straight.

36. LULA JANE HARRIS

A FEW WEEKS LATER, Lula Jane Harris looks back at me from the bathroom mirror in my old apartment. I study her. I was shocked the first time I saw her because, by a freakish twist of fate, she looks horribly similar to Junior's wife, Sharon.

Sharon had been a pretty cheerleader in her youth, but her features melted in her later years and the loss of her taut and peachy complexion created a softer facsimile of her former self. The woman I am looking at is no great beauty either, but she is a great improvement on the ruin that Junior left behind.

Like Sharon, I am now blonde. A visiting makeup artist recommended the change. "Black hair is harsh with facial scarring," she had said and I had appreciated her honesty. "Blonde softens things and these days, it's easy to maintain the colour at home."

I wear black-framed glasses that also help disguise the fact that my one cheekbone is lower and flatter than its counterpart. My scarring from the stitches is still vivid but I have creams and lotions and I know that the crisscross tracks will fade in time.

And now, it's time to start putting things into motion.

The first thing I do is get in touch with my niece, Emma. Joe helps me find her, and he comes with me to meet her.

My hands are shaking on the drive there and I can hardly sit still. I keep tugging at my seatbelt. How can I explain abandoning her like I did? Never mind that I don't even know how to talk to a ten-year old girl.

"Treat her like an adult," Joe says when I tell him what I am thinking. "And tell her you're sorry. Kids have a great capacity for forgiveness."

"What if I've scarred her for life? What if she has abandonment issues forever because of me? First she loses her parents and then her aunt doesn't want her."

"Her aunt's lifestyle at the time wasn't conducive to raising a child," Joe corrects me and he reminds me of Cedar who had said the same thing. "You used to be a big-time career girl but not any more. Things change and now you know what really matters. The truth is, if she's going to be screwed up forever by the things that happened to her, then that's her issue. I've seen kids in the same situations react in completely different ways, it depends on who they are." Joe is a lot more mature and serious than Eno had been and it took me a while to get used to it.

"True," I say. "My parents died and I never felt like they abandoned me."

"No, but you did bury yourself in work and you hid in relationships that couldn't last," he comments, and I feel slighted.

"What the fuck, Joe? You spend your spare time psycho-analyzing me? I don't need a shrink, I thought you were my friend."

"I am your friend," he says calmly, handing me a cigarette. "Which is why I point things out to you, from time to time. I care. People who don't care will say you're wonderful no matter what you do, because they don't care. I care."

"Yeah, and if I do the same to you?"

He laughs and grins at me. "Bring it on, lady, I've got big shoulders. But my point is, you've changed. Things are different for you now, things matter that didn't before. You never wanted to see her before but now you do."

"I do and I don't. I'm terrified."

"Understandable. Well, hang onto your hat because we're nearly there."

We pull up outside a plain yellow semi-detached house with a neatly kept front garden and a white picket fence.

"They've got a picket fence," I say, panic-stricken by this symbol of normalcy.

"Relax Lulabelle, we're just here for a meet and greet, okay? No pressure. Breathe. No one expects you to be the perfect auntie right out the gate."

"I do," I mutter under my breath and I follow him up to the front door.

The woman who answers the door is not what I was expecting. I had a different kind of mom in mind, the kind with plump hips, wearing a shapeless peach or beige cardigan, with cropped, sensible, greying hair.

This woman is tall, boyish and skinny, with long red hair pulled back from her face in a ponytail. She has pale green eyes and freckles and she's wearing slim fit jeans and a sleeveless black tank top. She's friendly enough. "Hi, you're Lula, come on in. I'm Bev, Emma's foster mom."

Joe had looped her in that Julia was no more.

I follow her inside the house and find an artist's haven of pottery, knitting, drawings, sculptures, and paintings. "We're very organic," Bev explains, "very tactile. Creativity is crucial to children and helps nurture their souls. We make our own yoghurt and we grow cucumbers and kale and tomatoes in the backyard. We ride our bikes as much as we can and Em decorated her room all by herself. Handmade is so much nicer than store-bought, don't you think?"

I gurgle something and Joe grins. Bev and I are about as different at two people could be.

"Breathe," Joe whispers as we watch Bev calling Emma in from the back garden.

"Oh Joe, she's lovely," the words catch in my throat as Emma runs through the kitchen and then she stops short, a few feet away from me.

We look at each other, and neither of us says anything.

"This is your Auntie Lula," Bev says brightly. "The one I was telling you about. How about I get us some lemonade and we sit under the tree in the back? It's lovely out there."

"You don't look like my mom," Emma says and I nod.

"I used to look much more like her," I say, which was and wasn't true. We shared some similarities but, in fact, we were a study on how two people could share a few features, except one was stunningly beautiful while the other was plain at best.

Emma has inherited the best of her mother and father. She has dark curly hair that she's wearing in a French braid, an oval face with a little roman nose and large brown eyes. I try to summon the feeling that she's related to me, but I can't.

"I used to look more like her," I say again, "but I was in an accident. The doctors had to give me a new face. I'm still getting used to it too."

She comes up to me and I kneel down.

"You see these lines," I point out the railway track scars around my mouth and eyes, "they had to sew me back together."

Bev swings around as if not approving of such graphic honesty but Emma runs her fingers lightly across my face.

"Did it hurt?" she asks.

"Yes, it hurt very badly," I tell her. "It still does."

"Let's go outside," Bev says.

"I'll help you with that," Joe takes the tray from her.

Emma leads the way, pointing out beans and potato bushes in the sizable vegetable garden.

"We can't have the big tomatoes," she says, "because the birds eat them. We have to plant cherry tomatoes instead. I don't like them as much."

"They aren't easy to eat," I say. "If you bite them wrong, they spray everywhere."

Emma thinks this is hilarious and Joe shoots me a look like he's trying to tell me that I am doing well, but I am nearly dead with stress and exhaustion and we haven't even been there ten minutes.

Emma stops and looks at me, and her gaze isn't quite as friendly as it was when we first arrived. "Can I ask you something?"

"You can ask me anything you want to."

"Why didn't you come to Mom and Dad's funeral? There was no one there except for me and the priest and another lady from the police. I didn't even have Bev. I came to stay here later."

We sit down on the grass in the shade of a big oak tree and I search for the right words.

"It was very wrong of me," I say. I know I had lied at the time about having some work emergency, but the truth was that I hadn't wanted to acknowledge Emma's existence. I didn't want to have to reject her in person and it was easier to simply pretend she wasn't there.

"Since we're being honest with each other, Emma, I'll tell you the truth. Before my accident, I wasn't a nice person."

"Are you a nice person now?"

"I am nicer than I was," I say. "And I'm trying very hard. I don't care about my job like I did before. I care about you and I'm sorry I let you down. I'd like to make it up to you by being a good aunt."

"Do I have to come and live with you? I like it here."

"This is your home. But if you guys don't mind, I'd love to come and visit sometimes and hang out with you and Bev."

She and Bev noticeably relax when I say this and, truth be told, so do I.

"You can teach me art stuff and gardening," I tell her. "And do you know something? I haven't ridden a bicycle since I was fourteen. You'll have to remind me how."

Emma laughs. "Who can't ride a bicycle? That's funny. Look, I'll do a handstand. I am one of the best in my class at gym."

She braces herself and, in that moment, with her little feet neatly placed together, and her hands outstretched, palms facing down, I see that she is my sister's child. Jan used to stand exactly like that, with the same expression of concentration on her face.

I'm so sorry, Jan, I think and I swallow back tears. *I took you for granted. I thought you'd always be around. I never acknowledged your life or your death. I felt like you didn't need me and so I walked away. But you were my sister and I'm sorry.*

Coming face-to-face with the relentless immensity of my selfishness makes it hard to concentrate on Emma but I tell myself this isn't about me and I clap as she does the perfect handstand.

"Excellent," I applaud her.

"I'm very good," she says matter-of-factly. "I am on the school team. Watch, I will do a cartwheel."

"What was your job, Lula? Before the accident, I mean?" Bev asks.

"I was VP of the copywriting, marketing, and advertising division for a large multi-media company," I explain and Emma is instantly bored by the turn of conversation and she waves a hand at Bev to interrupt us.

"Can I go and phone Neela? Neela's my best friend," she informs me. "She's dying to hear about you."

"Ten minutes," Bev says and Emma rushes off.

"I'm timing you," Bev calls out. "She and Neela can talk for hours," she says. "Even after seeing each other every day at school. But I guess we were the same at that age."

"I wasn't," I admit. "I always had my nose in a book. It used to drive Emma's mother crazy when we were kids. I've always been a loner."

Bev looks at me. "And yet now you want to be a mom?"

"I want to be family to Emma," I correct her. "I want to be someone she can rely on. I just want her to know that I'm here for her in any way that she wants. Do you think I damaged her?" The question is foremost on my mind and it shoots out before I can stop myself from asking.

Bev shrugs. "Hard to say. She's got lots of friends at school. Her grades are good, she eats well, she's happy and energetic.

She had nightmares for about six months after she came to live with us and she wet the bed for a while but that stopped. She seems fairly resilient. I keep an eye on her artwork to see if there are any warning signs about low self-esteem or things like that, but, as I say, she appears to be happy. The thing is," she says and she pauses and puts her hand on her flat belly, "things may change. I'm pregnant. Only six weeks. I have a history of early miscarriages, so please don't say anything, and Emma doesn't know about the other attempts. I don't want her to think I'm trying for a biological baby because she isn't enough. I love her as much as if I had given birth to her myself, and the last thing I want is for her to feel unwanted in any way. But if I do carry this child to term, then she will feel unsettled and you being a part of her life will help."

"What about your husband?" I ask, feeling like I am intruding. "Do he and Emma get on well?"

"His name's Jackson and they get on like a house on fire," Bev says. "He's a long-distance trucker, so he's gone a lot but she loves him and he thinks she's the bees knees. They like to go fishing together which is incredibly sweet to see."

"Neela says you sound cool," Emma comes running back. "Do you want to see my room?"

"I'd love to," I get up. "Bev said you decorated it yourself?"

"Bev helped, but I did most of it. The colours and everything," she skips ahead and I follow behind her, leaving Joe and Bev under the tree.

I am reassured by Emma's room. Her paintings are intricate and far more detailed than I would have imagined and she has a real talent for drawing. The walls of her bedroom are pale green and lilac, and her slatted wooden bedframe is a patchwork of bright colours and patterns.

"I painted it," she says proudly when she sees me looking. "Jackson said I could use as many colours as I wanted."

"It's beautiful," I say. "This is a lovely room."

Half an hour later, Joe and Bev come to find us. "Sorry squirrel," he says to Emma, "but we need to start heading out."

"Squirrel!" Emma giggles. "But I wanted to show you our lake before you go."

"There's a lake near here?" Joe is surprised. "I didn't know that."

"Yeah and it's got a really funny name—"

"Let me guess," I say and my heart flutters like a trapped bird. "It's called Ecum Secum."

They stare at me in surprise. "How on earth did you know that," Bev asks.

"Because she's a white witch," Emma says. "With magical powers since her accident. She can move things with her mind."

"I wish," I say, smiling at her. "No, I met a woman in ... in hospital and she told me there's a lake near here. I forgot about it until now."

Joe gives me a funny look. "Well, squirrel, we'll have to look at it another time, I'm late for work and you don't want me to get fired now, do you?" He grins at her and Emma shakes her head.

"Will I see you again?" she asks me and there is doubt in her voice.

"Oh honey, yes," I say. "Absolutely. You're going to be sick of me in no time."

"Can I phone you?"

"Maybe Auntie Lula doesn't like being on the phone," Bev says remembering what I had said earlier, giving me a way out.

"Bev's right," I agree. "I'm not much of a phone person but you can call me anytime, twenty-four seven."

"Twenty-four seven," Emma repeats. "Do you have her number?" she asks Bev.

"Her? Who's her? The cat's mother? You mean Auntie Lula? Yeah, I do."

"The cat's mother," Emma giggles. "I never know why you say that."

"Can I have a hug?" I ask, astounding myself.

"Yes." Emma holds out her arms and I kneel down and hug her and unexpectedly, I am crying. "Oh honey," I apologize, not wanting to alarm her with my tears. "I'm crying because I'm happy to meet you, that's all."

"That's okay," Emma says and she pats me on the head. "Adults can be very emotional."

This has me laughing and blowing my nose at the same time.

"It's true, we can. Thanks Bev," I am unsure what to do, shake her hand, hug her or just walk away.

"No prob," she says and she gives me a quick hug. "It's all good. Emma and I were a bit nervous too, weren't we sweetie? But it's been lovely."

There doesn't seem much more to say after that and Joe steers me towards the car.

"You did good, Lulabelle. You tired?"

"Shattered. I could sleep for a week."

"How's the pain?"

"Comes and goes," I say. "But for the most part, it goes, for which I am grateful. Thank you, Joe. I couldn't have done this by myself."

"Yeah, you could have," he is confident. "Give yourself a break. But I'm happy to help out. She's a great kid. And good old organic Bev's solid too. Emma really lucked out, trust me."

He drops me off at my apartment. I need to find a new place to live and I have started packing up. I let Marcello's mother and her friends come in and raid the place and it was like they had died and gone to heaven.

"Chanel! Dior! Givenchy! Oh my god! Are you for real?"

"Take, take, take," I told them. "As much as you want. You're helping me, please, take."

"If you twist my arm, honey, then trust me, I can take," Marcello's mother said and she yelled down the stairs for her son to bring up a big empty box.

But even with their efforts to clean me out, I was left with more than enough stuff to last a lifetime. I had also given a lot to Isabelle/Ella and before our visit, I had thought about making up a gift bag for Bev but I was glad I hadn't. She wouldn't have wanted any of it and it would have been entirely the wrong message.

The first thing I did when I got home from the hospital, was settle a score with the sofa on which I was attacked. I wanted to set fire to it and watch it burn but since that wasn't practical, I slashed it with a Stanley knife and ripped it to shreds. I stabbed it, shouting obscenities and imagining Junior's face. Marcello hadn't said a word about the mess and he helped me stuff the foam and torn fabric into garbage bags and he took it all away.

Between that and giving things away, there is more space in my apartment and I love it. Purgatory has cleansed me of my need for stuff.

I only use the TV to check up on the weather and the news. I buy a new phone but I keep my old one, the one with Junior's numbers on it, if they are still the same, since it might come in handy.

I lie down on my bed to rest for a moment and I fall asleep. I dream that Jan and I are being chased through a dark forest that turns into a snake-infested swamp. There's a guy coming at us with a machete and he's gaining ground. It feels so real that when I wake, my clothes are wet and sour with sweat and I pull them off.

I stand under the shower for a long time, with the water as hot as I can bear it. I haven't wanted to take a bath since I got back from Purgatory and I'm not sure why.

I can't stop thinking about the guy with the machete. The danger is far from over.

37. REVENGE, PART ONE

AFTER I LEAVE THE HOSPITAL, the second item on my to-do list, after meeting Emma, is to buy a gun. I don't tell Joe about the gun. I buy a semi-automatic pistol online and my hands are shaking the first time I hold it.

"Here's how you load it," the federal firearms license dealer shows me. He works out of a pawn shop downtown and I pick up the gun from him. "Here's how you hold it."

"And the silencer?"

"It fits on like this," he demonstrates.

"I'm afraid of loud noises," I tell him, feeling the need to explain the silencer but he doesn't comment. He just hands the gun to me.

"It looks mean," I say, turning it over in my hand. I feel dizzy for a moment. Me, as a gun-toting femme fatale hadn't featured on my list of life's aspirations but then again, I hadn't envisaged any of the events of the past six months. The gun feels solid and reassuring.

"It's not a toy," the guy replies. He never asks me why I want it. "You should go to the shooting range, out by Main Road, and get some practice."

I take his advice. I am terrified at first, but it hardly takes any time before I am filled with a surge of power that I haven't felt since Junior and I were the King and Queen of mean.

I aim my gun at the target and I fire, imaging Junior's face in front of me. I've been rendered powerless since the day I was axed by that greaseball slob, but now, with the surgeries complete and my shiny gun to protect me, I'm starting to feel in control again.

The next thing I do is fire up the cheap laptop I bought from the pawnbroker. I have no idea how cyber tracing works but I figure it's wise to not use my own computer. I set up an account with the email name *justiceman6667* and I draft a letter to Dr. Richard Silino. Luck had been on my side the day he gave his email address to a nurse within my hearing.

> Silino, I know that you are a drug addict. Heroin, specifically. I also know that you killed a dealer, Foxtrot Four. I am going to ask two things of you:
> 1. Go to rehab and get clean.
> 2. Give me the contact details for Healey.
> You should know that I could kill you but I am choosing to spare your life for the sake of your children.
> If you do not go to rehab, I will inform the police and the hospital authorities of your addiction. If you tip off Healey, I will inform the police and hospital authorities of your addiction.
> I am giving you the opportunity to make things right.
> You have six hours to respond, from the time this message leaves my mailbox. If I don't hear back from you in six hours, I will inform the police and hospital authorities of your addiction.

I sit back. I read the letter a few times and I press send. I would love to make Richard suffer for what he did to Grace but she wouldn't have wanted that. Richard is a good father, and I have to respect Grace's wishes.

It doesn't take long for a reply to appear on the screen:

> Who the fuck is this? What do you think you know? You don't know anything about me.

I was expecting that and I have my reply ready:

> You hide your stash in the downstairs washroom in your house. This is not a bluff. Give me your assurance or I will contact the police and the hospital authorities and when I say assurance, I want to see a booking reservation in your name with a recognized clinic. You can say it's mental exhaustion. No one has to know the real reason but if you don't cooperate, I will rat you out. And if you think you can rush home and hide your stash, it's too late. I've been in your house, and I've got photographs.

The last is a bluff but there's no way he can know that.

> You hide your drugs in a cookie tin, under rolls of toilet paper. And, on the basis of the photographs, I will report you to the police and they will give you a blood test. Now give me Healey's deets and agree to my deal.

Cyber silence follows and I wonder if I have misjudged him. Or is there any possibility that he can know it's me? I light a cigarette and wait, smoking in quick drags. This time, the silence is lengthy and finally, ten minutes before his time is up, I receive a message. The message contains a telephone number and a street address for Healey. And, a screenshot confirming that Richard will be checking into a rehab centre in three days' time.

Satisfied? he asks.

Yes. I reply. But I'm keeping my eye on you.

I wish I could do more. What if he doesn't go to rehab? What if he relapses afterwards? This part of my payback plan is annoyingly vague but I can't see another way around it. I had to give the guy a second chance, for Grace and the children's sake, but Richard deserved to pay for killing Foxtrot Four who, in turn, could have saved Isabelle.

But Isabelle is happily back as Ella, and I have Healey's contact details and that will have to do for now.

38. VISITING AUNTIE MIRIAM

THE NEXT DAY, I do something I haven't done in decades. I get on a bus. I am going to visit Agnes's Auntie Miriam. I find the old-age home easily enough and I stand outside and light a cigarette, wondering what I should say and I decide to play it by ear. "I'd like to see Auntie Miriam," I say. "I'm a friend of Agnes's."

The woman at the reception desk is very chatty. "Yeah, Agnes, poor girl, too terrible what happened. And to Josh too. We had no idea they even knew each other. He was such a good kid, a hottie, let me tell you. We all thought he was headed for the big time, what with his guitar and all. He was really good. And then, shot to death in a parking lot. They say it was drugs but I don't believe it for a moment, he was a good kid. The violence in the city these days, guns everywhere—"

"Auntie Miriam?" I interrupt her.

"Just finished her mid-morning snack. She hasn't eaten in the dining room since Agnes died. She loved that girl more than anything. I liked Agnes but if you ask me, she was a bad influence. I mean look what happened to Josh. I just can't see him being involved in something like that, but Agnes, well, she had a bad side. Her own mother—"

"Auntie Miriam's room number?" I ask.

"Yeah, right." She peers at a screen. "Number 65, door at the end of the hallway. Agnes's mother said she had it coming..."

I slip away quickly and I hear Miss Chatty yammering on, even though I've walked away.

I stand outside Auntie Miriam's door and I knock. "They took the tray already," a quavering voice says.

"I'm a friend of Agnes's," I call out, hoping I won't give her a heart attack saying that.

"Agnes! Come in, dear, come in."

I open the door and see a tiny birdlike woman sitting in an old-fashioned wing chair with a knee rug tucked around her legs. "I would get up," she says, "but my old bones are too tired. Forgive me, dear."

"I'm Ju—I mean Lula," I say. "I'm very pleased to meet you. I should have brought you flowers or cupcakes. I'm sorry, I didn't think. I will, next time."

She laughs and waves a hand at me. "Don't be silly. Flowers! I don't have the energy to throw them out when they die and the cleaners are useless. And cupcakes…. All they do is feed me here. It's a wonder I'm not seven hundred pounds!"

She would hardly weigh seventy pounds soaking wet. She's bent over at the waist, with sloping shoulders and a perfect, old ladies' crone face, with creases and wrinkles and folds, and stray hairs sprout from her chin like a cat's whiskers. Her beaky nose curves down to meet her chin and her mouth is a sunken cave. But when she looks at me, her eyes are bright and sharp.

"How did you know my Agnes?" she asks. "You're a bit too old to be one of her friends, if you don't mind my saying so."

Her brain is clearly bright and sharp too and I decide to tell her the truth. "It's a strange and unbelievable story," I warn her.

"Try me, dear. It's less easy to shock me than you might think."

"A man nearly killed me, and he put me into a coma. While I was in that coma, I went to Purgatory. I met Agnes there."

"Go on."

I am not sure what to say next so I start at the beginning. "Agnes has a job there, she's what's called an Introducer. She helps new arrivals who don't realize where they are. She was very kind to me and we became friends and we met every day for coffee even after she had done her job. I really enjoyed her company. She's funny and kind and intelligent and she's a good person. She was my friend, when I needed one the most."

"Why is she in Purgatory, not Heaven?"

"I don't know exactly. I think she wants to join Josh, but she can't move on yet. He wasn't there, in Purgatory. I'm not sure if it's a matter of time or how it works. Purgatory is comfortable, so maybe it's her choice."

"Did she seem happy to you?"

"She's okay. But she misses you. She worries about you. And she feels bad for what happened to Josh."

Auntie Miriam snorts. "That boy." She speaks slowly, sucking on her teeth for emphasis. "Everybody thought he was such a movie star but I wasn't a fan. Shortly after he started working here, ladies started missing expensive pieces of jewelry. No coincidence. He thought he was a charmer, Josh did. Ask the nursing staff and they'll be googly-eyed. The sun shone out of his you-know-what, as far as they were concerned."

She pauses and closes her eyes and I'm not sure if she's going to continue or if she needs to have a nap.

But her eyes snap open and she carries on; her voice has dropped to nearly a whisper and I have to lean in close to hear her. "I knew he and Agnes were seeing each other although she didn't know that I knew. I hoped he would move on. I knew it would break her heart if he did, but then she could get on with her life. Maybe she's in Purgatory because she doesn't realize yet that he wasn't the right one for her. He wasn't in love with her, not like she was in love with him. He was her first love, but he was just using her."

Her head droops again. "Too good for him, my Agnes was. She never had enough love in her life. Her mother was mean to her and I never understood why. She picked on Agnes for her weight, how she stood, how she chewed. Agnes couldn't do anything right, not from the time she was born. If you ask me, it was because her mother hated Agnes's biological father and she hated being reminded of him. He was a lot like Josh, only he had money and he dumped her when she got pregnant. Cheryl thought he'd marry her, so she got pregnant on purpose, that's the kind of person she is. But he dumped her."

"Did Agnes ever see her real father?"

"He wasn't interested in her. She tried to meet him a few times but he never showed up. I hated him for that. Eventually she gave up. Poor Agnes, life never gave her any breaks."

"She had you," I say. "She loved you very much."

"She was a good girl," Auntie Miriam says, and two enormous tears roll down those amazingly wrinkled cheeks. "I loved her too. I miss her every day. She visited me often, and I loved seeing her. We'd sit and watch Shirley Temple movies. Cheryl never even had a name picked out for her and so I named her after a cousin of mine who died young. Agnes Anne. She was my girl."

"I'm sorry," I say.

We both fall silent and I look around the room. I had witnessed its destruction during the Viewing but it had been put back to together so perfectly that no one would ever have suspected what had happened.

Auntie Miriam has fallen asleep.

I am not sure what to do. I see the cushion on the bed and I grab it and go into the tiny washroom, clutching my purse. I close the door, sit on the side of the bathtub, unzip the cushion and dig around inside. It isn't hard to find the drugs and I stuff them into my purse. The bundles are each bound with a plastic band and they aren't very heavy. I make sure I get all of them and I zip up the cushion and snap my purse shut and I flush the toilet and wash my hands.

The washroom is fitted with numerous handles for Auntie Miriam to hold onto when she uses the toilet and I am sure she cannot shower unattended. The soaps are hypoallergenic and antiseptic and the place feels sterile and depressing. I can't wait to leave and I creep out and put the cushion back on the bed.

I kneel down close to Auntie Miriam to say goodbye and that's when I realize that she is dead. She has gone to join Agnes in Purgatory. I know it, as sure as eggs are eggs, as Aunt Gwen used to say when I was a little girl.

Fuck! Talk about bad timing! I sit down and try think about what to do but my mind is completely scrambled. How will I explain my presence? How will I explain how I had known Agnes? As Auntie Miriam had pointed out, I didn't exactly look like one of Agnes's pals.

"You could have waited until I left," I whisper to Auntie Miriam.

I think back to the chatty receptionist. She hadn't so much as asked for my name and I hadn't signed in. The woman had looked at her screen for most of the time and I don't think she got a good look at me at all. And fortunately, I am wearing a large hat to protect my scarred skin from the sun, as well as a scarf to hide the scars on my neck and chest. My hair is tucked away and I hope my glasses are distracting as opposed to identifying. Even if the home has cameras, which I doubt, I look fairly anonymous.

I go to the washroom and grab a tiny hand towel. I rub everything in the washroom that I might have touched, the door handles, the bath where I sat, the taps. Other than that, the only thing I had touched was the front door to Auntie Miriam's room. I hang the towel neatly back in place.

"I'm sorry," I whisper to Auntie Miriam on the way out, and I close the door and wipe the handle down with my scarf.

I am hesitant to walk down the dark, narrow hallway and I don't want to brave the busy reception area near the dining room. But I can't just stand there, staring at a closed door.

I suddenly freeze. An old lady with a walker is shuffling towards me. She is looking down, concentrating hard. I am a deer in the headlights of her geriatric path, and I'm convinced I will be interrogated by the old duck and revealed to be a drug-carrying, Auntie Miriam-killing maniac, but the old lady veers off to the left and I hear a door open and sunshine briefly floods the hallway.

There is a side door that leads outside! Escape! My armpits are soaking wet and my hands are shaking. I pull my hat down low and fumble around in my purse for my prescription sunglasses, exchanging them for my regulars.

I slip outside. The old lady is sitting in the sun with her face upturned and her eyes closed. I say a quiet prayer to whichever deity helped me out and I tiptoe past as speedily as I can. I don't even pause at the bus shelter but walk a long stop further.

I am not sure what I am afraid of except that one mistake can lead to another. From the old-age home's perspective, the series of events is this: Mr. Healey trashes Auntie Miriam's room, shortly thereafter, a conservative, older woman shows up out of the blue, wanting to visit Auntie Miriam and claiming to be one of Agnes's friends. And then Auntie Miriam dies. Alarm bells will be sounded. I am annoyed at this glitch and I silently apologize to Agnes for calling her great aunt's death a glitch, but my plans are only beginning to fall into place and I can't let anything go wrong.

39. SILLY BUNNY

I GET HOME AND SURPRISE MYSELF by grabbing my Chanel Coco Mademoiselle Scented Foam Bath that retails for over a hundred dollars a bottle. I had thought I was done with bathing and that I would be taking showers for the rest of my life, but apparently not. I feel oddly guilty at this indulgence but I remind myself of all the things I had missed about Earth when I was in Purgatory, and I tell myself I deserve these small delights.

I soak for ages in the hot, scented water, trying to remind myself of the other things I had missed and I realize that my wish list is primarily a bunch of things I've never done, but still want to do. I'll make a list and I hope I'll be able to interest Emma in some of my ideas.

I get out of the bath and pull on a brand new Samantha Chang chemise that I discovered in the back of my closet. The delicate flower-patterned silk and rose pink lace feels soft on my skin and life, at that moment, makes perfect sense.

I jump when the phone rings, startled out of my happy reverie. I figure it must be Joe or Isabelle checking up on me, or maybe it's Emma, phoning to say hello. But it isn't. It's Junior.

I never should have answered. The caller ID said Private Number and maybe, in my haste, I thought that Joe was calling from an unlisted phone, but he had never done that before, and as soon as I accept the call and hear the silence at the end of the line, I know I have made a terrible mistake.

"Ju-Lula," Junior finally says mockingly. "Did you think I wouldn't find you? You're still in the same apartment, you silly bunny."

I keep the phone pressed to my ear and I rush over to my purse. I flip it upside down, emptying it of its contents. The heroin spills out onto the floor and with it, my pistol. I flick the safety catch off and crawl with my back against the wall, so I'm facing the door with my gun pointing dead ahead. For all I know, Junior's standing on the other side, with his muscle man for company, ready to kick the door down. My hand holding the gun is shaking and I pull my legs in close and balance the gun on my knees.

"What do you want?" I urge my voice to be calm but I sound terrified and I hate myself for that.

"Nothing. I don't want anything. I'm just calling an old friend. Saying how do. And how are you, Lula? Your face is all nicely fixed?"

"What do you want?" I ask again and he laughs.

"Nothing. For now. Nothing. But hey," he gives a weird chuckle. "I'll be sure to keep in touch."

He hangs up and I'm left alone with the terrifying silence that fills my apartment, nearly suffocating me.

How did he get my number? It's supposedly unlisted. And me, I am unlisted, Lula Jane Harris. How did he know about Lula? Did Richard tell him, as revenge for the rehab email? But Richard couldn't have known I was behind that, and he didn't know about Lula and as far as I know, he doesn't know Junior. The only people who know about Lula are Joe and Isabelle and Emma and Bev. It suddenly feels like too many people know. I don't know what to do.

I sit like that all night, with my back against the wall, thinking.

40. ON THE RUN

THE NEXT MORNING, in the darkness of predawn, I pack a small suitcase. I pull on a large floppy sunhat and sunglasses. I'd rather look ridiculous than be recognizable. I call a cab and slip out of the apartment. "Westside Mall," I tell the driver.

"You're a bit early," he says. "The mall doesn't open for hours."

He's in the mood to chat but I am not interested. I ignore him and silently hand him a couple of twenties when we get to the mall and I watch him drive away.

I withdraw a thousand dollars from the ATM. It isn't going to get me very far but it will have to do for now.

I sit on the sidewalk and wait until Emma will be up and having breakfast. I call her and Bev picks up. "Bev, it's me, Ju-Lula." Darn, I had nearly said Julia again. I hate to admit it but Joe was right, I should have picked a name closer to my own. "I have to go to Florida for an operation on my knee. I'm leaving today and I wanted to let Emma know. I'll be gone for a while."

"Yeah, sure, nice of you to call. Hang on. I'll get her. Em, honey, your aunt's on the phone."

"Coming!" I hear her footsteps getting louder.

"Hi Auntie Lula! How are you?"

"I'm fine, sweetie. Well, sort of. You know my sore knee? Well, I've got to go to Florida and have another operation."

"Why Florida?"

"There's a great doctor there, and he says he can fix it. I'm hoping that maybe one day you and me can rollerblade and do things like that together, and I need my knee to be good."

"I can already rollerblade," Emma says confidently. "I can teach you."

"That'd be fantastic. I'd love that more than anything in the world. I'll be gone for a four weeks, it's a big operation but I'll be sure to call you as much as I can, okay?"

"Okay. I better go, Bev's waving at me, I'm going to miss the school bus."

"Sure, off you go, and Emma, I just want to say how happy I am that you're my niece. I'm very lucky."

She giggles. "I'm lucky too. Goodbye, Auntie Lula."

She puts the phone down and I'm about to call Joe but I change my mind. It will be easier to text him. I don't know if I can trust him, even though it breaks my heart to think that.

I tap out a message about Florida and my knee, and send it quickly before I can change my mind. I'm aching to call Joe and tell him I need his help, tell him that Junior's back and that he had been right, that Junior was the one who had beaten me senseless. But I can't tell Joe that I want to exact my own revenge and that's why I lied. For a moment I had mistakenly thought that I was in control, but Junior seems to be holding all the cards and, right now, I can't be sure whose side Joe is on either. How else would Junior have known about Lula?

Most of the stores are still closed and I join a few unwashed homeless-looking fellows in the food court while I wait. How my life has changed. I study my cellphone. Is it friend or foe? Is it equipped with a tracking device? How would I know? All I do know is that people's phones can be used for that very purpose, and I turn mine off. I dig my old phone out of my purse and make sure that it's also powered off.

As soon as the store with wigs and hair accessories opens, I buy a black wig, with a bobbed style and bangs. I head for the drugstore, and select a vivid red lipstick, Truckstop Fire Blossom. I pick up pair of sparkly, dangly star-shaped earrings and I can't help but smile at what my former self would have said about my choice. I keep my head down at the register and try not to worry about my already dwindling funds.

I can't stop thinking about the security cameras aiming their beady little eyes at me but there's nothing I can do except pull my hat down and go about my business. I don't want either Junior or Joe to find any evidence of my having been at the mall, although hopefully, it wouldn't be the first place they would look.

I rent a non-descript white Honda and I study the form but it doesn't tell me what I need to know.

"Listen," I say brightly to the pimply-faced boy, "I'm trying to get away from my boyfriend. He's this crazy jealous guy who wants to get married but I need time to think."

The boy looks bored to tears and he's hardly listening to me.

"He can't track the car, can he?" I continue. "I mean, do you guys have GPS thingies on your cars?"

He bursts out laughing as if this is the funniest thing he's heard in ages. "Uh, no, Ma'am," he says. "We can't afford no fancy shit like that. But hey, if you're thinking of stealing the car, I got a copy of your driver's license."

"I'm not going to steal the car," I smile at him. "I just need to get away and I want to make sure he can't follow me."

"He can't. And listen, your secret's safe with me. Anyone comes looking for you and I won't say I seen you, okay? He sounds like a nut. Find yourself a new guy, if you want my two cents."

"I think you're right," I say and I leave the store.

I buy a disposable cell phone, grab a muffin and coffee to go, and I head out to check my new ride. I sit there for a moment, wondering what I might have missed. I can't think of anything, so I start the car and set off to find Beatrice's house, on the edge of Ecum Secum Lake. I turn on the radio just in time to hear "Survivor" by Destiny's Child and I sing along with my girl Beyoncé. I'm loud and I'm off key, yes, but the window's down and the warm summer wind is blowing through my hair.

41. ECUM SECUM LAKE

THE HOUSE IS NOT EASY TO FIND. Chuckery Hill Road is a tiny, unmarked side lane that I first mistake as being someone's driveway but then I see a street sign.

Beatrice hadn't given me a number and I only find the place by accident. I am trying to do a U-turn at the end of the lane, thinking I must have gone past the house when I pull into a tangled and overgrown driveway, and I spot an old house at the far end of the property.

I lean forward, clutching the steering wheel in a way that reminds me of Shirley the Driver, and I bite the inside of cheek as I edge the car forward slowly. I am glad for the weeping willow trees that swing closed behind me like a curtain, and I pull up next to the house and get out of the car.

I take out my gun and I walk around the house. The back garden is close to the edge of the lake and it's hard to imagine that this is the same lake that Emma mentioned, and that she's on the other side. Granted, it is a huge lake.

Beatrice's place is utterly deserted and it's sealed tight as a beaver's bottom, another one of my Aunt Gwen's sayings when I was a kid.

I have no idea how I am going to get in. Someone has boarded up the place, and it looks impenetrable. I bet it was Beatrice who had taken care of locking up her house before taking her own life, because with Beatrice, the job got done properly. But coming up against this fortress is something I hadn't considered and I give myself a mental slap on the wrist. I poke around for a while but there's simply no way to get in. I need a hammer.

I get back into my car and I put on the wig and pull my hat down tightly. I apply two coats of the startling lipstick and I add the earrings. I manage a three-point turn in the overgrown driveway and head back towards a Walmart that I had passed along the way.

I buy a heavy-duty hammer as well as a chisel type of tool, and some gardening gloves. I load up on canned goods and crackers, a tin opener, bottled water, and a flashlight. I find myself in an aisle with blackout curtains, guaranteed to block out every light and I grab them on a whim. I throw a roll of duct tape into my cart and add a sleeping bag. I figure I'd better stop shopping before I bankrupt myself. I am taken aback by the bill. Who says Walmart is cheap?

When I get back to Beatrice's house, I scout around and pick a window that faces away from the road, towards the lake. I pull off my wig, wipe my forehead and spend the better part of two hours dismantling the boards that might as well have been welded into place. I curse Beatrice more than once for her diligence and I can just see her, feet up on the desk, crunching on an apple, telling me to stop being such a girl.

Finally, covered in sweat, with my hands aching, I get the boards off. I peer inside the window but it is dark and I can't see the interior. The glass windowpane is still intact, and I'm going to have to smash it even although I'm wary of the noise it will create. I pick up a stone and wrap my scarf around it. I hold the bundle against the glass and tap it with the hammer. A small crack appears and I repeat the action, and I am rewarded when a fist-sized piece of glass shoots inwards.

I pull on my gardening gloves and I manage to soundlessly clear enough glass to undo the latch and open the window. I have finally found a way to get into the house. I'm relieved about this because the afternoon is quickly moving towards evening and I want to be settled inside before nightfall.

I grab the flashlight and my gun and I climb inside the window. I am standing in Beatrice's bedroom and the place is perfectly tidy, marred only by a thin film of grey dust on the bedside table. A brightly-coloured quilt covers the bed and there is a red and blue striped lampshade on the bedside table. Everything is neatly organized, just like Beatrice's office in Purgatory. The evening sun floods the bedroom with light but the rest of the house is as unwelcoming as a dark cave and I am grateful that I bought a good flashlight.

The kitchen is pristine, save for the layer of dust on the counter and in the sink. I open the cupboards and find stacks of plates and bowls and an eclectic variety of drinking glasses. Another cupboard holds mugs and in another, I find a collection of margarine tubs that mirror the ones in Beatrice's office in Purgatory. There are dozens of them in a stack, with their lids tucked to one side and there are empty jars of Sanka. An ornamental shelf displays a tiny stuffed toy cat inside a glass bell jar, exactly like the one Beatrice has in Purgatory.

The fridge is empty. I try a light switch but there is no electricity. I turn on a tap and after some hesitation, the water sputters out, a little rusty but soon clearing. I know I need to explore the rest of the house but the darkness and the stillness are oppressive.

My heartbeat is speeded up and loud in my ears and while it's cool inside the house, sweat gathers along my hairline and runs down my face. I hold the gun and flashlight in front of me, thinking that I look like some stupid cop in a TV show but I don't care. Safety before ego.

A spacious living room houses an ancient TV set and clearly, Beatrice liked her sofas. There are four of them, two-seaters, placed around the perimeter of the living room. There is a huge pile of board games next to the TV set, and I smile when I see the Scrabble. Yes, it's the same set.

Beatrice loved seashell ashtrays; there are half a dozen of them and they are spotlessly clean.

The walls are lined with artwork, the kind you'd see at a cheap yard sale: a watercolour of a bicycle leaning against a brick wall with a bowl of fruit on the windowsill behind it. In another painting, a stormy sunset looms over a ploughed field with random hay bales rendered with an oddly skewed perspective. Then, a group of white horses runs wild against a black background and, within the confines of a thick, gilded frame, a red cardinal looks demented with a sideways glance and one beady eye.

I am reminded of the first time I met Beatrice and I was caught out studying her office. "Enjoying yourself?" she'd asked. "Very nosy, aren't you? Nosy parker."

I apologize to Beatrice for criticizing her taste in artwork and I carry on, finding a small washroom at the bottom of the stairs. Raised blue seashells decorate the ceramic tiles and the blue shower curtain has peach-coloured seahorses and starfish. Small, framed Norman Rockwell prints hang on the wall, with children up to their cheeky antics.

There is a full roll of toilet paper in the holder, and this makes me smile. Beatrice couldn't leave without having every single thing in place.

I go upstairs and stop short. This, I did not expect.

I am in the main bedroom, which is decorated in shades of hot pink, bright orange, and sunshine yellow, although the colours have faded somewhat. A king-sized bed is positioned close to a baby's crib that has a mobile hanging above it. A white dresser is set to the side, and it is stacked with diapers, baby powder, bottles, and pacifiers, all covered in a thick layer of dust. In the crib, lying flat, is a tiny pink onesie, with booties at the feet and a bonnet at the head.

Another dresser with a large ornamental mirror is backed against the opposite wall of the room and I shine my flashlight on it and nearly have a heart attack.

There's a ghost in the room and she's staring at me like a deranged escaped mental patient. I nearly fire my gun at her until I realize it is me and I lower the gun. My hands are shaking and I wipe my palms on my jeans. The mirror is blown-out, with black spiderweb cracks and the wooden surface is covered with blackened silver-backed hairbrushes and long dead make-up jars and pots.

Time to blow this creepy pop stand. The floor is thickly carpeted and I don't make a sound as I rush down the narrow stairs, happy to be back in the normalcy of the living room with its floral sofas. I walk through to the kitchen and back to the bedroom with the quilted bedspread. I am tempted to sit on the bed and rest but I need to get my suitcase and the rest of my supplies out of the car. The day has flown and it's nearly eight o'clock at night.

I get everything inside and I tape the blackout curtain to the inside of the window just in case any neighbours across the lake will be alerted by a light in the abandoned old house.

I sit in the eerie silence and torchlit shadows, thinking that the pounding of my heart must surely be echoing throughout the entire house. I can't do this. I can't stay in this house. A cat gives a feral cry outside my window and I jump in terror and my eyes fill with tears. My great idea isn't turning out to be all that great and I might have to find a hotel instead. But I don't have enough cash for a hotel and Joe and Junior will be able to find me. I have no choice but to stay here. I fold my arms tightly across my chest and let the sad tears run down my face.

And then I hear Beatrice talking to me as loudly and clearly as if she is in the room with me. "Oh, for fuck's sake Julia, where are your big girl panties? I wouldn't have taken you for such a ninny. It's just a house. It's a refuge and you'll be safe. Relax, sunshine. Get some food into you and get some sleep."

I laugh and the vice of tension that gripped my body like an iron maiden melts away. I start unpacking and making myself at home.

I take the dry goods to the kitchen and I open a can of peaches and clean off one of Beatrice's forks. I stand in the flashlit kitchen, feasting on the sweetened fruit and the insane sugar rush restores my mood. I can do this thing. I *will* do this thing.

I finish my meal and rinse out the can so as not to attract ants. I spread my new sleeping bag onto the quilted bed and I lie down.

"Beatrice," I whisper quietly. "If you're Viewing me, which I hope you are, then thank you for letting me stay here. I'm wearing my big girl panties and there'll be no more panic wobbles."

I swear I hear her laugh. "It's all good. Don't worry, Julia, you're safe now."

Taking her at her word, I turn off my flashlight and fall fast asleep, a sleep plagued by nightmares of men with bloodhounds chasing me and Jan and Emma through tangled, hostile woods. My bare feet are shredded to bloody ribbons and we can hear the awful baying of the hounds as they close in on us. We aren't running fast enough and gap is closing.

When I wake, I am not sure which is worse, the terrifying dream or the reality I face.

42. TAKING CARE OF BUSINESS

I**T IS STILL DARK OUTSIDE** when I wake to the sound of my alarm. The blackout curtain works like a charm. I dress by the light of my flashlight, then I switch it off and pull the curtain aside. There is no sign of the coming dawn.

Hoping that I am ready for what lies ahead, and praying that all will go according to plan, I get into my car and drive west.

The previous day, I had texted Healey from the Walmart parking lot. *Do you want the drugs Agnes & Josh stole from you?*

The reply was quick to come. *Yes. Who r u?*

First give me Cockney's name & deets.

This time the reply took longer. *No.*

Okay. No deal.

I waited. Then: *He will meet u with me. Where?*

Where you killed Agnes & Josh. 4:30 am. Just you & Cockney or no deal. No wingmen and $350,000.00 cash. If you're late, I'll leave.

See u there.

I am the first to arrive. The parking lot is deserted and the world has yet to wake up. I am hoping that the early hour will work to my advantage, and that these guys will be less prepared than if they'd had more time to plan things.

I am wearing my black wig, my sunhat, black jeans, and running shoes.

A black SUV pulls into the parking lot. I lean against my car, a bag slung over my shoulder, my arms crossed.

The SUV parks close to me and the window rolls down. Healey's in the driver's seat. I walk a couple of steps closer to him.

"You're the…"

He never gets to finish his sentence. I shoot him twice in the head.

He falls face first onto the steering wheel and I have a clear view of Cockney who is sitting shotgun. He throws his hands up in instant surrender. His hair is a Mohawk, and snakes and ladders are tattooed on his neck and skull, and his fingers are shiny with thick gold rings.

"You killed Tracey's mother," I say. "Didn't you? You killed her on her birthday."

"The bitch stole from me," he shrugs. "She knew what would happen. It's on her, not me."

"And you supplied the bad drugs at the rave that killed all those kids?"

"I never forced them to take the drugs," he says. "If it wasn't me, someone else would have supplied. Listen, I've got a big bag of money here for you, let's not be stupid about this."

"This is for my friends," I tell him and I shoot him twice in head.

I hear a noise coming from the back of the SUV and I swing around. Two men are sitting in the back seat, frozen. I recognize them from Agnes' Viewing. They are the dickheads who helped trash Auntie Miriam's room.

"You want some of this?" I ask, waving the gun at them and they shake their heads, their hands held high.

"Get out and move Healey," I tell them and I keep the gun on them. This is taking longer than I had thought it would, although I hadn't believed for a moment that Healey and Cockney would come alone.

The parking lot is hidden from the lakeshore by a hedge and I pray that no one will drive down the small side street but the clock is ticking and the dog walkers and early morning cyclists will soon be out.

The two men scramble out of the SUV. The one man opens the back while the other grabs Healey. "Help me," he calls out to his partner. "He's fucking heavy." They lug him around and toss him unceremoniously in the back.

"We have to get Stan too," the one man says to me. "We can't drive off with a fucking dead man sitting in the front seat."

"Be quick."

I didn't have to tell him that. Seconds later Cockney is lying in the back next to Healey. The same guy jumps into the driver's seat and turns on the ignition.

"My money?" I ask, keeping my gun on them with my right hand and holding up the bag with my left.

"Here," the other guy leans into the back of the SUV, grabs a bag, and walks towards me.

"You got our stuff?" he asks, and I gesture to the bag at my feet. Maybe I get distracted for a moment because quick as a flash, while I am thinking about the exchange, he ducks around and grabs me from behind, putting his hand over my mouth and holding me around the waist.

I have been breathing heavily through my mouth the entire time, so when he clamps his hand across my face, my lips are wide open and in a split second all I can taste are his stubby, revolting, nicotined fingers in my mouth. I bite down as hard as I can, breaking the skin and drawing blood, and he howls, lets go of me, and then he bends over, clutching his injured hand.

"You stupid fuck," I say, spitting out blood and saliva. "Get away from me!" He backs up, holding his hand and I snatch the tote of money he dropped and unzip it quickly. It's filled with stacks of used $100 dollar bills. "Get into the car and get the fuck out of here," I say, and the man sitting at the wheel, with the engine revving, nods vigorously.

"What about our H?" the other man whines, clutching his hand to his chest.

"Just be happy you're alive," I tell him. "Now fuck off before I shoot you too. And you know I will." There was no way I was going to let them have this heroin and ruin the lives of other people.

"Ian, leave her alone, man, come on, we've gotta get outta here."

Still clutching his hand and scowling at me, Ian walks slowly backwards until he reaches the car, then rushes over to the passenger side and climbs in. The driver throws the car into gear and guns it out of the parking lot.

I get into my car and I look at my watch. The whole thing has taken less than fifteen minutes. I throw both bags onto the back seat. Hands shaking, I put the car into drive and curse when I stall the engine. Focus, concentrate. Restart the car, get moving.

I had been relatively calm while the whole thing was happening but now that it's over, I am flooded with nausea. I want to throw up the early morning coffee I bought from a gas station on the way but I don't want to stop, and I force the bile down and make myself carry on. I can't get the taste of blood out of my mouth and I use the dregs of cold coffee as mouthwash, and I spit out the window.

I head back towards Beatrice's house, and my nerves start to settle a little.

I have settled the score for Tracey, Samia, Agnes, Auntie Miriam, and even Josh. My chest fills with a sense of righteous satisfaction and I grin, once again reminding myself of Shirley the Driver. That thought makes me laugh out loud and next thing, I am cackling like a crazy woman. Hysteria or relief, it's hard to tell. I should feel some guilt for killing two men but I don't feel anything apart from satisfaction. They had it coming, both of them.

Suddenly ravenous, I pull into a diner next to a gas station. I lock both bags in the trunk and I go inside. I order a full breakfast of bacon and eggs with pancakes and a bottomless cup of black coffee. Someone has left a copy of *The Sun* newspaper on the table and I pick it up while I wait for my breakfast to arrive. I flip through it, finding nothing of any particular interest until I see a small story at the bottom of page five.

Plastic Surgeon Dies In Heroin Overdose.

It is a small story, no more than a paragraph really. Doctor Richard Silino, 47, was found dead in a motel with a syringe still in his arm. He had accidently overdosed.

I supposed he must have been partying before going to rehab and he went too far. I am not sorry he is dead. Were it not for Grace, I would have killed him too.

My breakfast arrives and I eat it slowly, savouring every bite while I sip my coffee.

Healey, Cockney, and Richard are taken care of. Dealing with Junior is not going to be nearly as easy.

43. PLANNING THE NEXT MOVE

BACK AT BEATRICE'S HOUSE, I hunt around for a good hiding place for the money, and I finally stash it under the mattress in the crib. I lay the money out flat and when I replace the mattress with the onesie and booties, you'd never know it was there.

I pull on a pair of thick rubber gloves and I dig a deep hole in the backyard under one of the trees. I put the bag of drugs inside it and I slice the packets open. I've wrapped a bandana around my face, to make sure I don't inhale anything by mistake. I pour gasoline on the drugs, making sure I ruin them. I had thought of weighing the bag down and dropping it into the lake but I didn't want to cause any kind of toxic waste to the fish, in the event the drugs leaked. Nor did I want to take the risk of anybody getting their hands on the drugs ever again. Once I make sure they are well and truly destroyed, I cover up the hole and go inside for a cold water scrub down.

It's time to plan Junior's demise.

Junior has a wife and three kids. I cannot remember how old the kids are. I know he told me at one time but I had no interest in them then.

Junior's wife, Sharon, owns a small couture boutique and she considers herself to be quite the style maven. Meanwhile, I consider her to be parochial at best, with an embarrassing fondness for reviving antiquated eighties' trends. She and Junior were high school sweethearts who married young. I saw pictures of their wedding, with Sharon emulating the late Princess Diana in a satin meringue dress with linebacker shoulder pads. The ten-foot train of seed pearl-encrusted fabric required an army of peach-clad bridesmaids to follow behind her as she arranged herself regally. She even wore a tiara.

While Junior and I were conducting our glorious two-year affair, I had not given any thought to Sharon and the children except to regard them as an occasional annoyance when Sharon put a kibosh on our plans because she wanted to do things like have a family Christmas.

Thinking about it now, I am baffled as to why Sharon put up with the whole thing, since we were far from discreet. But I guess at the time, she had no choice. Or, she only had two choices: put up with it or get a divorce. And then, once the great but tiny man was toppled from his perch, she was waiting with open and forgiving arms. But given that she was the one with the money, I didn't understand why she didn't dump him for a better model of husband and father.

I am quickly bored at Beatrice's house and I decide, on a whim, to drive past Junior's home. I had been there several times before, for cocktail parties, or the odd occasion when I had to wait for him in the living room while he ran into his study to get something, avoiding his kids' outstretched hands like a tourist avoiding beggars in India.

"Daddy's home!" they screamed with needy delight, following him, shrieking their commentaries at the same time while he fired off a few vague answers and we'd rush out as if we had narrowly escaped the gallows.

Sharon always managed to disappear when I was there, apart from the cocktail parties where she behaved as I didn't exist at all. In fact, I had admired her ability to block me out, while smiling graciously and playing the role of the perfect hostess.

I wonder what she made of the whole cuff-linked genitalia affair. It seems that her capacity for forgiveness is endless. That, or her ability to bury her head in the sand.

It takes me about an hour to get to his mansion in the leafy suburbs and when I pull up, I see a party is in full swing. A children's birthday party. I get out of the car and stroll up to take a closer look.

I am wearing my black-wig, red-lipsticked disguise and I fit right in with my summer dress and strappy sandals, my hat pulled down low, and my sunglasses in place.

I walk up the driveway as if I have been invited. It turns out to be the oldest boy's birthday, a kid called J.J., which is short for Junior Junior, but everybody mercifully agreed it would be a crime to actually call the boy that. So J.J. he is and now the little tyke is turning twelve.

"Welcome," a caterer offers a tray with a selection of drinks and I take an orange juice. "Everyone's out back."

"Great, thanks." I give him a great big smile and walk down the hallway and out into the enormous backyard where kids are jumping in an out of the swimming pool. A row of barbeques is fired up and ready for the first round of hamburgers. A kids' movie is showing in the gazebo for the younger lot who are sitting with their nannies while their parents laze on loungers or stand around chatting in civilized clusters. Two tables are loaded with snacks of both the kiddie and adult variety. I take a moment to hang out at the snacks table while I scout around. I can't see Sharon or Junior but I spot J.J. on a trampoline, doing summersaults and backflips and he's pretty good.

None of it is very interesting and I can't see anything that will be helpful to my cause. Sharon's pair of little pom-pom Pekinese are yapping and darting around like tiny fluffy hens while Junior's enormous Doberman, Snitch, is napping.

I walk back through the hallway of the house and that's when I spot Sharon and Junior. They are at the far end of the hall and they are chatting to someone, but I assume they will be heading my way soon. I duck into the kitchen that is a hive of frenzied activity, with the caterers opening containers, mixing things, and yelling at each other.

A pastry chef is intent on putting the finishing touches to a Nascar-style birthday cake. The car has J.J. on the hood, doors, and roof. The bonnet even has an accurate picture of the kid.

No one notices me and I sidle around the marble island in the centre and ease my way past the double-door, stainless steel fridge. The fridge is covered with photographs and colourful magnetic letters that spell out the children's names. There are schedules and reminders, along with notes from the school and, in the centre, there is a large, old-fashioned paper calendar with names penciled onto the days. Soccer, ballet, gymnastics, book club for Sharon, and hey, wait a minute, there's Las Vegas for Junior. He is going to be in Vegas for a week, three days from now. *Junior, Vegas, Annual Poker, Venetian.* All in Sharon's neat writing.

I know I should get the heck out of there, and I'm pushing my luck by staying but there's something I can't resist doing. I move the magnetic letters around and spell out: *silly bunny was here.*

I whip out my phone and take a picture of my artwork then I saunter back out into the hallway. Sharon and Junior are now at the other end, closer to the swimming pool, about to go outside. I walk away, as casual as can be but I see Sharon looking in my direction, and her body language tells me to pick up the pace.

I walk briskly down the driveway, hop into my car and drive off quickly, relieved that Sharon had not seen fit to chase after me and ask me who I was.

I am filled with glee. Junior is going to Vegas. And so am I.

44. MAKEOVER

I LEAVE JUNIOR'S HOUSE and I find a small park in the area. I pull up under a tree and switch on my phone. I send Junior a text message with the picture on his fridge. I would just hate for him to miss it.

The last time he had called me, it was from a private, unlisted number so I sent the message to the old number I had for him, and I didn't have to wait long before I got confirmation that it was still in use. *Think you're clever, JuLula? You bitch. This time I will kill you dead no doubt.*

I turn off the phone and drive back to Beatrice's house and on the way, something occurs to me.

Junior had lied about his alibi to the police. He said that he had been in Vegas at his annual poker tournament the night I was nearly beaten to death. But it hadn't been a year since it happened; it wasn't even six months.

I wonder if I should forget my own vendetta and take this fact to Joe, but Joe would want to know how I knew and besides, Junior would simply have his friends come up with another lie or say that they have two annual tournaments a year, or something like that.

No, I need to continue as planned.

I stop at a library and research flying with firearms. Apparently, I can take my pistol if I put it in my check-in luggage, and I need to declare it at customs. And I have to check it's okay with the airline I am flying with.

I go to the mall, and change back to my blonde self and I clean off the glaring red lipstick.

I go into the bank and withdraw five thousand dollars from the teller who counts out the cash with careful concentration. This trip is going to be expensive but it will be so worth it. I have the tote with the drug money, but I am wary of using it so soon after Healey and Cockney have been killed.

I find the Flight Centre, get the gun situation clarified, and I book myself a flight for the following day, paying in cash.

Then I get a haircut and some colour done. The blonde got blonder and we added some thick stripy highlights.

"You're sure this style is what you want?" the hairdresser studies the picture I show her. "It's a bit old-fashioned, if you don't mind my saying so. What you've got is much nicer."

"I'm sure," I tell her. "And if I hate it, we can change it. One thing about hair is that it grows back."

"Thank god it does," the hairdresser agrees, sanitizing her comb, "or I'd be out of a job."

After my hair makeover, I shop for clothes to match my new hairstyle and I find exactly what I am looking for, the exact cut, colour, and style, and I even find a purse to match.

Then I stop by an optician to see if they can fit me with a disposable contact lens so I won't have to wear my glasses and they find a match for my poor damaged eye.

The list is checked off.

And now, all I can do is wait. I consider buying a book to read or a magazine, but I can't concentrate on anything except my plan.

45. VEGAS

WHEN I LEAVE BEATRICE'S place the next day, I duct-tape the blackout curtain to the outside wall. I can't replace the heavy wooden boards but I do what I can to seal up the place. I thank Beatrice again for her hospitality and I drive to the airport and check the rental into the short-term parking.

My luggage passes through customs without any issues. Clearly it is not unusual for people to travel with firearms in their checked-in suitcases.

Once again there is nothing for me to do except wait, which is one of my least favourite non-activities. And once again I run through the plan I have in mind. One thing is for sure, I'll need Lady Luck on my side and I hope the gods and goddesses of good dice are with me.

As soon as I arrive in Las Vegas, I pick up a rental car and drive to The Best Western Plus Casino Royale. The hotel is on the Strip and close to the Venetian. I check myself in and then I go shopping for the supplies I'll need to carry out my plan.

Once I have everything, I set out to find myself the perfect escort. I pick up a bunch of cards and escort catalogues, or whatever they are called, and start my search. I need the right escort—a real leggy beauty, a class act—and as it happens, I don't only need one, I need four.

I start calling, using a new burner phone I picked up.

I have a list of questions and if there is a weird pause or silence, I thank the woman for her time and I hang up. I need someone with savvy, a woman who has her wits about her. I also need women with great glamour shots that Junior and Teddy, Junior's best buddy and partner in crime, will find irresistible.

Finally, after nearly four hours of fruitless calling, I realize this is much tougher than I had thought it would be. I hadn't been concerned with this aspect, figuring that escorts would be easy to find, but it's proving to be a worrying challenge.

I leave my hotel and walk to the Bellagio where I have a discreet conversation with the concierge who helps me out. At least I hope it was a productive discussion. I will wait to see the escorts in person before I start doing any celebratory dances.

46. THE PLAN IN MOTION

THE NEXT DAY I PUT ON my alter-ego black wig outfit and I sit in the lobby of the Venetian, waiting for Junior and the boys to arrive. They're impossible to miss. They rock in, loaded and rowdy, and I can only imagine what the plane ride must have been like with this noisy crowd of overgrown frat boys.

I'm familiar with Junior's boys because back in the day they had thought I was the hottest thing since sliced bread, but after what I did, sending out that photo, I understandably never heard from any of them again.

I think back to the night I was given that horrendous beating, how the second man just stood there watching. I try to match him to one of Junior's buddies but none of them fit, they are too tall and skinny or too short and fat. I wonder who Junior got to do his dirty work with him, and perhaps it says something about these guys that they weren't willing to be a part of it.

I watch them check in. They wheel their suitcases across the expanse of gold and cream marble and wait for the elevator. Junior's like a five-year-old kid at his birthday party, grinning and chirping like a hamster on speed. The boys are all eager to get their game on, party hard, get wasted, have fun. They are all about fun; meanwhile I nearly died. I lost not only my face, but the life I had built for myself. It may not have been the best life, the most well-lived life, that's for sure, but it was mine. I don't feel an ounce of remorse for the revenge I am going to exact.

I stay where I am until I see them come back down and leave the hotel. I go to the washroom and change my look to blonde and pretty, and I approach the front desk to work some magic.

Once I get what I need from the concierge, I return to the washroom and switch my look back the red-lipsticked brunette and I wait for a shift change, to make sure I won't be recognized. I hand the envelopes to the new concierge. "For Junior Loach and Teddy Whyte, can you make sure they get them? I'm not sure which rooms they're in?"

The concierge taps the keyboard and nods. "Yeah, they're here. No problem, I'll get someone to slip them under the doors. That's more reliable than waiting for guests to respond to a message and come to reception. Most people get so caught up in having a good time that they don't even notice phone messages."

I thank him and leave. And once again, all I can do is wait.

47. THE ESCORTS ARE PREPPED

"YOU NEED TO LET ME KNOW if you hear from them," I had told the escorts I had managed to hire. "You'll phone me, right, as soon as you hear? If they call, sound hot and eager, keep them interested. And if you don't hear from them, you need to let me know that too. I'll still pay you, but I need to know either way."

Much to my relief, I had found four perfect escorts and the puzzle pieces of my plan were all slotting neatly into place. The women told me they got it, no problem. I had met with each of them separately, so none of them had any knowledge of the others, and I was my blonde self the whole time, dressed in my spiffy new getup.

The day after Junior arrives in Las Vegas, two of the escorts call me, within twenty minutes of each other. "He's in," one of them reports, referring to Teddy.

"Good. Did he give you a room number and a time?"

"Yeah, Room 1209. He said six p.m."

Teddy is right next door to Junior.

"He's super keen," the next escort says about Junior.

Why am I not surprised? "Room 1211?" I double-check.

"Yeah, for six p.m."

"Great." I meet them and pay them, and they both tell me it is the easiest money they have ever made.

I meet the next two escorts separately. "You're on," I tell them and give them a room number and a time, and I pay

Teddy's escort in advance. "You'll call me once he's sorted?" I ask the one who is meeting Junior's.

"Don't worry," she says. "I'll get him good and ready."

I thank her and tell her I will pay her when I see her.

48. REUNITED WITH JUNIOR

THE FOLLOWING EVENING, shortly after sunset, I wait in my rental car in the parking lot. I have checked out of my hotel and I am waiting to hear from Junior's escort.

I've never been a nail-biter but I am chain-smoking cigarettes one after the other, and I am snapping gum so hard my teeth hurt. I am going crazy waiting for the call. As it gets closer to the time, I haul the suitcase out of the trunk and I lock the car. I approach the hotel, wheeling the large suitcase, with my phone in hand and finally, the call comes. Game on.

I wave off the bellboy who offers to help me with my luggage and I make my way up to Junior's room. The escort I've hired opens the door. "He's out cold," she says. "He drank the champagne like it was a soda, didn't notice there was anything in it, and then he fell asleep."

"Thank you," I tell her and I pay her.

She picks up her purse and leaves. I had told her I was Junior's wife and that I wanted to catch him cheating so he wouldn't be able to lie to me any more. She had nodded casually when I told her to put sleeping pills into his drink, and I realized the less said, the better; all she cared about was being paid.

I had pulled a classic switch hustle. I had sent the glamour shots to Junior and Teddy and those were the girls they had spoken to on the phone. But a second, different set of leggy women arrived for the hookups. There were no glamour shots of these girls and no one would have any idea who they were or where they could have come from. I instructed the first set of girls to be in the public eye during the time the whole thing was going down and, when questioned, they were to say yes, they had dropped their shots off, and they'd spoken to the guys on the phone but neither Junior nor Teddy had set up an actual date. The second girls would be ghosts in the night and as for the concierge at the Bellagio, he had seen exactly what I wanted him to.

I look at Junior who is lying on his back, snoring.

I pull him across the bed, using the satin coverlet to drag him and he flops easily into the suitcase. I tuck him in, all nice and cozy and I hope he will have enough air. I don't want him to suffocate before I have the chance to kill him.

I also hope he won't wake up in the elevator and start banging around.

I slap some duct tape across his mouth and bind his hands and feet. Granted there is not much space inside the suitcase for banging or thrashing around.

I ease the suitcase upright on its wheels and I give the room a careful once over. I have removed the girl's glamour shot and I have worn gloves the whole time I have been in Junior's room, but I am still worried. Did I miss anything? I can't torment or second guess myself. I have been careful and cognizant; I need to trust the plan.

The ride down in the elevator takes a lifetime. I am joined by an elderly couple and a family with four young kids who are excited by the prospect of a buffet dinner. It is a tight squeeze and my breath is trapped in my throat until we reach the ground floor where I exhale and take a big gulp of air.

I exit through the main doors and I am relieved when none of the porters or valets stop me and offer to help. I wheel the suitcase to the car and I open the rear passenger door.

One thing I have not calculated is how heavy the suitcase will be with Junior in it. After a number of tries, I realize there's no way I'll get be able to get it onto the back seat. Sweat is pouring down my face and I wipe it away. I'm stuck, and I have no idea what I am going to do.

"Want some help?" A burly man stops.

"Yes, please," I say. "Too much shopping. And my trunk is already full. I know I should have split this into two smaller cases, but this just seemed easier. Thank you for your help."

By the time I am finished babbling, the man has hefted the case into the car and he shrugs and smiles.

"Piece of cake," he says.

"You're a lifesaver," I tell him as he leaves, and I am well aware of the irony of what I have just said. I wipe my forehead with a tissue and I drive away with Junior in the suitcase on the backseat of my car.

I drive until I am out of central Vegas, and I pull into a dimly-lit side street and turn off the engine. I get into the back of the car and open the suitcase without too much difficulty, having practiced this maneuver.

To my relief, Junior is still breathing, and he is out cold. I roll the suitcase out from under him and he falls onto the backseat, and I check the bindings on his hands and feet.

For good measure, I stretch the seatbelt around him and manage to get him buckled in, just in case he wakes up and gets any ideas about trying to lunge at me even with his hands tied.

I cover him with a blanket, and he looks like a sleeping kid.

I put the suitcase into the trunk of the car and I hit the highway and drive into the desert, taking my carefully mapped out route. My car is full of gas and things are going well.

But I start shaking uncontrollably. My whole body is vibrating, and it is hard to breathe and my chest feels tight. I am overcome with dizziness and I can't see and there is a loud, high-pitched ringing in my ears. I pull over onto the dirt and lean my head on the steering wheel.

I have missed something. I know I have. I'll be caught, tried for murder, and put away for the rest of my life. And what on earth am I thinking? I have a man bound, drugged, and gagged in the back of my car and I am planning to kill him in cold blood. I can't do this. This is wrong, evil, on so many levels. I'll have to drop him off somewhere off the Strip and hopefully when he comes to, he'll just think it was a sex game that went wrong or something. There's nothing that will lead them to me. I'll leave Vegas and get on with my life and put this whole mess behind me.

But then I turn and look at Junior on the backseat and it all comes back to me. The humiliation, the beating, the pain, my ruined face, my damaged body. His phone calls, his brutality.

No. He is not going to get away with it. He's not going to win. And if I let him go, he'd come after me again, no doubt about it. I have no choice. I have to kill him. I can do this. I will do this. I repeat my mantra again. And I tell myself the same thing I told myself in the hotel, that I need to trust myself, my plan is sound. I take a few deep breaths and drink some water. My head clears and my heart slows down and I feel resolve settle into my bones. I sit up straight and start the engine.

And I carry on driving, out into the desert.

49. JUST DESERTS

WHEN HE COMES TO, Junior is sitting on the ground in front of the car, with his hands behind his back, securely tied to the front bumper. His legs are spread out in front of him and his ankles are tightly bound. I am sitting cross-legged in front of him, wrapped in a thick blanket.

The desert night is cold although it is high summer. Junior is illuminated by a flashlight that I am aiming at his face.

"Hey baby," I say, and I turn the flashlight on myself.

It's safe to say that Junior is not happy to see me. "What the fuck? Sharon?"

"I look like her, don't I?" I say and at the sound of my voice, he goes ashen. It's satisfying to watch the colour drain from his face.

"Julia? What the fuck? Why do you look like Sharon?"

I shrug. "It just worked out that way. Trust me, when I first saw myself, I wasn't too ecstatic. A leftover cheerleader from the eighties isn't what I would have chosen, but the surgeon did what he could with the pieces you left, and this is the result. But," I add, and I casually wave my hand around, "it worked out fine for me."

He peers into the darkness that surrounds us. "It did? We're in the middle of fucking nowhere," he says and then he realizes what that means.

"Yeah, the middle of nowhere," I say. "Just you and me. Isn't this romantic?"

"You fucking bitch," he says.

"Gee. Even now you can't be nice. I'm waiting for the charming Junior to appear, the one who can sell anything to anyone, anytime, anywhere. I know he's in there. You'll bring him out as soon as you realize how serious I am and that this isn't a joke."

As if to make my meaning clear, I take out my gun. And in that moment, I see him realize that I am not joking.

"Julia," he says quietly, "I—"

"I was right," I interrupt him. "Here comes Mr. Nice Guy. 'Julia,'" I mimic him, "'I'm sorry for what I did to you. C'mon, baby, let me go. We'll leave here and be the best of friends and everything will be hunky and dory, like I never tried to kill you twice."

"Julia," he says and his voice is even, "I was going to say that I will never regret having beaten you to within an inch of your motherfucking cunting life and if I had the chance, I would do it all again, only this time, I'd do it even more slowly and I'd make sure to hurt you much, much more."

"I guess I should be relieved that we're having an open and honest conversation," I reply. "I thought you'd try and sell me a story, like you did when we met."

"I never sold you anything. You think I'm a terrible person? No more than you. We're a match made in hell. You think what I did to you was bad? I can never go anywhere, EVER, without people thinking about that photo when they see me. How would you like that?"

"You fired me," I retort. "You didn't even have the decency to do it yourself or give me any kind of warning or do it in a way that would have been kind. You took away the career I spent my whole life building. You took away every single thing that mattered to me, and you did it in the worst possible way. And then you went to breakfast with your little buddies, while I was walking home by myself, fired, with nowhere to go and no one to be with. You took away our friendship that day too. We were lovers, friends, allies, business partners. You amputated me, Junior, and you threw me out like garbage. You got what you deserved with that photo."

We sit in silence for a while after that.

"So you're pretending to be Sharon," he says. "Like that's going to work. Sharon does a thousand things in her day. She'll have more people to alibi her than the police will know what to do with."

I shrug. "Yeah but at least it won't have been me here. Remember J.J.'s birthday party? I took Sharon's driver's license. You guys should be more careful, the house was wide open and no one even noticed me."

"Right, *silly bunny was here.*"

"And look," I say brightly and I unwrap my blanket, "all Sharon's clothes. I bought the same things she was wearing that day, right down to the purse, although I got a knockoff because my days of Michael Kors were over the moment you canned me. But I've been Sharon all the way and my alibi back home is tighter than a duck's ass."

"The girl in my room, she came from you?"

"Yeah. And Teddy's too. I got him one so you wouldn't feel special, being singled out. I thought if Teddy bought it, you would too."

"But the girl who showed up wasn't the same as the one in the picture?"

"There were lots of girls," I say. "I wanted to change them up, create confusion. They came from different places, so if you're thinking that either of Teddy's girls will be helpful to the police, think again. The girls don't know anything about each other, or about you."

"And now you're going to kill me."

"Yeah, I am. Any final words of wisdom for the world?"

He sighs. "You may or may not want to believe this but being with you was the best time of my life. You were beautiful and powerful and you had the greatest fuck-you attitude ever."

"Ah, now we reach the point where you try to sweet talk your way out of this."

"Like I said, you can believe it or not. And, believe this or not, I was gutted when they let you go. It wasn't my decision. There wasn't anything I could have done about it. It wasn't personal."

"It sure as fuck felt personal. And if you were so gutted, why didn't you tell me yourself? Why didn't you text me afterwards or contact me or anything? Oh yeah, you were gutted alright."

"I wasn't legally allowed to," he says. "It was a mandate. They told me I had to stay away from you."

"They? Who the fuck is they?"

"The Board of Directors and the human resources department. They said if I did, I'd get fired and I wouldn't get any kind of package either and you might think I've got money but I don't, it's Sharon's. So I couldn't get in touch with you even though it nearly killed me."

"And yet, talking about killing, you managed to find me and try to kill me, not once but twice. Really, Junior, do you think I'm an idiot?"

"I'm telling you the truth. I may have tried to kill you but I've never lied to you. Think about it. Think about us. What we had was spectacular. Don't you think I would have been with you if I could have? Don't you think I would have warned you, if I could have? I couldn't do anything, my hands were tied."

"A situation you find yourself in once again," I point out.

I am silent for a moment. What he said made sense. I had seen people walked off the property in a matter of minutes, and I had always felt smug, incredulous at their stupidity for having let it happen. And it was true that we were told not to get in touch with anybody, but to let a cooling down period create some distance and perspective. It had never bothered me before because I had thought those who were fired deserved it in some way and besides, I never got close to anybody I worked with; everyone was replaceable.

"But why me? Why was I fired?"

He shrugs. "They bought the Buffalo Bills and couldn't afford them. They needed to make cuts to save money and they brought in some numbers guys who looked at the books and chopped a whole bunch of people. You weren't the only one let go that day, hundreds were, across the country. You would have seen it in the papers if you weren't so busy trying to humiliate me."

"But still," I say, "there must have been something you could have done—written me a note to say you'd be in touch, something."

"And you would have kept your mouth shut?"

He has a point there.

"Julia," he says "I mean it, we were special you and me. Things got out of control when it all went down. Let's face it, we're dynamite together and instead of blowing up the world, we blew up each other. I'm sorry I tried to kill you. But can you imagine my humiliation? I couldn't go to work, I couldn't face my friends or the guys at the golf course, anyone. You destroyed my life and so I tried to destroy you. But if you go back to before you got let go, it was so great. You were the best friend I ever had. Being with you, my whole life made sense. I didn't have to be the good husband, or the good father, or the good buddy. I was just me, nasty me, who got off on being powerful. You made me feel like I was a god. When I had you on my arm, it was like the whole fucking universe was mine. And fucking you was incredible. But it wasn't only that. You were my soul mate. You were. Tell me you didn't feel that too?"

"Of course I did, you idiot. Why do you think I was so shocked when you dumped me like you did? I also thought we had something real. But clearly we didn't."

"But I've explained that," he says and he sounds desperate. "There was nothing I could do. Nothing."

I can't think of anything to say to that.

"You know my best memory of us?" he asks. "Remember

that charity ball that went on for hours and we stayed up all night? We drove down to the lake and watched the sun come up. It was cold as a witch's tit, but you looked incredible. You were wearing that gold sequined dress and we held hands and watched the sunrise."

Bastard. Why did he have to bring up that? It was a magical moment, one I had even told Cedar about.

"Everything was golden," he says. "Nothing else mattered. It was just you and me, with the rest of the world fast asleep. I didn't want anything or anyone except you."

"Yeah, that was a good time," I say and my voice cracks.

"We can have that again," he says and his voice is quiet and sure, but I laugh.

"Yeah, really, Junior? And how can we do that?"

"I've got money now. After what the company did you to you, I found a way to shave off a couple of mill that I've got in a Swiss bank account. I figured if they did that to you, they could do it to me too, and I didn't want some little payoff. I wanted it to be worth my while, all the work I've done for them. They're so stupid, they'll never even realize what I did."

"So what, you and I, we'll run away together?"

"Yes. Leave today. Do you think I care about Sharon or my kids or anything? I don't. I only care about you. We could go and live in Monte Carlo or anywhere you like, start again, just you and me."

"Sure. And I'd sleep soundly at night, next to the man who tried to kill me twice."

He winces. "Look Julia, like I said, I reacted to what you did. I know how terrible it must have been for you that day they let you go, but you should have trusted me. You should have believed that I would have come to you as soon as I could. Nothing mattered to me except you."

"You seemed pretty happy at home the day of the party," I tell him. "Mr. I've Got Everything. Great wife, great kids, great house. Mr. Perfect."

"You were gone! I didn't have anything left except for Sharon and the kids. What did you want me to do, sit around crying? For fuck's sake, Julia, think about it. What else could I have done?"

"But I don't even look like Julia anymore."

"You're still you. And you've got that killer body. Oh man, I'll never forget that day on the stairwell. I get hard just thinking about it. Come here, feel me, if you don't believe me."

I cannot believe this guy. I am there to kill him and he wants me to feel his hard-on. Feeling stupid but unable to help myself, I shrug off my blanket and edge towards him, keeping my gun trained on him. I reach down and the crazy bastard is right, he is hard as a rock, with that little cock straining at his underpants.

I undo his belt with one hand, unzip his pants and stroke him. I lean down and take him in my mouth, pulling away just before he comes.

He groans. "Why are you stopping?"

"Because I want to kiss you."

I lean into him and we tongue like teenagers, kissing for what feels like hours and then I lean down and finish what I started.

Junior. There has always been something electric between us, something irresistible. I wipe my mouth and move away from him, and wrap myself in my blanket.

"Come on, Julia," he says, his voice low and disarming. "Let's run away together. You and me. We'll rule the universe and be happy. Tell me you've ever loved anybody like you love me. We were made for each other and you know it. We'll put the past behind us and conquer new worlds. Get into movie making, try some different shit. We're a powerhouse together, baby and you know it."

I look at him and I am, insanely, about to consider it, when I see something. His lying twitch. His bottom lip does that little thing, that little sideways jig it does when he is lying. I watch him and I see it do it again.

I laugh. "Well done, Junior. You nearly had me."

"What do you mean?" he sounds panicked and so he should.

"Remember I told you how your voice changes when you lie? There's another thing you do too. Your bottom lip does this little twitchy thing and you did it now."

"What the fuck? You don't believe me now because of some facial muscle spasm? You've got a gun on me, I'm surprised my entire face isn't going crazy."

I sigh. "Nope. Not buying it. But hey, at least you went out with a bang."

"You're seriously going to kill me? Come on Julia, we're soul mates."

And there it is again, that twitch and this time even he is aware of it, and he bites his lower lip, catching it between his teeth as if he can save himself that way.

"Interesting," I say, sounding quite disinterested. "Where was I before you tried to sell me a bill of goods? Right, I was going to kill you. Time to get back on track."

"You fucking bitch. You cunt. Fuck you, Julia Redner, and the horse you rode in on. You're right, you crazy fucking bitch, if you think for a moment that I was in love with you, you're dreaming. You're the craziest fucking bitch I've ever met."

"Eloquent," I say and I get to my feet.

"And I lied," he shouts. "I could have got in touch with you but I didn't want to. I was glad to get rid of you. You were like a fucking anchor around my neck. I never met a woman as clingy or needy as you. You were like fucking seaweed, strangling me. And it wasn't the Board of Directors or human resources or the money men who axed you, it was me! Me! I had the power and I'd enough of you and I wanted you gone. We were nothing, you and me, nothing! And I was sick and tired of you. You know the worst thing about you, Julia? You are so fucking boring. Boring! I hated being with you by the end, I hated it. Boring, vain Julia, thinking she's Anna Wintour. You're a legend in your own lunch box, Julia."

"I've never owned a lunch box in my life," I tell him.

I go around to the back of the car, letting him rant his heart out, and I throw the blanket into the back. I walk back to Junior and he looks up at me. "I know about your pretty little niece," he says. "Kill me and she's dead too."

The shock of what he says brings me to my knees and I crash onto the hard desert earth, skinning the palm of my hand. I nearly lose my grip on my gun but I grab it tightly.

"What?" I say. "What did you say?"

"If I disappear, my buddy, the big guy who helped me out with you, he'll take care of your niece."

I am about to throw up. It hadn't occurred to me that Junior might know about Emma. I don't know what to do.

"You're lying," I say and I watch him carefully for tics but there is nothing and I can hardly think straight.

Emma. I have put Emma at risk. How could I not have thought of that? And then it happens. The facial tic. Junior's bottom lip twitches.

"You're lying again," I say, so relieved I want to throw up. "You know about Emma but you haven't said anything to anyone about using her as insurance. Why would you have? You had no idea I was going to get you. You felt safe and secure. You underestimated me. But how did you find out about her?"

"Evan followed you. You, and that cop, Joe."

"Evan who?" I ask, but he grins and shakes his head.

"Evan who?" I repeat and he looks at me with pity.

"Hard to say," he says, "when I'm trussed up like a turkey and freezing to death."

I look at my gun for a moment and then I take aim and shoot him in the thigh. The scream he makes is ungodly and earth-shatteringly loud. I rip off a piece of duct tape and slap it against his mouth, which is tricky to do, since he's writhing around like a lizard that's just lost its tail.

I wait for him to stop thrashing around and he finally slows down. Tears are streaming down his face and I can see he's struggling to breathe through the snot and mucous.

"I am going to ask you again," I say. "I will take your tape off and you will tell me Evan's full name. I don't believe you said anything to him about using Emma in the event of your disappearance but I need to know who he is. And if you don't answer me, there goes your other leg. And after that, I'll work my way through the various parts of your anatomy until you do tell me."

He nods mutely and I take the tape off and he can't get the words out fast enough. "Evan Anders. He's the security guy at my golf club. After you sent the pic to the whole world, I got drunk at the club and he drove me home that night, and he said he could help me." He babbles like a kid.

"Evan Anders," I say. "Thanks. I'll be sure to reach out to him. And now it's time for you to shuffle off this mortal coil, you evil piece of shit."

But then I remember there's something else I needed to ask him. "Who tipped you off about me changing my name? And who gave you my unlisted number?"

"A cop in the department. She likes to party and I got pictures of her with her face in a fishbowl of blow. And before you shoot me again, her name is Theresa May and good luck to her with you on her tail. So listen Julia, let's be reasonable, even if I'm not the greatest guy on the planet—"

He starts begging again and I slap the tape back on. I go around behind him, so I am leaning across the hood of the car, and I aim the gun at the back of his head, wanting to shoot away from the car so as not to get any blood on it.

"Sayonara, baby," I say. "Just so you know, I am going to kill you now." I pull the trigger and the bullet passes through the back of his head and explodes out of his forehead.

"Now you've lost your face, just like I did," I tell him conversationally as he slumps forward.

I have worn gloves the whole time in the car, even when I first picked it up from the airport. But I dig in the trunk and put on a new pair, not wanting to transfer any gunshot residue to the steering wheel from the pair I was wearing when I shot Junior. I drop the old pair into a plastic bag.

I grab a bottle of bleach, a rag, and a garbage bag from the trunk and I walk back to Junior. I make sure to stay out of the path of any blood spatter.

I cut the tape holding him to the bumper and roll him away from the car. I remove all the tape from him and crumple it up and put it into the garbage bag. I remove his clothes, cutting them off with a knife, and I stuff them into the bag too.

"There's a little matter of DNA to get rid of," I tell his dead body and I uncap the bottle of bleach and I pour a load onto his privates. I lean down and scrub a bit, making sure that I clean him off properly and then I rinse what's left of his face with a generous shower. For good measure, I get a second industrial-sized bottle of bleach from the trunk and I make sure he is soaked from head to toe, back and front.

I step away from him. There isn't much left of the man formerly known as Junior. He lies crumpled on the desert ground, pathetic and no longer a danger to anyone. I roll his body into a small gully that I know is behind where I was sitting.

I take a deep breath and I look at the clear, starry skies above and I hear a coyote call out and it sounds like a victory cry. My life is finally my life again and I am going to make the most of it.

But first I need to cover my tracks and get the heck out of here. I get into the car, put it into reverse, and drive it a few metres away. I examine the front of the car with my flashlight but there is no blood to be seen. I drive off, glancing at my watch. I am running later than I had planned, but I hadn't factored in a make-out session with Junior.

Dawn is a fiery glow on the horizon of the eastern sky and the Joshua trees are hunched silhouettes. I think about Junior, lying alone and naked in that desert ditch. I had chosen my location carefully, and I had scouted it out a few days earlier.

It was not a place for hikers or tourists or even local traffic. It was just an old, unused road that led out into the desert and the odds on them ever finding Junior were slim to none. And even if they did, he was clean as whistle as far as evidence went.

I drive for an hour and I pull in at a gas station with a car wash. I get the vehicle detailed, paying extra for super gloss and a double wash inside and out. There is another car being buffed and polished and I'm glad I am not the only conspicuous customer. While I am waiting, I throw the garbage bag into the trash, making sure no one is watching me.

I get back on the road and look for a place to get rid of the suitcase. After a while, I pull into a run-down strip mall and drive around to the back parking lot. Just as I expect, there are dumpsters lining the shabby place and I make good use of them, triple-checking that I leave no evidence of myself behind.

I remove the ammunition from my gun and I put the bullets and pistol into the airport regulations box and tuck it among my clothes.

Then I drive to the airport and return my vehicle. I check in and wait for the flight that will take me home. I'd love to have a drink at the bar but I need to stay out of sight as much as possible. The time for celebrating will come later.

50. SKEPTICAL JOE

B Y THE TIME I ARRIVE HOME at Beatrice's place, it is late in the afternoon. I thought I would feel tired and want to sleep but I am too wired. I keep thinking about how things went, still wondering if I missed anything.

I change out of 'Sharon's' clothes and stuff them into a brown paper bag. I have a poor man's shower at the kitchen sink, and I scrub my face and body. The water is ice cold and I am shivering by the time I am done. I check the time. The mall will still be open. I drive to the hairdresser.

"I hate this look," I tell her. "You were right, it's too old-fashioned. Can you change it? Do anything you like, I don't care."

"You're lucky I got a cancellation," the woman says. "Charlene will shampoo you. I've got an idea for a style I think you'll love. Think Audrey Hepburn."

And I do love it. I leave my frumpy suburban look behind and I walk out, styling a modern shorn feathered look. I stop and have a burger at the local diner, and by the time night falls, I am beginning to feel tired.

I drive home and as soon as I am tucked up in my sleeping bag, I fall fast asleep. There are no men chasing me, no forests, no machetes, and I enjoy the sound dreamless sleep of the vindicated.

When I wake up, I make a small fire in the backyard in a steel bin I get from Walmart. I burn Sharon's license, the receipt for parking the car at the airport, all the clothes, the black wig, the spangly earrings, the sunhat, and even the shoes. I take the ashes and the bucket and dump them in a field where no one will find them.

Next, I take my gun to the firing range and do some practicing and I get the pistol cleaned.

I make myself wait for three long, boring days before I rejoin the real world. I want to make sure that the timing isn't suspicious, Junior vanishes and then, *voilà*, out I trot.

Finally, I run through a mental checklist a few times and I make the call. "Joe?" My voice is tremulous.

"Lula? Where are you? We've been going out of our minds with worry. You never picked up your phone. It kept going to voice mail. We realized we never got the name of the clinic you were going to. Ella and I have been going crazy."

"I can explain," I say. "Can you meet me at the Starbucks at the Westside mall?"

"Yeah, sure, I'll be there in half an hour."

I rehearse my story a few times while I wait for Joe. This is going to be a real test. Joe is no dummy and I have to be absolutely convincing. The palms of my hands are wet with sweat and I am shaking. He looks so concerned and happy to see me that I feel bad for all the lies I am going to have to tell him.

He orders a coffee. "You changed your hair," he says. "Looks good. How is your knee? Why didn't you pick up your phone? Where was the clinic? Lula, we've been out of our minds."

"There is no clinic," I tell him and his brow narrows and he sits back in his chair. "And you were right. It was Junior who tried to kill me the second time. I didn't tell you because there was no way you could prove it, and I thought he was done with me and that he'd leave me alone. I thought that if I accused him of anything that it would just stir things up. So I lied. I am sorry Joe, I couldn't go there."

He is silent. He sits there listening, his coffee untouched, looking at me.

"But he didn't leave me alone," I say, and my eyes fill with tears. "He called me, on my new cell, and he called me Lula. He knew. He said he was coming to get me and this time he would make sure I died."

"Why didn't you call me?" Joe asks. "I would have protected you."

"I panicked. I needed time to think. I was worried that I would put Emma in danger. All kinds of things were going through my head." I look at him. "I didn't even know if I could trust you, Joe. How did Junior know about Lula? No one knew about that except for you, and Emma and Bev."

"And you thought I told Junior?" He looks angrier than I have ever seen him.

I shrug. "What would you have thought?" I'm dying to tell Joe about Theresa May but I can't. That's a secret I'll have to carry to my grave. "I got paranoid Joe. I lost trust in everybody. I don't know, I even thought maybe Bev told Junior to get me out of the picture, so she could keep Emma. And I thought maybe you had made a mistake and let something slip about me, or maybe someone overheard you talking about my new identity. Or I thought maybe your partner Dan had been bought off by Junior. I had all kinds of ideas on how everybody on the planet could have betrayed me. I see now that I was just filled with panic, but wouldn't you have been? Put yourself in my shoes."

He thinks about that for a moment. "Yeah, maybe. I'll get to the bottom of how Junior found out," he says. "It could have been a cop in the department. Or someone at the district attorney's office. I'm going to find out. But where have you been?"

"Off the grid. I'll show you. A woman in the hospital told me about a place her aunt had near Ecum Secum Lake and how the place was tied up in inheritance battles and it's been standing empty forever. I rented a car, drove myself there, and that's where I've been, the whole time."

Joe picks up his coffee and takes a swallow. "All this time? You've been hiding out in an abandoned house all this time?"

"Yes. I know I should have called but I needed to time to think."

"And you're coming to me now."

"Because I realize I can't stay in hiding forever and I don't know what to do. He's going to kill me, Joe. Please, help me. I need your help."

"Have you heard from him recently?" Joe asks and I don't like where this is going.

"Not since he sent me a text message. He called me and then he sent me a text to say he is going to kill me. I can show you."

"Junior's not going to kill you," Joe says. "As a matter of fact, he's gone missing."

"What do you mean, missing? What happened?"

"You sure you've been here in town all this time?"

I start to get angry. "Of course I have. Where else would I be? I've been driving around in my rental car, going out into the country, hanging out here at the mall. Gets tired fast, I'll tell you that. Then, I did some shooting at the range and that's the extent of my exciting life since you saw me. What's the story with Junior?" I ask.

"We don't know for sure. He went to play poker with some buddies in Vegas, an annual thing, and someone comped him a stripper and next thing, he's gone."

I think about mentioning the fact that Junior lied about the annual poker tournament, using it as an alibi for not being around when someone tried to kill me, but I figure the less I say about the whole thing, the better.

"Knowing Junior, he's on a sex binge with her somewhere," I suggest, but Joe shakes his head.

"They found her. She said they did the dirty, but when she left he was still alive. We've got footage of her going down in the elevator, and Junior wasn't with her.

I'm taken aback that they found the woman. I had banked

on the glamour shots confusing things. But it didn't matter, she had kept her mouth shut, thank god. *Thank you,* I tell the woman silently. *You didn't give me up.*

"Funny thing," Joe says. "All the evidence is pointing to Sharon."

"Sharon? His wife?" I am shocked. "Well, he did humiliate her repeatedly, so I guess it makes sense that she would finally snap."

"She's a soccer mom," Joe says. "Her little dress shop and her family mean everything to her. I can't see her having killed her husband. He was a shit but she loved him. Anyway, she's got about a hundred alibis for the time he went missing."

"But then why do they think she was involved?"

"Because someone who looked like her was scampering around Vegas, flashing her driver's license."

"And you think it was me? You're saying it in as many words, Joe. If that's what you think, say it."

"It's just odd how you disappeared the same time he left town, and then he comes up missing and you show up asking for my help."

"I disappeared after he sent me this!" I show him my phone with the message *Think you're clever, JuLula? You bitch. This time I will kill you dead no doubt.*

"Trace it, you'll see it came from his phone. I disappeared after he phoned me and after he sent me this." I had, of course, deleted the text that I had sent Junior with *silly bunny was here* on it.

Joe is studying me. "Come to think of it," he says, "you do look a bit like Sharon." He screws up his eyes and cocks his head to one side. "Put a different haircut on you, take off the glasses, and you could pass for her. I never noticed it till now."

My face turns ashen. "Joe? What the fuck? You can't seriously mean that. And how do you think that makes me feel? Now I'm going to think of Sharon every time I look at myself in the mirror. That's enough to make me want to kill myself."

My horror at him having connected the dots of Sharon's and my appearance makes the depths of my emotion ring true and Joe raises his hands in surrender. "I went a bit too far there," he says. "Forget I said that. But I'll need to see where you claim to have been living and I'll need you to come down to the station with me and put this in a formal statement."

"Of course," I say and I get up. "Let's get this done so I can put it behind me and get on with my life. I'm not going to tell you that I'm sorry he's missing. He's scum. How can I be sure he won't pop up again and try to kill me? You don't even know for sure that he's dead. Missing isn't dead."

Joe shrugs and we leave. He follows me to Beatrice's house and we climb in through the window and I show him around.

"Creepy," he says. "I wouldn't stay here, not if you paid me a million bucks."

"I was desperate," I tell him.

I take him upstairs, careful not to look at the crib where the drug money is stashed but Joe can't wait to get out of there and I needn't have worried.

"Not for a million bucks," he repeats as we stand outside in the garden and he rubs his hand across his face. "I had this weird *déjà vu* in there. And I felt like a bunch of ghosts were watching us. Did you feel anything?"

I shake my head. I am certain he will ask me for details of the woman in hospital who mentioned the place and I am ready to say that I can't remember exactly, I only remembered what she had said about the location. But he doesn't ask me anything else; he is keen to leave.

I follow him to the station in my car and, once I am there, I continue my rant of the possible dangers of the reappearance of the missing Junior and I get quite wound up.

By the time I have repeated my story over a dozen times and endured countless interrogations, close to eight hours have passed. I sign a statement and nearly everyone believes my story. The cops check the mileage on my car and it supports my claims of having driven around aimlessly. My gun is checked, as well as my story of having recently practiced at the firing range and everything ties up neatly.

"You're free to go," the Deputy Chief tells me and I thank him.

"What are you going to do now?" Joe asks as he walks me to my car.

"I am going to go back to my apartment and I'm going to have the longest, hottest bath ever. Washing with cold water out of a kitchen sink sucks, I'll tell you that. Listen, Joe," I stop. "You still think it was me, don't you?"

"We're friends," Joe says awkwardly. "I never want that to change."

"But it has."

He sighs. "There's something weird about this whole thing," he says. "I can't put my finger on it. But I'm still here if you need me."

I get into my car and snap the seatbelt in place. I open the window and Joe leans his hand on the door trying to find the right thing to say but he can't come up with anything and he steps back. He looks tired and drawn and I feel bad for what I am putting him through.

"You're a good friend to me, Joe," I say. "Love to Ella. Will you ask her to give me a call?"

"Yeah, sure," Joe says and I look at him, wishing there was something else I could say to fix things but knowing there isn't. I drive off and when I look in the rearview mirror, he is still standing there, watching me.

I've lost him and that hurts. But it couldn't be avoided and I did what needed to be done.

PART III: **HERE AND THERE**

51. PURGATORY

I FIND NO PEACE back at my apartment. I can't rid myself of thoughts of Junior's last call to me when I was so terrified. I try to soak in the tub but I am restless and nothing soothes my nerves. I am determined to get some sleep and I take not one but a couple of sleeping pills. I want to be transported into the land of sound and dreamless sleep, but instead I bounce back to Purgatory.

I come to in one of the white hallways and hear a beeping sound and I nearly get run down by Shirley the Driver who barrels past me, grinning.

"What the fuck?" I say, looking around. "What am I doing here?"

"Welcome," Agnes says popping up next to me. "This is Purgatory and I am Agnes. I will be your Introducer."

I grab her and hug her. "Agnes! Good to see you! But why the fuck am I here? Did I die again? Did two sleeping pills kill me?"

"Calm down, calm down," Agnes pats me on the back and extricates herself. "Glad to see you're still your usual hysterical self. You didn't die. You're here to check in, that's all. Calm down, grasshopper, and follow me."

I am soon back in the caf with the others, inhaling the aroma of a fresh tray of Tracey's cookies and there are mugs of coffee all round.

"I am so happy to see you," Samia says excitedly. "We've been Viewing you the whole time. Could you feel us?"

I shake my head. I don't want to disappoint her but I cannot tell a lie. "But I did feel like Beatrice was talking to me, in her house," I say.

"Yeah, I was," Beatrice says in her gravelly voice. "I told you to stop being such a ninny. And before you think I'm a basket case, what with the upstairs bedroom and the baby stuff, that was my sister's. Her infant was stillborn and she lost her mind. We always lived together, her and me. We inherited the house from our granny. Anyways, my sister gets pregnant, no husband, just a one-off thing and we were both happy about it, thought it'd be nice to have a kid around. Then it goes and dies and takes my sister's mental faculties with it. She lived in that room for thirty years, exactly like that. After a while, I never went up there. She came down when she needed something and that was it."

"That's very sad," I say. "Thank you for loaning me your house. I don't know what I would have done without it."

"It worked out the way it was meant to," she replies.

"How are you feeling about things?" Cedar asks me and I jump. I didn't notice that he was there too and I focus on not punctuating my tale with any profanities.

"Good," I say. "I feel good. The only thing I miss is Joe. You know, Eno. He knows what I did and I think he can't forgive me."

"It goes against his moral principles," Cedar says. "Vigilante justice."

"He won't ever forgive me?"

"He will try, but he'll feel like he can't trust you."

I am silent. That hurts.

"A bit rich coming from a tweeker drug addict," Tracey comments.

"Joe's not Eno," Cedar says. "He's the good man that Eno wanted to be."

"I thought he was my friend," I say, and I am stupidly close to tears.

"There is always a price to be paid," Cedar says, but he says it gently and I feel a bit better.

"Auntie Miriam's gone to heaven," Agnes informs me. "She stopped by here and we had a great time together but she moved on. Which is fine. I'm happier knowing she's in a good place. Thank you for that."

"She nearly gave me a heart attack when she died," I tell her and the others laugh.

"Yeah, we could see that!" Samia comments.

I turn to Grace. "I'm sorry Richard overdosed," I say, but she shakes her head.

"I'm not. You didn't see it, but he was getting crazy at home. He even hit my sister. This way she gets custody of the kids and he's no danger to Beatrice when she grows up, which always worried me. They're moving to a smaller house, which is better too. I never wanted them to grow up to be spoiled rich kids."

"You got Mr. Cockney good," Tracey says. "Thanks. I wish there was a way we could have proven it wasn't Mom's boyfriend who killed her. He spent all this time in prison. But he's such a drugged-up loser, it's not like it's any loss to society."

"And thank you," Samia chips in. "From me too, for killing Cockney. I never wanted to die and embarrass my family like that."

I don't know what to say so I nod and change the subject.

"I never saw your Cadillac," I tell Beatrice.

"It's in the garage, through the side door of the kitchen. Listen, Julia or Lulu or whatever, if you like, I'll give you the house."

I gape at her. "You can do that?"

"Yeah, there are always ways. Earth people call them miracles." She grins at me. "You can redecorate, you have my permission. I might be wrong but I don't think you love my artistic leanings."

I blush and she continues.

"And that way, Emma can come and stay with you sometimes, if she wants to, and you'd be near to Bev and her school."

"That's fantastic. But…"

"But what? I know the house isn't in that bad a state."

"The house is great. I love it. But I don't know if I want to go back."

This has the others staring at me open-mouthed.

"Why not?" Cedar asks. He is the first one to speak.

"I'm lonely," I admit and it's not an easy thing to say. "I have been so lonely my whole life and I never realized it. I worked like a demon so I would never have to admit to myself how alone I was. And then I met you guys and you were the closest friends I ever had. But now, I don't have anything. And I've lost Joe and Ella."

"You haven't lost Ella," Cedar says. "And what's more, she needs *you*. She doesn't have any family either, remember? Right now, Joe's telling her that he thinks you got rid of Junior and she's reading him the riot act for giving you a hard time."

"She is?" I sit up straighter.

"Yeah, and trust me, she's got a tongue on her. She would have been bounced out of my office a dozen times by now. And her take is so what if you got rid of Junior, he deserved it. So, you've got her and you've got Emma. It would be a great loss to Emma if you left her."

"She's got Bev and Jackson and a new baby brother or sister."

"She does, but you're her aunt and as she grows older, she'll need you more than she'll need Bev, you'll see. She'll become like a daughter to you. And you never know, you could fall in love, have a kid of your own."

I burst out laughing. "Um, I'm too old, Cedar, to have a kid."

"No, you're not. Remember what Beatrice said about miracles."

"Yes, well, please let's not fill the nursery yet," I tell him hastily. "It's not like I ever wanted kids. In fact, I never did. But so what, I've got Ella and Emma. Two people are not exactly going to keep the cockles of my heart warm at night."

"The circle will grow. Being with Emma and Bev will force

you out into the world and you'll meet new people. And you'll do well at your job because you do love to work hard, but this time, you'll make friends. And you'll enjoy the work too. You might find this astounding but you'll have fun at trade shows and conventions. Real, actual fun."

"Go Cedar!" Agnes is grinning. "He's right," she says to me. "Friends grow in increments. One at a time. And you don't need as many as you think. Loneliness is terrible, trust me, I know better than anyone, but it won't be like that forever."

"Listen to you guys, kicking me out," I say. I'm crying and I blow my nose on a Kleenex that Grace hands me. "What about the sins I committed? I just killed a bunch of people."

"You didn't see the sign when you came in?" Cedar asks.

"No. And besides I thought you couldn't see the sign."

"I was just messing with you. Of course I can see the sign. Go out into the hallway, it's there. It will answer your question."

I go out and there is the sign.

Ezekiel 25:17

I go back to the caf.

"It says Ezekiel 25:17. How I am I supposed to know what that is?"

"You haven't seen *Pulp Fiction*?" Agnes is horrified. "It was one of Samuel L. Jackson's finest moments." She gets up and closes her eyes. "The path of the righteous man is beset on all sides by the inequities of the selfish and the tyranny of evil men. Blessed is he (or she)," she interjects, "who, in the name of charity and good will, shepherds the weak through the valley of the darkness, for he is truly his brother's keeper and the finder of lost children." She opens her eyes, points at me and raises her voice. "And I will strike down upon thee with great vengeance and furious anger those who attempt to poison and destroy my brothers. And you will know I am the Lord when I lay my vengeance upon you."

She sits down. "You were the Lord's weapon of vengeance," she says.

"Wow," I say. "That was impressive, Agnes."

"You know the Bible?" Tracey is incredulous.

"No, dufus, I know *Pulp Fiction*. But my point is that Julia doesn't have to feel guilty."

"*Pulp Fiction* took some liberties rephrasing what the Bible says," Cedar comments. "But Julia, I would encourage you to embrace Agnes's interpretation."

I want to hug him.

"Are you going to stay Lula or go back to Julia?" Samia asks.

"Go back to Julia. It's who I really am. But what is odd is seeing myself in the mirror. I still expect to see my old self."

"I never got used to it," Grace says. "It is strange." It helps, her saying that, and I nod.

"You want the house or not?" Beatrice is brusque.

"Beatrice, I would love the house. Thank you, that's huge. What's going to happen to all of you? Will I see you again?"

"Of course you will," Cedar is hearty about it. "At one point or another. We'll meet up eventually, have no doubt."

"Oh dear, I'm starting to fade," Grace says. "Thank you, Julia. I'm finally ready to move on—" and next thing she is gone.

"And she ain't coming back," Beatrice says. "She's moved on up, and good for her."

"I am ready to move on too," Samia says in a small voice, and Beatrice nods.

Samia looks at me. "See you when I see you," she says and her voice quavers. "I'll have a latte ready." And with that, she vanishes too.

"Yeah, well, I'm not ready to be a heavenly body, but I got a bounce coming on," Agnes says. "Love you, Julia. Have fun in the real world. Give them shit and take no prisoners."

"What she said," Tracey adds and they both bounce and I am left with Cedar and Beatrice.

"Where's Jaimie?" I ask.

"Wandering the halls, looking for a mirror," Beatrice says. "Pretty boy needs some time to realize a few things. Now Julia, don't get weepy again. Like they said, we'll see you soon enough. I'll be waiting with the Scrabble board and for god's sake, do some practicing, girl."

She leaves and it is just Cedar and me.

"Cedar," I say, and my voice fills with tears.

"Ah, none of that," he says and he gets up and hugs me. "You are one of my success stories."

"Of course I am," I tell him and we grin.

"I love you Cedar," I say, but I say it out loud to my empty bedroom, with no one there but me, and a full moon shining down through my window.

But in my hand, I find a feather necklace.

ACKNOWLEDGEMENTS

Many thanks to my beloved Inanna Publications, particularly to my incredible Editor-in-Chief, Luciana Ricciutelli, for making my most important dreams come true. You are beyond amazing. And, as always, huge thanks to the wonderful Inanna Publicist, Renée Knapp.

To my family, thank you for all your love and support, and thanks in particular to Bradford Dunlop for reading every version of every story and for encouraging me on this creative journey. Thank you, also, for all my lovely author portraits.

Thanks to Samia Akhtar for being a muse for the Samia in this book, and for a wonderful friendship.

And, while I have worked in magazines for many years, it's important to note that angry, feisty, arrogant Julia Redner is a complete work of fiction—all my real life editors have been kind, generous, professional, and lovely people.

Thank you Rogers Media for letting me go after nearly six years on the job — the anger I felt certainly fuelled this book into life!

Grateful thanks to early supporters of the book: James Fisher, John Oughton, Jacqueline Kovacs, Suzana Tratnik, Liz Bugg,

Miguel Ángel Hernández, Rosemary McCracken, M.H. Callway, Jade Wallace, and Shirley McDaniel.

Slogans for the signs outside Cedar's office are taken from various sites on the Internet.

Thanks to the Mesdames of Mayhem, without whom, Agnes would not exist. She started out as a short story for Thirteen O' Clock and I had to know what happened to her. Many thanks to the Toronto writing community, the Sisters in Crime, the Crime Writers of Canada, and the Toronto Public Libraries. The camaraderie makes all things possible.

I thank and acknowledge the support of the Ontario Arts Council and the funding supplied by the Writers' Reserve program that helped support the writing of this book.

Photo: Bradford Dunlop

Lisa de Nikolits is the award-winning author of seven novels: *The Hungry Mirror, West of Wawa, A Glittering Chaos, The Witchdoctor's Bones, Between The Cracks She Fell, The Nearly Girl* and *No Fury Like That*. Her short fiction and poetry have also been published in various anthologies and journals across the country. She is a member of the Mesdames of Mayhem, the Crime Writers of Canada, Sisters in Crime, and the International Thriller Writers. Originally from South Africa, Lisa de Nikolits came to Canada in 2000. She lives and writes in Toronto.